# The Duke's Easter Lady
## Irene Loyd Black

**ZEBRA BOOKS**
**KENSINGTON PUBLISHING CORP.**

*FROM THE AUTHOR:*

*The Duke's Easter Lady* is fiction. The historical events are factual, but are not necessarily written in the order in which they happened.


ZEBRA BOOKS


are published by


Kensington Publishing Corp.
475 Park Avenue South
New York, NY 10016

First Printing: March, 1993

Printed in the United States of America

*TO PRUE,*
*With Love.*

# Chapter One

A raw, vibrating silence hung over Fernwood Manor's drawing room. Only the ragged breath that escaped Emma Winslow's flared nostrils penetrated the enveloping quietness. Her guest, Elwood Prescott, her late brother's solicitor, sat on the edge of a red leather chair twice his size, looking as if he were afraid to breathe.

Emma pulled her gaze from Prescott, and with quick steps moved across the room to stand before a long narrow window which opened out onto snow-covered moors. Beyond the moors, hillocks with snow lying deep in their corries, thrust upward. A blue sky hung like a protective quilt over the highest white peak.

*Uncanny,* Emma thought, *snow on Good Friday.* Tears clouded her eyes. Easter was about hope, a new beginning. A new beginning indeed; in a very short time she would be leaving Fernwood forever.

Turning back to the solicitor, she vented her anger, lest she burst. "And who is this Consuelo deFleury with whom my sister and I are to live?"

Two weeks earlier Prescott had been the bearer of other bad news. Lord Charles Winslow, Emma's brother, the seventh earl of Wickersham, had been killed fighting a duel over his lightskirt. Never mind that he had a wife and daughter; fighting duels and doing other exciting things were Charles's way of life.

According to primogeniture law, entailed Fernwood could only pass to a male relative, this time to a distant cousin of whom no one had ever heard. Until Charles Winslow had passed from life.

"Consuelo deFleury is your late mother's cousin, third removed," quailed Mr. Prescott. "She lives near Brighton, at Craigmont by the Sea."

"Never heard of her. Mama never mentioned—"

"On-dits have it that she has not visited London for thirty years."

"Is she daft?"

"Perhaps there's a reason for her not visiting London, but I do not feel it my duty to apprise you of your family history." The solicitor took a long breath, as though in preparation for a dive into deep water. His voice shook when he said, "I fear there is more . . ."

"You fear there's more! Do you not think this is singularly enough? I never thought I would be leaving Fernwood."

"Surely you knew that if Lord Winslow did not produce a male heir that on his death a Winslow male of some sort would crop up from somewhere."

"Of course I was aware of that, but Charles was young and he planned more children . . . as soon as Margaret regained her health."

Unlikely even if he'd lived, thought Prescott. Rumors had flown for years that Charles was a spoiled pup, a rakehell of the first order, a man who would give any woman a constant case of the vapors.

Prescott sank back into his chair and eyed the woman before him, without doubt the most beautiful creature in all of England, even shabbily dressed in a faded blue morning dress. How he wanted to run his fingers through the thick folds of glistening black hair that hung halfway to her waist, resting between narrow shoulders. She was tall, with a regal carriage, and her eyes were the deepest blue.

Prescott could hardly blame her ladyship for her anger. She was twenty and three, and on the shelf, just because her brother would not allow her a Season. For years she had managed Fernwood with the help of an overseer—and no help from Lord Charles. His Lordship had even established a home in London, claiming it was because of his wife's poor health.

Prescott sighed and started again, "There's more—"

Emma went to sit in a chair on the opposite side of the fireplace, inside of which a cozy fire crackled and popped. Cold chills ran up and down her spine. Placing her hands over her ears, she said emphatically, "I don't want to hear it." But her hands did not keep out the hateful words.

"You must," the solicitor said, and plunged right into his prepared speech, while pulling from his portmanteau a sheath of papers. "Two weeks before the unfortunate duel, Charles came to me in the middle of the night and asked that I add a codicil to his will."

Emma started to speak, but the solicitor refused to be interrupted. Lifting his quizzing glass, he peered down at the papers. "The codicil states that you are to marry His Grace Ashton deFleury, the Duke of Attlebery."

"Who!"

"The Duke of Attlebery."

Emma could not credit what she was hearing. Just as she had never heard of her mother's Cousin Consuelo, she had never heard of the Duke of Attlebery, and said so, and then she asked in a strident voice, "Why would Charles want me to marry this . . . this Duke? My brother refused every gentleman who wanted to pay his addresses to me."

"It wasn't Charles's idea. It seems that he lost quite a large sum of money to His Grace at White's gaming tables, and when he could not pay up, His Grace suggested your hand in marriage instead." Feeling more relaxed now that the worst was over, the solicitor chuckled. "A very careful man, that Duke, but not a trusting one. He left nothing to chance. He accompanied Charles to my place on the night I mentioned and insisted that the debt, and the payment of that debt, be written into your brother's will. And His Grace further insisted that Lord Charles cut you and your sister from his will entirely should you refuse to live at Craigmont with your mother's cousin. No, the careful Duke left no string untied. In truth, Lady Emma, you are left destitute, with no choice but to marry deFleury."

Emma glared at him, unbelieving, noticing only that his white cravat was askew and that his waistcoat was embroidered with bees and butterflies. She watched as if she were detached from her body as he took a tin box from the waistcoat pocket, opened its lid, and sniffed snuff into his nostril. Then he said, "It was almost as if His Grace had a premonition about fate."

"He probably arranged for the duel to happen."

"I thought about that, but later, when I called on His Grace, I dismissed the idea."

Emma straightened. "You know the Duke. Well, then, you can talk some sense into his empty head. I have no intention of marrying him . . . or anyone else. I'm too set in my ways to make any man a suitable wife."

The solicitor smiled. Most any man would be too fragile for such strength, and he, himself, was too bald to approach such a gorgeous creature. She would set him to quailing with one stony glare from those blue eyes. Right now, she looked like a big black cat, with a white face, about to spring. "You . . . you underestimate yourself."

"Well, no bother. I'm not going to marry the Duke, and that is that. Given time, I will think of some way to get out of it." She stopped for a moment. "By the by, what is this Duke like? I need to know if I am to deal with him successfully."

"A nabob, I hear, and of course he is the talk of the Ton.

There's not a mother among the lot who would not give her eye teeth to nab him for her daughter. It is bruited about that he is like that with His Majesty King George." Prescott held up two fingers as if they were glued together. " 'Tis said he came by his dukedom because of that friendship . . . and for other reasons, not because of anything brave he did."

"Go on," Emma said.

"Gossip has it that he is nasty, pleasant, handsome, plain, noteworthy, talkative, and silent."

"Mr. Prescott, will you stop bandying words." Emma then declared roundly, "I care not a fig about the gossip. You've seen him; you've talked with him. Now tell me what this nasty, unworthy, silent, and talkative Duke is like?"

Prescott sucked in air as if he needed the extra oxygen to assuage his nerves, then expelled it with force, after which he said with true conviction, "Handsome and ruthless."

Emma had not expected such candor. She did, however, hold her anger. Decorously, she offered the solicitor tea. Not that she wanted him to stay, but she had been brought up with a modicum of refinement. Mostly she wanted time to pull her thoughts together, to absorb the pain of leaving Fernwood before plotting against this ill-fated betrothal, if one could call it that. Prescott said he would love a spot of tea before returning to London, and Emma rang for a maid, who immediately appeared, bobbing as she entered.

"Minnie Lou, bring tea for Mr. Prescott," Emma said, and went again to stand by the window. She did her best thinking there, and think she must. She pressed a hand across her lips to still their trembling.

Once again silence permeated the big room. The maid brought the tea, and the solicitor sipped without fanfare, the cup and saucer when they came together making not a sound. Emma wished that he would go. He had brought enough bad news. Had it been only two weeks since he had come to tell her that Charles, twenty-nine, had been killed in a duel?

They had buried her brother in the West Wycombe grave-yard, with the small church in its center. She had been angry then, at the senselessness of his death . . . but now this news the solicitor had just delivered sent her anger out of control. How dare Charles cut her and her sister off without a shilling if she, Emma, did not marry some monstrous Duke?

For a moment Emma thought of the past; she had been a mere three and ten, Francine still a baby at seven, when their father, the sixth earl of Wickersham, and their mother, Countess Winslow, were killed in a carriage accident. Charles had inherited the estate and the earldom, but, having been brought up the only son, he had been doted on all his life, and the sense of responsibility had escaped him. At twenty, he had married Margaret Hanover, a sweet but weak woman, with good lineage, and they had had a child, a daughter, Prudence, now eight. After that, if gossip could be believed, it was as if there were no marriage.

Charles had boasted that there would be a son to inherit Fernwood and the earldom, but now Emma doubted that after Prudence was born he had ever again visited Margaret's bedchamber. There had been one mistress after another.

Ruminating about the past would do no good, Emma told herself. She turned back into the room to find Prescott standing, ready to leave. Emma said quickly, "I beg your forgiveness, sir. I'm afraid I have been dreadfully rude."

Prescott bowed. "I regret infinitely that it was I who brought you this bad news. I do hope the alliance with His Grace will not be as painful as you seem to expect. The gossipers have him very rich, and he said himself that he had just returned from India, where he had transacted business."

"A pox on His Grace. He will see many summers before I marry him. I will accuse him of cheating my brother at the gaming table. I will tell him . . . oh, I can think of any number of things to say to him."

12

The solicitor bowed again and hurried toward the door. With his hand on the knob, he said in a apologetic voice, "Lady Emma, the new owner will take possession of Fernwood two weeks from this day." As if afraid he would be struck by a flying object, he darted out the door, closing it noiselessly behind him. Emma watched him walk with great speed down the path to his carriage, climb in, and take the ribbons. And then they were off, the horse's hooves burrowing in the soft snow.

*Two weeks! Two weeks! Two weeks!* pounded her brain.

She had to plan, but that she could not do as long as her thoughts were running together. For a moment it seemed there was no fighting spirit left inside her. She was whipped, drained. The past two years had not been lucrative for Fernwood. Rain had not come, and the crops had dried in the fields. The reserve blunt had been used to keep Fernwood going, and neither she nor Francine had had a new gown in those two years.

Without plan or conscious thought, for her mind refused to work, Emma reached up and yanked hard at the window covering, tearing it from its rod. Yards of dark-blue silk puddled at her feet. She stooped and gathered it into her arms, then rang for a maid. When Minnie Lou came, Emma asked that she find Francine and send her at once to her bedchamber. The maid bobbed and left the room, as did Emma, climbing the winding stairs to the second floor. There, she went to the book room for the latest copy of *The Lady's Magazine,* in which there were two hand-colored plates of the latest Paris fashions. If she and dear Francine had to be shoved off on an unsuspecting cousin, they would go in the latest style.

Now that Emma had a plan, the pounding in her heart and in her head, subsided considerably, allowing her to arrange her thoughts in a more constructive pattern. Always sensible and levelheaded, she did not like to feel out of control, as she had when dealing with Prescott. But that was because so many things had happened at once, she told herself.

She opened the door to her sitting room and went in. It was a pleasant room, furnished with handsome mahogany furniture, with gold and brass inlay ornamenting the curved legs. Fire in the grate emitted warmth. Light for sewing flowed through wide windows.

An ormolu clock on the mantel showed it to be eleven o'clock. Francine had not yet arrived. This did not surprise Emma. Her sister was probably hiding out somewhere reading and primping. Most likely applying lemon oil to her freckles, and gilt paint to her toenails. Emma smiled. Francine, at seventeen, was on the edge of maturing into a woman.

Emma pushed the chairs and settee back from in front of the fire and spread the blue silk on the floor. She then took up the *Lady's Magazine* and sat at her writing desk, studying the plates. She did not hear the door open, and it was not until Francine spoke that Emma knew she was in the room.

"Did you send Minnie Lou to fetch me?" Francine asked.

Turning to the voice, Emma smiled. Francine was a slender girl with huge gray eyes, and outrageous red-blond curls framing a lightly freckled, round face. As always, Francine had a ready smile. She held in her hand a basket filled with colored Easter eggs.

"Thank you for coming," Emma said. "Have you been coloring eggs?"

"Yes, for the tenant children. This will probably be our last Easter here, and I want to make it a special occasion for the little urchins."

Emma heard the break in Francine's voice and knew her pain. Francine loved the children of Fernwood and had laughingly said she would marry and have a brood of her own. This thought disturbed Emma. She had not yet faced

14

the problem of Francine's come-out, now that there was no blunt at the ready.

Before the two drought years, Emma would have simply taken money from the estate, with or without Charles's permission. She had long ago determined that he would not be allowed to prevent Francine from having a Season, as he had prevented Emma.

*"Tis a shame,* Emma thought, *that a woman cannot make a suitable marriage without a proper Season, and it's too bad that the expense is so enormous.*

At the moment, Emma could not readily think of a plan for Francine, and she did not want her to know just how much was bearing on her mind, such as a marriage contract their brother had signed with some mysterious Duke. She knew, however, that she must needs tell Francine *where* they would live after leaving Fernwood. "When will the hunt be?" Emma asked.

"Sunday, after we return from church. I hope the snow has melted by then." Francine's gaze dropped to the material spread on the floor. "What are you doing, making yourself a new Easter gown?"

"No," Emma said truthfully, and a little sharply. "I don't need a new Easter gown."

"Oh, but you must. Everything is new for Easter; it's a new beginning. Besides, if you do not wear *something* new, crows will befoul your old garments and bad luck will follow you all of the new year."

"That is an old superstition—"

"I believe it."

"Then I shall make you a new dress for Easter. Helga can help me. After I have studied these plates, I will cut a pattern."

They did not use the blue material; it was Emma's favorite color but not Francine's. She preferred green she said, and Emma told her to go to the green salon and fetch the window coverings. "Enough for a bonnet, too," she added.

"But Emma," Francine protested, "will not the new Earl object? After all, *he* now owns Fernwood."

"Balderdash," Emma retorted. "Fernwood is not his until he takes possession two weeks from today, and Mr. Prescott did not say in what condition he would inherit Fernwood. We shall use as many yards of the window coverings as we like to make a new wardrobe for both of us, and the lace tablecloths will be excellent for evening dresses and elegant palatines."

Emma's enthusiasm spread to Francine, and she left, laughing, and was soon back with fabric from the green salon, a delicate muslin with a satin stripe. "Let me measure you," Emma said, placing a string under Francine's bosom where the waistline would be.

"I will be the best dressed lady at church Sunday," Francine said, and when Emma told her that they both would be suitably dressed when they went to live with Cousin Consuelo at Craigmont by the Sea, Francine exploded with, "Who is Cousin Consuelo?"

"That is just what I asked Mr. Prescott. It seems she is our mama's cousin, and we are to live with her when we leave Fernwood."

A long, terrible silence ensued, and then Francine asked, "Will we be terribly poor?"

"Not terribly so. While cutting and snipping, I have come up with a plan. As soon after Easter so as not to break propriety—and seem disrespectful—we will gather the things which belonged to Mama and Papa personally and take them into Town. The money we derive from the sale should finance your Season; you will marry a rich husband, and we will move from Craigmont into Town."

*And I will not be forced to marry that odious Duke.*

Selling her mama's and papa's things had just occurred to Emma, and painful as it was, she thought it an excellent plan. She would insist that His Grace give her six months, or maybe even a year, before they were married. Of course they

16

would never marry. She would see that things changed during that time. Francine would be securely married. . . .

"But Emma, should you not have a Season and a husband first? You don't want to be an ape-leader, do you? No gel would. How awful!"

"Do not worry about me," Emma said. "Let's concentrate on your future." Emma knew, given time, she could outsmart the Duke. She much preferred being an ape-leader, even though it was an undesirable state for any woman, meaning it was to be her fate in hell to lead apes, as to being married to some egotistical dandy of which she had never heard. And she did not care if the gossips did claim he was rich.

The measuring, cutting, and pinning continued, and when Emma was satisfied that Francine's Easter dress would be exactly like the plate in the French magazine, she sent for Helga, who said if someone would take care of her other chores she would have the gown stitched long before sunrise on Easter Morning.

When Francine and the maid had gone, Emma, having kept her feelings in check in Francine's presence, paced the floor of her sitting room. Through the door she could see her bedchamber. Red velvet bed hangings, lined with white satin, framed the bed she had slept in practically every night of her life. Emma ground her teeth together, but refused to cry. It was suppertime. She would go and eat, and tomorrow she would cut material for carriage dresses, morning dresses, walking dresses, everything she and Francine would need when they went to Craigmont, and for later, when they traveled to London for Francine's come out.

On Easter she would go to church, but she would not pray for a new beginning. Why should she? she asked herself. Everything she wanted was at Fernwood, and Fernwood was lost to her forever.

*Chapter Two*

So that Ian, Fernwood's coachman, might be home with his family on Easter morning, Emma chose to drive the Standhope to church. It was as if it had not snowed on Good Friday. The countryside had returned to a sweet green, the wild cherry trees had recovered from their battering, and cottage gardens were filled with color — yellow jasmine, purple crocus, and a profusion of red and white busy lizzies.

As the Standhope bounced along, thoughts tumbled through Emma's mind, not about the glorious Easter morning and its meaning, but about what would happen to her and Francine. There was so much that needed to be done, the new wardrobes, the trip into Town to sell her mother's possessions. Emma thought to share her thoughts with Francine, but decided against it. She could hear Francine saying, "Sister, you worry overly much. I think it's exciting, a new place to live. Are you not tired of the sameness at Fernwood?"

Of course Francine did not know of the ruthless Duke's and their dead brother's marriage plans for Emma.

Emma gave her sister a fond glance. Dressed to the nines in her new green-striped dress, with bonnet to match and locks of red-blond hair curled around her face, Francine, in Emma's opinion, was beautiful. She smiled at her own thinking and admitted to being prejudiced. She had practically raised Francine.

"Is it not a beautiful day?" Francine asked, and Emma gave a reluctant "yes" in response.

Last night Francine had been out with the tenantry children, building a bonfire in celebration of Easter morn; yesterday, she had helped the servants clean the manor, in the old-fashioned belief that one should make ready for the resurrection. And this morning, beside Emma's breakfast plate there was a painted egg, representing a new life.

Emma thought about His Grace Ashton deFleury. She was positive he had tricked her brother into the game of chance in which he had won Emma's hand in marriage.

A profitable marriage for Francine was the only hope, and as beautiful as her sister was today, there should be no problem in finding her a rich husband, Emma reasoned. And mayhaps if he had plenty of blunt, he would not mind that Francine was not dowered.

They passed through the minuscule village of West Wycombe. A winding road led to the top of the tree-covered hill overlooking Wycombe Valley, and then, around the bend, the parish church of St. Lawrence came to full view. Brilliant sunlight glistened on the gold-leaf ball atop its tower, and on the white tombstones in the churchyard.

It was the only church Ladies Emma and Francine Winslow had ever attended. This day, from the tower, five bells chimed the call to worship the Risen Christ. Emma was proud of the Church's history and was pleased to be a part of the stability it exuded. It dated back to the eleventh century, and one of the bells in the tower bore Joseph Carter's name, the date 1581. In 1763, when the church was rebuilt, the *Royal Magazine of Gentleman's Companion* said that "It is reckoned the most beautiful Country Church in England."

Emma pulled the reins and guided Shelly, the horse, to the front of the church and pulled them to a stop, where a young lad came to tether the horse, another to let the step down. Giving a bow, he greeted them with, "The Lord has risen."

"The Lord is risen," Francine said, and as they stepped down onto the ground, she said to Emma, "Sister, I do hope a crow does not befoul your gown."

It seemed to Emma that everyone was celebrating the old traditions of Easter except her. But she could not help her feelings. This was not a good year. She wore a morning dress of the palest blue sprigged muslin, outmoded by several Seasons. A matching bonnet partially covered her long black hair. Looking around, she saw Easter finery everywhere, and people were laughing.

"Emma, who is that man?" Francine asked. She pointed to the right of the church.

"Where? Francie, don't point."

"Leaning against the tree. Not far from brother's tombstone. He's a stranger . . . and he's staring at us."

"Lots of strangers pass these parts. Perhaps he's traveling to Oxford and stopped to observe Easter. Most likely he is staring at your beautiful Easter dress."

The tall man standing in the middle of the graveyard did not look to Emma like someone bent on celebrating Easter. She felt his searing gaze as the distance closed between them, and his half-smile left no doubt in her mind what he was thinking. Burning with indignation, she looked straight ahead and quickly entered the church. But the stranger's gaze followed her; she felt the heat on her back.

Inside the church, colorful spring flowers adorned the nave and the side chapels, but on the altar itself there were only pure white lilies and dark green yew branches, signifying immortality.

Emma led the way to the family pew, and when she and Francine were seated, she saw through the window her brother Charles's tombstone. Not wanting to revive her anger toward her brother, she directed her gaze and thoughts

20

to the pulpit, which carried an eagle with outstretched wings, to hold sermon notes.

Around the Italian-style font was entwined a serpent, the symbol of evil. Over the chancel arch was a painting of the Royal Coat of Arms of the mad King George III. Emma could not help but pity King George. The quidnuncs said terrible things about him. Nonetheless, when the congregation settled, the organ played and the people sang *God Save The King.*

Total silence prevailed, the candles were lighted, and songs of the resurrection were sung, after which the Vicar, a small man with a booming voice, filled the church with Christ's victory over the cross, the unfailing love in His heart, His ability to forgive. Emma heard the Vicar repeat Christ's words as He hung on the cross. "God forgive them, for they know not what they do."

The Easter message.

She fidgeted and squirmed, and looked through the window at *that* tombstone. Then the sermon ended, and by the time the long closing prayer came to an end, Emma's discomfort had become so great that she could not stop herself from turning to look to the back of the church, as if something or someone was willing her to do such an unmannerly thing. Feeling a nudge from Francine's elbow, Emma quickly righted herself and with great determination kept her eyes, but not her thoughts, on the vicar.


That one look, that brief glance, was what His Grace Ashton deFleury had been waiting for. He had seen his intended walk into the church and thought her regal carriage exquisite. Still he wanted to see her face. Throughout the church service he had glared at the back of her head, willing her to turn and look at him. He smiled to himself, for Lady Emma Winslow was as beautiful as any chit he had ever seen. Charles Winslow had not lied.

Lord Charles Winslow, before his untimely death, had been the Duke of Attlebery's friend, and often he had expounded overly much about his beautiful sister, laughingly calling her a Blue Stocking. "How capable," he would say, and then in the next breath he would declare that she was so intelligent, and so stubborn, no man would want her for a wife.

"She's even good at figures, and well read," Charles had extolled, until meeting Lady Emma Winslow had become an obsession to Ashton deFleury. He wanted to marry this gel whom no man would wish to wed. At one and thirty, it was time he took a wife, and the last thing he wanted was a hoity-toity thrust on the marriage mart by an overly anxious Ton mama.

Slipping from the back pew and out the door, he then hurried to his traveling equipage. His steps were light, and he puckered his lips and whistled. He told himself that he had not cheated Winslow; the chap just happened to be a rotten card player. Now, in a fortnight, Lady Emma Winslow would be at Craigmont, ready to pay her brother's gaming debt.

The egg hunt with the tenant children had been a huge success, so Francine reported. A fine meal of roast lamb and mint sauce, various vegetables, custard tarts sprinkled with currants, Easter cakes, and, of course, boiled Easter eggs, was enjoyed by the household staff. As was the custom at Fernwood on Easter day, Ladies Emma and Francine dined with the staff at four o'clock in the afternoon. It was then that Emma broke the news—as if they did not know—that within a fortnight she and Francine would leave Fernwood.

"Upon the death of Lord Charles a Winslow cousin inherited the estate, and we shall be leaving." Emma tried to keep the emotion from her voice, for the last thing she wanted was tearful servants protesting the unfairness of primogeniture.

Nonetheless, tears were shed and regrets expressed. Emma cautioned the servants to be as loyal to the new master as they had been to Lord Charles. Almost in unison the servants stated that Lord Charles had had little to do with Fernwood, that it was to Emma they had looked for guidance.

Relieved that the painful duty had been dispensed with, and happy to see the Easter day draw to a close, Emma repaired to her sitting room and began cutting more patterns for her and Francie's new clothes. Earlier in the day she had brought more copies of fashion magazines from the book room. She was not long in her task when Francine, wearing a plain day dress and her hair in a white nightcap, pushed the door open and stuck her head in, horrified to see Emma working.

Stepping inside, she exclaimed, "Sister, do you not know it is still Easter Sunday?"

Emma smiled. "I have observed Easter in a way that I am sure was pleasing to our Lord, and now I have things to do. I vividly recall that somewhere in the Good Book it says that if an ox is in the ditch on the Sabbath, pull the ox out."

Francine cocked her head to one side and eyed her sister, grinning mischievously. "Are you sure the Good Book says that?"

"I'm sure. Maybe not in those exact words . . . but today the ox is in the ditch."

"Why so?"

Emma looked at her sister. Certainly their leaving Fernwood, and all that had to be accomplished before they could do so, had not yet soaked into her head. "Never mind, Francie, in the time it would take me to explain, I could cut two more patterns."

Francine poked at the fire, then sat in the chair opposite Emma. Even though the snow was gone, with the disappearance of the warm sun, the evening had become quite chilly. The fire blazed; she reached for a chunk of coal and pitched it onto the grate.

Emma thanked her, and when Francine remained mysteriously silent, Emma, raising a dark brow, asked, "What is it, honey? What's on your mind?"

"I was thinking of this Consuelo woman. What's she like? Do you suppose she will be uppish and treat us like poor relations . . . or even servants?"

Emma realized that Francine was on the edge of plunging from the secure haven of childhood into cold reality, which was slower to come in the country than in Town. Emma remembered all too well when, at eighteen, it had happened to her. Becoming worried about her future, she had begged Charles for a Season, and he turned his back on her. Her pleading did not help, and he finally gave her an emphatic "No."

She had lived in the *real* world since then.

Emma could not bear to point out the many possibilities that leapt to her mind as she considered her sister's question. The remark the solicitor made, "It is not my duty to apprise you of your family's history," came to Emma's mind. So from the start, mystery shrouded Consuelo deFleury, and Emma thought she would have to be devilish queer not to have visited London in thirty years.

Because Emma did not know what to say, silence hovered in the room. Finally, she took a long breath and made a solemn promise, "If we are treated as servants, we will leave Craigmont and move into Town. I shall work for a modiste, cutting patterns, maybe even start my own shop and make clothes for ladies of quality."

"Oh, Emma, you couldn't. Mama would expect—"

"Then Mama should have raised her son, the heir, to face responsibility."

"You're angry with Mama, too, aren't you?"

24

Emma tried but failed to keep the sharpness from her voice. "What do you mean with Mama, too?"

"Well, it is obvious that you are angry with Charles, and he's dead. You're angry with Mama, and she's gone. What about Papa?"

"Him, too," Emma said, setting her chin in an implacable line and thinking that Papa had the same responsibility as Mama in the upbringing of Charles. No, she thought, Papa had *more* responsibility. He was the head of the family.

"Sister," Francine said tentatively, "I hate to see you so angry with all these dead people. Can't you forgive—"

"Never. Well, maybe Mama and Papa, but not Charles." She shook her head. "I'll never forgive Charles for making us leave Fernwood. He should have had a male heir."

*And I'll never forgive Charles for promising a ruthless Duke I would marry him.*

Francine rose to go, and Emma, noticing her bare feet, and indeed her toenails were painted gilt, laughed and said, "Cousin Consuelo may have a spate of vapors when she sees you've painted your toenails. You know ladies of quality do not do that."

"I'll wager she won't give a fig about my toenails. She'll most likely be old, half-blind, and can't see my feet, much less my toes." At the door, Francine turned back. "Emma, promise we won't be separated."

Emma felt tears scald her cheeks, but she gave her sister the best smile she could muster. "I promise."

After Francine was gone, Emma put away her patterns and made ready for bed, pulling the red velvet window coverings against the outdoors. She needed a good night's sleep. Tomorrow, besides cutting more patterns and getting someone to help Helga with the sewing, she, Emma, would start gathering the things she would take into Town to sell.

Feeling exhaustion overtake her, Emma thought for a moment she would order hot water for a bath, but then decided just to wash, using the porcelain basin and water from the ewer. It would not be cold beyond bearing. And this she did, and then she donned a thin white nightdress, climbed up into the four-poster bed, and buried herself in the feather mattress.

But sleep did not come easily. She stared through the darkness at the ceiling, seeing the scrolled squares with her mind. The chiffonnier, the Adam fireplace came into her blind view; until, finally, the tiredness of her body and her tensed muscles dragged her down into a fatigued sleep that forced her coiled body to unwind and rest.

*Only then, when Emma was at peace, did the* Dream *come.*

*She stands at the foot of a huge cross, on which a man wearing only a loin cloth has been crucified. His arms are outstretched, as if to encircle the world, and blood oozes from his hand where the nails have been driven. Darkness closes in, and then a brilliant, blinding light engulfs the cross and the man. Slowly, the circle of light grows larger, until Emma can see two smaller crosses flanking the larger one, and on these two men hang, dying by degrees.*

As in the Easter story. thinks Emma. But why am I here?

*Frightened, Emma starts to leave, stumbling through the overwhelming blackness. Even the trees are invisible, but she can hear them whispering: "Father, forgive them, for . . ."*

*She stops and looks back; the crosses have disappeared, and in their stead are decaying buildings, without roofs, the white stone walls half crumbled.*

*Sitting atop one of the walls, her feet dangling over the side, is a little girl who looks no more than eight. Clasped in her small fists is a lighted candle. Her head is bent over the candle, and her lips are moving.*

*Transfixed, Emma stares at the child, whose invisible face is circled with a halo of blond curls. She seems familiar, but her identity escapes Emma. Again the trees move and whisper, this time a prayer of supplication.*

*Then the child, the talking trees, and the crumbling walls disappear. Emma is alone in the darkness.*

# Chapter Three

The dream did not awaken Emma, nor did the clock's striking twelve times, evidence of her total exhaustion of the past days. It was her lady's maid, Hannah, who disturbed her deep slumber.

" 'Tis midday, m'lady. I come to see if yer might be ailing?"

The rattle of curtain rings drawn against brass rods cut through Emma's mind like a sharp knife. Suddenly bright sunlight filled the room, and shadows danced on the walls, and on her bed of tumbled covers. Grimacing, she pulled herself up against the curved headboard and combed her black hair back from her face with her fingers. "W-what time is it, Hannah?"

"The clock just struck twelve times, m'lady. Did you not hear it? It being so late, I took it on meself to order breakfast fer yer—"

"Twelve o'clock," Emma shrieked. She bounded from the high bed and went quickly to her dressing room, unbuttoning her nightdress as she went. "I don't have time to eat. Of all the times for me to sleep late . . ."

"I know. The whole of the house is talking about it. Never have we witnessed yer being so tired out as to sleep like yer was dead."

Emma shuddered at the thought. Bending over the basin,

she splashed cold water on her face and rubbed the sleep from her eyes. "Stuff," she muttered when she saw in the looking glass they were red and swollen.

"No need to worry," she said aloud as she brushed her long, black hair. After ten strokes she tied it at the nape with a riband, then declared her toilette finished.

Emma had never been one to primp overmuch; for, in truth, it was not necessary for her to do so to be beautiful, a fact, it seemed to Hannah, that everyone knew except Emma.

Hannah also knew that her ladyship had the reputation of being kind and considerate with the servants. Only when it was absolutely necessary did she become firm.

Emma said to Hannah, "Please hand me a morning dress from the chiffonnier."

"What color, m'lady."

"I don't care, as long as it covers me." Emma quickly donned white pantalettes and slippers, and when Hannah brought a pale pink dress, made with a high waist and laced around the neck with ribbons, Emma, her thoughts elsewhere, slipped it over her head without notice.

"Ahhh," the maid expostulated. " 'Tis a sight fer sore eyes, yer are, m'lady, a dress the color of a peach, and the sun on yer hair makes it glisten like'n a raven's wing."

Emma gave a little laugh. "That's the first time I've been compared to a raven." She recalled what Francine had said about a crow befouling her dress, because it was not new in celebration of Easter. The *dream* came faintly to mind, but Emma shrugged it off, thinking that mayhaps guilt for not listening to the vicar's Easter message had caused it. Or could it have been the mutton stew she had eaten for supper?

A dream was a dream, she told herself, and, not having time to think upon it, and refusing to admit that the dream disturbed her, she thought instead about Francine's concern about Consuelo deFleury, this obliterating everything else.

29

Because of Francine's questions, Emma had decided that it would be foolish to go to Craigmont to live not knowing what to expect. She and her sister might even be thrown into a dungeon.

Emma laughed at the thought; nonetheless, some time during the past night, when crosses holding crucified men and little girls praying over a candle were not trampling her mind, the plan to send one of the servants into Town to make enquiries about Consuelo deFleury had materialized. It seemed odd to Emma that she had not, until now, heard of her mother's cousin.

Although that was entirely possible, she told herself. In the country, morning calls were not made as they were in London, where members of the upper orders thrived on gossip about everyone except themselves.

Why had her mother not told her of her cousin? Or about her son, the ruthless Duke? Emma recalled the look on Elwood Prescott's face when he had said it was not his duty to apprise her of the gossip about her mother's cousin.

*I shall request that enquiries be made into the personal life of His Grace Ashton deFleury, the Duke of Attlebery.*

A knock on the door sent Hannah racing to admit a maid with a tray loaded with Emma's breakfast, stewed kidneys, thinly sliced pork, fried to a crisp, eggs, a plate of flat biscuits, and gooseberry jam. Steam curled from the spout of a silver coffee pot. "I don't have time . . ."

The aroma stilled Emma's tongue. Feeling her mouth start to water, she dug into the food as if she had not eaten in a week. Between bites she told Hannah to find Ian and ask that he come to the belowstairs receiving room.

"Yes, m'lady." Hannah bobbed, then left in a swirl of rustling black bombazine.

She would go into London herself, Emma mused, but she had no "companion" to accompany her, nor did she have an entree into the London's Upper Ten Thousand. Usually one had an aunt, or even a distant cousin, who would welcome a country relative to her home and sponsor an introduction into society. Emma had no one. Of course there was Charles's widow, but Margaret had not even traveled to Fernwood to attend her husband's funeral, and the little girl, Prudence, had not, in all of her eight years, been to Fernwood more than twice. It was unheard of that a lady of quality go into coffeehouses where men passed gossip, smoked cheroots, and told bawdy jokes. And Emma had to think of the future when Francine would come out into society. No, it would not do for her to go, even in disguise, something she had considered greatly.

"I must do with Ian," she said aloud, "and I will send Frank with him. Mayhaps they can keep each other out of trouble."

Emma quit the room and went quickly to the receiving room, where she found Ian. She could not remember when the short, portly man was not Fernwood's coachman, and she remembered how, as a child, she had giggled when his heavy jowls shook like jelly when he talked. Today, dressed in gold and blue livery that was about to pop its buttons, sporting many capes and holding his three-corner in his hand, he stood awkwardly not too far from the door through which he had entered.

Emma greeted him with a forced smile. "You don't have to stand, Ian. Please sit." She motioned him to a chair and went to sit opposite him. The room was pleasantly warm. The early morning fire had died to smoldering red coals.

After explaining her plan, she said, "Go where the coachmen and footmen go while waiting on their lordships. Servants know more about the upper orders than the upper orders know themselves, and I want every on-dit you can squeeze out of anyone."

"Yes, m'lady."

Emma raised her voice slightly. "Do not blab what is going on at Fernwood. Should you do so, you will suffer a crushing set down."

Ian shook his head, mumbled a solemn promise of loyalty, and then brazenly asked, "M'lady, I don't take your meaning. Why do you want this information?"

"I will tell you with the conviction that you will not tell a soul. When Lady Francine and I leave Fernwood we are forced to live at Craigmont, in Sussex, with Consuelo deFleury. Last evening when my sister asked if we would go there as poor relations, maybe even be treated as servants, the thought even entered my mind that we might be thrown into a dungeon. These troubling thoughts set off an explosion in my mind. If such a fate is in store for us, a juicy on-dit like that is bound to be floating high among the Ton."

"But yer of the nobility. She can't make a servant out of yer," Ian protested.

"It has happened, even to members of the aristocracy."

*When one finds oneself without a feather to fly with, as I am at the moment,* Emma thought as she rose from her chair.

Ian jumped to his feet and dipped in a half bow. "Good day, m'lady." He moved toward the door.

"Ian, take Frank with you," Emma told him, sure that she could count on the head groom to keep quiet about the matter. He was a quiet, conscientious man who had never been known to say more than two words in succession.

"I'll be glad to have company, m'lady," Ian said.

As if it were an afterthought, Emma nonchalantly added, "And His Grace Ashton deFleury, the Duke of Attlebery, keep your ears tuned for news of him. His Grace is Consuelo deFleury's son."

"Yer wish is my command, m'lady. We'll leave immediately."

"Return tomorrow before nightfall. I will give you a voucher for a night's lodging."

"Never ye mind, m'lady," Ian said, "I 'ave a brother who'll welcome us . . . and yer ladyship, you can depend on me to

32

be mum about what is happening to yer and Lady Francine. I'd give me right arm fer yer ladyships."

Emma smiled. She knew the coachman was sincere. *If he doesn't fall into his cups.* "Go to the Thatched House Tavern. I hear it's a favorite of the pugilistic, and that is bound to draw members of the nobility."

"I will go to the Thatched 'ouse Tavern, m'lady, and as many others as need be. Good Easter Monday to yer."

The coachman bowed again and left.

*Good Easter Monday!* Emma had forgotten. In days past, on this day lads took round a chair decorated with flowers and greenery, and in it lifted the women of the house three times, expecting to be rewarded with a pence or so. It had been great fun when she had been the age of Francine. Regretfully—and she would only admit the regret to herself—she considered herself entirely too old for such foolishness.

Taking up a silver bell, she rang it crisply, and Fernwood's housekeeper appeared, bobbing and practically stumbling over herself, making Emma suspect she had had an ear to the door.

Ellie Snapp was a tall, slender woman around forty, a spinster, always immaculate and elegantly turned out in starched bombazine, over which she wore a white apron trimmed in lace. She *was* the housekeeper, and in charge of the household. A very important position, she often reminded members of the household staff. And she often imparted to them that the white apron and starched cap set her apart.

*Or is it above the others?* Emma thought, smiling.

"I'm ready for my instructions," Snapp said, sitting herself primly in a chair, as she did every morning of the year. Never before, she mused, had she had to wait until midday to see the lady of the house. But she listened intently as Emma pleasantly told her how she expected the household this day to be run, ending with, "Most especially Helga must

33

needs continue stitching on the new clothes, and if she needs help, engage others to assist her."

"Yes, m'lady," Snapp said, giving a quick bob and leaving immediately

That done, Emma went looking for Francine, finding her on the north terrace, her face flushed, her red-blond hair flying. Before she could enquire the reason for her sister's obvious happiness, Francine blurted out with great exuberance, "Gregory Banks and Claude Mason came to lift me, and when I ran into the house, Gregory followed and brought me out."

Emma laughed. "I suppose you locked the door when you went into the house." This was the fun of the lifting, the girls pretending they did not want to be lifted.

"Of course I didn't lock the door. "I'm not a slow top."

"Did you give him a pence?"

"No, I gave him a kiss."

"You shameless flirt," Emma teased, but the brightness emanating from Francine's gray eyes caused her, Emma, to lift a dark eyebrow quizzically. A flutter of concern materialized but left when Emma did not invite it to linger. She changed the subject entirely. "Francine, I must needs visit the tenantry today, to tell them goodbye. I've put it off as long as I can. Will you come with me?"

Francine was delighted.

The visits took the remainder of the day, and when they returned, Fernwood Manor glowed under a full moon, and under miles and miles of shimmering, star-studded, blue sky. Dew glistened on the grassy moor, and beyond that, hillocks, covered with swaying trees as black as indigo, rose majestically.

In the manor, mullioned windows framed lighted candles, and gray smoke curled from chimney pots atop the steep, slate roof.

Emma felt her heart lurch, and she began to be glad that time for leaving was nigh at hand. One did what one must do, and did it quickly. She listened to the night sounds, frogs croaking in the pond, crickets chirping, and from somewhere the sound of an owl hooting into the night.

No matter how much she tried to stop the thought, Emma wondered what it would be like at Craigmont by the Sea.

It had not been an easy task, the visits, saying goodbye to the people who had farmed Fernwood's 5,000 acres as long as Emma could remember.

Even so, Emma felt a sense of satisfaction: Each tenant had a small, well-kept, well-run cottage, surrounded by a profusion of blooming flowers, space for a vegetable garden, and outbuildings for their own animals. Children played in the small yards. Laughing, they had run to meet Francine, calling, "Lady Francie, Lady Francie." And when the equipage had pulled away, little hands flailed the air, saying goodbye, and tears spilled over onto Francine's cheeks.

Now, quiet and pensive, she asked, "Sister, what do you suppose Ian and Frank have found out about Consuelo deFleury?"

*And about Ashton deFleury,* Emma thought.


In London, in the Thatched House Tavern in St. James's, the third stop for the coachman and groom, Ian asked veiled questions about Consuelo deFleury. No one admitted knowing or even having heard of Consuelo deFleury. When asked *why* he wanted to know about someone no one had ever heard of, Ian lied, feeling that loyalty to his Lady Emma required him to do so.

But Frank was not as careful. After three tankards of cheap ale it seemed to Ian that the groom's tongue was tied in the middle and loose at both ends.

"They might make servants out of m'ladies, or even pitch them in a dungeon," Frank said, his words slurred from too much drink.

Ian was sorry beyond measure he had told the sapscull groom the purpose of their mission. He gave Frank a hefty nudge in the ribs, to no avail.

The groom continued: "We be from Fernwood. Ever 'ear of Consuelo deFleury?"

He received another nudge in the ribs, this time hard enough to bring a loud "ouch" that transcended the din and echoed off the rafters, from which hung lighted lanterns beaming circles of yellow light onto the stone floor.

Frank jumped to his feet and centered himself in one of the circles, dancing and prancing like a pugilist, swinging balled fits in front of his face, and at Ian. "Yer broke me rib, and I be for settling this right 'ere, instead of tomorrow on the field of 'onor. My fists's me weapon."

Ian groaned in disgust.

"Come on, Ian, yer ain't a coward, are yer?"

Ian looked up at the groom, thinking him paper-headed, a fool. Tall and willowy, he looked like a bean pole; the orange breeches stretched over matchstick legs made him look very much like a scarecrow.

A crowd had gathered inside the tavern, forming a circle, laughing and shouting encouragement at the groom, while throwing shillings into the circle of light. Ian recognized in the crowd pugilists Gentleman Jackson, the ex-champion of England, and the terrible Randall; their laughter was the loudest, their bulk the heftiest.

Ian had to think of a way to get out of there, and at the same time save face. He thought about hitting Frank and knocking him out, but realized that even when standing full height, his arms would not reach the groom's face.

*There's only one way to do this.*

With his three-corner secure on his head, his eyes squinted, his back bowed like a bull, Ian, leading with his left shoulder, ran into Frank's middle, folding the groom as if he were a loosely filled sack of grain.

Ian straightened to his full height, and, with Frank's long

arms dangling down his back, and his orange-covered spindle shanks dangling down his front, marched through the door to the unmarked curricle, where he unloaded the groom without consideration of his comfort. Laughter and clapping coming from inside the tavern, causing Ian to swear vehemently. Her ladyship was bound to hear of this. Quickly he bounded up into the carriage, took the ribbons, and guided the horses onto the cobbled street.

Ian did not know what to do next. He positively could not allow Frank into another coffeehouse.

Along St. James's, gaslight burned in the smoky haze. Ian decided they would go to the Cocoa Tree in Covent Garden, where mostly clergymen gathered for coffee, tea, or spirits, whatever suited their fancy. And gossip. He reasoned that since Lord Charles had only been recently buried, gossip among the black robes might be rife about his lordship's family.

But first, Ian decided, he must needs do something with Frank, who was snoring with gusto. He was tempted to dump the drunk-as-a-wheelbarrow groom beside the road and let him find his own way back to Fernwood. But being a kind man, the coachman did not dwell long on the dumping. He stopped the carriage and took from its boot a length of rope, with which he hobbled Frank's feet, then tied his hands behind him. Knowing the snoring would soon turn to swearing, Ian could not help but enjoy a little levity as he drove to his destination.

In the Cocoa Tree a fashionably dressed young woman dispensed tea and coffee in bowls, and young boys served the customers, offering each a copy of the London *Times*. Ian took his paper and went to sit on a bench by a long table situated by a window. He opened the paper and pretended to read, and when the boy brought his bowl of tea, which cost a shilling, Ian sipped the hot liquid slowly, and carefully. He did not want to burn his tongue, nor did he want to spend another shilling for a second bowl. Peering over the top of the paper, he eavesdropped, surreptitiously he hoped.

But the clergymen's mumbled voices ran together. *This will never do,* he thought, and moved closer to a black-suited man with his gaze focused on the door. Time dragged and Ian was ready to give up. Closing his eyes, he mumbled into his tea, "Please let someone mention Consuelo deFleury, or speak about the Duke of Attlebery, or about her ladyship herself. Any moment Frank will be yelling his lungs out."

For Ian, praying was the last resort, and he often felt guilt about that, but the awful feeling of failure as a sleuth was creeping up on him. He rose to leave, and just then the door creaked, and a man of considerable height entered and headed straight for the table occupied by the lone man.

The waiting man stood and greeted the newcomer with a hug and a kiss on the cheek, calling him brother.

Ian moved a table closer, sat down, and ordered another bowl of tea. What else could he do? He could not sip from an empty bowl.

"This day Countess Winslow was removed from her home to Bedlam, leaving the little girl," the newcomer said.

The other man sighed deeply. " 'Tis a shame. A Parson's life is not an easy one."

The words so shocked Ian that he spilled in his lap the fresh bowl of hot tea. "Demme, the devil take me," passed his lips before he could remember that just moments before he had been praying. He turned to offer an apology to the men of the cloth. "I'm sorry to be so awkward," he said, "and I'm sorry not to control me mouth."

The men went on talking, acting as if they did not hear Ian, and he knew he had lost his chance to start a conversation with anyone in the Cocoa Tree. Desperate, he blurted out, "Consuelo deFleury, do yer 'appen to know 'er?"

"Never heard of her," was the short, crisp answer, accompanied with a look of disdain.

"His Grace Ashton deFleury, do yer know 'im?"

The men of cloth didn't answer, just shook their heads as if this man belonged in Bedlam along with Countess Winslow. He thought of taking their shoulders and shaking them until they listened to him. But that would not do, he decided. It would only draw more attention to him, and to his enquiries.

It was time for him to leave. He must needs return to Fernwood with no more news than the late Lord Charles Winslow's widow had departed this day for Bedlam.

A bellow much resembling something coming from an angry bull pierced the air, and Ian knew Frank was awake. Quickly he dashed from the tavern and returned to the carriage where he found the groom fighting the ropes with all his might, his temper out of bounds. "You jackanapes. I bound I'll take yer fer this," he said, and Ian laughed.

It was late. He untied the groom, then took from his pocket a round timepiece and confirmed the time. Weary, he decided to go to his brother's place of dwelling near the docks, and on the way he would administer a strong set down to Frank about his loose tongue.

But Ian found it unnecessary to scold the groom. The sleep had killed the ale in Frank's veins and he sat in deep silence, which was more to his nature. Upon arriving at their destination, they ate a bowl of kidney stew graciously afforded by the tenant of the humble dwelling, and then the groom went quickly to bed, taking up his snoring again.

A tattered quilt attached to a rope divided the room in half. On the day side, where food was cooked over a grate in the fireplace and a tin wash pan held water for washing, Ian, tears spilling from his eyes, sat at a wobbly table and talked to his younger brother. "Jack, I've failed me ladyship." With the back of a plump hand he swiped at the tears that had run down onto his heavy jowls.

Jack arched a dark brow. "Fustian, Ian, I can't imagine yer failing anyone."

"Oh, but I 'ave." Ian stopped for a deep breath, and a

39

deep sigh, and then he told Jack about what had this night transpired, even telling names. He did not know how to explain his important mission without using the names of Consuelo and Ashton deFleury.

Upon hearing the name Ashton deFleury, Jack's eyes lighted up and his voice rose to a high pitch. "Yer mean His Grace Ashton deFleury, the Duke of Attlebery?"

Ian stared at him incredulously, and then he jumped to his feet, almost upsetting the table that held the leavings of kidney stew. "Jack, I pray yer know 'im." He grasped Jack's arm. "Pray tell me about Consuelo deFleury, about Craigmont where she lives."

Learning about the Duke of Attlebery was not as important to Ian as learning about Consuelo deFleury, the woman who might make servants out of the Ladies Winslow. That was the person his ladyship wanted to know about. In truth, if he remembered right, he had been taking his leave before her ladyship mentioned the Duke, which proved she had hardly any interest in His Grace.

Ian shook his head, thinking that the Duke was probably a fop anyway.

"What's so important about thet place?" Jack asked.

"Me ladyship fears she will go into service if she goes there. Tell me this Consuelo be a good woman who won't 'arm me ladyship and her sister."

Jack threw his head back and laughed boisterously. "Yer should have come 'ere in the first place, and saved yerself all that time at coffeehouses. I know plenty 'bout the Duke of Attlebery. A strange man, they say. Keeps 'is own counsel. Comes to 'is office ever day at the dock . . . and I 'ear he don't like to be called His Grace—"

Ian frowned. "About Consuelo deFleury?"

"Not that me and the Duke's bosom bows, but where I work, I 'ear things."

Jack worked at the West India Dock. He was a darkly handsome man, considerably intelligent, and it was only natural, Ian surmised, that his brother would be sought out for gossip.

"What kind of things, Jack?" Ian asked.

Jack stood and stretched. "Settle down, Ian. I'll fix us a posset. I believe yer in need of one." With slow ease he put a pan of sweetened milk on the coals, then withdrew from a box near the fireplace a bottle of wine, adding it to the milk, curdling it. "They call him a nabob."

"What's thet?"

"A rich man who has made his fortune in the trades. Ashton deFleury's own ships sail between England and India."

"But he's a duke," Ian protested.

Jack laughed. "Being the bastard son of the old eh what king got 'im the title; 'is fortune he made hisself. I 'ear he hates the uppity Ton, but thet don't stop the Ton mamas from chasing him for their daughters."

Ian hated to appear stupid to his intelligent brother, but he wanted to know things. He thought if he waited a moment Jack would tell him without being asked, and when it did not happen, Ian blurted out, "Who's the eh what king, Jack? And stop bandying words. I care not a fig for the duke. Tell me about 'is mother . . . Consuelo deFleury."

"One question at a time." Jack poured the posset in tin cups and handed one to Ian, then sipped slowly from the other. "Mad King George. Ain't yer 'eard? 'e follows everything he says with "eh what." Little wonder they think the old man is a lackwit."

"About Consuelo—"

"On-dits 'ave it that when His Majesty got this Consuelo deFleury in the family way she left London and ain't been seen since."

Ian's spirits dropped. "That's all yer know about 'er?"

"No, I 'ave knowledge of more. She's on friendly terms with Prinny's Mrs. Fitzherbert, and with Prinny's daughter, Princess Charlotte, 'eir to the throne."

41

Ian did not know whether that was good or bad for his ladyship. "Do yer think she be looking for serving gels?"

Jack cocked an eyebrow. "Could be. I 'ear 'er protection was cut."

"But if she's got a rich son—"

"Thet's another matter. They don't rub well together. The Duke lives in a sky-'igh townhouse in Mayfair, and never darkens the door of Craigmont."

At Craigmont, a three-storied country manor, His Grace Ashton deFleury, the Duke of Attlebery, sat in the elegant bookroom of his apartment and stared at the simmering coals in the fireplace. He had been riding and wore buckskin riding breeches, a spencer of impeccable tailoring, but no riding coat.

And his collar was open, exposing tangled hair that grew on his expansive chest. Although a fastidious dresser, he hated anything formal. Many times he had crossed the street to avoid greeting one of London's dandies, such as Beau Brummell, who, in His Grace's opinion, made no worthy contribution to humanity.

Ashton deFleury had worked almost as long as he could remember. He had signed on his first ship when he was five and ten, and when he was one and twenty he bought his first freighter. His leathered complexion was evidence of his years serving as captain of his own ship.

Now, each of his ships had a proven, seaworthy captain.

Leaning back in his chair, His Grace's weary eyelids dropped over smoldering hazel eyes that could become as keen as the brain behind them. He was a tall, well-built man, with straight sun-streaked blonde hair that grew rather long-ish on his neck. Much out of mode, but His Grace did not give a fig about that.

Propping his feet on a stool, he listened to the waves pounding the Sussex shore. He should feel peaceful, he argued to himself, but an anxious heart beat against his rib cage. Anytime now, his future wife would arrive at Craigmont.

Producing an heir, the age-old duty of titled men, was not the reason for His Grace wanting a mate. He was lonely. Upon making the decision to marry, His Grace had pensioned off his mistress of many years, telling himself that he wanted to be worthy of Lady Winslow.

Now, restless, he left the chair and paced the floor. This day the leather-bound books that reached from floor to ceiling, in beautifully carved cases, held no appeal. He felt hot blood flush his face, and as he envisioned Emma as he had seen her on Easter morning, beautiful beyond measure, with her tiny waist, and her bosom pushing against the bodice of her faded dress, desire filled his loins.

A light knock stopped His Grace's pacing and his rambling thoughts. To his abrupt, "Come in," the door opened and a liveried footman handed forward a salver, on which a sealed missive rested. He then turned to leave, but His Grace stopped him. "I may have a reply."

The missive bore the solicitor, Prescott's, signature.

His Grace read: "Enquiries are being made in London about Your Grace, and about Consuelo deFleury. A reliable source reports that Lady Emma Winslow fears her departed brother, Lord Charles Winslow, sold her and her sister into servitude at Craigmont, and the source further reports that Lady Emma Winslow fears they might even be thrown into a dungeon."

"This is good," His Grace said. *When her ladyship learns her fears are ungrounded, she will be most anxious to become my wife.* There was more to the missive, and His Grace read on: "I regret to inform you that Dowager Countess Margaret Winslow, Lord Charles's widow, was this day admitted to Bedlam. Daughter Prudence is here with me. Please advise what I am to do with *this* child."

Ashton was saddened by the news about poor Countess

Margaret. But he had feared it would come to this. Quickly he turned to his writing desk and penned his reply: "Take little Prudence to Lady Emma Winslow, at Fernwood, before she departs for Craigmont. And make enquiries of a private hospital for the Countess, secretly, of course."

Handing the sealed envelope to the footman, His Grace ordered that it be delivered to Prescott before first light on the morrow. The footman left, and His Grace turned back into the room. He could not stop the elation that washed over him.

Sunday, the banns would be read. . . .

# *Chapter Four*

Emma put the last stitch in her moneybag, and swore, *sotto voce*. A deep frown creased her brow. Ian's report had not been favorable. The strange Duke was as daft as his mother, Consuelo deFleury, who was probably a dried-up old cakey who was still wallowing in her shame for having the mad king's by-blow.

"I suppose Consuelo deFleury is the skeleton in the family closet to which Prescott alluded," she said aloud.

Holding up the moneybag, made from scraps of material left from Helga's sewing, Emma was pleased. The sale of her mother's valuables—and a few she had stolen from the estate—had gone very well. There was enough, she was sure, to support Francine's London Season. And the new clothes now packed in several boxes would do them in style.

"Almack's here we come," she said to the empty room. She counted the money again. All one hundred pounds of it. Her head whirled, and she was tempted to bypass Craigmont and go straight to London. She poked the money into the bag, then tied it around her waist. Dressed only in white pantalettes and a white bodice, she danced around the room. Gay excitement welled up inside her. The money made the difference. Now, she would welcome the chance to outwit the Duke of Attlebery. Marry him, indeed!

"You pea-goose, Emma Winslow, you can't fritter the

morning away," she said. She stopped her dancing and from the chiffonnier took a blue morning dress and slipped it over her slender body, but when she looked at herself in the looking glass, her high spirits disappeared and her heart dropped to the pit of her stomach, to rest in a pool of horrified dismay. *I look enceinte.*

For a long moment she stood and pondered what to do. It was imperative that she hide the money on her person, else a maid, or even one of Consuelo deFleury's spies, would find it. And Emma did not discount the possibility of highwaymen robbing them on their way to Craigmont.

Emma started to remove the stuffed bag, and then the most marvelous idea stormed her mind. She giggled. *Let the ruthless Duke think I'm in the family way. That will cook his goose.*

A knock on the door leading into the hall took Emma from her plotting, and into her sitting room. It was Hannah, she knew, the knock was Hannah's alone. She bade her come in.

A bob preceded Hannah's hurried words, "M'lady, a carriage comes. Suppose it's the new earl? I remember thet yer said yer want to take leave before—"

"I most certainly do." Emma ran to the window and yanked back the curtains, scraping rings against rod, and her spirits dropped further. It was not the new Earl. It was her dead brother's solicitor, and so far when the man had come to Fernwood he had been the bearer of bad news.

This day, walking up the shadowed lane that led to the Manor, Prescott carried a small suitcase in one hand and held the hand of a little girl with the other, and he was walking so fast the child could barely keep up.

Quickly Emma went belowstairs to the receiving room, where she opened the door and peered out, looking not at the solicitor but at the little girl. After a moment she recognized her as her niece Prudence. Charles's daughter.

Emma had seen her niece only twice in the child's eight

years. For some inexplicable reason Charles had kept his family away from Fernwood, and he had never invited his sisters to visit his London home located in Hanover Square. So why was Prudence suddenly here? Had not Charles left directives for the child's life, as he had for hers and Francine's?

Emma watched, and as the man and child drew nearer, she felt her heart break. Dressed in black from head to toe, including hightop shoes of the lower orders, Prudence very much resembled an urchin, not unlike the children who swarmed the streets of London, selling flowers to make money for bread.

Tears streaked Prudence's unwashed, stonelike face. Emma could whip up anger toward Charles, but not toward this innocent child, who was another victim of Charles's careless way of life.

Emma walked down the steps and reached out her arms in welcome.

"Aunt Emma," Prudence said very properly, while ignoring Emma's outstretched arms, "I do not like my name. The children in school call me Prudy, or Prude. I hate it. So will you please call me Prue . . . or Joy, which is my other name."

Emma cleared her throat to dislodge the huge lump. "As you wish, Lady Prue Winslow. You know that is your proper name, do you not? Your late father was the seventh Earl of Wickersham, and your mother's a countess."

"That does not matter a whit. When we went into mourning for my father, we gave everything to the less fortunate souls of London. My mother says I am to always remember the poor in the world and not hold myself above them."

*And did she not teach you to bathe?* Emma wondered. She looked at the solicitor, who stood with his eyes rolled upward in a gesture of hopelessness. He had released Prudence's hand, as if to say: Take her Lady Emma; she's all yours.

Taking the little hand, which was balled into a fist, Emma led Prudence up the steps and into the foyer, where she rang for a servant. When Hannah appeared, Emma asked that the child and her small bag be taken upstairs to her, Emma's, rooms, adding, "And order hot water for a bath. I will be up directly."

When the maid and child were gone, Emma turned on the solicitor, who had meekly followed them into the house. "I should like an explanation. Why is the child here at Fernwood when you know all too well that tomorrow Francine and I depart for Craigmont . . . to God knows what."

Prescott shifted his weight from one foot to the other. His eyes were focused on something beyond Emma's shoulder. "I—uh, brought her here on the Duke of Attlebery's orders."

Emma's mouth fell open. "The ruthless Duke again! What right . . . is he taking over my niece's life, along with everyone else's?" Ian had told Emma that her sister-in-law had been removed to Bedlam, but she had assumed the child would have been sent to live with her maternal grandmere, not sent to an aunt who was practically a stranger to the child.

"Sadly, with her mother in Bedlam, you might call the child an orphan. She has no means."

*Nor do I*. Emma thought. "About the Duke—"

"I sent a missive, apprising him of the situation. His reply was that I deliver Lady Prudence Winslow to Fernwood before your departure to Craigmont."

"Why did you confer with Ashton deFleury regarding my late brother's daughter? Why did you not come to Fernwood at once? Or take Prudence to the Countess Margaret's mother?"

"My instructions came from His Grace—"

"But you are the solicitor for Charles's estate."

Prescott smiled. "I am now His Grace's solicitor. Quite a lucrative account."

Emma wanted to spit. At every turn Ashton deFleury was in charge. "I don't take the meaning—"

"Often I didn't get paid. More than once His Grace stepped in and saved your brother. I don't know where Winslow's blunt went. Now, I must needs look out for myself."

That was outside of enough for Emma. She wanted Prescott gone, and she said as much in a cutting voice, "*I* will not be needing your services, Mr. Prescott, so you may leave."

"The child?"

"You may rest assured Lady Prudence will be taken care of . . . without His Grace's help."

Prescott gave a half bow, his eyes cast downward. "Yes, Lady Winslow." With his coattail flapping behind him, he skittered down the steps and down the lane toward his traveling equipage.

*Like a scared rabbit.* Emma thought. She watched the horse and carriage until it disappeared from sight, and then she slammed the door and hurriedly ascended the stairs. It was outside of enough that she should have to appear at Craigmont with a child requiring . . .

Emma thought for a moment; she did not know what children required.

"But I do not have windmills in my head. I know your thinking," she said to His Grace, whom she had never seen, did not want to see, and who was, she was sure, a purse-proud, domineering jackanapes. No doubt he wanted her saddled with formidable obligations so that she would be forced to do his bidding. "Well, we shall see about that," she said, visualizing a bacon-faced old man with mean eyes, who sniffed snuff and spilled it on his cravat. Never mind that Prescott had called him handsome.

She left then to go deal with Prudence. Upon entering the room where Prudence waited, sitting in a chair with her skinny legs dangling over the seat's edge, Emma managed a smile, which was not returned. Big gray-green eyes, framed with dark lashes that curled upward, met Emma's. "Aunt Emma, I do not want to burden you with my presence."

*My God,* thought Emma, *is this a child speaking?*

"Prue, your presence could never be a burden. You are my brother's child, and I am sorry that we have not been together more. It would have made this reunion so much easier."

"I know, but Mamma did not wish it. She did not like Fernwood, and what my Mama wanted, my Papa wanted. He loved her very much."

Emma doubted that, but she would not for the world disillusion a child of eight. "I'm sure your Papa did love your Mama, and I am sure a bath would be in order."

Prudence stood and removed the ugly black bonnet, releasing yellow curls that framed a small, round face. Emma reached to touch a curl and felt her hand shake. For a brief time she was taken back, but to where she did not know. A hot, smothering feeling engulfed her, but the feeling passed as quickly as it had come, and as she helped Prudence undress she told her that on tomorrow they would depart to a wonderful place called Craigmont, where they would live with Cousin Consuelo deFleury.

"If it is so wonderful, why are you worried?" Prudence asked.

Emma started to lie and say she was not worried at all, but instinct told her Prudence would know better. Tears brimmed the little girl's eyes, lodging on her long lashes. Emma gathered her into her arms and for a while sat in the chair and held her.

"The unknown worries grownups, but not children. From now on you must needs let your Aunt Emma do the worrying."

"I did the worrying for Mama, especially after she became so ill." Prudence pulled back and looked unblinking into Emma's face. "Do you believe in miracles, Aunt Emma? Like at Easter, the miracle of the resurrection."

Emma was speechless, and Prudence went on, as if talking to herself, "When Jesus rose from his tomb, He gave the world hope. Mama says we must needs always have hope."

"Of . . . of course I believe —"

"Then, you will understand."

"Understand what?"

Prudence jumped from Emma's lap and went to open the small suitcase, which, Emma supposed, held the child's worldly possessions — what she had not given to the poor.

Emma waited.

From under more black garments, Prudence withdrew a half-burned candle. "I believe in miracles. I believe God will make Mama well, and being a realistic person, and knowing how sick Mama is, I've set the time for next Easter." She held the candle in her small hands. "I suppose I should light it, but I don't think God will care."

Emma watched as she bowed her head of golden curls. Her lips moved, but no sound came from them.

The silence filled the room, and Emma. The place in the hollow of her throat began to beat so fast that she felt she could not breathe. Then, before her eyes, Prudence's face became blank, the golden curls a halo.

Emma gasped for breath, her body began to tremble, and the awful darkness engulfed her. Once again she stood in the forest, where trees whispered, and this child . . . this child sat on a crumbling stone wall, her head bent over a candle.

## Chapter Five

It was the Ladies Winslows' last evening at Fernwood. With a footman's help, Emma packed the carriage in which they would travel to Craigmont. There was hardly room left for her to sit, much less Francine and little Prudence. She wished they could take a baggage carriage. That, however, was out of the question. The new earl would probably send the Bow Runners after her for taking the carriage with the noble crest emblazoned on its panels. But it was most certainly not her intent to arrive at Craigmont as impoverished relatives.

She would sit on the box and handle the ribbon herself, Emma decided. She had intended to take Ian, but then she would worry about how he would be returned to Fernwood.

Having done all she could do, Emma went to bed. She slept fitfully, and in the early morning hours, between midnight and dawn, making sure she did not awaken Prudence, she bounded from the bed, dressed quickly, and went to the outbuildings where the farm animals were kept. First, she caught two unsuspecting geese, hobbled them, and left them flopping and squawking on the ground. Then she loaded into the farm cart two goats, and two pigs. Having no coop in which she could put the geese, she put them in the cart with the pigs and goats. Stealthily she crept to the door of the chicken house.

Holding the catcher—a long, stiff wire crooked on one end to fit around a chicken's leg—she snared from the roost a plump pullet whose squawking woke the other chickens, and pandemonium broke loose. She quickly closed the door to prevent their escape and continued her task undeterred until she had caught twelve sleek, white, fat pullets, which were four months old and would soon be laying eggs. "Don't squawk so loud, and stop your flapping," she scolded as she stuffed the last one in the coop.

A loud cock-a-doodle-do set forth from the top roost. A huge black-and-white cock was stretching his neck and voicing his objection to the disturbance. Or for losing twelve of his flock over which he has been lord and master, Emma mused. She told the crowing rooster to be quiet else she would take him to Craigmont with the pullets. When he did not heed her warning and let out another long boisterous crow, she slipped under the roost and grabbed his leg, careful not to let him spur her. "You have nothing to squawk about, so behave yourself," she said as she pushed him into the coop with the pullets. "How lucky can a male be?" she wanted to know, smiling.

For some inexplicable reason, His Grace Ashton de-Fleury, the Duke of Attlebery, came to Emma's mind. She imagined him a randy *old* Duke who kept twelve lightskirts for his pleasure. Even though she was a country miss, she was not unaware of what went on in the world of the upper orders. It was expected of the nobility to keep mistresses, sometimes more than one. She regarded this with disdain.

Another thought crept into Emma's mind, and she said aloud, "If His Grace is so anxious to become leg-shackled that he would trick my brother into a game of chance, why has he not sent a carriage to transport Francie and me to Craigmont? He seems adept at running things, like ordering little Prudence be brought to Fernwood.

"Well, I'm not joining the Duke's lightskirts, nor will I marry His Grace to produce an heir to inherit his dukedom."

She was sure that was what he wanted; all titled men did. But she would not be a party to such an alliance. Her menagerie of fowls and animals, and the money she had managed to gather, would guard against her doing anything against her will.

The coop of chickens would ride atop the carriage, she planned, and the farm cart would be pulled behind the carriage. In time there would be more chickens, more geese, more pigs, and more goats, which she would sell. She felt the moneybag tied around her waist for assurance. A noise from behind made her turn.

It was Francine, her red-blond hair a tangled mass of curls, her feet bare. Covering her face was a paste made of barley flour, bitter almonds, and honey. Called Roman balsam, it was supposed to fade freckles. Emma had her doubts. She smiled at Francine. "Careful," she said. "It's not safe to walk in here."

"Sister, I saw the farm cart, and now the chickens. Are we boarding Noah's Ark?"

"At all times we must needs be independent. If conditions at Craigmont are unacceptable, then we, you, Prudence, and I, shall depart for Town. Of course we will sell the chickens and animals before seeking a place to live."

Francine laughed a tiny laugh. "I think that would be a capital idea." Becoming suddenly somber, she flung her arms around Emma. "Oh, Sister, I'm so frightened."

Emma was frightened, too, but she was trying to keep the fright hidden. Hugging Francine, she spoke in a voice depicting false high spirits, "Don't be frightened, Francie. Remember, you told me that the change would be exciting, a new beginning."

"I've found that I don't want a new beginning."

Emma was quiet for a moment, and then she said, "Francie, sometimes things are out of our hands. We must needs trust God, who, I am sure, has a plan for us."

Emma wished she could believe what she was saying. In truth, she thought that God had forgotten all about them.

"I want—"

Emma cut Francine's words short. "I predict that by next Easter our lives will be as happy as they have been at Fernwood."

She believed no such thing.

"Do you think so, Emma? I pray that Gregory will find his way to Craigmont . . . or into London—"

Emma forced a laugh. "Little one, I believe you are suffering your first spell of puppy-love. When you have your come-out and meet all those handsome rakes, who, I am sure, will be paying you their addresses, you will have forgotten all about farm-boy Gregory."

Francine gave a wan smile but did not say more.

"Come on," Emma said, taking hold of her arm. "We must needs get dressed. First light will be upon us shortly. It is a full day's journey to Craigmont."

They went quietly inside the house and crept up the stairs. Emma did not want to awaken the servants; she could not bear telling them a last goodbye. "Wear the green satin traveling dress," she told Francine. "We want Cousin Consuelo to see right off that we have means."

They parted, and Emma went to her rooms to face once again her eight-year-old niece who was pushing thirty in her demeanor. Prudence had refused to sleep in a room alone, and Emma had finally agreed to share her bed with her. Sometime in the night Prudence had awakened her, sobbing her little heart out, a child, not the grown-up she wanted to be. Emma had held her close to her body for warmth, and comfort, and told her to believe in the Easter miracle, and finally the sobbing stopped, and the child slept.

Now, she sat in the same chair she had sat in yesterday, dressed in the same black dress, the same black high-top shoes, her golden curls hidden by that awful bonnet. Resting beside the chair was the small suitcase she'd brought to Fernwood.

*I can't take her to Craigmont like this.* Emma thought, and prevailed upon the little girl to give up the mourning clothes. "No, Auntie Em, I can't. I must needs wear mourning clothes." She looked at Emma straightforward. "Why are you and Francine not wearing black? It is proper according to society."

Emma did not want to tell her that wearing black would be a constant reminder of her anger toward her brother, and that she did not need to be reminded. "It is not as important in the country as it is in Town, Prue, and black is so depressing. When we pass through a village on our way to Craigmont we shall purchase for you a beautiful dress . . . and patent slippers with bows."

"No," was the simple answer, and Emma managed not to despair. Prudence was, after all, a child, a very stubborn one, she was learning. Consuelo deFleury must needs accept that.

Emma reasoned again that it would have been better for Prudence had she been sent to live with her maternal grandmother. What she, Emma, knew about raising a child could be put in a thimble, proof of which was her allowing Prudence to sleep with her. That was unheard of among the upper orders. *But she was so frightened.* She took a moment and bent to hug the child, and then she hurried to wash and dress.

She had chosen a dress of bishop's blue silk, cut fashionably low to show a goodly amount of cleavage. Tied under her bosom with a ribbon, the skirt fell loosely over her waist, made thick with the stuffed moneybag.

Emma found herself hoping the Duke *would* be at Craigmont, to witness her condition. He would not be there when they arrived, if rumors could be believed, but soon he would be. When he came to collect her brother's debt.

Planning ahead, Emma had wrapped scones and thin

56

butter cookies in brown paper. It would be their breakfast. She gave a cookie to Prudence, then rewrapped the others. Down the road it would save a stop at a posting inn.

Emma had yet to decide which hat to wear. Standing in front of the looking glass, she chose at first a Gypsy, plain straw and tied with a ribbon, but she thought that not quite the crack and chose instead a Cossack, which had a rounded crown, with the front edged with pearls, and with feathers at one side. She poked at her long black hair until it was secured underneath the high crown, with only a few wisps on her neck. The purple ostrich feathers curled under her chin, in the style very popular with the ladies of the upper orders, so she had read in fashion magazines.

Leaving the Gypsy for the next lady of the house, she turned away from the looking glass and saw that first light had quietly invaded the room. It was time to leave.

Holding Prudence's little hand, Emma quit the room without looking back. Her chin was set in an implacable line, for she refused to let it quiver, as it was prone to do when her heart pounded in her breast. Quietly she pushed words from her mouth, "We must needs leave quietly, lest we wake the servants."

"Where is Francie?" Prudence whispered.

"She will meet us belowstairs."

At the end of the hall they turned right and descended to the lower level by way of the servant's stairs. From under the door that opened into the kitchen a sliver of light danced on the stone floor. Emma frowned, and when she pushed open the door, the swollen eyes of her dearly beloved staff stared at her in solemn silence. Then a single sob, and a floodgate of wails suddenly opened, until Emma thought perhaps she was attending her own wake. "Now stop this," she scolded, her gaze scanning the faces. "And whoever awakened you?"

"The chickens, m'lady," they said in choked unison.

"The rooster crowing," said a footman, already dressed in Fernwood's livery of blue and gold.

Hannah stepped slightly forward, rustling her bombazine. "But we wuz awake, m'lady. We could not allow yer to leave with yer stomach empty."

Emma smelled for the first time the wonderful aroma of cooked porridge, eggs, ham, and hot bread. The scent filled the room. She blinked back tears and swore *sotto voce:* "I'll be demmed if I cry." Forcing laughter, she thanked the servants and asked that they enjoy the sumptuous meal. To those who had not met Prudence, Emma presented her little niece without explanation.

"We want to serve yer," Hannah said. And they did.

They sat at a long table in the formal dining room, and the servants brought the food on silver platters, in the most eloquent style. Hanging from the ceiling, a Wedgwood chandelier held lighted candles, and fresh flowers, picked from the garden and placed in Wedgwood epergnes, graced the table's length.

*We should have entertained more at Fernwood,* Emma thought, quickly reminding herself that it was too late for regrets. Of course when the sixth Earl of Wickersham and his Countess, Emma's Mama and Papa, had lived, they had entertained extravagantly.

*It was when Charles married and deserted Fernwood that the entertaining stopped.*

She looked at Prudence. The child ate as an adult would eat, primly wiping her mouth with her serviette, sipping her tea quietly, speaking only when spoken to.

Francine sat pensively quiet, picking at her food, and Emma thought that any moment her sister would start to cry.

"If we leave soon, there will be time for a picnic along the way," Emma said. She rang a bell and a footman appeared.

"Yes, m'lady."

"Please, James, see that a picnic basket is prepared. We have decided to make our journey to Craigmont a wonderful, joyous journey."

The footman bowed, "Yes, m'lady." And then he left, smiling, his shoulders squared, his steps quick, as if he could not do his mistress's bidding fast enough.

"Mama and I picnicked in St. James's Park," Prudence said, her eyes big, her voice animated, happy for a moment.

But the moment of happiness was short-lived, Emma noticed. The somberness returned to Prudence's little face almost immediately, and she said, "I wonder if they will take Mama on a picnic —"

"Of course they will. And, Prue, I see no reason why we can't visit your mama soon, maybe share a picnic lunch with her. Craigmont is not awfully far from London."

"Oh, do you think so, Auntie Em? I know Mama would love to see me, and I would dearly love to see her."

"We shall certainly try."

Emma hoped that she had not spoken too quickly. What if the people in charge at Bedlam refused Margaret visits from her daughter? She pushed the worry aside. Prudence needed to be able to hope, and to plan.

One by one the servants came and lined themselves against the dining room wall, watching their departing mistress with adoring eyes. Emma knew it was past time to depart. Giving a small, forced laugh, she stood. "This has been most wonderful, and I shall feel happy about your kindness for the whole of the trip . . . and even beyond that." Then without thinking, she made a promise she was not sure she would keep. "I will return to Fernwood to see all of you."

*Dear God get me out of here.*

Emma's bravado had exhausted itself. She gathered up her hat, plopped it back onto her head, and headed for the waiting carriage.

Standing by the carriage was Hannah, holding a small cardboard box in her hands. " 'Tis me things. I won't need much."

"What do you mean, won't need much?" Emma asked,

and then, "Hannah, you can't go. Consuelo deFleury will cast us all out."

"Then I will be there to catch yer, m'lady. And I will be your spy." The maid climbed up onto the box to sit by Emma.

"I won't need a spy," Emma protested, knowing it was of no use to argue with Hannah, unless she wished to have the loyal maid physically removed from the box. After making sure Francine and Prudence were squeezed inside the carriage, she climbed up and took the ribbons. Urging the horses to a trot, down the long lane they went, toward the main road.

Emma refused to look back. She knew the servants were gathered on the lawn, whispering, some still crying. She could not bear it.

Ponderously the carriage bounced along, followed by the farm cart, and daylight stealthily crept upon them. Morning dew shimmered on the grass and on the wild flowers along the roadside, and the sun rose to their back. Somewhere ahead of them was Craigmont by the Sea . . . and Consuelo deFleury.

Now that they were on their way, Emma became anxious to arrive at their destination. Pushing the horses toward London, which they skirted, they joined travelers on the New Road that led to Brighton, a six-hour journey from London.

Scudding clouds rolled away behind the carriage, while ahead, a smooth, macadamized road swallowed up the pounding hoof beats of horses pulling elegant carriages to the resort town of Brighton. They stopped for the picnic she had promised Prudence, and several times to rest and water the horses, and to feed and water the fowl and animals. Prudence, for a while, rode on the box beside Emma, usurping Hannah. Then she became sleepy and asked to ride inside the carriage, which she did, resting her head in Francine's lap.

It was late evening when they reached Brighton, and Emma was weary and scared. Never had she journeyed so far from Fernwood. Seeing a man in front of the theater situated along New Road, Emma reined the horses in. The small man wore skin tight pantaloons of a purplish tint, a white waistcoat, and a black box coat. A cape hung carelessly off one shoulder. Emma thought he might be an actor, perhaps performing on the stage this very night. "Sir, could you be so kind as to direct me to Craigmont?"

His gaze swept blatantly over Emma, the packed carriage, the chicken coop, the farm cart, while a faint smile slowly curled his thin lips.

Emma gave a stern look. What was so terrible about asking directions? "Well," she said when he did not right away answer, "do you know where Craigmont is located or not?"

Obviously just now seeing the emblazoned panels, the little man's expression changed to one of respect. Bowing from the waist, he said, "I do, m'lady. It is rather complicated, and I think I must needs make a drawing."

He turned and went back into the theater, and several minutes passed before he returned to hand up a folded piece of paper to Emma. "M'lady, are you certain Miss deFleury's expecting you?"

"At this moment, I do not know what to think, but I shall soon find out." Emma thanked him for his trouble, cracked the ribbons over the horses's backs, and guided them in the direction the crude map indicated they should go.

They traveled north, parallel to the Sussex Coast. A gay sea wind whipped their faces, and Hannah complained profusely, until Emma threatened to put her off to walk.

They passed through Worthington, and almost immediately the road veered to the right and they entered woods, passing through tall iron gates over which "Craigmont by the Sea" was displayed in huge letters. The gates clanged shut behind the carriage, as if they had been trained by some mysterious force to open, then shut quickly behind the carriage, making the Winslows Craigmont's prisoners.

Like an enchanted ribbon, the road twisted and turned. Lush with tall trees, plants and vines, there was the humid, flowery odor of a giant hothouse. High above the carriage, tree limbs touched, making an archway. Like the roof of a church, Emma thought. At this turn, or around the next bend, surely they would come upon Craigmont.

As they traveled deeper and deeper into the woods, Emma's heart began to pound, for she did not like the darkness. Somewhere it was still light, she knew. It was late spring, and days were longer. At last the trees thinned, and Emma saw ahead a patch of blue sky. She urged the horses to go faster and soon they came to the edge of a massive clearing. Pulling the horses to an abrupt stop, she bent forward and stared.

In the middle of the clearing, perched on a small incline, with terraced gardens sloping to the sea, sat a magnificent four-storied manor house built of yellow brick. A thing of beauty, exquisite beyond Emma's understanding. She caught her breath. A hundred rooms or more, she guessed; its very size was frightening.

Late sun sparked tall, narrow windows, and from more than fifty chimney pots gray smoke curled upward, forming a purplish cloud over the steep roof. Behind and beyond the manor, still more tall trees loomed ever skyward.

The road to the manor, made of crushed white stone and flanked on both sides by horse chestnut trees, broadened and curved, so that a carriage would approach head-on. No longer in a hurry, Emma drove slowly to the wide sweep of steps that led up to a spacious veranda.

Through an open door, she saw a man wearing white hose, knee breeches, black tails, a pristine white shirt with extremely high collar points pressing into fat jowls. When she pulled the horses to a stop, he stepped out onto the veranda and slowly approached the top step, glaring through his quizzing glass. Before Emma could introduce herself, he announced explicitly, "Miss deFleury is not receiving."

And when he managed to twist his captured jowls loose from the' collar points so that he could view the whole of the packed carriage, the passengers, the chickens, geese, and animals, his face flushed beet red, and he further stated, "We are not in the market for produce."

Emma, drawing herself up, set her chin in an unrelenting line. "This produce is not for sale. Would you please be so kind as to tell Miss deFleury that Ladies Emma, Francine, and Prudence Winslow have arrived from Fernwood." After a nudge from Hannah, she added, "With abigail Hannah."

The butler snorted and went back into the house.

Emma had never felt so unwelcome in her life. She swore under her breath. Were they to sit there all night? Finally, lest she explode, she said, "If Charles were here, I'd wring his neck."

"Oh, please, m'lady," Hannah pleaded, "do not speak of the dead. They might come back to haint yer."

"Charles would not dare show himself before me after what he has done. He's probably groveling at St. Peter's feet, begging forgiveness."

Hannah shook her head. "Jesus Christ and Mother Mary."

"Don't swear, Hannah," Emma said in a low voice.

"I'm not swearing, m'lady, I'm praying."

"Then do it quietly. We must needs not let Consuelo de-Fleury know we are frightened."

The butler at last returned to tell Emma to please take the farm cart, *and* the chicken coop to the stables. Emma thanked him kindly, then asked if her sister and niece, who were so cramped inside the carriage, might please wait in the receiving room until she had seen to her fowls and animals.

The butler reluctantly acquiesced. Emma hopped down off the box to let down the step for Francine and Prudence. No, she would not do it. It was the duty of a footman. Turning to the staid butler, she asked very politely. "Please fetch a footman."

Another snort, but the fine-dressed man disappeared again, bringing a footman when he returned. In deadly silence the footman put down the step and offered a hand to Francine and Prudence.

"M'lady, Hannah said, "if yer don't need me, I feel disposed to stay, too. Me backside can't take much more of this box."

"Do so," Emma answered. "And please keep an eye on little Prue. Just find a place and sit quietly. I should not be overly long."

Holding her belongings in her arms, Hannah scrambled down to join Francine and Prudence, and they all trooped behind the butler into the house.

Emma regained the box and cracked the whip over the horses' backs; the resounding pop joined the sound of booming waves beating against the shore.

At the back of the manor, trees and resting benches dotted a grassy, well-kept lawn. Emma could not see a stable anywhere, or outbuildings of any kind. At Fernwood they were everywhere. Common sense told her to stay on the road. She passed over a little bridge that spanned a narrow stream and again entered woods.

The road wound through the copse, and there, in another clearing, were the stables, almost as large and as magnificent as the manor. Just not as tall.

There was not a chicken house in sight.

Circling the stables, for the doors opened away from the manor, Emma pulled the horses to a restive stop and waited for a groom, who eventually came, his eyes wide, his mouth gaped.

By now Emma had had her fill of people who acted as if they had never before seen a chicken coop atop a crested carriage, or a farm cart with animals and geese. "I'm Lady Emma Winslow," she said in way of introduction. "The butler said that I should deliver these to the stables."

The groom cocked an eyebrow in a questioning manner and just stood there.

Emma added loftily, "I shall return to the manor, to be received by Miss deFleury."

That helped the groom find his voice. "M'lady, what am I to do with . . . with these things?" His arm raised, he pointed imperiously to the farm cart.

Emma climbed down off the box and looked around. "Does not Craigmont have a chicken house, or a goat pen? The geese can be turned loose; they will return periodically, bringing little goslings. Of course the pigs will need their own pen, so they can reproduce."

Just then the tearing thunder of hooves on dirt and the dolphin-like blowing of a horse's breath drew Emma's attention. Looking up, she saw a rider approaching on a long, sleek black horse. Reining in, the exceptionally tall man riding the horse dismounted with alacrity and handed the reins to the groom. With masculine assured grace he moved toward Emma, who had no idea who he was. His intense gaze was focused directly on her.

Probably the overseer, she thought, hoping he might be of more help than the groom. "Can you suggest where I might put my chickens . . . and my animals?" she asked.

"Your what?"

Emma heard a squawk and looked around. One of the geese had worked free of its bondage and was standing on the ground, its wings spread for flight. She dove for the goose, and missed.

The goose, however, did not miss the man standing directly in its flight pattern, who, when hit in the face by flapping wings and clawing feet, lost his balance and ended up on his backside in the stable yard.

He swore loudly, "The devil take me."

"I'm so sorry," Emma said, running to help him up. "My goose was frightened. Are you injured?" She wondered if the man could talk with any intelligence. So far he had not said a word, except what, and to swear.

Laughter was the response, and then, "No, I'm not injured, and if you were anyone besides who you are, your goose would be cooked for supper."

He pulled himself up to full height, which was tremendous, Emma noticed, and brushed the dust from his riding breeches.

Emma gave a quick answer. "You do not know who I am, nor do I know you. I don't believe we've been properly introduced."

He walked to stand before Emma. Lifting her hand, he brushed it lightly with his lips before saying, "Lady Winslow, I am Ashton deFleury, your future husband."

# Chapter Six

Emma's hand flew to her mouth. "You're not the ruthless Duke?" *Of course he is; he just said so.*

"You've been listening to the quidnuncs," he accused, smiling as he walked closer to the carriage and farm cart. The gentle smile turned to uproarish laughter.

Emma could see nothing comical about her situation, and she said so. "What's so demme funny?"

"You, Lady Winslow . . . what does this mean? Where did these goats and pigs come from?" His gaze fell on the chicken coop atop the carriage. "And what are you going to do with chickens? And the goose that attacked me?"

She stared at him without blinking. If he were so witless . . .

His gaze fell on the other goose. "I see there's another soldier primed for attack. Did you bring two of everything?"

"So they can multiply," Emma retorted in a superior tone. "These animals . . . the geese, and the chickens came from Fernwood. I would like a place to put them. I'm sure they are thirsty, and hungry." When he did not answer straight away, she prodded him, "Well, hurry."

His Grace stood with his legs slightly apart, rubbing his clean-shaven chin. "I'm giving your request considerable consideration."

He was no longer looking at the animals and fowls,

Emma noticed. His gaze was moving over her, from head to toe. So she engaged in some deep scrutiny herself, looking him up and down.

He wasn't old, as she had expected. His looks were passable, his height was formidable, his buckskin breeches fit his muscular physique too tightly, and he wore no coat. He didn't dress like a duke, she decided.

But foremost Emma wanted to know *why* he was at Craigmont when she had it on good authority — Ian's words — that he never darkened Craigmont's door. Quickly she decided to wait to ask him about that. At the moment, her fowls and animals needed attention.

"Are you, or are you not, going to answer my question?" she asked. Before he could start laughing again, if that was his intent, she added, "And I don't appreciate your laughter."

"Never talk to a man when he is thinking," His Grace said, still stroking his chin.

Emma could have sworn that his big hand had been hiding a smile, for, when he dropped his hand to his side, white teeth showed, and his hazel eyes twinkled with what she suspected to be hilarity.

"I think," His Grace said, "I shall send them to Brighton. They should bring a goodly price. Or would you prefer they be returned to Fernwood, along with the crested carriage you stole."

"You had better think again," Emma said. "And I didn't steal anything —"

As if she hadn't spoken, His Grace turned to the groom, whose small beady eyes had been watching them from around the corner of the carriage. "Feed and water them, Samuel, then take them into Brighton. I don't believe they would survive a return trip to Fernwood."

"Yes, Yer Grace," the groom said.

Out of the corner of her eye, Emma had noticed a hayfork leaning against a stable door. Lightning quick she had the long-handled, five-pronged instrument in her hand, pointing it at the groom. "One move to remove my property to Brighton and I will stab you through."

The Duke swallowed. Lord Charles had said his sister was stubborn and high strung, but he had not prepared him for this. His Grace chuckled to himself. Even angry, she was beautiful, this gel whom Lord Charles had said would drive any man to despair. His gaze lingered on white bosom above a low-cut neckline. She *was* driving him to despair, but not in the way Lord Charles had anticipated. He longed to take her in his arms, to hold her forever, to kiss her as he had never before kissed a woman. He calculated the time. It had been one week since the banns had been read the first time, twice more, each Sunday the next two weeks, and he and Lady Emma Winslow would marry. Two weeks seemed like two years to His Grace.

He pulled his gaze away from her ladyship, who was still holding the pitchfork menacingly. With a touch of obsequiousness, he addressed the groom, "Find a place for Lady Winslow's *property*. Move horses out and use stables if need be. Tomorrow, a chicken house will be erected . . . and a pig pen . . . and a place for the goats. The blasted geese can go to the devil."

"Yes, Yer Grace," said the scared groom, skittering quickly into a stable, and out of sight.

Turning to Emma, His Grace asked, "Are you happy, my love, that you can keep your precious animals? After we are married, you will see what a kind person I can be."

"I am not your love . . ." She discarded the fork and gave a mock curtsy. "I'm ever so grateful, Your Grace. Now what did you say about *us* being wed?"

He smiled at her. "I'm certain the solicitor informed you about my agreement with your brother Charles. I am perfectly willing to carry through with my end of the bargain. Two weeks, I think, will be ample time for you to prepare for a grand wedding, if you prefer one of that nature."

Emma walked closer and looked up at His Grace. "You tricked my brother into that agreement, Your Grace, and I will need time to forgive and forget."

Emma was stalling for time. She had no notion of forgiving and forgetting what her brother had done. She straightened her dress and pulled it tight around her stomach to show its thickness. Lifting her chin, she waited for His Grace's surprised reaction. He would not be wanting to get leg shackled to a gel already in the family way.

His Grace was all seriousness, with just a trace of a grin showing on his sun-browned face. "How many pounds did you stuff in your moneybag? And are you not ashamed of yourself for stealing the new Earl's candlesticks?"

Shocked and humiliated that His Grace knew her secrets, Emma's anger exploded in the most ferocious way. "Are you a mind reader?" she asked scathingly, and when his grin broadened, she whipped round and started walking as fast as she could on the road that circled the stables. Taking a path that wound through the backyard, she hoped to come to a door through which she could enter the manor house. She must needs check on Francine and Prudence, and of course Hannah. If the old cakey was as weird as her son, they might not stay the night.

It was not until Emma stumbled that she realized His Grace was two steps behind her. He caught her before she hit the ground and lifted her up. He was extremely tall, but she was a tall woman, and their faces were only inches apart. Thinking he was going to kiss her, she gave his shin a hefty kick with her booted foot. "Put me down, you jackanapes," she said. And he did, with grim determination showing on his countenance.

Emma did not know whether he was determined to kiss her, or to put windmills in her head. Looking at the back of the house, fifty windows wide, plus many, many doors, Emma realized she had no idea which door to open. Fernwood was a cottage compared to Craigmont by the Sea.

Reluctantly, she turned to His Grace. "Which door do I open?"

"Where are you going?"

"You should know. You were following me."

"I was following you to wherever you were going."

Emma regarded him with scathing animosity. "I wish to join my sister, and my niece, who are supposed to be waiting in a receiving room."

"Then I think it a capital idea for us to enter by the front doors. That is where the receiving room is located, and 'tis the usual way guests enter Craigmont."

Taking her arm, His Grace directed her to the right, to a path that wound through a garden where roses bloomed and honeysuckle emitted the most wonderful smell. Emma sucked in a deep whiff.

"This is Consuelo's rose garden," His Grace said. He walked beside Emma, and again she, although angry beyond bearing, was aware of his height. Even so, his steps were smooth and fluid.

*Like a panther's.*

An awful lump of desolation filled Emma's throat. She felt drained of the spirit that had kept her going these past weeks. First light of this day seemed eons back. And she was hungry. Nothing had worked as she had planned; His Grace knew her secrets, and now she had to face Consuelo de-Fleury.

Emma could not imagine anything worse at this hour of the day, and she prayed that the old cakey would, as the butler had said, not be receiving, that somebody would feed her, Emma, and let her and her family start anew in the morning. When she could think better.

"What is your mother like?" she asked His Grace, not to be friendly, but because she wanted to know.

"Stubborn as a mule, domineering, and at times downright obstinate."

"How awful, to speak of your mother that way."

His Grace's laughter floated out onto the cool night air. "Just wait until you hear what she has to say about me, her adoring son." His demeanor became suddenly serious. "I think you will like her, Emma. She speaks her mind. One never has to wonder what she is thinking."

Emma noticed right away that he had called her Emma, not Lady Emma, or Lady Winslow. She gave him a sideways glance and saw a handsome face that looked as if it were holding back a smile, and brilliant, calculating eyes that knew more than they should. A chill danced up and down Emma's spine. Little wonder he was called ruthless. She felt like a fly about to be sucked into a wicked spider's web.

*Not if I can keep my wits about me.*

On the veranda, in front of the huge carved doors, now closed, Emma said to His Grace, "I wish to meet Consuelo deFleury alone."

"Are you certain, love?" the Duke asked, a frown wrinkling his brow.

"I'm certain. And I am not your love."

His Grace bent and kissed her on the forehead, cupping her chin in his big hand. Smiling, he removed her hat and handed it out to her. "Burn it, it's atrocious. It hides your lovely hair."

Emma jerked the hat from his hands. "I'll thank you not to interfere with my dress."

"Two weeks, Emma," he said. "It seems a lifetime."

"It will be a lifetime before I marry you, and I would also thank you not to take such privileges as kissing me."

Drawing her to him, he kissed her again, this time a gentle kiss on the lips. She felt his warm breath on her face, heard the groan that escaped his throat, and then he suddenly released her. She raised a hand to slap him, but he caught her wrist, holding it in a viselike grip.

"I would not want you to slap me." He grinned that crooked grin again. "It might precipitate my turning you over my knee."

"You wouldn't dare!"

"Don't tempt me."

His laughter as he turned and walked toward yet another entrance to the house only fueled Emma's anger. Knowing she needed a moment to let it cool before meeting another deFleury, she turned and looked toward the sea, at the sloping gardens, their colorful flowers now a dim, shimmering hue in the twilight. Gold streaked a purple sky, made that way by the last rays of the day's sun, and black waves spiraled upward from the undulating sea, coming down to pound the craggy shore. The sounds, and the smell of the fresh sea air, sent Emma's senses reeling, and for a long moment she forgot what had sent her to Craigmont, and what she had found when she arrived—the ruthless Duke.

The lapse of memory lasted only a moment. She could not stop the feeling of disquiet. How did His Grace know her every move, unless he had spies everywhere. She discounted the idea that he was a fortune-teller, although she had read of people having the gift of reading minds.

The opening of a door drew Emma's attention. Turning, she saw the staid butler in his knee breeches and long-tailed coat. And the high collar points. She must needs not forget the high collar points. Bracing herself, while holding her hat in her hands, she stepped through the expansive aperture into a great foyer.

The butler said in a condescending voice, "Miss deFleury is waiting—"

"Lady Winslow," Emma said, just in case he had forgotten to whom he was speaking.

"Lady Winslow," the butler repeated.

Emma swept past him, then stopped. Surely she had stepped back in time, into a great hall, where the king met his knights. She lifted her gaze to a scrolled ceiling two stories high, with beams the size of one hundred year old trees.

Carved mahogany balustrades framed steps of a great curving stairway. Expensive paintings, not portraits of ancestors, hung on the walls. Turkey carpet, in shades of blood red and deep blue, ran the length of the great hall, and up the stairway.

While Emma stood in awe, the butler went ahead of her. Her feet were rooted to the floor, and she was overcome with the feeling that she was in a house that held many secrets.

Again she visualized Consuelo deFleury a dried-up old cakey, eccentric, stooped, using a cane for support.

*And Charles sent me here to live.*

The butler's voice seemed far, far away. "Lady . . . Lady Winslow . . ."

Emma forced her feet to move, and she marched behind the butler the length of the vast hall, passing on each side doors opening into elegantly appointed rooms, all as spacious as the great hall, and lighted with glistening crystal chandeliers swinging from high ceilings.

"This was the banqueting hall, in the old house," the butler said, and Emma was pleased to know that he could speak to her in a civilized manner. Before reaching the stairway, which Emma had expected to climb, the butler turned right and entered a room not so brightly lit. "Lady Emma Winslow," he announced with proper dignity, after which he left.

Emma saw across the room a beautiful woman standing near a marble fireplace, over which hung a portrait of herself, probably painted when she was young. But no more beautiful, Emma thought, than the woman now crossing the room. As slender as a young girl, she moved with much grace. She was dressed to the first stare, in black silk imprinted with tiny red roses, with rushing around the neck and hem, and a train that trailed behind her as she glided toward Emma.

Emma's homemade dress of bishop's blue paled beside the wonderful French creation the approaching lady wore.

As she drew near, Emma saw a delicate face framed with snow-white fantastical ringlets, while the rest of her hair

74

rested in a bed of curls on the top of her head, and wisps curled on the back of her long, swanlike neck.

*So much for an old cakey.*

"I'm Emma Winslow, ma'am." Emma took the hand extended to her, and was immediately stricken to fear with the eyes that blatantly stared at her through a jewel-rimmed lorgnette. Although the large hazel eyes, the same color as her son's, swam in sadness, behind the sadness was strength . . . and what Emma perceived to be a palpable dislike of the person to whom Consuelo was speaking, Emma herself.

Emma cringed.

"I'm Consuelo deFleury, and I prefer to be called Consuelo, not ma'am," she said in a cultured, well modulated voice. "Welcome to Craigmont, Lady Winslow. I understand you have come to wed my son. I must needs warn you against it."

Emma returned Consuelo deFleury's gaze unwaveringly. "I have come to Craigmont because my spoiled, thoughtless brother willed that I do so, lest the small stipend he left to my sister and me be cut off." She stopped to take a deep breath, then continued, "And I have no notion of marrying your son, Miss deFleury. It is my belief that he tricked my brother into playing cards with him; therefore, I am not honor bound to fulfill their silly marriage arrangement."

Emma knew she was going to swoon but could not stop the sinking feeling of total exhaustion. There was nothing left inside of her with which to fight. This day and the past weeks had been too much for her. Before her eyes the chandelier that swung from the high ceiling became a mass of whirling, brilliant lights, a cone-shaped vortex of eerie winds were sucking her up, up into a shimmering, tangled web of secrets. Consuelo's face, framed with white hair, the Duke's laughing eyes, his happy laughter, invaded her being. She felt her hat slip from her hand. *I must needs find Francine and Prudence.*

Fighting with all the strength that was left in her, Emma

pushed their names from her throat, hearing only the echo of strangled sounds, "Francine . . . Prudence . . ."

And then a cold, penetrating darkness was there to claim her. *Like in the trees that whisper.*

"Take that demme stuff away," Emma said, slapping at the hand holding foul-smelling hartshorn under her nose. She was lying on a white sofa in the room where she had swooned. A broad wrinkled face with small beady eyes floated dimly between her and the scrolled ceiling.

Surely, Emma thought, she had died and gone to hell. She tried to ask the ugly woman with the hartshorn who she might be, but words would not come. She heard a gasp. Consuelo's hands shot up to cover her face as she said, "The poor thing is *enceinte*. That accounts for the swooning."

"I knew that no good would come from their coming here," said the hartshorn woman, clucking in an all-knowing, all-seeing way.

"She is *not* enceinte," a booming voice declared, and Emma jerked herself up as if she had been shot. His Grace was marching authoritatively into the room. Emma giggled. *If he should fall, he'd make a long splatter on the beautiful carpet.*

A hand pushed Emma back onto the sofa and started waving the bottle again, and the awful odor of hartshorn burned inside her nostrils. This time it was held where Emma could not slap it away. Much to her chagrin, she coughed and sputtered, and things became clearer.

"She's not *enceinte*," His Grace said again, closer now.

"And how would *you* know that?" Consuelo retorted. "Her stomach bulges, and that usually means—"

"That's her moneybag. She feared she would be placed in servitude at Craigmont, or worse yet, thrown into a dungeon. She planned to escape to London."

"That is a lie," Emma said, bouncing up again. And this time she made sure that no one could push her down. "I

76

feared I would be robbed by highwaymen on my journey from Fernwood."

Emma looked at His Grace, obviously studying the situation.

He said, "We must needs get her upstairs to bed." He moved in Emma's direction, as if to pick her up.

Most likely in *his* bed, Emma thought. She recoiled instantly. "Oh, no you don't. I am perfectly able to walk; besides, I do not need to go to bed. I want to know where you've put Francine and little Prudence."

His Grace acquiesced, but stood guard. He looked to Consuelo for an answer to Emma's question.

"We haven't *put* them anywhere," Consuelo said. "They are in their quarters, and very happy if the upstairs maid can be believed."

"And Hannah?"

"She will be in the maid's quarters next to little Prudence. I have put her in charge of the child's needs."

Emma was instantly on her feet. "Hannah is *my* maid. I can't remember when she did not take care of *my* needs."

It was then that Consuelo introduced the broad-faced, hartshorn woman as Miss Van Winters. "She will attend you," Consuelo said.

"Why, Miss deFleury? So she can spy on me? So you will know my very thoughts." Emma fought back the tears that threatened to spill out of her very tired eyes.

His Grace spoke. "Consuelo, can you not let Hannah — ?"

"No. Lady Winslow needs a proper lady's maid. Before her come-out she must be trained to meet society . . . if we are to find a proper husband for her."

His Grace and Emma spoke simultaneously, Emma saying she had no intention of coming out into society to look for a husband, that she was *too* old and too independent of nature to take a husband, and His Grace saying that *he* would be marrying Lady Winslow as soon as the banns had been read the third time.

Consuelo smiled at her son. "She has informed me that she has no notion of marrying you, Your Grace, so I shall see that a proper husband is found." Pausing for a moment, she tilted her white head to one side and rested a long, slender finger on her chin. Her hazel eyes twinkled. "To be presented at Court will be the first order, after a decent wardrobe has been provided. With her beauty, men will swarm to pay their addresses. I feel it incumbent upon myself to do my duty by my cousin's daughter."

*Why do I feel that Conseulo is enjoying this immensely?* thought Emma.

"Your duty be demmed," His Grace said with pardonable vehemence. "Lady Winslow will marry *me*. It has been decreed."

Emma thought she wanted to be on Consuelo's side. Locking her gaze with his, she asked, "By whom? My thoughtless brother? He was not the King of England when he added that ridiculous codicil to his will."

His Grace dismissed Consuelo by turning his back on her. He said to Emma, "I refuse to discuss our affairs in front of Consuelo and a housemaid. I respectfully request a private audience with you, Lady Winslow, on the morrow. Will you come to my book room soon after breakfast?"

Emma could see no harm. If he kissed her again, she would somehow manage to slap him, showing him that she could be as stubborn as he. She believed in getting things settled, so she agreed pleasantly and watched as he marched from the room, shoulders back, steps long and quick. He was not laughing.

When he was gone, it seemed to Emma that life had been sucked from the room. A Cheshire-cat smile played on Consuelo's beautiful face, and Van Winters stood like a statue, her hands folded in front of her. How Emma wished she could read *their* minds. Consuelo turned to Van Winters. "Have two footmen bring the chair and carry Lady Winslow to her quarters."

Emma could not believe what she was hearing. How utterly ridiculous! She reached for her hat and crammed it back onto her head.

# Chapter Seven

Emma had heard that a sedan chair was dandy Beau Brummell's favorite transportation around London. She felt like a fool riding in one, and her sympathy went out to the two footmen struggling to keep the chair level as they climbed the stairs. For an instant she entertained the thought of hopping down and climbing the stairs by her own volition, and she only thought better of it when, looking below, she saw Consuelo deFleury's keen eyes on her and the ascending chair. Emma was too weary for a set-down this night. And of course Hartshorn Van Winters was walking beside the chair, in soldierly fashion. Watching and listening, Emma was sure.

Van Winters directed the footmen. "The west wing."

"Where are Francine and little Prudence," Emma asked, and when Van Winters did not answer, Emma added in a firm voice, "I will not be separated from them."

Giving an inane smile, Van Winters said, "Did you not have separate quarters at Fernwood Manor?"

"Prudence had only been there one night, and she slept with me."

"It will be different at Craigmont."

"On whose orders?"

"Miss deFleury's."

I guess that is that, Emma told herself. It seemed that

Consuelo deFleury was in charge of everything and everybody. But this did not worry Emma, for she had in just the last few moments decided that she would soon leave Craigmont and go to London. Living here would be like being locked in Newgate, with Consuelo as the jailer and Van Winters as the guard. Emma had not forgotten the unsettling flash of dislike in Consuelo's eyes when they met. No doubt she had greeted Francine and Prudence in like manner, maybe even worse.

Emma said to Van Winters, "Please fetch my sister and my niece to my quarters."

"After you've had your supper."

"I suppose those are Consuelo's orders," Emma retorted.

Another inane smile. "Yes."

This was outside of enough for Emma. She told the footmen to halt at once and to lower the chair. And to all who wanted to listen, she declared, "I am not some child to be ordered about."

They had reached a huge landing from which several doors opened. Emma bounded to her feet and, looking about, wondered which door to open. Resolutely she started toward one, not caring where it would lead her. After only two steps, she felt the floor coming up to hit her in the face. Her head swam, and her stomach made a strange connection with her throat. She was going to be sick on the beautiful carpet was her last thought before blessed darkness again claimed her. She heard Hartshorn Van Winters talking, but could not discern the words, probably giving orders to the footmen to throw this malcontent into the dungeon to join Francine and Prudence.

Emma was barely cognizant that she had been thrown over someone's shoulder, and the next thing she knew, she was in a soft white bed with white hangings. Van Winters was holding her head over a pan and saying, "If you're going to be sick, don't soil the bed."

"I'm not going to be sick on your bed," Emma said with a

goodly amount of disgust in her voice. "Fetch my sister and my niece." Reaching down, Emma felt her money bag, just in case *someone* had the notion to steal it.

Emma was not too sick to plan; an array of thoughts tumbled through her throbbing head. Tomorrow she would gather her chickens and her animals and sell them in a village on her way to London. The geese were probably lost forever in the woods.

There was enough money for Francine's entry into the marriage mart, where a rich husband would be found. She had heard that a lady of the upper orders—most likely a heavy loser at the gaming tables, Emma thought—could be hired as sponsor-companion, claiming her new ward to be a cousin with good lineage. And that one could obtain through a good sponsor a subscription to Almacks, a must if one expected to reach the top of the Ton. And that was where a rich husband for Francine most likely would be found. And if need be, she, Emma, could work as a modiste, secretly, of course.

So deep in thought, Emma had not noticed that a maid had brought a tray holding a silver tureen, setting it on a table near the bed. She watched as Van Winters ladled into a flat soup bowl a rather thick soup, which had a mouth-watering aroma.

"This will make you well," the woman said, and Emma was on the verge of sitting up and taking the bowl when she decided to bargain. So she set her chin in such a stubborn line that Van Winters would have no doubt that she, Emma, meant what she said.

"After I have seen Francine and Prudence, I will eat."

"Have you always been this difficult?" Van Winters asked.

"I'm used to giving orders, not taking them," Emma told her.

The maid drew herself up. "At Craigmont, Miss deFleury gives the orders."

Nonetheless, Van Winters quit the room, and in what seemed to Emma to be forever, she returned with Francine and Prudence following in her wake.

"Sister, are you ill?" Francine asked worriedly, and Prudence ran to her and hugged her so tightly Emma could hardly breathe. She pulled herself up in the bed, hugged Prudence back, and felt love fill her heart, squeezing it tightly. "How good to see you, and to know that both of you are all right."

"Did you think we wouldn't be?" Francine asked.

Emma frowned. "Consuelo deFleury—"

Francine cut in, "Consuelo—she asked that I call her that—was wonderful to me. She even said that I would be presented at Court." She smiled at Prudence who had positioned herself on the edge of Emma's bed. "And she was ever so nice to little Prue."

"Yes," Prudence piped up, "Miss deFleury said that I would meet Princess Charlotte, that the Princess likes to share with the poor as I do. Princess Charlotte's the Prince Regent's daughter, and heir to the throne."

Prudence, as if guilt rode her for forgetting her mother for one instant, cast her eyes downward. "Most important, Miss deFleury said that she would see that I get to Bedlam to see Mama before next Easter, when Mama will be well."

"I told you I would take you to see your mama, perhaps even have a picnic with her," Emma said a little shortly.

Francine's voice showed her excitement. "And Mrs. Fitzherbert, the Prince Regent's illegal wife, lives in Brighton, and she makes morning calls at Craigmont."

"Did Consuelo tell you that Mrs. Fitzherbert is the Prince Regent's illegal wife? I should think she would not pass on dits about a friend."

"Oh, no," Francine said. "I read about the marriage at Fernwood. Prinny married her against the King's wishes, and he claims she's his wife and be demmed His Majesty's

83

wishes."

Emma gave a look of incredulity, but before she could reply, Van Winters pushed the bowl of soup toward her. "You promised you would eat—"

"I shall, and you may go now, Miss Van Winters. I'd like a private coze with Francine and Prudence."

"After you've eaten. I must needs report to Miss de-Fleury."

Emma protested. "Miss Van Winters, I am not a child."

Van Winters grunted hugely in disbelief, and Emma took the bowl and started ladling the soup into her mouth as Van Winters had ladled it from the tureen. "If you would only slow down," Van Winters said, "you might taste it."

After that, Emma did eat more slowly, and it was indeed the most delicious soup she had ever eaten, even though she did not feel inclined to say so. When the bowl was empty, she handed it to Van Winters and thanked her graciously.

*Lord, let her leave.* Emma prayed.

As soon as Van Winters had taken up the tray and quit the room, saying she would return shortly and prepare m'lady for bed, Emma said to Francine, "I can't wait to leave this place. I have the most wonderful plan."

Francine walked about the bedchamber, her eyes darting hither and yon. "Your quarters are much like mine. Aren't they extraordinarily beautiful?"

For the first time Emma noticed the fire on the grate, the ormolu clock on the mantel, the smell of lemon oil. Around the Adam fireplace were two lovely chairs covered in white brocade. Even the huge chiffonnier was of pickled white wood.

Only the rug showed color, Emma noticed, and the deep mahogany wood and paintings of flowers, in vivid colors, against the white walls were striking. Windows with white coverings stretched across one wall.

Prudence went to sit in one of the chairs that flanked the fireplace, while Francine languidly ventured into the next room, calling back. "Oh, Sister, 'tis *sooo* beautiful, deep sofas and chairs, a writing desk and wonderful tables and lamps, and yet another fireplace."

Emma did not care about the rooms where she would only spend one night. "Francine, did you not hear me? I have a plan. We cannot stay here."

In a flash Francine was back in the bedchamber. "I don't take your meaning. Are we returning to Fernwood . . . that's impossible."

"Yes, *that* is impossible. We are going to London for your come-out. Remember, I told you that if things did not work out at Craigmont—"

"But they have. It is Consuelo's wish that I be presented at Court, and you, too, Emma, if you will agree."

Emma felt trapped. Obviously Consuelo had not shown dislike for Francine, or for Prudence, as she had in that one brief glance she had bestowed on Emma. *And she has so impressed them with her kindness that I will be forced to stay at Craigmont.*

What was Consuelo's purpose? Emma wondered. With her obvious dislike of her, Emma, even taking Hannah from her, why would Consuelo deFleury want the Winslows to stay at Craigmont?

Or was it only Francine and Prudence she wanted to stay, Emma mused. Tears pushed at her eyes as half under her breath, she said, "I hope she does not think I will leave them."

"What did you say, Emma?" Francine asked.

Emma made a quick decision. She would know more after her audience with His Grace on the morrow. "I think that we must needs think on this another time. But I caution you, do not discuss anything of a personal nature with anyone. I have the oddest feeling that here even the walls listen."

Francine and Prudence prepared to leave, and Emma felt a wrenching in her heart. She did not want to be left alone with Hartshorn Van Winters, and she could not bear another minute in bed. She bounded out of bed and declared that now that her sister and niece had seen her quarters she would very much like to see theirs. In truth, she wanted to know *where* they were, that, indeed, they were all right.

"It isn't like Fernwood, is it, Sister?" Francine said as they walked a wide, dimly lit hall which Emma thought would never end. "No place will ever be like Fernwood," Emma said.

Emma held Prudence's hand, and they walked in silence after that, until Francine stopped at a heavily carved door that held her nameplate. "I am in here."

They went in, and what Francine had said was true; the rooms and furnishings were almost identical to Emma's, except the bed hangings and the window coverings were a deep green against white. "It *is* beautiful," Emma admitted, and she did not tarry long. "We'll meet on the morrow, mayhaps at breakfast."

They parted, and Emma went with Prudence to see her quarters. "I have a huge bed-sitting-room combination, and a school room. And Hannah is right next door," Prudence said, seemingly pleased.

"Are you frightened?" Emma asked.

"No, because Hannah is close by. She seems to like me, but I'm sorry she was taken away from you."

"As long as you are happy, I won't make a fuss," Emma said, and then she added, "Prue, promise me that you will tell me if things aren't right. That's the only way I can know."

"I'm sure they will be, Auntie Em. Miss deFleury mentioned getting a tutor and using the school room. I think I will like that more than a public school, where they might ask questions about Mama."

When they came to the rooms and Emma stepped inside, she immediately knew that these had once been the ruthless Duke's rooms. Everything was so typically masculine; animal paintings on the walls, replicas of war weaponry, even a toy soldier holding a gun.

*Consuelo did not know Prudence would be coming to Craigmont,* thought Emma, *else this place would have been perfectly prepared for a little girl.*

"Auntie Em, would you stay while I say my prayers?" Prudence asked.

"Of course, darling, and perhaps you can ask God to guide me in a very important decision that I must needs make."

Emma only made the request to placate Prudence, and she felt like a hypocrite. Of late there had been so much pain, so much anger, she did not know what she believed any more.

Again Prudence prayed silently. Crouched on the floor she sat back on her legs and feet, her small hands reverently holding the lighted candle in her lap. Her eyes were closed as her lips moved, but not so much as a whisper invaded the quietness that enveloped the room. A shiver passed over Emma, and a damp coldness, as she had experienced when traveling through the woods. Pulling her gaze from the praying child, Emma walked to the window and looked out.

Below was the rose garden, and the eastern part of the terrace which rose to a smooth grassy bank that stretched to the near woods. Everything was so beautiful, softened by the darkness, frosted by moonlight, which showed only the barest shape of things. Emma started to turn away but quickly turned back. Her eye had caught a glimpse of a woman walking in the rose garden. As she watched, the woman bent and picked a rose and smelled it. She was dressed in black, and a black veil covered her hair, falling to rest on her shoulders. Emma watched as she walked beyond the grassy knoll and disappeared into the woods.

The same feeling of disquiet that she had felt when this day she entered Craigmont Manor swept over Emma. She scolded herself, saying there was nothing wrong with a woman walking in the rose garden. But why did she go into the woods at night?

When Emma left the window, Prudence had extinguished the candle and was beginning to undress. "Auntie Em," she said, "will you stay while I get ready for bed? I'm sure Hannah will come soon, but I'd much rather have you. I don't need help, just company."

"Of course I will stay," Emma told her, amazed at the deftness with which the child could rid herself of the ugly black dress and slip into a white batiste gown that she pulled from a small set of drawers beside her bed. The white gown buttoned high at the neck and came down to cover her small feet.

"How long have you been dressing yourself?" Emma asked.

"Since I was four. Even though I had a nice nanny, Mama took care of me until then. When she started getting sick, I helped take care of her. She had a lady's maid, but Mama preferred that I do for her. I think she just wanted me close."

*Oh, dear God, such pain as this child has suffered.* Tears clouded Emma's eyes. "Come here," she said, and she hugged Prudence and told her she loved her. Then she picked her up and carried her to her narrow bed, beside which stood the toy soldier with a gun. "You watch over her," Emma said to the toy soldier, and Prudence laughed.

"Good night," Emma said, and left. She followed wide halls, praying she would not get lost. On the way over she had mentally spotted identification points, a particular painting, a resting bench, and they served her well now. Finally reaching her own rooms, she realized that she had changed wings. Prudence's rooms faced east, overlooking the rose garden; while, from her window, Emma could see the sea. She went to the window, lifted it, and listened to the waves and smelled the fresh air.

Standing thus, Emma did not hear the door open behind her and when she turned, she was startled to see Van Winters turning back the white coverlet on the bed. "I didn't hear you come in," Emma said.

"I move quietly," the maid said, and Emma could believe that, for she had no doubt the woman was a spy. But for what reason? What had she done that deserved being spied upon?

"I have ordered water for your bath," Van Winter said. "Tomorrow you have an audience with His Grace."

Emma noticed that she spoke "His Grace" almost reverently.

"That I have," Emma said sarcastically. "I can hardly wait to tell *His Grace* that I shall be leaving Craigmont immediately."

The maid turned big eyes on Emma, silently looking at her as if she had jumped over the edge, and Emma laughed. If Hartshorn Van Winters was going to spy on her, then she must needs give her something to report to Consuelo, and to the ruthless Duke.

In the Duke's chambers, His Grace was seeking advice from Dodge, his dapper valet, who was a noted rakehell of the first water, but, if he were to be believed, very successful in bringing gels to toe. For years he had regaled Ashton deFleury with his tales of conquest. According to Dodge, not an upstairs maid between London and Craigmont was immune to his charms.

"Always an upstairs maid, very pretty, very young," he would say. Being class conscious, the valet considered scullery maids beneath his station. "More to my liking is a lady's maid, who has picked up the ways of the upper orders," he often said, and Ashton would grin and nod his head in agreement.

"I know nothing about charming a gel, I've never cut a dash in society, and evenings of cloddish insipidity are not my liking either," His Grace said. He much preferred passing his time in his book room, reading, and even with all his shortcomings, he had many times been chased by desperate

Ton mamas.

His only experience with gels was with his mistresses, who were willing to settle for an expensive bauble and a house in which to live. Seemingly thankful for his raging virility, they had not expected him to be charming.

Now, he regretted that, and it was in desperation that he had summoned Dodge from London to Craigmont. Living and dressing casually as he did in the country, he did not need a valet when he was at Craigmont. He was more than capable of taking care of himself. At age eight he started dressing himself and looking after his own clothes. In Town, his busy work schedule demanded he keep a man to assist him, so he kept Dodge. And Dodge kept His Grace entertained.

It was through the valet that His Grace learned all the Town on-dits exchanged during the upper order's morning calls.

"Maids always have an ear to the door," Dodge would say.

Gossip from the coffeehouses and the taverns also reached His Grace through Dodge. It had been the valet who had told him Lady Winslow feared she would be thrown into a dungeon at Craigmont.

His Grace smiled. Her country innocence endeared her to him. Her stubbornness, however, was something else, and he said as much to Dodge, "I don't take her meaning. I told her the banns had been read, and still she doesn't seem to give a fig."

Dodge, a small plump man of forty or more years, with a receding hairline, sat across from His Grace. His brow wrinkled, he leaned back in his chair and stroked his chin, on which a sparse white beard grew. He leveled his smoky blue eyes on the Duke's face. Then, after what seemed an eternity to His Grace, the valet asked. "How old is this chit?"

"Three and twenty."

"On the shelf, you might say. Why did you not pick one

who is not yet set in her ways?"

"She *is* stubborn. But I did not want a younger one. I appreciate maturity. Seize it, Dodge—"

"Stubbornness is not a good quality in a woman, but if you refuse to withdraw your suit, you must needs deal with it."

His Grace started to speak, but the valet held up a silencing hand. "You didn't take her wishes into consideration."

"What do you mean? I sent the solicitor to explain to her that her late brother and I had come to an agreement."

Dodge gave a knowing grin. "You and her brother made the deal. How would you like to be treated as a chattel? You shoulda asked her, courted her. Every gel likes to be courted, even the young ones. Your Grace, you must needs turn on your charm."

His Grace did not agree. "Burn it, Dodge, I understand that that's not done in proper society. A gentleman meets a gel, in this case a woman, and he asks her father, or, in this case, her brother, to pay his addresses to her."

"You skipped all that."

"Skipped what?" His Grace asked, perplexed and not just a little annoyed. This should not be such a complicated matter.

"You didn't meet her, and give her a chance to see you."

His Grace's words were crisply given. "More than once I asked Lord Winslow for permission to pay my addresses to his sister, and each time he refused. But he would not stop talking about her, tantalizing me to the point of distraction. Finally, I took drastic measures and coaxed him to the gaming table."

"You proceeded to win her one way or the other, the other being at the gaming table." Dodge clucked and looked pityingly at His Grace. "That's how you win in business, not in the game of winning a chit."

A deep sigh escaped His Grace. It was such a bumble broth. So far Dodge had only told him what he had done wrong, not how to persuade Emma Winslow to marry him. He pulled on a bellrope and when a footman appeared, he asked that ratifia and two glasses be brought to the book room. "And later, bring a supper tray for two."

After the refreshments had been brought and the footman had disappeared, the two serious-minded men lifted their glasses and continued their serious conversation. Dodge was the first to speak. "What were you wearing when Lady Winslow first laid eyes on you?"

His Grace looked down at his buckskin riding breeches, his dusty riding boots, his open shirt, then looked askance at the valet. "Why, this . . . this, what I have on."

"That is very unfortunate. No riding coat, I suppose."

"No riding coat."

"I can see that I have my work cut out for me. You must needs dress like a member of the nobility, all the crack, in the trim, as they say. Women love clothes more than they love the men wearing them."

His Grace cocked an eyebrow. "Are you sure you know what you are saying?"

"Indeed I do know of what I speak. As you know, I am a man of experience."

"Lady Winslow is a country miss," His Grace said, for a moment lost in thought as he remembered her wholesomeness, her kind, sweet, pretty face, her thick black hair, her eyes that were almost violet in color. He remembered also her temper as she held the pitchfork. Desire to be in her presence, desire to hold her in his arms, to kiss her as a husband would kiss his wife filled him to the point of desperation. "Demmet, Dodge, tell me how to marry the gel, not how to dress."

"To marry her, you must first win her. Unless you want to kidnap her and hold her as your love slave."

His Grace sputtered. "I would never take any gel against her will."

"Then be patient. Give her time. I can see she's a special

person, so treat her special, court her with flowers, with sweet whisperings, and take her on proper engagements, to the opera, on walks on the beach, all the time holding her hand, touching her in unobtrusive ways . . . as long as you don't break propriety. Steal a kiss now and then, to awaken that part of her, which, as a virgin, has not been disturbed." Dodge stopped to smile, then went on, "But don't act on that urge. Remember she is a lady of quality; she will bear your heir."

"I can only try," was His Grace's response. For years he had doubted his valet's wild stories about his many conquests. Now, he could see where they might be true. But would all this tomfoolery work for him? He was not a patient man. He wanted to marry Lady Winslow *now*.

Sighing, he lifted his glass and took a long swig, and silently he prayed for courage, and for patience.

# Chapter Eight

"What gown will her ladyship wear this morning?" Van Winters asked.

"What difference? I'm only going for breakfast," Emma replied, with as much pleasantry as she could muster this early in the morning. Beyond the window gray fog roiled upward from the sea.

"Even so, you must needs dress appropriately at Craigmont. Now, which dress—"

"I don't give a fig," Emma said, and then something suddenly came to mind. "The Duke doesn't dress appropriately for his station. When we met at the stables I thought he was an overseer."

"You must needs not follow His Grace's example. He is the rebellious sort. Always has been."

"In what way is he rebellious?" Emma thought mayhaps she could pry information from Hartshorn Van Winters that would be helpful when she talked with the Duke after breakfast. She repeated, "In what way is he rebellious?"

"Which dress—"

Emma took from the chiffonnier a blue-sprigged muslin, slightly faded, but the pattern was one of her favorites.

Displeasure showed on Van Winters's face. She held the dress up for Emma to slip over her head, then she pulled and straightened and smoothed.

"Stuff," Emma said. "I am not used to this kind of pampering. I am perfectly capable of dressing myself. At Fernwood, Hannah did not—"

"You are not at Fernwood, and Hannah is no longer your lady's maid. She has been delegated to watch over Prudence, and that is only a temporary thing."

Emma whipped around. "What do you mean, temporary? Hannah is not temporary."

"She does not know one thing about being a lady's maid. She can fetch and carry but a household maid can do that. Most likely she will be returned to Fernwood, as will the eighth Earl of Wickersham's carriage."

"Neither Hannah nor the carriage will be returned to Fernwood," Emma said with conviction. Then she was silent. She would not be reduced to discussing her wonts and not wonts with this hoity-toity maid. She should have taken Francine and Prudence straight to London, and she would have had it not been for the stipend from her brother's estate. But now that she was here, she must needs think of a way to leave. She turned to Van Winters. Mayhaps she could give her a clue on how to outsmart the Duke of Attlebery. "What did you mean, Miss Van Winters, when you said His Grace always had been the rebellious sort?"

Immediately becoming puffed up with importance, Van Winters raised her brows and pulled a knowing look. "He was born that way, from what I hear. I was not here for the birthing, but I came soon after."

"Surely he wasn't a stubborn *baby?*"

When Van Winters compressed her lips together, as if no one would pry another word from her, a brilliant idea came to Emma. "Please, Miss Van Winters, give me an example." She paused for a dramatic breath. "As you know, His Grace expects that we shall soon be married—according to an agreement between him and my dead brother—and I must needs know how to please him. You can be of great help to both of us."

Van Winters cut her small, sharp eyes to Emma. "Did you not tell him that you would not honor your brother's agreement?"

Emma gave a small laugh. "You know us gels, Miss Van Winters. We often say things in anger that we are not quite sure later on that we mean."

That was an outright lie, Emma thought. She had meant it when she said she would not marry the Duke because of a silly agreement her brother signed. He, Lord Charles Winslow, had not lived his life as was expected of a titled man, so how could he think to dictate how she should live hers?

Van Winters began, "His Grace was a terror when he was yet a boy. At eight he locked his governess from his room. He refused a tutor, attended public school, and at fifteen he refused to attend Oxford, as Miss deFleury so desperately wanted him to. He went to work instead, taking his books with him, saying he would educate himself. And I hear he is a real bookworm."

Emma creased her brow worriedly. "It seems that he did an awful lot of refusing."

"Miss deFleury despaired of him. Knowing it would do no good to argue, she cut the apron strings and let him go." A pause, and then, "It wasn't until he refused the dukedom that King George offered him that she got her hackles up."

"He didn't want to be a duke?"

"That is the word that reached Miss deFleury. She was beside herself. Finally she left Craigmont and went to London."

"I thought she had not set foot in London for over thirty years, before His Grace was born."

"That one time was all. And it was only assumed she went to London. She went alone . . . at night, driving a post chaise, an armed guard beside her."

Emma smiled. Not at the story; it was pretty dramatic, but at the enthralled look on Van Winters' face, as if this thing had happened to her. Mayhaps, Emma thought, the woman had no life except the one she lived vicariously through the upper orders.

But Emma still thought the maid a spy, and she cautioned herself to be careful about what she said to her. "Did you learn what transpired in London?"

"Not a word. But soon after she went to London, we, the staff, learned that Ashton deFleury had been honored with a dukedom by the King. We could only guess that she finally told him who sired him."

Emma's mouth gaped. "He didn't know his father? Then his not knowing caused the rebelliousness. I hear that is very important to one, especially a man of honor."

"I should not be repeating gossip," Van Winters said, showing contriteness.

"I won't repeat it," Emma promised.

She had learned that neither on-dits nor servants' gossip, could be trusted. Maybe King George had sired the Duke, and maybe not. Other kings had had by-blows, and later made them dukes. From the dresser she picked up the brush and began stroking her long, black hair, looking at but not seeing herself in the looking glass. Other thoughts ran through her mind, and she wished she had more time to think things through before going down to face Consuelo deFleury. And later, the Duke.

"I will brush your hair," Van Winters said. She took the brush and expertly gave Emma's hair a hundred or more strokes, and then she pulled the black tresses back and twisted them into a bun on the back of Emma's head. With a pair of scissors, she snipped until tiny wisps curled around her ears. "That's the way m'lady should look," she said. "It's all the crack in London, I hear, and it shows your blue eyes to advantage. His Grace will notice."

"I don't care what His Grace notices," Emma said.

Van Winters clucked. "Lady Winslow, do not mislead yourself. When His Grace Ashton deFleury sets his mind to something, do it he will, matter not what obstacles stand in his way."

"No man, matter not his lofty title, will marry me against my will," Emma said. She went back to the looking glass and, being a fair person, said to the maid, "I am pleased with the way you dressed my hair."

Van Winters grinned proudly, and then looked critically at Emma's faded dress. "Miss deFleury will cast out the homemade gowns you brought from Fernwood."

Emma's temper, which lay just beneath the surface, flared. "My gowns are perfectly fashionable. I cut the patterns myself."

Van Winters pretended to straighten the skirt of Emma's dress one more time. " 'Tis very pretty, but Miss deFleury has a fetish about everything at Craigmont being up to snuff."

Determined to have some sort of say, Emma blurted out, "Mayhaps that is why His Grace does not visit more often."

"He comes once a month and dines with his mother. He used to come more often and stay longer, but Miss deFleury kept trying to get him leg-shackled to some chit. So he now only spends one night when he comes, and he makes it plain that he is only here to check on her health. Of course this time, he came to await his future bride, which is you."

Emma didn't reply, and saw the disappointment on the maid's face. Future bride, indeed. Most certainly she would address *that* subject with the Duke. Van Winters opened the door and stood back. "There's a stairway that leads to the morning dining room. I shall show you the way."

After traversing many halls, they came to a door that opened out onto a large landing. From there, Emma saw below the morning dining room. Consuelo deFleury sat at the head of a long table on which candles burned and fresh flowers bloomed in their light. Prudence sat to Consuelo's right, and was smiling a rapt little smile, her soft mouth slightly open.

As Emma watched, Consuelo bent her head to the child and said something in a conspiratorial manner. Prudence was laughing.

Emma's heart squeezed shut with the fierce protective love she had developed for the child. She let her gaze shift to the room of gargantuan proportions. A bright carpet lay on a highly polished dark wood floor. Equestrian paintings, one of which was of His Grace's black stallion, hung on the walls, and in the fireplace coals smoldered. Large windows afforded a view of the gardens and of the sea. The fog had cleared, and rippling waves shimmered in the sun.

"The other door on the landing leads to the third floor, where Miss deFleury has the east wing, and His Grace the west," Van Winters said as they walked down the curving stairs. At the bottom, she disappeared behind a serving screen. Emma walked toward the table. Consuelo peered through her long-handled lorgnette at her, and a frown appeared between her sharp hazel eyes. She opened her mouth to speak, but Emma would never know her intended words, for Prudence, squealing with delight, scrambled out of her chair and ran to greet Emma, flinging her little arms around her waist.

Emma patted her head of yellow curls. The child wore the ugly black mourning dress that touched the top of her ugly high-top shoes. "Good morning, Auntie Em," she said. "I've been waiting for you. Miss deFleury wanted me to eat before the food became cold, but I told her I didn't care if it did get cold, I would wait for you."

Laughing, for she could not let Prudence see that Consuelo's frowning greeting troubled her, Emma bent and kissed her niece, then spoke pleasantly to Consuelo. "The food is on the sideboard," Consuelo said. "We serve ourselves."

There was a touch of derision in her voice and Emma quickly went to help herself to the food. A liveried footman stood at the end of the sideboard to lift the sparkling silver-domed lids from the equally sparkling silver bowls and platters.

Rustling bombazine behind Emma alerted her to step aside. A maid wearing a black dress, white apron, and white cap, brought hot food, taking the cold away. Emma was overwhelmed. There was tea, in a huge silver urn, and piping hot dishes of scrambled eggs, of bacon, another of fish, and on its own special heater, porridge, and ham and scones.

On a table draped with white linen there were various pots of jellies; fresh fruit, piled high on silver platters, sat on a separate sideboard.

Emma filled a bowl with porridge, then taking ham and scones, she asked the footman to bring a cup of tea to the table. She went to sit beside Prudence, smiling fondly at her and asking, "Prue, did you sleep well?"

"Yes. I was very comfortable, and Hannah was very attentive. But she is terribly worried."

"About what?" Emma asked.

Prudence took a bite of scrambled eggs, chewing and swallowing her food in a most ladylike fashion before talking.

"That she will be sent back to Fernwood. She's heard rumors."

Emma responded with alacrity. "If it is not Hannah's wish to leave Craigmont, she will not do so. If she leaves, we, you, Francine, and I, shall leave."

Consuelo cleared her throat and announced in a prideful voice, "I have sent for a modiste, Madame Lacont from Brighton. I've used her for years, and can vouch that she is better than any modiste in London. New wardrobes will be made for the three of you."

She looked directly at Emma, who responded quickly. "Miss deFleury, we have new gowns, Francine and I. And little Prue insists on wearing mourning clothes."

Consuelo blushed slightly. "Lady Winslow, I do not

100

mean to be hurtful, but I have examined the clothes you brought." She shook her head. "They will not do in Town."

*So Hartshorn told me right,* thought Emma. She pulled herself up and set her chin in a stubborn line, staring directly at Consuelo. "I don't take your meaning. Our gowns are of the latest fashion. I cut the patterns myself."

Emma, angry beyond measure, was on the verge of leaving, and she would have had not Francine swept into the room, wearing a dress Emma had never seen. It was made of fine cambric and followed closely the lines of Francine's slender body. Topping the dress was a low cut pelisse of green-shot sarcenet.

She carried a reticule of the same shade of green, and a smart Oatlands hat showed off her lovely face. Emma had never seen her so ravishingly beautiful. She felt betrayed but could not say why.

"I'm going to Brighton with the footman who is to fetch the modiste," Francine said.

"Not alone," Emma said.

"Of course not, pea goose. Consuelo has assigned the most marvelous lady's maid to me. I now have my own abigail, Emma, and she will accompany me everywhere. It is not proper for a lady to appear in public unchaperoned."

"Where . . . where did you get that dress?" Emma asked.

" 'Tis one of Consuelo's. We're the same size. Isn't it outside of enough that she would lend me one of her gowns . . . until the modiste stitches new wardrobes?"

Then, as if she had just now noticed the tears that clung to Emma's long eyelashes, Francine hurriedly added, "Not that the gowns you and Helga made for me are not all the crack . . . but, Sister, it is so nice to have gowns made by a real modiste. And little Prue has agreed to shed her stark black for only a touch of black to show her mourning."

Emma looked at Prudence, who was shaking her head and smiling sweetly.

Emma looked at Consuelo and prayed to know what was

in the woman's mind. Was the owner of Craigmont playing a deep game?

Consuelo's demeanor gave nothing away, nor did the words which she spoke proprietorially, "You must needs hurry, Francine. The carriage will be round front any moment."

Never in her life had Emma wanted to spit and swear so badly. Under her breath she muttered, "Hell and the devil." She then quickly excused herself and, taking the first door on which her eyes fell, she left the room.

The door led to a small stoop. She stopped, sucked in fresh air, and surveyed the grounds. Before her was a wide splice of lawn, and beyond that woods. She would go to the stables and see about her chickens and animals, she decided, walking across the lawn. From behind her came a voice, "Lady Winslow . . . Lady Winslow."

Emma looked back.

Standing on the stoop was Consuelo, calling, "Lady Winslow, my *chère amie,* do not forget your audience with His Grace."

Emma spat, and it felt good.


At the stables, Emma found workmen building a house for her dozen hens and lone rooster. "Build nests," she told them. "The hens will soon be laying eggs."

The pigs and goats were in separate stables and seemingly faring well. They had been fed and watered.

"Nancy, she's the nannie goat, needs milking," Emma told the groom.

Grinning, he asked, "Do yer know 'ow to milk a goat? I work the stables, and never before 'ave we 'ad a goat."

Emma thought for a moment. "What is your name? I can't just keep calling you groom."

"Me name is Tom, m'lady."

"My name is Emma Winslow, and I suppose you must

needs call me Lady Winslow, else Consuelo deFleury will give birth to kittens."

"What . . . m' lady Win . . . Winslow?"

Emma laughed. "That's a figure of speech which means she would have a fit."

"Oh, I see," Tom said, joining in the gay good humor.

Emma looked around at the workmen. Other grooms were brushing horses, and in a fenced area a groom walked the black stallion His Grace had been riding when first they met.

"Well, Tom," Emma said. "I don't see anyone around here who looks capable of milking a goat, so I suppose that I will have to give poor Nancy relief. Her bag looks as if it will burst. Can you find me a stool and a pail?"

At Fernwood, Emma had watched the milkmaid milking the goats, and the cows, but she had never thought she would need to know how.

"M'lady, we don't 'ave a stool, nor a pail, that is, one thet's clean," the groom said.

Emma looked through a high window and spied a stump from which a tree had been cut. "Put a rope around Nancy's neck and lead her to the stump," she told Tom. Then she grabbed a feeding pail and went to sit on the stump, and when Nancy was in proper position, she pulled on her teats and prayed that milk would come.

"I think you squeeze," Tom said.

At last a stream started, making a loud noise when the milk hit the bottom of the tin pail. The audience with His Grace was far from Emma's mind. She said to Tom, "We'll feed the milk to the pigs. It will make them fat."

Steam rose up from the warm milk, and everything seemed to Emma to be perfectly in order. She did not know that behind her grooms, carpenters, and handymen had gathered, and were placing wagers on her success.

Behind this audience, the tall Duke stood peering over the tops of heads, a huge grin on his face. Never had he seen anything so precious, he thought, as his Emma sitting on a stump milking a goat. He could see her beautiful face; he could even see her laughing smile, which showed even, white teeth. His heart swelled in his chest, and a choking lump lodged in his throat. As he turned to leave, something flickered past his vision; a goodly portion of Emma's shapely legs were scandalously exposed by the pulling up of her skirt so that she could hold the milk pail between her knees. Immediately, wanting gorged his being. Sweet, excruciating pain filled his loins, and again he counted the times the banns must need be read. He delayed his departure and watched as she stood and handed the pail to the groom, then pointed to the stool.

The groom sat on the stump, placed the pail between his knees, as Emma had done, and began pulling and squeezing on the goat's teats. Once he stopped and said something to Emma, and she bent to instruct him, and when milk met milk, a loud whoop went up from the crowd.

Not wanting Emma to see him, lest she be embarrassed, His Grace ducked around the corner of the stable, and his long strides took him across the clearing and through the woods, on his way back to the manor. He swore vehemently. The desire in his loins had not abated.

# Chapter Nine

In his book room His Grace paced the floor. Would Lady Winslow never leave the stables? Why could she not be as anxious to see him as he was to see her? He retrieved from his writing desk the list of things he was, according to Dodge, supposed to do to win her heart. Instinct told him not to appear overly anxious, and he wondered if he should proceed as he would if he were negotiating a shipping contract. It was, after all, a contract for marriage.

"Dress according to your station . . . don't rush her," he read aloud from the list he had made from memory after his talk with the valet. That was as far down the list as he got before hearing a light knock on the door. He said as calmly as possible, "Come in."

The door opened, and there she stood, hair coming loose from its bun, straw clinging to the bottom of her faded blue skirt, even dirt around the hem. Her beautiful face carried a solemn look. Smothering a smile, His Grace jumped to his feet. "I'm glad you are here, Lady Winslow."

Emma gave a courtly curtsy. His Grace took her hand and lifted her up. "It is not necessary for you to curtsy."

Emma recalled that Ian, her London on-dit source, had said the Duke did not wish to be addressed as Your Grace.

"Your Grace," she said, "I did not come of my free will. I was summoned. Now that I am here, there is much I wish to discuss with you. I wish to leave Craigmont at once."

As if she had not mentioned leaving Craigmont, His Grace said, "And I have much which I wish to discuss with you."

His manner was extremely businesslike, Emma noticed, not at all like a man whose intent was courting. He took her arm and guided her to a red leather chair matching his own. "As you know this agreement with your brother—"

"Balderdash," Emma said.

His Grace looked abashed. "What did you say?"

"Balderdash . . . nonsense. That is what the agreement with my brother amounts to. He bargained with something he did not own—me."

Without answering, His Grace went to his writing desk, and stood there, shuffling papers, and while he was thus occupied, Emma sat in the red chair and let her eyes traverse the fine book room, with its elaborate leather furnishings, bright carpets, and burgundy colored, leather-bound books with gold spines. Sunlight cut it in half.

And then she scrutinized the Duke. Outside of looking bewildered, he made a fine dash; leathery, slim-hipped, and long-legged. This day he was dressed like a duke, in high fashion; an impeccably tailored, cut-away morning coat of blue superfine, an embroidered waistcoat, and skin-tight tan pantaloons defined every muscle from his narrow waist to the top of his low-cut slippers. He even wore a cravat, immaculately folded, pristine white, against his sun-browned skin.

Emma had no doubt that His Grace was a rich nabob as reported by Ian: a scoundrel, and a rake, given her opinion. The ruthless Duke; he looked the part, she mused. She watched as he took parchment and quill from his writing desk, moving afterward to sit facing her. And she saw something else; his chin was set in an indomitable line, and his eyes were sharply focused on her.

"Am I to understand," Emma said, "that you have had the banns read for our wedding?"

"That is right, Lady Winslow. Two more times—"

"Have them unread."

"What! Why, Lady Winslow, that would be scandalous. They would say I cried off. That is beyond the pale . . . something an honorable man does not do."

"Then say I cried off."

"Why? Why do you not want to marry me? I can well afford a wife."

Emma looked at him with a narrowed gaze. "You negotiated with my worthless brother. Not with me."

His Grace took obvious offense. "Emma, the late Lord Charles was a worthy man. May I tell you about him?"

"I know all that it is my wish to know," Emma said harshly. "Now about this marriage."

"I negotiated a marriage contract with your guardian, which is a Ton custom."

Emma thought for a long moment, and then she looked straight into His Grace's eyes. "It is not my wish to marry *any* man, and should there be a marriage, it would not be a *Ton* leg-shackling."

"I don't take your meaning," His Grace said. "Marriage is the natural state for a woman. Every gel wants—"

"This gel doesn't. Should I marry, it would be for love, not for convenience, or to produce an heir. I could have loved when I was ten and seven, or perhaps as late as twenty, but now I am entirely too old to conform to the role of subservient wife. And I am entirely too bossy."

Emma laughed, and the Duke raised a quizzical eyebrow.

She said, "Did you not hear Tom, the groom who was helping me milk Nancy, teasing me about being bossy? Well, that is the way I am, and no man would bear it."

"I did not mean for you to see me watching you milk the

107

goat," the Duke said apologetically. "I was afraid it would embarrass you."

"Doesn't matter," Emma said. She wanted to get this business over with. The Duke was burning her with his gaze. She reached down to pick a straw from her skirt, and to brush the dirt from its hem. "It's settled then. The banns will be unread by reasons that I do not care to disclose." After a pause, she added, "Perhaps if I loved my husband, I would not be so bossy and he could bear me. But as I said, I am too old to change, and I am not in love."

His Grace said, as if talking to himself, "You are too angry with your dead brother to even consider loving someone."

Whether His Grace meant for Emma to hear his remark or not, she heard him, and retorted quickly, "I love Francine, and little Prudence."

His Grace sat upright in his chair and began writing. He saw how hopeless it was to try and reason with his intended, so he had no choice but to treat this contract as he would treat any other. He began writing: "I propose we state that the wedding has been postponed until a later date."

"How much later?" Emma asked, thinking that all she needed was time to introduce Francine into society and find her a rich husband.

"A month."

Emma scowled. "A month isn't long enough. I must needs put Francine first, introduce her into society, and find her a suitable husband. *A rich one.* And little Prudence is now my responsibility." A thought came to Emma. Prudence, being practical, had said that she had asked God for an Easter miracle, and the next Easter was almost a year away. "A year," Emma said quickly. "And that only means at the end of the year this agreement can be renegotiated."

Emma was pleased with herself.

His Grace's heart sank. He could not bear a year . . . and

then renegotiate! But Dodge had said not to rush her ladyship. He must needs somehow gain some leverage, he mused, and was silent for a long moment while he determinedly removed himself emotionally and thought as he would if he were negotiating a shipping contract. A thought, or plan, came to him. "Within that year you are to give me ample opportunity to win your heart. I am a fair man, Lady Winslow, but I am also determined. I want *you* for my soul mate. I am willing to prove myself."

His Grace saw no difference in expressing willingness to win her ladyship's hand in a year than promising a shipment of goods in a year's time. In this case, with luck, he would cut twelve months to two, three at the most. Even that length of time seemed a lifetime to him. Even with her admitted bossiness, she was the most delightful creature he had ever had the privilege to meet. *My Easter lady,* he thought, watching her as she sat there brazenly, as if she had come from her dressing room, dressed all the crack. Instead, she looked like a milkmaid, a very beautiful and charming milkmaid. He noted that she still wore her moneybag.

Emma rose to leave.

"Please don't go," His Grace said. "We should spend as much time as possible getting acquainted. A year is really a short while. If I am to win you, as is stated in the contract — which I think we both should sign — then I must needs —"

Emma finished for him, somewhat sarcastically, "You must needs be with me as much as possible." Well, she could see no harm in that. She felt totally immune to his prowess as a charmer, even though he seemed quite sure of himself. "I will cooperate," she promised, already thinking of ways to thwart his plan of marriage at year's end.

"Oh, that is very good. Now, do you mind if I ask you a few questions, which I will make note of?" His quill made a scratching sound, moving across the parchment with lightning speed.

Emma heaved a deep sigh. "Ask away, if I may then ask questions of you."

"Of course. How much money do you have in your moneybag, and what do you plan to do with it? And the animals, the chickens, and the blasted geese. What was your purpose in bringing them to Craigmont?"

"I do not plan to stay at Craigmont. I only came because of the small stipend from my brother's estate. But I see that I cannot stay. I will take the hundred pounds I have in my money bag, sell the animals and chickens—the geese are probably gone forever—and take Francine to London, where she will come out into society and marry."

*A rich husband,* she thought, keeping that part to herself.

"Then, I will work as a modiste, and take care of little Prudence until her mother is well."

Emma had no notion of working as a modiste. Francine's husband must needs be wealthy enough to "adopt" the whole family.

His Grace's laughter irritated Emma utterly, and his words even more so. "Lady Winslow, do you have any notion how expensive London is? Your measly pounds would not last a fortnight."

"At Fernwood—"

His Grace's voice once again was very businesslike. He leaned forward in his chair. "Lady Winslow, London is not Fernwood. Pray, let me advance you the cost of Francine's come-out. When her future is settled, we will be married . . . if I have by that time won your heart."

"And what if you have not succeeded?"

"Then you can work as a modiste and repay me."

"Will you write that down?"

"I most certainly shall, also the part about your giving me plenty of opportunity to win your hand in marriage. I want fair advantage. We shall both sign."

His Grace wrote as fast as he could. He could not be more

110

pleased, except that they were not to be married right away. Today would suit him better. But mayhaps courting would be an enjoyable experience. "I will add that I am willing to furnish an enticing dowry for your sister."

"That might bring on fortune hunters," Emma said.

"I will see that it doesn't."

And so the negotiations went. They both signed, and he asked for a kiss to seal their bargain. "Never too early to start to work," he murmured under his breath as he stole a second kiss, while daring to put his long arms around her, holding her to his heaving chest for just the shortest moment.

He smiled generously when she jerked away. "I'll thank you to remember that I am a gentle-born lady, not one of your paramours."

The kiss had burned her lips like fire.

"I'll try to remember," His Grace said, smiling.

After that, he locked the signed agreement in a safe, returned to his chair, sat down, and crossed his long legs in front of him. "You have questions?"

"Only a few," Emma said. "First, I would like to inquire as to what goes inside of Consuelo's mind. She has totally won Francine's and Prudence's favor, while alienating me with her coldness and indifference to my wishes."

His Grace looked pensive. "I wonder if anyone knows what goes on inside of Consuelo's mind. But I think you are imagining that she is cold and indifferent to you. You see, Lady Winslow, a year or so back Lord Charles spoke to me about his plight. In retrospect I believe he had a portent of his early death."

"What plight?" Emma asked.

"About yours and Francine's welfare if he should die."

"Stuff. He never gave any indication that he cared whether we lived or died. He knew we would have to leave Fernwood —"

"That is true, and he despaired of it. I spoke with Consuelo about your living here, and she was ecstatic, as was Charles when I told him. So I believe you are mistaken about Consuelo not caring for you. But, love, if I find this to be true, I most certainly will speak with her."

"She warned me not to marry you."

His Grace laughed. "I can believe that. She has said many times that I would make a horrible husband. I guess I was quite a task when I was in leading strings. I believe she wanted a daughter when I came along. Now she has three, and she wants to fuss. So let her fuss."

"I will not forebear her sending Hannah back to Fernwood, that is, unless it is Hannah's wish to go."

"Hannah will leave only if she wishes to leave, my love. But I do intend sending the Earl's carriage back to Fernwood. It does not seem fitting to keep it."

"But what will I use for equipage?"

"The grandest of carriages will be at your disposal, my very own, with the Attlebery crest. Nothing I own will be kept from you."

For a moment Emma's head spun, but she regained her composure almost instantly. She only had to remind herself that His Grace was trying to win her heart, which she had no notion of letting him win, not in a year, not ever. She rose to leave and gave a quick curtsy, dropping her gaze demurely. "Your Grace."

"That is not necessary," His Grace said, his voice firm. "And I prefer you call me Ashton. I never sought the dukedom."

"So I heard," Emma said, but she did not want to get into what she had heard. When His Grace did not respond, she was quick to remind him to have the banns unread.

"I will handle the matter," His Grace said as he accompanied her to the door, and as soon as his future bride was gone, he turned again to his writing desk, where he speedily

112

wrote: "The reading of the banns for His Grace Ashton de-Fleury and Lady Emma Winslow will continue until they've been read thrice. However, the nuptial vows will be read later than the set date. A notice will be sent."

That done, he put the sealed missive on the silver salver for Dodge to handle, and went to look for Consuelo, finding her on a bench in her rose garden. She raised her lorgnette to his eyes and greeted him with a gracious smile. "Come sit, Your Grace."

His Grace remained standing. A hot flush suffused his face. How many times, he thought, had he asked her not to address him as *Your Grace*. To no avail.

Forcing a pleasant demeanor, he said, "Consuelo, as you know, I plan to marry Lady Emma Winslow. She has told me that you warned her against marrying me."

"I did. And I am warning you against marrying her."

"Why?" His Grace's voice was strong and firm; his temper simmered just below the surface.

"I don't like Emma Winslow."

"Hell and damnation, why not? She is a precious—"

"I have my reasons." Consuelo compressed her lips and looked through her lorgnette at the blooming roses.

"What reasons?" he asked.

"It will do you no good to ask. I said I have *my* reasons, and I shall keep them mine. In truth, I would like to get her married off . . . but not to you. When you came upon me just now, I was thinking of possible suitors and Sir Arthur Stewart came to mind. I believe he is visiting Brighton right this minute."

His Grace exploded in the grandest fashion. "That jackanapes! He's a scoundrel of the first order. What . . . what can you be thinking?"

"I do not find Stewart as offensive as you seem to, and since Emma is past the preferred marriage age, one cannot pick and choose."

His Grace's heart sank. Stewart had every gel in Town panting after him. He seemed to know the right thing to do, the right thing to say. In truth, His Grace thought, the man had turned his womanizing into a work of art. "Well, Consuelo, since I cannot reason with you, I must needs trust Lady Winslow's good judgment to turn aside Stewart's advances, if he should so choose to pay his addresses to her."

"Oh, he will choose," Consuelo said smugly.

"What makes you say that?"

"Because Emma, with all her faults, is beautiful beyond measure, and Stewart loves beautiful gels, all beautiful gels. I am certain that he will favor us with his presence for supper, or some other such gathering at Craigmont, in the near future."

His Grace stared at her incredulously. "How do you know that? You've not had time to ask him—"

"Oh, but I shall. Just as soon as the modiste stitches appropriate gowns for my three gels. And possibly a new one for me." Consuelo rose from the bench and went to bend over an especially beautiful rose. She wore an elegant dusty rose long round gown which showed her youthful figure. "Look, Your Grace, isn't this a thing of beauty?"

She took a pair of small scissors from her pocket and cut the rose from the bush, then, smiling up at her son, proceeded to attach it to the lapel of his coat.

He flung her hands away and frowned ferociously. "You're a wicked woman," he said. Turning, he strode from the garden, swearing under his breath.

Consuelo smiled as her gaze followed her son's leaving, his straight back, his tall body moving like a prowling animal, never wavering to the right or to the left. So sure of where it was going. What's on his mind? she wondered, and she even imagined the swear words that spilled from his mouth. She knew so well his favorites. When he was but a boy, she'd tried to stop his swearing, but had failed. Tears then filled her eyes, and memories flooded her mind. "Ashton, oh Ashton," she murmured. "How dear you are to me. I would never hurt you."

Considerable time passed as Consuelo deFleury stood there, watching, and when there was nothing left for her to watch, except the slammed door quivering in His Grace's wake, she turned back to her beautiful roses, her thoughts then turned in another direction. There was so much to be done. A missive would be sent to Sir Arthur Stewart. . . .

Emma went directly from His Grace's bookroom to Prudence's quarters, where she was sure she would find Hannah. She wanted to hear from the maid herself if she favored returning to Fernwood. The distance was far, and as she walked the long, wide halls she stopped to look at paintings of flowers and of rose gardens. She pensively recalled the conversation with His Grace and felt no compunction whatever for having deceived him by letting him think that she would marry him after a husband had been found for Francine. She tossed her head of black hair to one side. Why should she feel guilt; he had tricked her brother.

She also recalled His Grace's kiss, and she cautioned herself to be careful. She had felt a minute amount of excitement not natural with her. Not a minute amount, a lot, she mused, being honest with herself.

When she was young, a neighboring farm boy had stolen a kiss when they were at the stables. She had felt absolutely nothing. He had come to work, she had told him, and then saw that he performed the chores he had come to do.

Emma thought about His Grace's remarks about it being all in her imagination about Consuelo taking her in dislike, and she wondered if possibly it were true. "I cannot be selfish and insist that Francine leave with me when His Grace has offered her such a wonderful opportunity for a come-

115

out. And Consuelo acts as if she has suddenly been given three daughters to pamper."

Emma corrected herself, "Two daughters."

At last she was at the door of Prudence's bed-sitting room. She knocked, then pushed on the door, finding the room empty. Hearing a voice next door, in the schoolroom, she stood unobtrusively in the door and listened to Prudence reading to Hannah. She had not known that the child was so accomplished, and marveled at her enunciation of words much advanced for her age. Hannah listened, as if enthralled.

Upon seeing Emma the reading stopped, and Prudence ran to greet her. "Auntie Em, Miss deFleury is looking for you. Miss Van Winters came and said that if we saw you that we were to tell you to come to the withdrawing room on the third floor."

"She knew I was with His Grace," Emma said.

"But she thought your audience with His Grace was over. They had no idea, so Miss Van Winters said, that you would be in his bookroom so long. And unchaperoned."

"They were welcome to come along as chaperons," Emma said sarcastically. Taking Prudence's hand, they walked to the table where Prudence had been sitting. "I'm happy to see you, Prudence, but it is Hannah I wish to speak with."

"Shall I leave?" Prudence asked.

"No, of course not. You may hear whatever I have to say."

Emma turned to Hannah and asked, "Do you wish to remain at Craigmont, or is it your wish to return to Fernwood?"

"I wish to stay at Craigmont," Hannah said, adding, "And fer good reason."

Emma studied her for a moment. "What reason is that, Hannah? Not to be my spy, I pray."

"To make sure m'lady's not poisoned."

Emma did not know whether to laugh or cry. The maid

116

looked genuinely frightened. "Hannah, no one is going to poison me."

"I would not be so sure if it was me. I hear talking between the upstairs and the downstairs maids."

Emma's heart skipped a beat and started to pound. "Hannah, don't beat around the bush. What —"

"They said thet Miss deFleury had taken yer to dislike and that yer days at Craigmont were numbered."

Emma wanted to deny Consuelo's dislike, but she knew it was of no use. Staff gossip was stronger than the sword. "Well, that doesn't mean they are going to poison me."

"Not if I work in the kitchen," Hannah said.

"Work in the kitchen! Why, Hannah, you've never worked in the kitchen —"

"Oh, but I ken. I have my plan. When yer eat at the table with the others nobody would risk tinkering with yer food, but should food or tea be brought to yer room, thet would be the time for dirty work. I will be the one to bring it to yer, and I will set it before yer, not giving that Miss Van Winters a chance at it. I'll even taste it before yer."

The maid's loyalty brought tears to Emma's eyes. Oh, how she missed Fernwood, and *her family* there. "Hannah, I will see that you work in the kitchen if that is your wish, but pray, don't mention that you are there to keep me from being poisoned. I'm afraid the staff at Craigmont thinks we are country bumpkins as it is."

She turned to leave, and Prudence asked, "Auntie Em, will you hear my prayers? I'll come to your rooms, if you want. I like to visit with you before I go to sleep. It makes Mama seem closer."

Emma looked at the head of blond curls, and the green-hazel eyes and her heart wanted to burst inside of her. Her innocence, and her faith that everything was going to be all right, was a miracle within itself. She tried to remember when she had been that young and couldn't. Too much stood in the way. "I'd love to hear your prayers, Prue, and come in time for a long visit. Mayhaps bring a book. I would love to hear you read."

Tears pushed at Emma's eyes. She left immediately and found her way to the stairs that led to the third floor, where she would find Consuelo deFleury waiting in her withdrawing room. *Dear God, what have I done to deserve this?* she prayed, and her thoughts turned to Charles, her brother who had not even tried to produce an heir to Fernwood. Her teeth involuntarily ground together. *If he had not been so busy womanizing . . . and getting himself killed over a lightskirt.*

Consuelo answered the door herself when Emma knocked. The door opened to a room beautiful beyond bearing. Rose silk-covered sofas and chairs, and open windows brought sloping gardens and a raging sea right into the room.

Emma's feet sank into plush carpet as she walked to the chair which Consuelo indicated was her place to sit. A puppet on a string, she thought, and it did not fit her personality at all.

Turning on Consuelo, she spat out her anger, "Why are you treating me this way?"

Consuelo walked to the chair closest to the one Emma sat in and sat down. "What way, my dear?"

"Don't bandy words with me, Miss deFleury. It has been obvious to me that you have had nothing but dislike for me since the moment I arrived at Craigmont. While, on the other hand, you seem to dote on Francine and little Prue, as if they were new toys. Or is that your mode of manipulation?"

Consuelo smiled a sweet smile. "My, you have a temper. Just like my Ashton. In the rose garden, only a short while ago, he was as angry with me as you are. And all because I do not think the two of you are suited for each other."

"I did not come here to discuss my relationship with your

son, Consuelo. That shall remain between His Grace and me. I came because you sent for me. Can we not hurry—"

"Of course, dear." Consuelo turned in her chair and looked out the window. "The sea . . . it is so beautiful."

Emma waited, while her anger simmered in silence.

Finally, Consuelo started talking, speaking as if Emma had not spoken to her in anger, as if Emma had not asked that very important question of why had she taken such a dislike to her.

"The modiste will arrive shortly. I should like you to be available for measurements."

"Is that all?" Emma asked. "Where did you think I would go?"

"Possibly riding with His Grace. Or disappear to the stables to care for your chickens and animals." She looked despairingly at the skirt of Emma's gown on which strands of straw still clung, and at the hem caked in dirt.

Emma pulled her legs back close to the chair, but her carelessness in dress was blatantly obvious. "I'm sorry," she said contritely, "I should have changed before I answered your summons."

Consuelo dismissed the subject as easily as she had introduced it. "My true purpose in wanting to talk with you is to learn if you have particulars about a governess for Prue. I've sent enquiries into Brighton. I've asked a dear friend of mine, Mrs. Fitzherbert, Prinny's illegal wife, to send three from which to pick. I was certain you would know—"

"I know nothing about children," Emma said, and then she quickly added, "Prudence should visit with the women. I will trust her judgment. Of course I will be present when the women are interviewed, and I will have the last say."

"That is odd, to let a child pick her governess, but I agree with you. Prue is an astute child, very personable, very innocent and believing. I only wish I could have just a smattering of those qualities."

Emma saw sadness behind Consuelo's eyes; it even seeped into her words. Anxious to leave, she stood. "I appreciate your wanting a governess for Prudence, and your interest in Francine. I must needs see that she has a good husband, and then I can think of my own future."

"I fully intend to find a husband for you, my dear. Three and twenty is not too old for marriage . . . to the right man."

Emma could not believe what she was hearing. "I do not want a husband," she said, and she quickly quit the room.

It was not until Emma was outside the door that she realized Consuelo deFleury had not answered the one important question: Why had the Craigmont recluse taken such a dislike of Lady Emma Winslow from Fernwood Manor?

# Chapter Ten

Emma prepared for bed. It had been a strenuous day, she concluded as she reflected back on the events that had transpired. She, Francine, and little Prudence had been measured for gowns by Madame Lacont and her four helpers, who had descended on Craigmont in early afternoon, their scissors and needles at the ready. "Within a week your three gels will have new wardrobes, even Court gowns," Madame Lacont promised.

When the measuring had been completed, Emma talked seriously with Francine about leaving Craigmont. She did not have the heart to tell her sister about Consuelo's obvious dislike for her, for fear Francine, out of pity, would insist they leave. Emma did, however, tell her that the Duke expected her to marry him. "To pay our brother's debt."

"Oh, sister, married to a duke!" Francine said.

"Anything can happen in a year," Emma answered.

In the end, they both agreed that Francine, and little Prudence as well, had a promise of a future if they stayed at Craigmont, whereas if they went to London without adequate means anything could happen.

As the day passed, Emma learned that breakfast and the noon meal were served on sideboards and left for an extended time; tea, which would be served in one's room, or, if preferred, belowstairs in the drawing room at half-past four.

Emma had had tea brought to her room. Hannah, much to Van Winters's obvious displeasure, was present and surreptitiously tasting everything in sight.

Supper was at eight at night, served in the dining room by elegantly attired servants.

"We will dress appropriately," Consuelo said, and Emma wore another of her homemade gowns which she thought very pretty, and very flattering. The gown brought no comment from Consuelo.

Francine wore another of Consuelo's gowns, and Prudence, as usual, wore total black.

Well-trained servants were in incredible numbers at Craigmont. They moved noiselessly, saying nothing to each other. Nothing like Fernwood, Emma thought, and she scolded herself for comparing.

Supper had seemed uneventful to Emma, more food than an army could eat, and pleasant conversation. Consuelo talked with Prudence about Princess Caroline, whom she knew well, she said, and promised that soon she would invite her to Craigmont for tea with Prudence. The Duke, dressed to the nines, and very handsome, Emma was forced to admit, joined them, and she felt his burning gaze on her until she lost her appetite.

But he did not mention the banns having to be unread, or about their coming marriage — which was not going to be — and she was thankful for that.

After the meal, His Grace approached Emma and asked, "Will you walk with me on the beach? The moon on the water is very pretty."

Emma declined, claiming fatigue, which was not altogether a lie. Turning from the look of disappointment registered on his face, she repaired to her rooms. Prudence came with her candle, this time as before, praying silently, then talking anticlimactically about the Easter miracle that would make her mama well. Emma listened, unbelieving, and when Prudence left she noticed the silence of the night more than she ever had. She felt terribly alone, homesick for Fernwood, heartsick over the inexplicable turn of events. Never before had anyone treated her with dislike, not even the servants at Fernwood after a severe set down, which, before she spoke, she always made sure was well deserved.

Now, the day was past, and Emma slipped a white night-dress over her head, then poured water from an ewer, splashing it onto her face. She dried with a thick towel, while her heart swelled in her breast until she thought it would burst. Holding back the tears — for ladies of three and twenty were too old to cry — she went to stand by the window. She tried desperately to deny her tears, but they came, unbidden, in torrents, and sobs like tiny avalanches assaulted her body. She thought about her mama and papa. At Fernwood, she had felt their presence. How she missed them. They had not been perfect parents, letting their only son escape responsibility, but neither had they criticized their daughters.

Emma's anger for her brother flared, and she vowed over and over that she would never forgive him. "Never, never, never," she said, and she vowed anew to outsmart the duke. His Grace was as much a culprit as her brother Charles.

Both were villains, and when she at last went to bed, she slept quickly and dreamed of her dead brother, and of the Duke of Attlebery. Both had horns, swords, and devil eyes, and she wore an armor their swords could not penetrate. Above it all hung a crucifix wrapped in writhing snakes.

The dream had no meaning, Emma told herself upon awaking, myriad events jumbled together, giving no ending. Dreams were like that, probably from one's unconscious self, and most likely relating to nothing at all, she reasoned.

Nonetheless, she slipped from the bed and found her diary which she had neglected since learning she would be leaving Fernwood, and wrote in detail about the dream, and then she recorded the dream about the man on the cross, the whispering trees, the child sitting on the crumbling wall, her head bent over a candle.

As she wrote, it became clear to Emma that *that* dream had been different. It had been like a play, acted out before her eyes, in proper sequence, the players real. Still, Emma had no idea what the dream meant. She remembered vividly the whispering trees and shuddered, and the strangest feeling came over her, as if something supernatural had entered the room. Emma knew that every manor in England had a ghost, but she was not ready for an encounter. Her hands were shaking; her brain felt thick and fuzzy. Lying back on the bed, she willed that she would again sleep. "And, pray, this time no dreams," she said as she listened to the waves sloshing high, breaking, then crashing down onto the shore.

The rhythm was astounding, and the sound lulled her to sleep. Yet another dream came, this time one which Emma could understand: her fine pullets had laid seven eggs in the corner nest of their new home. "That cannot be," she declared when she awoke. She looked beyond the window; dawn had not yet broken, purple mist rose up from the gardens, and from the sea.

Knowing that even the servants would still be abed, she bounded to the floor, grabbed from the chiffonnier a long pelisse and put it on. After slipping her feet into flat slippers, she quietly and quickly left the manor.

Emma did not stop to think. She knew that she must needs see if the dream had meaning, if there were seven eggs in the corner nest. Why, she asked herself, were the strange dreams coming to her. Especially at this time. Was she receiving messages from on high? She knew nothing about interpreting dreams, and never had she had portents of future happenings, or feelings that she was being visited by a higher power. She recalled that the dreams had begun when she learned she would be leaving Fernwood, coming simultaneously with her deep anger for her brother.

"A troubled mind brings troubled dreams," she said, as she sped across the emerald-sapphire grass, wet with dew. She then took the road through the copse that led to the stables, and there she darted into the newly constructed house where the twelve pullets and one rooster were on roosts. She moved quietly so as not to disturb them and headed straight for the corner nest.

Emma knew absolutely before she looked that she would find seven eggs, and that awful feeding of being visited by the unknown, by something supernatural, returned. The eggs were there, seven of them. Even though she expected to find them, she was stunned. Turning, she left as fast as she could, going back through the woods in the direction from which she had come, back to strange, unfriendly Craigmont Manor, she thought.

Emma's feet moved swiftly, and the sprawling manor soon came into view, four stories of mellow yellow brick beyond a smooth mossy lawn. Mullioned windows framed flickering candles, attesting that servants were up and about, servants to whom gossip was the breath of life. She wanted to turn and run; she stood for a long moment, then retraced her steps through the woods to the sweeping curve that would take her back to the stables. Her plan took her no farther than that.

Stopping again, she decided not to follow the road, but instead to walk deeper into the woods, along the narrow bridle path from which His Grace had made his appearance on his big black horse. She had no idea where she was going. Looking up, she saw dark, threatening clouds, roiling and scudding, as if angry. A strong breeze off the sea cooled her face, and ruffled her black hair up from her neck. Suddenly feeling cold, she pulled the pelisse together in front, shutting out her thin white nightdress. Trees, like tall images, their limbs intertwined, shut out the sky, and roots stretched across her path like tendrils ready to trip her.

Still Emma did not want to turn back. She pushed blindly onward, anywhere to escape the house where she felt so blatantly unwelcome. She could hear Consuelo's critical voice, ingratiatingly sweet as honey, horribly false.

She lost all track of time, and she found herself off the path on which she had started. In truth, she admitted in alarm, there was no path. A ground mist lay blue against the dark green woods, where, no doubt, the sun had not reached for days and days. Mayhaps years. She looked ahead of her, behind her, to the right, and then to the left. She heard the liquid spill of a bird's crystal clear song, and stopped and listened, mesmerized by the sound. Nothing in her life had prepared her for the sheer beauty of what surrounded her, and she wanted it to swallow her up, to hide her, the overpowering, mystical, wonderful woods.

She walked on and on until she realized she was indeed incredibly lost. No longer could she hear the wash of the sea. She was strangely not frightened. A calmness engulfed her as she walked in the direction she thought would bring her to the Sussex Shore, where, she reasoned, she could find the manor.

But the woods became darker, and it began to rain, hitting the leaves and sounding very much like the stealthy movement of a full-skirted gown. She wondered for a moment what progress the modiste and her helpers were making toward stitching the Town wardrobes. But her only real concern was for Francine and Prudence, and, of course, Hannah. What would they think when she did not come down for breakfast?

Emma only hoped that Hannah did not accuse someone of poisoning m'lady.

Walking on, she came full circle. She knew this because the moss still held her footprints. Tired, she sat and rested, then plowed deeper into the woods. At the top of a hillock she saw below a break in the towering treetops. The rain had stopped, and sun glinted on wet leaves and on limbs that waved in the wind.

Fighting the underbrush, hearing her clothing tear, she determinedly, as if pulled by some mysterious force, made her way toward the clearing. There she gasped and covered her mouth with her hand. She thought at first it was an apparition, born from her dream, for in front of her were ancient white stone walls, unroofed, half-crumbled. She fully expected to see three crosses holding crucified men, a child on a wall, praying over a candle, and to hear the trees whisper, "Father forgive them for they know not what . . ."

Emma's heart gave a small spasm, as if a suddenly caged bird had set up a sparrowlike thrashing in her breast. Her body began to shake, and she muffled a mewling cry that leapt from her throat, and then she was engulfed by a great empty silence.

A cry from Emma's throat did not penetrate the dense, enchanted air, and intuitively she knew she stood on sacred ground. There was a sense of timelessness, a sense of mystical sacredness as she walked through what once, she was sure, were rooms. Stone beds were attached to a wall, and there was the remains of a wellhouse where someone had drawn water. The cooking area had smoked-black walls; there was what could have been a chapel, with religious signs carved into the walls.

Emma lingered, looking for clues to her dream, but found none. Why would she dream about a place she had never seen? Why did she dream about seven eggs, when there was no relation between her pullets laying and the crumbling walls? Why had she dreamed that her brother and the Duke of Attlebery had horns and swords? What did her dreams mean?

Doubt that these were the walls in her dream did not enter Emma's thoughts; the imagery was too vividly imprinted in her mind. The silence deepened, holding her in its grip, and still the answer she sought did not come. All around her was that terrible darkness. She stood and pondered: *I know that some force is telling me something, but I know not what.*

And then she heard water gurgling and walked toward the sound, finding a narrow clear blue stream snaking downward. She bent and drank, then followed the shallow water a mile, or even more, she calculated. The trees thinned and spates of probing sunshine warmed her, and dried her clothes. Bluebells, not moss, grew beneath her feet.

The vibration and the sound of pounding waves were suddenly in Emma's ears. The little stream turned and trickled farther downward, but she went to the sound, to the top of a cliff, and there she saw the sea coming toward her in blue-black roiling waves. For a long moment she stood and let the mist hit her face, let the wind blow her long hair, while she sucked in deep breaths of fresh salt air.

It was as if she had walked out of a dream, and she found herself ridiculously laughing. She sat on a huge rock that hung over the beach and combed her tangled hair with her fingers. The hem of her pelisse and that of her nightdress were torn to shreds.

The placement of the sun told Emma that midday had come and gone. She would not have thought it, for it did not seem that she was in the woods that long. Now that she knew, hunger pains attacked her. She must needs think of which direction to go to find Craigmont Manor, she told herself, and was surprised to find that she was not sure. She rested a short while, then climbed down over the rocky shoreline onto the white sandy beach. Looking both right and left, she decided to go to the right and walked in that direction until she came upon a sign that read: Private Property—Stop Here.

Emma ignored the sign, beyond which was a bend of sorts, like an island the size of a drawing room protruding out into the sea. On the other side was a buoy painted white and green, and farther out a ship lay at anchor.

Emma stood and stared, and upon closer scrutiny of the ship, she saw a man standing on deck, peering out at her through a spyglass. After staring at him a considerable time, she walked on; the sky again became suddenly sullen, and she could not gather the angle of the sun. South was north as far as she was concerned, and east was west.

A little farther on, she stopped, wondering if she were not going in the wrong direction, and, starting to turn back, out of the corner of her eye she saw an overgrown path that climbed upward over huge boulders and shiny rocks. Without hesitation Emma ascended to the top ledge and saw twining into the woods a continuation of the path, at whose end was a cottage surrounded by a carpet of bluebells. Lichen climbed to its narrow windows and around its door.

By now frightened for having invaded someone's private world, Emma started to turn and retrace her steps, but then she reconsidered. Naturally curious, she climbed up and made her way to the cottage, around which trees and vines warred with each other, evidence that the cottage had not been occupied for a long time. And looking through one of the narrow windows, she saw that white ducking covered the furniture and other objects leaning against the walls. Black coals lay in the fireplace grate, as if they had grown tired of burning and had gone out because there was no one there to stoke them.

Emma tried the door and found it locked. So she turned and retraced her steps to the beach, where she went in the opposite direction, walking fast until she was around that small piece of protruding land which shielded the anchored ship, the green and white buoy, and the path that led to the cottage.

Emma did not know why she should be frightened, but once out of sight of the man on the ship, she began running. Her feet leaden from fatigue, her body weak from hunger, she did not hear the sand-muffled hoofbeats until a black horse came to a shuddering stop practically on top of her.

"Emma, I've been out of my mind about you," His Grace said as he slid from the saddle and reached his long arms out to Emma, who would have been pleased to have seen the devil himself, as long as it was not Consuelo deFleury.

His Grace wore a rain garrick and fawn-colored riding breeches; his blond hair was wet and stuck to his head.

Emma did not haughtily tell him that she was not his love, nor did she pull away when he pulled her to his long frame and held her against his heaving chest. She found his arms comforting. Aloneness gushed from inside her like a spring, and she wanted to tell him, anyone, about her mysterious dreams.

Knowing she would be thought ready for Bedlam, she refrained from doing so. "I saw ruins . . . crumbled walls . . ."

His Grace's arms tightened around her. He felt her weariness, her fatigue, her body growing limp. "The Abbey, destroyed by old Henry VIII. My God, Emma, have you been *that* deep into the woods?"

"How are Francine and Prudence?"

"All right. Worried about you. Why, darling, why did you leave without a word?"

"I'm so tired, but I should go . . . Francine . . ." Emma murmured.

"You must needs think of yourself," His Grace said in a protective way. He picked her up, laid her on the white sand, and then, propped up on an elbow, half-lay beside her. She was instantly asleep, and His Grace found himself filled with such happiness he had difficulty breathing. Just being near her, touching her, was the most wonderful thing that had ever happened to him. Asleep, she seemed so vulnerable. He let his gaze slide over her lithe body, noting the tattered hems of her garments.

He moved his finger down the side of her cheek, then bent to brush her half-parted lips with his. She wrinkled her nose and slapped at him, as if he were a fly. His Grace smiled, and when her breathing became deep and steady, he, overcome by temptation, decided to try another kiss.

Lightly, he told himself, but when his lips touched hers the fomenting passion in his veins pushed him beyond return and he held her tight, kissing her with fervor, with love,

130

with all there was in him. Dear God, he prayed, do not let me offend her sensibilities, her innocence.

Emma kissed him back. She wrapped her arms around his neck and a little moan escaped her throat as their lips met and lingered, and met again.

His Grace did not have a conception of heaven, but he was sure that when she snuggled closer to him, resting her sweet face in the crook of his neck, he had suddenly arrived there. She loved him as much as he loved her, he reasoned, else she would not have returned his kiss. To let his ardor cool, he looked out at the sea, and the scudding clouds moved over to let the sun shine on them. A perfect omen, he thought. Then time passed without meaning, and over the blue-black water, sea gulls dipped and dived, and on the shore, waves washed wet the sand beneath His Grace and his only love. Tomorrow, he would send the notice to the papers, announcing the date of their wedding. He pulled her to him and stole another kiss.

# Chapter Eleven

"I did not kiss you," Emma said with unbending dignity, her blue eyes dark and luminous.

His Grace gave a crooked grin. "On my honor you did kiss me, and with intense feeling. So I took it upon myself to have the banns read a second time." He did not tell her that he had requested the banns be read the required three times, that he had informed the papers that he would send notice when the date for the wedding had been set.

"Then, Your Grace, take it off yourself and have the banns unread. It is not my intent, or my wish, to marry you," Emma said, quickly adding, "Not right away. Not until Francine has her come-out and is settled with a nice husband." Emma almost reminded him that when that happened the agreement would be up for renegotiation, but she caught herself in time. At times she spoke too quickly, she knew, and silently threatened to bite her tongue off if she did not contain herself. They were at the stables, she gathering her seven eggs, and His Grace having just returned from a morning ride. Dressed in proper riding clothes, impeccably tailored, he stood tall and erect, one hand holding his black horse's rein. His gaze was focused on Emma. He was ruggedly handsome, she decided. It would have been so much easier to thwart his and her dead brother's marriage plans if he were stooped and used snuff, as she had imagined before coming to Craigmont.

This day Emma wore a well-worn blue morning dress, and a half-apron in which she had gathered up to hold her eggs. Looking up at His Grace she vividly recalled yesterday's dark woods, His Grace rescuing her.

After her rest on the beach, they had returned to the manor astride his black horse. She had sat in the saddle, with His Grace riding behind her, his big hands spanning her waist. She had asked why Craigmont did not farm its land, and when he said that Consuelo would not allow the trees to be cut, she had replied, "All this land for beauty's sake. Why, at Fernwood we grew crops . . ."

"Love, this is not Fernwood," His Grace gently reminded her, and after that, little or no conversation transpired, and upon arriving at the manor, Emma had gone directly to bed to finish her rest. Her only explanation to Consuelo and Francine was that she had been lost in the woods.

Emma was not sure about the kiss. She vaguely remembered feeling strangely warm when she awakened, and it was possible, she now told herself, that she *had* kissed His Grace. But she was not going to admit it. After all, one was not responsible for what one did when one was asleep. She smiled at His Grace, who was looking at her with a most peculiar look on his face, his hazel eyes like shards of green glass.

"What's wrong, Your Grace?" she asked. "Is it too difficult for you to understand a gel's desire to get her younger sister married and settled before she, herself, settles into married bliss?"

The Duke's eyes moved over her, riveting on her breasts, and on her mouth that begged to be kissed. Long lashes shaded her melting blue eyes and made shadows on her cheeks.

"I've asked you to call me Ashton," he said as two long strides wiped out the distance between them. His long arms reached, and Emma, before she could step back or sideways, felt herself crushed against his hard, heaving chest. "You won't forget this kiss, and you *will* kiss me back," he said before bringing his lips down on hers with unquestionable authority.

Emma knew her stubbornness in not admitting she had kissed this ruthless Duke had pitched her into this trouble and, for a moment, she tried to think of a way to stop the lingering, searing kiss.

But only for a moment, for yesterday's strange warmth returned in full force, and she found herself totally submissive, even to the point of contemplating placing her arms around His Grace's neck and pulling him closer.

She was not, however, given the opportunity. After kissing her until her breath was coming in small gasps, her heart thundering inside her head, and her knees about to give way, His Grace released her so quickly that she stumbled backwards, barely regaining her balance before falling.

It was then Emma realized her eggs had been crushed.

"See what you've done," she accused.

As if she had not spoken, as if she did not look a spectacle, His Grace said, "Don't ever again deny that you kissed me." He had never wanted a gel so demme bad in his life. He turned quickly and regained his horse's reins and led him to the cool-down lot for the groom to walk. He felt the need for a cool-down walk himself. Returning to his mistress even crossed his mind, but he knew he would not. With plans to be married, it would not be honorable. What he must needs do now, His Grace told himself, was to hurry to his rooms and retrieve the missive announcing his coming marriage before Dodge, his valet, put it in the post. He could not get married without the gel's consent.

This, His Grace did, and later he told Dodge that he did not understand women at all, and the valet, grinning wryly while taking a sniff of snuff, replied, "I will give you the whole of it, Your Grace. I have a feeling that before you marry Lady Winslow you will know more than you care to know about women."

The remark was little comfort to the Duke. His desire to marry Emma Winslow was stronger than *anything* he had heretofore experienced, and that included the acquisition of his first ship. So it stood to reason that he would win, he told himself. But when? He closed his eyes: *Pray, do not let it be long, for I don't think I can stand another such encounter as the one in the stable yard.* He felt the familiar ache, and said angrily, *sotto voce,* "This is ridiculous."

But he went on with his thoughts. He visualized her in his townhouse in Grosvenor Square, tall, regal, elegant, waiting for him to come home from the office. Never would he stop at White's, or any other club strictly for gentlemen. Not when he would find her waiting. She would not want to go out to some social gathering; instead, they would dine at home, with candlelight, and later, he would carry her to their bedchamber. Always their bedchamber, for he would not sleep away from her, as was fashionable. He would make love to her and hold her through the night. . . .

He quit his bookroom and repaired to his dressing room, where he sat for a shave, and then listened to the sage bachelor-womanizer's advice on how to win Emma's heart. Meticulously, the valet selected proper clothes His Grace would wear to impress her. "You must needs give her time," the valet said.

"Fustian, you've told me that before," His Grace complained.

The valet turned and looked straight into His Grace's face. "I can't say it often enough, Your Grace. You must needs give her time. Do not rush her. Let her see what a wonderful catch you are. Let her see that half the gels in Town are after you."

"More like their mamas," His Grace said, "and only because of my success in shipping." He vividly recalled the time an over-eager Ton mama brought her daughter, dressed to the first stare, to his office — in an area she had no business being — on the pretense she had ordered a shipment of rare birds, and they had not arrived. He had told her he did not deal in birds, and that he only dealt with merchandise brokers.

As His Grace donned his clothes, he thought about Consuelo's plan to get Lady Winslow leg-shackled to Sir Arthur Stewart, a preposterous idea that did not bear thinking upon. He did not understand Consuelo. Even before he had seen twenty summers she had pushed to get him leg-shackled to some London chit vacationing in Brighton. One of Prinny's crowd, of course, and this he could not abide. Because of her matchmaking he had for a time stopped his visits to Craigmont, but then, out of guilt, had resumed them.

Why had Consuelo taken Lady Winslow in dislike, he asked himself. It was singularly queer. Other than Emma's stubbornness, he could not find fault with her. And in a way His Grace could understand the stubbornness. Forced to shoulder a man's load at Fernwood, survival had become Lady Winslow's main focus in life. Her love had been expended on Fernwood, and on Francine, when she should have been thinking of herself, a life of her own, which would mean, of course, a good marriage. He smiled when he recalled her denial that she would marry any man, and then she had changed her mind, saying that when Francine was settled they would be married. That was as it should be. Every gel needed a husband to love and protect her. If he could only convince her that she needed him.

His Grace could even understand Emma's anger with her brother, and it disturbed him immensely. Shaking his head, he quoted something he had read in one of his big books, "Anger eats away the vessel that holds it." He did not want that to happen to Emma. He wished he could tell her how wrong she was about Lord Charles, tell her the whole of it, why he had stayed away from Fernwood. But the time was just not right; Emma's anger was still too raw, too blatantly unforgiving.

His Grace's mind turned back to Consuelo. He had never

known her to be unkind to another human being, not to a servant, not to an animal. Life had not been easy for her, yet she had never complained. When London cut her, she cut London from her life, never looking back, and seemingly not caring. She had come to Craigmont to raise him, she had said, and at Craigmont she had stayed. The thought crossed His Grace's mind that mayhaps she had given up on his ever marrying and giving her the grandchildren she so desired. Mayhaps she was angry about not having grandchildren. Mayhaps that accounted for her instant love for Francine and little Prudence.

But not for Emma.

The thought entered His Grace's mind that if he owned Craigmont, he could forbid her to invite Stewart inside its doors. But Consuelo had been given Craigmont by her wealthy father, a member of French nobility, and the monies that maintained it came from his estate, which was considerable.

There was nothing for it, His Grace decided, but to talk with Consuelo again about Emma. He would pour out his love for her ladyship, and pray that Consuelo would take pity. Not that he needed her approval to marry, but sweet, sweet Emma did not deserve to be disliked.

Another thought came to His Grace. He would hurry the Ladies Winslow's departure to London, where Francine would surely shortly find a husband.

Dressed to the nines, His Grace, after thanking his valet, quit the room and went to find Consuelo, expecting to find her in her upstairs drawing room. He knocked, received no answer, and continued his search by descending the stairs to the second floor, although he had no idea what she would be doing on that floor. On the square landing, which was as large as a normal-sized room, he encountered Prudence and was pleased to have a chance to visit with the lonely little girl. His planned conversation with Consuelo could wait. "Good morning, Prudence," he said, smiling down at her. She gave him a set-down look and said, "Mr. deFleury, I do not like to be called Prudence."

His smile broadened. "What shall I call you?"

"Prue. I hear you do not like to be called His Grace, so I shall call you Mr. deFleury."

"And I shall call you Prue."

She started to leave, and he sought to detain her by putting a big hand on her small shoulder. "Prue, will you stay and coze with me? I've been searching the manor and you are the only lady I've laid eyes on. I'm quite lonely."

Big eyes looked up at him. "Mr. deFleury, I understand, for I am always lonely. I miss Mama . . ."

Instantly His Grace felt tears cloud his eyes, and a lump the size of an egg formed in his throat. Reaching down, he embraced her. She was so thin. He lifted her up into his long arms and carried her to a small sofa that sat against the north wall. Many times, when he was no older than Prudence, he had sat there. He remembered too well the loneliness.

"Life can be very trying when one has only eight summers," he said.

"I had a wonderful life until Mama became ill. She laughed a lot and loved me completely. Papa was not home overly much, business kept him away, but when he did come home he was the sweetest man to Mama, and to me. He was killed in an accident."

His Grace looked at her, dressed in black from head to toe, the black startling against her fair skin. She sat with her small hands crossed demurely in her lap. He wanted so much to comfort her, but his ineptness with women reached to children as well. "I knew Lord Winslow well, Prue. He was a fine gentleman. He so often spoke of you with great fondness."

This brought a smile to the wan face. "I have accepted Papa's death. Mama told me that only our Lord rose from the grave, and for me not to expect Papa to do the same. So I don't. But I *know* Mama will be well by next Easter."

His Grace looked askance. "How do you know, Prue?"

"Because I believe in miracles, like the ones the Bible talks about, and I am petitioning God for a miracle, that Mama will be well by Easter. She was very sick, but I think a year should be adequate time, don't you, Mr. deFleury?"

The seriousness of the child's faith, and her grownupness, squeezed His Grace's heart. She was asking him if a year was adequate time, seeking reassurance he could not give, for he had never heard of anyone who went to Bedlam returning. He began to prepare her for that by saying, "Dear child, oftentimes we must needs accept that which we cannot change."

"But God can," she said adamantly, and His Grace thought for a moment. He could not shatter the child's dream, and he silently prayed, *How can I help,* and, like on a whirling wind inside his head, the answer came. He would have Countess Margaret moved from the government-owned hospital for the insane to a private institution, and he would right away do that. Even so, he held out little hope. He had heard that patients at Bedlam were bled daily, to remove the tainted blood, and oftentimes they became so weak they died. He castigated himself for not thinking sooner of moving Countess Winslow, and his only excuse was that he had been thinking only of himself, and his quest for a wife.

His Grace also knew the history of Margaret's illness. He looked at Prudence. His heart was not large enough to hold the sorrow he saw in her sad eyes, so much like her papa's.

He promised Prudence, "If there is help for your mama, I will find it. Mayhaps a better place, where she will get better care, where there will be doctors who specialize in illnesses of the nerves."

"See," Prudence said excitedly. "Already He is answering my prayers. Thank you, thank you so very much, Mr. deFleury. What they say about you is not true at all." She threw her arms around his neck and hugged him.

His Grace laughed outwardly and hugged her back. Inwardly, he was afraid to ask, but did. "What do *they* say about me?"

"That you are a nabob, that you live in a world by yourself, and that your only goal in life is to make more and more money, without giving thought to helping the poor. Mama told me the rumors that floated around in Town."

This hit His Grace in the face with great force, like a storm at sea when he had thought to be blown away. He had heard the saying, *From the mouths of babes,* and, at that moment, he came face to face with his true self. The rumors were the truth. Money had been his God, until he decided to marry Emma. He promised himself that he would do better, but he could not forget his desire to marry Emma. So he said, "Prue, there is something I want very much. Will you pray for a miracle for me?"

"An Easter Miracle?"

"I would prefer it sooner. I want very much to marry Lady Emma Winslow."

"Do you love her?"

"With all my heart."

"Then, I will pray for a union between the two, that is if Auntie Em wants to marry you."

The child's answer made him smile. "It must needs be honorable," she said, and he told her that it was. She left then, going to her rooms to read to Hannah, if the maid had managed to slip away from the kitchen. Soon a tutor would be hired, Prudence said, but until then she did not want to lose her skills. Feeling much lighter in spirit, His Grace continued his search for Consuelo, finding her belowstairs conferring with Madame Lacont and her helpers.

"Come in, Ashton," Consuelo said, and began immediately expostulating about who would wear which gown to what grand ball, or rout, or assembly. He had never seen so much fabric, cotton twills, stuffs, sarcenets, satins, and silks. Gowns of all kinds were in the making, and Consuelo exuded happiness. Enthusiasm spilled from her words when she said, "I've assigned one seamstress to work entirely on little Prudence's new wardrobe."

His Grace thought about the black mourning garb the child wore, and shuddered.

"And the Court gowns will be divine," Consuelo said, her eyes positively gleaming. She held up two half skirts with three layers of fabric over hoops narrow at the sides, protruding very far out in the front and back.

His Grace's right brow shot up. "They go to Court in this?"

Consuelo laughed giddily. "Of course not, pea-goose, this is the undergarment. A satin skirt decorated with silver embroidery will top a tulle skirt with a silver lace furbelow. Over the satin skirt will be a shorter top skirt, made of silver-spangled tulle and decorated with garlands of flowers. Then that will be . . ."

"That's outside of enough," His Grace exclaimed, feeling nothing but pity for a gel who had to wear the outlandish garment. His Grace knew that a young gel's entry into the polite world was officially marked by a Court Presentation. But that usually happened when she was sixteen or so, when her school years were behind her. *Not at three and twenty,* he thought. He asked, "Why would Emma be needing a Court dress?"

"Every gel with proper standing is presented at Court before her come-out," Consuelo answered. "Their names have been sent as candidates to be privately presented to King George. We are very fortunate in that we are personal friends of His Majesty, even though he has become a little addled."

"He still has his lucid moments," His Grace said, remembering that the last time he had visited with His Majesty how sharp his mind was. "Emma does not need a come-out," His Grace said. "Presentation at Court is a capital idea, if she so desires, but a Season in Town is nothing short of a husband hunt."

Consuelo tilted her head and smiled. "Well?"

"Fustian, Consuelo, Emma is promised to me. As soon as

141

Francine is settled with a suitable husband, we are to be wed. A come-out is entirely unnecessary, a waste of time, as well as waste of energy for the poor gel. She is as fragile as a rose."

This brought a tremendous laugh from Consuelo. "Fragile! Emma is as strong as an ox. When she came to Craigmont her nerves were in tatters, her energy expended from having managed a producing farm for many years. Rest will cure her. She deserves a Season of pretty clothes, of men fawning over her, falling at her feet. I predict . . ."

Jealousy roiled inside His Grace. "I don't give a demme what you predict, Consuelo. Lady Emma Winslow does not want a come-out, and should she acquiesce to one it will only be because she wishes to please you. She has spoken to me about your dislike for her, and I came looking for you to again protest—"

"*That* does not enter into the matter. She deserves a Season. And I predict further that she will find a fine husband, most likely Sir Arthur Stewart. I think they are perfectly matched."

"A pox on Stewart. He's a blumberbuss, cheeseparing chucklehead. I will call him out and kill him before I will let him have my Emma."

Enjoyment of the purest kind showed on Consuelo's face. "She is not your Emma. Not yet."

His Grace was beginning to think it was he whom Consuelo did not like, and he thought back as to what he had done to her to bring on such spite. Nothing immediately came to mind. He decided to bargain. "Consuelo, I do not take your meaning. I think you are wrong to push a come-out on Lady Winslow. It is the last thing she desires. She's too sensible."

"She hasn't said so. Not once."

"As I said, she begs to please you . . . because of your dislike for her. In your presence, I will inquire as to her wish, and I will assure her that it can be entirely her choice . . . not yours."

They were sitting in a small sitting room a distance away from where the modiste and her helpers were working. A closed door afforded privacy. Consuelo stood, looked at the Duke, and smiled. "I'll wager fifty pounds, to be given to Help the Climbing Boys of London."

His Grace jumped to his feet. "Fifty pounds it is, but why to the Climbing Boys of London? I thought you hated all things that smacked of Town."

"I'm too old to hate," Consuelo said, a note of finality trailing her words.

His Grace gave her a quizzical look. What was on her mind? He did not ask. Of late, she had seemed so strange, so different. Never before had he heard her mention being "old." Lifting her hand to his lips, he kissed it, strangely feeling compassion. "Say at tea this day. Will you have Emma there? I shall ask her about the come-out, though I know what her answer will be."

"Don't be too sure," Consuelo said, a lilt to her voice.

Ignoring Consuelo's last remark, His Grace quit the room and repaired to his quarters, where he penned a missive to his solicitor, asking that proceedings be started to move Countess Margaret Winslow to a private institution, with all cost charged to Ashton deFleury's shipping company. He further advised Prescott to locate a doctor who specialized in the nervous disorder from which the Countess suffered. "I hear there's one of extraordinary skills in Paris, a Dr. Reneau. Get him."

Skipping a space, His Grace added to the missive: "Inquire into the most worthy charities . . ."

Prudence had started him thinking.


Tea was served on the first floor, where all rooms were elegant, but not as elegant as the drawing room, whose great expansive windows overlooked the gardens, and the sea. Unless the weather was foul the windows were raised, allowing in the sounds which came in such a stated rhythmic pattern they were soothing rather than disturbing to one's ear. This day, brilliant sunlight cast shadows across the rose-colored chair in which Consuelo sat, and across her sleek skirt made of rose satin. Rose was her favorite color. Her gowns, as well as the furnishings in Craigmont, attested to that.

Before her the tea table stood draped in a snow-white cloth, holding cakes and crumpets; a silver kettle of hot water resting on its little flame, awaited His Grace and Lady Winslow. Delicate china cups and saucers and small tea plates were beautifully placed near the tea pot.

As Consuelo awaited Ashton and Emma she thought about the conversation with His Grace when she had mentioned feeling old. She had not meant to say it, especially not in front of Ashton. But of late she had felt old. And loneliness had crept into her soul. Having the Ladies Winslow at Craigmont had pumped new life into her veins, and she wondered if their coming, even under painful circumstances, had not been the answer to her prayers.

She thought about the cottage, the happiness it once held. She smiled, remembering so much, but before she could go on with her ruminations, a faint knock caused her to jump, For a slight instant, she thought it might be *him,* so deep in thought was she.

It was His Grace. She looked at the clock which at that instant chimed one time, indicating that it was half after four. Ashton was never late, and today he was dressed so splendidly. She went to him and lifted a jeweled hand for a perfunctory kiss.

"Are you prepared to lose the wager?" she asked.

"It is not my plan to lose," he assured her.

He would win the wager. Of that he was sure. Since he and Lady Winslow were to be married, there was no reason for her to suffer a come-out. Looking up, he saw her enter, and caught his breath. She wore a new gown, one, he was sure, Consuelo had insisted the modiste finish before tea time.

Made of some soft fabric, purple with a bluish tint, the gown matched her violet-blue eyes. Several puffs, each tied with a deep-blue ribbon, constituted the sleeves which stopped at her slender wrists.

Standing there in a regal stance, she reminded him of a stately tall oak, exuding strength, and then he brought himself up. One should not compare one's love with a tree, and he tried to think of something more romantic. He should read more of Byron's poems, or Keats, he told himself.

He went to her and executed a leg, and when she curtsied to him, he felt embarrassed. Being a duke did not at all suit his self-image. "Pray, don't," he said, lifting her up and kissing her hand.

A firelike spark shot from Emma's hand to her elbow; she felt her face flame. His Grace's intense eyes were daring her to forget his kisses. She jerked her hand from his grasp and went to sit near the tea table, taking the cup held out to her by Consuelo. Taking a scone, she bit hard into it, while swearing under her breath.

"You look lovely today, my dear," said Consuelo, and Emma forced a smile and thanked her graciously for the new gown.

Consuelo poured and handed a cup to His Grace. He took it, set it down on the tea table, then leaned back in the chair and crossed his long legs. "I do not imbibe overmuch in tea," he said. "I only came to collect a wager."

Emma gave him a questioning look. "From whom? Not I, I hope. You broke the eggs I planned to sell."

Emma watched a slow, knowing grin soften His Grace's rugged, sun-browned face as he hooked his thumbs in his waistcoat pockets and said, "I believe two people were involved in the crushing of those eggs. That is, if you are speaking of the incident in the stable yard."

*He knows demme well I'm speaking of the incident in the stable yard,* thought Emma, feeling mortification sweep over her. From her flushed face the awful hot shame moved down onto her neck and then to her shoulders. She could even feel it in the pit of her stomach.

Consuelo leaned slightly forward in her chair, while carefully holding her tea cup so as not to spill the tea. "Stable yard? Ashton, what are you talking about?"

His Grace's grin turned to laughter. "I shall offer Emma the privilege of telling about *her* eggs."

"There's nothing for it," Emma said so quickly she almost twisted her tongue around her words. "I dreamed there were seven eggs in the corner nest of the chicken house, so I dashed out at daybreak to see . . . and sure enough there in the corner nest were seven eggs. I told His Grace who had just returned from his morning jaunt about my dream, and he accused me of being a witch. He said only witches dream dreams that come true. So he broke my eggs . . . which I intended to sell."

Emma looked at His Grace and smiled. He was no longer smiling, or laughing. His keen eyes told her he was thinking of a retort to her lie. "You are a witch, a lovely witch."

"Thank you," Emma said. She drank her tea, and Consuelo drank daintily from her cup.

"Did Francine and little Prudence not want to come to tea?" Emma asked.

"I asked them to have tea sent to their rooms, or to enjoy a repast in the rose garden."

"Why?" Emma asked.

"Because His Grace and I have something we wish to discuss with you."

Emma then recalled the mention of a wager. "What is it about a wager?"

Consuelo started to speak, but His Grace raised a silencing hand. "Remember Consuelo, you promised that Emma would be asked about a come-out without your interference. I'm quite sure she is capable of making up her own mind that it is outside of enough for a betrothed gel to suffer a come-out."

"Suffer a come-out? Is it something to suffer?" Emma asked.

" 'Tis nothing but a husband hunt," His Grace said. "Men would be fawning all over you, and since it is understood that we are to be wed when Francine is settled with a new husband, it would be deceitful of you to *pretend* you are looking for one for yourself. Now, to be presented at Court . . . that's a capital idea. His Majesty is a dear friend . . ."

*He may have even sired you,* Emma thought, shutting out His Grace's fine, somber voice. She looked at Consuelo, who had a slight smile on her face, and wondered what the woman was thinking. She, Emma, did not care about a come-out. At three and twenty she was entirely too old. She did not want a husband. Her well-preserved anger surfaced, anger at her dead brother, anger at this nabob sitting across from her petitioning her not to suffer a come-out, the man who had made a marriage contract to marry her without consulting her. No one owned her, she vowed with conviction.

Since this grand offer had been made by Consuelo, she *would* come-out into society the proper way, Emma decided. She even thought she might enjoy attending a grand ball, a soiree, or going to Almack's Assembly Rooms, and she might even enjoy men fawning over her. "I would love a come-out," Emma said unequivocally. "To be one of the Beau Monde would be to my liking, I am sure."

Emma looked at His Grace's tight-set jaw. He was looking at her incredulously, and his hazel eyes blazed furiously. Her instant reflex was to duck. Laughing, she said, "Your Grace, you look as if you've been visited by the manor ghost."

He glared at her. "I'm talking to a witch. Why do you want a come-out? For spite? I've asked for your hand in marriage."

"You asked my brother. You didn't ask me."

Consuelo interrupted. "Ashton, I believe you owe me."

His Grace jerked his gaze around to Consuelo. He then reached his hand into his coat pocket and pulled out a fifty-

147

pound note and slammed it into her extended hand. Even if she were his mother, he wanted to wipe that silly grin off her face. His voice was strong and sure when he said, "Lady Winslow is my betrothed and, come-out or no come-out, we *will* wed."

"Would you like another wager?" Consuelo asked.

The tiny laugh that followed His Grace as he slammed from the room did nothing to soothe his temper.

# Chapter Twelve

It had been only after Emma had seen the exquisite stitching of the trained seamstresses that she realized how terribly "homemade" the gowns she had brought from Fernwood must have appeared to Consuelo deFleury. One morning as Emma pondered on this, a wonderful idea came to mind. At least she thought it wonderful. She could not bear being idle, so she would offer to help with the sewing, thus staying busy and learning a trade at the same time. If a rich husband could not be found for Francine, then she, Emma would be prepared.

While finishing her toilette she decided that it would also behoove her to learn all that she could from Consuelo before she, Emma, left to live in London. And that would fill some of her time while waiting. Sometimes she regretted having been so busy at Fernwood.

Of course here at Craigmont she checked on her animals each day, and spent time with Prudence when the child was not studying, or taking lessons on the pianoforte. Francine was busily exploring Brighton. She went there on every kind of equipage headed in that direction, and then returned to tell Emma everything she had seen. And they talked about being presented at Court, and about Prudence's welfare.

A fine tutor had been hired for her and a properly trained governess. "Prudence must be exposed to the finest books,

149

and to a governess who speaks properly," Consuelo had said, adding, "Pray she does not pick up Hannah's terrible cant, and her horrible misuse of the English language. That woman belongs in the kitchen, or even Bedlam. Who does she thinks she is, tasting all food that is brought to your rooms?"

Emma hid her smile and determinedly stilled her tongue. In fairness, she reminded herself of all the wonderful things Consuelo was doing for Prudence, and for Francine.

*And for me, too, although grudgingly,* Emma thought.

Coming out of her dressing room, Emma encountered Hartshorn Van Winters with a brush in her hand. "I've already brushed my hair," Emma said.

"Your hair has not been dressed. I shall create something Parisian, and it is time I instruct you in ways to go on in society. 'Tis my duty. And pray remember the rules of the Ton are stringent, and must needs always be obeyed."

She took Emma's arm, guided her to a chair in front of the floor-to-ceiling looking glass, and began brushing, twisting, and puffing her long black hair.

"Now, in Town one does not —"

Emma rudely stopped her. "On whose authority are you giving these instructions? And how do you know how to go on in London society when you've been at Craigmont all these years? Where did you learn all this you are going to tell me?"

"Miss deFleury requires all her lady's maids to know the rules of the Ton so that when we serve her house guests we will act properly."

"Did you work in London?" Emma asked.

"Oh my, no." Van Winters pulled herself up. "Miss deFleury gave me my instructions, and she learned her exquisite manners in Paris."

"In Paris! I didn't know Consuelo had lived in Paris," Emma said.

"Well . . . she has never spoken of *that* part of her life, but her father was a Parisian, a man of address, and with blunt."

By now extremely curious, Emma decided to pry from the maid Craigmont's secrets. All servants knew family secrets, and no doubt Van Winters knew *who* was on the anchored ship, and about the cottage hidden in the woods. "Why do you suppose Consuelo never talked about *that* part of her life?" Emma laughed, trying to appear nonchalant. "Is there a family scandal? And up the coast, I saw an abandoned cottage. Who used to live there?"

Emma watched in the mirror Van Winters's reaction. The maid shrugged her shoulders, put that knowing look on her face, and said, "Miss deFleury would be mortified to even think one of her loyal servants talked behind her back."

Knowing positively that the maid did not know anything to tell, else she would blurt it out to prove her importance, Emma did not pursue the subject further, and silence ensued while Van Winters brushed and twisted. "This style is called the *puff and sentiment*."

"Where would I wear *this?*"

Giving a proud smile, Van Winters pushed and combed and patted. "To Almack's I would think. And I must get on with instructions of the proper comportment of the upper orders."

"Why does Consuelo think I need such instructions?"

"She says that you are a country miss, that even though you are of the nobility, you have been stuck in the country all your life."

Emma could not deny the truth of that. But she was not totally without social graces; she had been exposed to harp lessons, and to proper dance. After all, she had been almost grown, three and ten, when her parents were killed.

Emma could not stop herself from asking, "If Miss de-Fleury appreciates Town so much, why did she leave thirty years ago and not return?"

More silence, and another ridiculous twist of Emma's hair, with Emma watching in horror. Finally Van Winters began again, prefacing her remarks with, "The same rules apply in Brighton, of course. In winter, Prinny's crowd flock here."

"Please go on Mrs. Van Winters," Emma said. "And please get on with the dressing of my hair."

Van Winters sighed deeply. Very theatrical, in Emma's opinion. "I'm only doing my duty, m'lady. If you would just not interrupt, asking questions that only Miss deFleury can answer."

Emma said she was sorry and Van Winters went on, "In Town, never be seen driving St. James's Street where all the men's clubs are."

"Why ever not?" Emma asked.

"It would be considered behavior unbecoming to a lady of quality. It would make one the object of every rakehell's wicked stare." She paused to wink. "If you know what I mean."

"Go on," Emma said.

"Your abigail will walk two steps behind you; you must needs never go out unchaperoned; you must not dance the waltz at Almack's without first obtaining permission from one of the patronesses."

Van Winters stopped to offer her own advice, bending close to Emma and saying in a very low voice, "Ladies have been warned to be aware of the waltz. Even men of great purity cannot be trusted."

Emma said, "I see," and smiled. "Tell me what a waltz does to a man that he would act against propriety."

"They hold a gel too close, and they get . . . you know."

Emma was about to laugh. "No, I don't know. Stop holding back. I want to know."

"His breath gets hot against the gel's cheek, and other parts of his body acts up. Things might happen that a gel should not know about until she's married, and then she's supposed to cover her head."

"Cover her head when her husband is making love to her?"

152

"That way she can keep her innocence. Afterwards, she can pretend *it* never happened," Van Winters said.

For a moment Emma thought about His Grace making love to her with her head covered, and she burst out laughing. *He would rip the cover away and say demme your innocence.*

" 'Tis not Tonnish to laugh when one is receiving instructions."

"I'm sorry," Emma said, straightening her face and refusing to meet Van Winters's eyes. "Pray, do go on."

"Never wear a warm pelisse or shawl; that is beyond the pale."

That was outside of enough for Emma. "Why in the world not? If one is cold . . ."

"Society believes that the very lightest of wraps should suffice in every type of weather."

There was more, but Emma was busily thinking that if having a come-out meant she had to be a scapescull and freeze herself to death on a cold night, then she should reconsider her decision, which had been made to spite His Grace.

Van Winters's next remark sent Emma into another spasm of laughter.

"To achieve social success, one must gain the approval of Beau Brummell —"

"The dandy?"

"If the Beau takes a liking to you, he can assure your place as a reigning toast of the Ton."

"Balderdash, who would care what that dandy thought?" Emma said, and received another set-down look from Van Winters, who reminded her that, "Ladies of the upper orders do not swear."

"They don't? Surely you jest," Emma said.

Van Winters raised her hand. "My honor."

"Then I shall *try* not to break propriety; however, I cannot promise."

"It is a tragedy to be cut by society," Van Winters said, her voice instantly soft and meditative.

*Like Consuelo,* Emma thought, but she did not respond. In truth, she was bored with the subject of going on in society, and she was bored with the terrible hairstyle Van Winters was concocting. She would not be seen dead in puffs that made her look as if she had just seen a ghost.

And then the very worst happened.

Before Emma could stop her, Van Winters took from her pocket a package of white powder and started sprinkling Emma's raven black hair. "Don't," Emma said, too late.

"This is complete to a shade," the maid said as she added curled feathers to the powdered erection. And then came the scented red silk roses, which she took from a box. The odor tickled Emma's nose as meticulously Van Winters searched for just the right spot in the puffs to bury the roses.

An excellent plan worked its way into Emma's hysterical thoughts. She would search out His Grace and show him the *complete to the shade* hairstyle she would be wearing in Town, and should they wed, what he would live with daily. That should damper his seemingly obsessive desire to legshackle her. Turning to Van Winters, she asked, "Do you know where I might find His Grace at this hour?"

Both brows shot up on the maid's broad, brown, wrinkled face, and she pursed her lips.

Emma read her thoughts clearly and, deftly crossing her fingers behind her back for the lie, added quickly, "I would like to show him your wonderful hairdressing skills."

That prideful smile appeared again. "Most likely in his bookroom. I hear he keeps his nose buried in a book, when he's not riding that black horse."

Emma quit the room and hurried down the long, wide hall to the landing, then turning, she climbed the stairs to the third floor. She went to knock on the door over which hung a copper plate that read simply *Ashton deFleury.* After giving a discreet knock, she heard a disinterested, "Come in." Which she did.

His Grace sat with his long legs propped on a leather stool, his troubled eyes staring blankly at a big, open leather-bound book. She knew instantly that he had had a set-to with Consuelo, and she wondered why he came to Craigmont at all, for it seemed he never came out winner in the confrontations.

"Are you still smarting over losing the wager to Consuelo?" Emma asked.

The Duke jumped to his feet. "I thought you were Dodge."

"Well, I'm not. Does Dodge wear yellow dresses with embroidered flowers?" She started to curtsy but remembered his reprimand the last time she had bowed to him. Now, he came to her and took her hand, kissing it and holding it much longer than necessary. She felt a quiver slide down her spine, and immediately jerked her hand free. *She* was in control of her emotions, and *she* would remain so.

Since first she met His Grace, Emma had at times thought her body starved for affection. Or was she just lonely, missing the staff at Fernwood, missing Fernwood, she wondered. Still, there was that longing, that creeping warmth, so unfamiliar.

"My love," His Grace said. He reached to embrace her, but his reach was not as quick as Emma's feet. She stepped aside, and His Grace stared at her. Obviously he was fighting for control when he said, "Your hair . . . Emma, it is lovely."

"Your Grace, you can tell a better lie than that." And then she said, "If we should wed, this is what you would look at every day, for I plan to be a very proper lady of the Ton."

His Grace groaned, and they both broke into hysterical laughter. Emma felt tears wet her cheeks, she saw a decade of years fade from His Grace's somber weather-brown face. His green-hazel eyes shot sparks of life and happiness, and that wonderful happiness spilled over onto her.

"Do you realize," he said, "that this is the first time we've laughed since we met. It makes one feel exhilarated."

Emma rushed to peer into a looking glass she had spied hanging on a wall, and the laughter began again. Coming to stand behind her, His Grace slowly pulled the pins from her hair, letting each puff languorously fall its full length. The roses and feathers he placed on a nearby table.

Then, with long fingers he silently combed and stroked each strand of raven hair, occasionally looking in the looking glass and smiling. His brooding hooded eyes spoke to Emma, and she found herself being sucked up into their spell. She thought of his depth, his love for books, his spurning of the Ton, his ability to succeed in the trades. And his strength against Consuelo, yet loving her. Undoubtedly, Emma thought, His Grace was different from any man she had ever met.

A secret smile lingered on Emma's lips. She reminded herself that she had not met many men. Standing there studying his reflection, enjoying the touch of his fingers in her hair, she had to work hard to find fault. That he had tricked her brother to bring about their so called betrothal seemed insignificant.

At the moment.

"I asked Prudence to pray for a miracle," His Grace said.

Emma turned from the looking glass and moved away from His Grace. *Mayhaps I can think better,* she reasoned. Cocking a dark brow, she looked at him askance. "For a miracle? What —"

"That Francine will soon find a suitable husband, and that we, you and I, will soon be wed. The banns have been read, and we only have to send notice of the date the vows will be taken. Oh, Emma, I want you so. Do you not feel the same way?"

"*That* would take a miracle," Emma said. She wanted desperately to change the subject. "Poor little innocent Prue. I want to tell her that her mother will never leave Bedlam, but I don't have the heart. Mayhaps by next Easter, which is the deadline she has given the Lord, she will have accepted the Countess's illness."

"Mayhaps," His Grace said. Tension sliced the air, and she thought for a moment he would address Prudence's faith, but he did not, and she, to relieve the tension, said that she must needs leave. "It's against propriety for me to be here."

Emma did not give a fig about propriety.

And neither did His Grace. "You are not in London. If the servants talk, and they surely will, we shall say they were mistaken, that the woman who came to visit me was my courtesan, a blonde, wearing a black wig of the most outrageous fashion."

Emma laughed and pretended shock. "You don't *really* have a courtesan!" And then she pretended he had answered. With her hand over her mouth, she said, "Oh, you do! Pray, tell me what's she like, what is her life like?"

His Grace was laughing. "Are you thinking of making that another venture to prove your independence?"

"That's a capital idea."

"I wouldn't know about a courtesan's life. I've never been one," His Grace said, hoping to succinctly dismiss the subject. He was almost sorry he had brought it up. He would not lie to Emma if she probed, but he had much rather not discuss his past dalliances.

"I must needs go," Emma said again.

"No . . . not yet. I have not shown you my apartment."

He took Emma's hand, and they went through deeply carved double doors into a huge drawing room furnished in comfortable deep maroon sofas and chairs. Exquisite tables of varying sizes, and holding precious objects and illuminating lamps, were spaced here and there, as if the one doing the placing had just put them where they were needed. Emma knew better. Consuelo had been the decorator, and she had exquisite taste.

A black marble fireplace, with a black marble mantel, glistened from a recent rubbing, and on the mantel sat a gold inlay clock. It had stopped.

As they sauntered in silence from room to room, Emma observed. Like the rest of Craigmont, she had never seen anything so grand. Colorful Turkey carpets covered wood floors, gold-leaf mirrors and expensive paintings hung on the walls. His Grace smiled when she ah' d and assured her that the furniture was much too elaborate for his taste.

"I'm seldom here, so I saw no reason to argue with Consuelo. I love the book room. She saw that it held great books."

When they came to His Grace's bedchamber, Emma felt her face flush and she averted her gaze from the huge four-poster bed with huge plush pillows. It was silly, but she was unable to control her thoughts, which were not at all lady-like. She counted the rooms, eleven in all; there was even a small kitchen in which His Grace's valet could whip up a meal, and a sun-filled morning room where he, His Grace, could eat if he did not wish to go belowstairs. Emma thought of the simplicity of Fernwood.

"She spared no expense," she said.

"That's Consuelo," was His Grace's simple reply. He went to yet another door and, taking a key from his coat pocket, unlocked it. "This is my sanctuary into which no one except me is allowed."

"Then, why are you allowing me to enter?" Emma asked.

"Because you are a part of me."

The very resonance of his voice startled Emma. No big fanfare; no big exaggerated declaration of love, just a profound statement. "You are a part of me."

So serious was the Duke that when Emma stepped inside the room, she half-expected to find an altar where daily sacrifices were made, where His Grace prostrated himself before some mythical god.

She found a room filled with sunshine, and walls covered with paintings, the ocean, the woods, the yellow brick manor house, Craigmont, flower gardens, beautiful roses that seemed to be about to burst into full bloom before one's eyes.

The Abbey Ruins of Emma's dream had been painted.

"You painted these?"

"Yes," His Grace answered.

At the far end of the room, on an easel covered with a canvas cloth, was his work in progress, His Grace said. Long strides took him to it, and Emma followed. He gingerly removed the cloth, and she gasped. Staring back at her was a portrait of herself, her eyes a deep misty violet blue, the wind sweeping her black hair into a streak behind her head, and whipping and twisting a thin gauze skirt around her knees. She was bent to unwind the skirt, but seemingly the wind could not be conquered. In the right hand corner was the word "Fate."

Emma gave His Grace a questioning look. Without hesitation he answered, "The wind cannot be conquered, neither can our love. It is as Fate decreed."

He looked lovingly at the painting. "Here, you are struggling with that which you cannot control, just as you are in real life."

Emma did not like it; she did not like the core of her being exposed. How did His Grace know so well her feelings? Turning away, she sought other paintings on which she could focus her attention, finding one of a man on a beautiful white horse. She thought at first it was His Grace, but then saw that there was only a slight resemblance of him. "Who is he?" she queried without thinking, knowing before she asked.

Silence was His Grace's response. Deep thought lines creased his brow, and his deep brooding eyes stared unrelenting down at the man on the horse.

Then, almost reverently he said, "My painting was meant to show his strength."

"Your father?"

"Yes. And as you can see he is not His Majesty King George as the gossipers would have you believe." He smiled, and his mood changed. "I've never denied it, for I enjoy immensely the on-dits of London's upper orders. You will learn that fashionable teas are nothing short of gossip broths."

Emma was stopped when she had uttered no more than, "Who—"

"That is for Consuelo to tell you, if she ever chooses to do so. I can only say he was a brave, wonderful man. I regret . . ."

He stopped there, and Emma, sensing his pain, did not probe further. She doubted that she would ever know the whole of it.

"I painted the man on the horse from memory. I was near twenty and one. He had long since gone out of my life."

" 'Tis a wonderful painting," Emma said, and they moved on to examine more paintings.

His Grace said, "I began painting when I was eight because I was lonely, and I only paint when I am at Craigmont."

"Where you are lonely."

"Yes, especially when I was younger."

"The portrait of Consuelo over the belowstairs' fireplace mantel, did you paint that?"

"No. He did. Isn't it wonderful? He captured her timeless beauty, and her strong character. She *is* quite a remarkable woman, Emma."

"You love her very much, don't you?" Emma asked.

"Yes, but lately I fail to understand her. She seems a different person. Her taking you in dislike for no reason is incomprehensible, and wanting to get you leg-shackled to that cheeseparing Sir Arthur Stewart is beyond thinking upon. The man is a cheat, a scapescull. I think she has windmills in her head."

"Is that why you looked so somber when I surprised you in your book room?" she asked. "Thinking about me with Stewart?"

His Grace placed a hand on Emma's shoulder. "That, and I had just received a missive in which she informed me that I was expected to be present at a delightful little party in Craigmont's ballroom two nights from now."

And then he sputtered, "Little! Consuelo has never had a *little* party in her life, and, of course, Stewart will be present to fawn over you."

# MORE PASSION AND ADVENTURE AWAIT... YOUR TRIP TO A BIG ADVENTUROUS WORLD BEGINS WHEN YOU ACCEPT YOUR FIRST 4 NOVELS ABSOLUTELY *FREE* (AN $18.00 VALUE)

Accept your Free gift and start to experience more of the passion and adventure you like in a historical romance novel. Each Zebra novel is filled with proud men, spirited women and tempestuous love that you'll remember long after you turn the last page.

Zebra Historical Romances are the finest novels of their kind. They are written by authors who really know how to weave tales of romance and adventure in the historical settings you love. You'll feel like you've actually gone back in time with the thrilling stories that each Zebra novel offers.

## GET YOUR FREE GIFT WITH THE START OF YOUR HOME SUBSCRIPTION

Our readers tell us that these books sell out very fast in book stores and often they miss the newest titles. So Zebra has made arrangements for you to receive the four newest novels published each month.

You'll be guaranteed that you'll never miss a title, and home delivery is so convenient. And to show you just how easy it is to get Zebra Historical Romances, we'll send you your first 4 books absolutely FREE! Our gift to you just for trying our home subscription service.

## BIG SAVINGS AND FREE HOME DELIVERY

Each month, you'll receive the four newest titles as soon as they are published. You'll probably receive them even before the bookstores do. What's more, you may preview these exciting novels free for 10 days. If you like them as much as we think you will, just pay the low preferred subscriber's price of just $3.75 each. *You'll save $3.00 each month off the publisher's price.* AND, your savings are even greater because there are never any shipping, handling or other hidden charges—FREE Home Delivery. Of course you can return any shipment within 10 days for full credit, no questions asked. There is no minimum number of books you must buy.

Emma contained her laughter. "Mayhaps I shall enjoy that."

"No!" His Grace declared angrily, and then he added unequivocally, "Only over my dead body, and Stewart's as well. Somehow I will outwit Consuelo and her grandiose plan."

"How —"

"I must need give it thought," His Grace said, grinning that rakish grin of his, and Emma felt his finger bite into the tender flesh of her shoulder.

# Chapter Thirteen

Emma had never seen anything like it. Craigmont was in sixes and sevens as every footman, every maid, and most especially the chef, prepared for Consuelo's *little* gathering.

"Of course it is not a formal ball; that will come in London," she said, and she explained to them one morning at breakfast, "My girls will not make a grand entrance . . . that would be usurping your real come-out in London. But you will greet guests with me at the door."

Emma wanted to ask who would chaperon them in London, sponsor the ball, get vouchers from Almack's, but she knew she was worrying unnecessarily. Consuelo would take care of those details. Silence, Emma had learned, served her better.

*If Consuelo could only like me, as she does Francine and Prudence. If only I knew, or could even guess, what I have done to make her dislike me . . .*

These thoughts caused a heavy darkness in the core of Emma's being, slicing through her heart like a knife. She felt cheated because she was not excited like Francine and Prudence, who could talk of little else.

And one would think the party was for Madame Lacont and her helpers. Their fingers fairly flew over the gowns for Emma and Francine. Even Prudence, so she would not feel left out, Consuelo said, would make a brief appearance. Her white dress would have black *mourning* bows.

Emma was glad to see the end to the child's retreats. Prudence's precise, old voice now had an occasional lilt to it, and she often laughed and skipped as children her age should do. She even helped Tom milk Nancy. Prudence mimicked her bleat, and the goat stood perfectly still, yellow eyes wide, ears laid back, as if she were being relieved of her milk by royalty. All this did not mean that Prudence had forgotten her nightly supplication to a higher power for her mother to be well at Easter time.

Only a child would give God a timetable, Emma thought one night as Prudence lighted the candle and bowed her head of yellow curls. Most likely she, Emma, would not know a miracle if it smacked her in the face, she often told herself. Mayhaps there were miracles all around her. Francine was doing well at Craigmont. Consuelo had won her over completely. One morning at breakfast when Emma and Francine were left alone, Francine had said, "Sister, isn't it just beyond thinking about?"

And Emma, in turn had asked, "What is beyond thinking about?"

"Consuelo's party, her little gathering. I understand there will be dancing in the belowstairs ballroom, and such wonderful food. Have you seen the haunch of beef the chef has on the spit? He says it will take two days to roast it properly."

"Francie, I will make an effort to view this miraculous happening," Emma said, feeling guilt because there was resentment in her words. "Consuelo's party does not interest me overmuch."

But Francine was persistent. "Emma, I wish you could get excited. Have you not seen our gowns? They are the most wonderful creations. All the crack. I can't wait to float across the floor of the ballroom . . . that is if someone asks me to dance."

"Pea-goose, of course you will be asked to dance. Mayhaps your future husband will be in attendance."

"Oh, I should hope not."

"Why ever not? That is our goal, is it not?"

"That is *your* goal, Sister. My goal is to savor life to its fullest, to go to Almack's, to King's Theater, to soirees, and to routs." Francine looked across the table at Emma, into her eyes, and Emma, knowing there was more, asked, "Then what, Francine? A rich husband?"

Words spilled from Francine's mouth, as if she had rehearsed them for months on end. "Then I will marry Gregory Banks."

Emma felt faint. This was not the plan. What had happened to Francine? Of course Emma knew. Consuelo had influenced the impressionable gel. *For spite, because she does not like me.*

A day or so earlier Francine had told Emma that her freckles were an asset to her beauty. And Consuelo had declared positively that her riotous red-blond curls would catch every young blood's eye who walked down Bond Street.

Francine had been trying to fade her freckles since before she had seen ten summers, and she had been straightening her curls since she was three and ten.

Emma felt her anger flare, that she had failed with Francine and Consuelo had succeeded, but she did not further pursue the subject. She rose from her chair, went around the table, and gave Francine a sisterly hug. Laughing a hollow laugh, she said, "I wager one of those young bloods walking down Bond Street will make you forget your farmer boy."

Emma recalled having said similar words at Fernwood. She had believed them then, before Consuelo; now she could only hope.

She bade Francine goodbye and went to visit the modiste, to see the gowns Francine had raved about. "Madame Lacont, may I help . . . since the gowns are a rush order."

The modiste raised a questioning brow, then spoke with a heavy French accent. "Every gown for Madame deFleury is a rush order."

She was a pleasant woman, with a fair, unlined complexion, and a figure most younger gels would die for. The gown she wore, one of her own exquisite creations, Emma was sure, hugged the right places, moved when she moved, rustling with every step. She swept across the room, away from Emma, and right away returned with a shimmering Clarence Blue satin gown draped over her arm.

"This is yours," she said. "You may sew pearls on the bodice." She stood looking at Emma. "Why do you wish to sew garments? Ladies of quality embroider."

"I very much want to learn to do different things. Embroidery, which I've done for years, bores me."

Emma had never embroidered a stitch in her life, thinking it a waste of time.

Left alone, Emma sat by a window and sewed away, her full attention focused on each tiny pearl and its proper placement. The slick satin felt smooth and wonderful to her touch, and she visualized wearing the blue gown while floating, as Francine had called it, across the ballroom floor . . . in His Grace's arms. They would even dance the scandalous waltz, and if His Grace got out of line she would slap his hand and tell him to keep it to himself.

Barely escaping ramming a needle into a finger, Emma pulled herself up and rearranged her musings. She would float across the floor with Sir Arthur Stewart.

*And His Grace will be mad with jealousy.*

And so it went, musings and plans, until the night of the little gathering at last arrived. For minutes on end, Hartshorn Van Winters had brushed and combed, and brushed and combed some more, until Emma's hair was a perfect bun on the back of her head. Around which Van Winters twined a string of pearls matching those on the gown.

165

"M'lady, a lady's maid who can dress hair is a rare find," Van Winters said.

Emma smiled. "And a lady who can withstand all the effort is a rare find."

Too modest to let Van Winters see her naked, Emma went into the adjoining room to remove her clothing and slip the blue satin gown over her head, returning immediately. For a long while she refused even a glance into the looking glass. She loved to feel the wonderful fabric against her skin. She listened to it whisper as she walked, and when finally she looked into the mirror, she gasped, for never had she seen a gown so utterly divine. The blue satin glimmered in the candlelight, and shadows danced when Emma moved. The neckline was low, showing a deep V between her breasts, and tiny puffed sleeves, covered in pearls, capped her shoulders.

"Sir Arthur Stewart will get a eyeful when he looks at you," Van Winters said, showing a proud smile. As if she had made the gown herself, Emma thought. From the rouge pot, the maid took a minuscule portion and smoothed it onto Emma's already flushed cheeks. "Upper orders do not blacken their eyebrows," the maid said. "But m'lady doesn't need it. I've never seen the like. They are as black as a black mare's tail, and your lashes, too, m'lady."

Emma placed her hand on her cheek and examined her face in the looking glass. The blue in the dress *had* set her eyes to sparkling. She took a cloth and wiped her cheeks, leaving only a trace of the rouge, and then with a small brush she brushed her heavy black eyebrows into an almost perfect partial circle above her blue eyes, making them seem even larger than they were.

"What's he like?" she asked Van Winters.

"Who?"

"The gentleman you just mentioned . . . Sir Arthur Stewart."

"Handsome rake, almost as handsome as His Grace." The

maid's knowing smile appeared. "But you won't get to compare this night. I hear His Grace refuses to honor Consuelo with his presence."

Emma felt her heart skip a beat. She fixed the maid with a mild stare. "Where did you hear that? Did His Grace tell you?"

"The abovestairs maid told me, but swore me to secrecy — "

"The abovestairs maid! I bound Craigmont servants gossip more than anyplace I've ever been."

"More than at Fernwood?" the maid said, her brow raised.

Emma started to challenge, but changed her mind. When she arrived at Craigmont she had found that everyone, even Consuelo, knew everything about her, and about Fernwood. His Grace had even known about her money belt, which she had later stuffed under her mattress. The information had had to come from Fernwood.

Van Winters, obviously in a loquacious mood, chattered on, "Craigmont's head groom goes smelly, smelly around Fernwood's housekeeper, the one who wears a white apron to prove she's above the other servants."

"That would be Snapp. She always had an ear to the door," Emma said with resignation, then added, "All right, I concede there's no difference in the two staffs. Both are a bumblebroth of gossip. But what does that have to do with His Grace not attending Consuelo's party?"

"Just that. He won't be there. They say that he's madder than a wet hen because Sir Arthur Stewart will be there, and he absolutely, positively will not attend. The upstairs maid heard him thundering away about it to his valet. It seems His Grace doesn't want Sir Arthur Stewart fawning over you."

Emma remembered His Grace saying he would find a way to outwit Consuelo, but refusing to attend the party, in her opinion, would not stop his adversary from doing whatever he wanted to do.

She left and went to check on Prudence, and when she entered Prudence's large bedchamber-sitting-room Emma's mind was in total shock at the picture-perfect little girl dressed in a long white dress. There were tiny black bows on the sleeves. The full skirt was covered with bows. Pantalettes with yards of fine, gathered lace showed below the long skirt. Her slippers were black patent with black bows. She ran to Emma.

"Auntie Em. Princess Charlotte is coming with Mrs. Fitzherbert. Consuelo taught me how to give a courtly curtsy, and after a short time at the party, just so everyone can meet me, we are to return to the upstairs drawing room where the servants will serve us a repast and we can have our own party."

*Consuelo does indeed know how to make a child feel important,* Emma thought, then she remembered the somber look on Prudence's face the morning she arrived at Fernwood and could not resent Consuelo's seemingly miraculous effect on Prudence. She bent and hugged her niece tightly, holding her for a long time. Prudence plopped a kiss on Emma's cheek and told her how utterly beautiful she looked, and Emma felt tears sting her eyes. She left quickly, leaving Prudence to be brought when she was sent for. Consuelo's instructions.

Unobtrusively Emma descended the winding stairs, seeing below at least a thousand candles burning in sparkling crystal chandeliers, spilling light onto a floor highly polished for dancing. From far off the delicious smells of food wafted up to assault her nostrils, and she knew that the great haunch of beef, and other wonderful food, was being set on the sideboards in preparation to feed the guests.

Francine was there, laughing and talking with Consuelo, who was dressed in the most gorgeous gown Emma had ever seen.

Elaborate embroidery covered bloodred fabric that dipped to show the top of her youthful white bosom. She moved with the grace of a panther, and one would hardly know she moved at all if she did not change locations, going here and there, checking.

Emma heard her say to Francine, "I wonder where Emma is. She should not be late," and Emma wanted to scream that she was not late. She quickened her steps and was soon in place, at Consuelo's side.

"Oh, there you are," Consuelo said, her eyes traversing Emma from head to toe. "Madame Lacont did a beautiful job in making your gown."

"Thank you," Emma said. She complimented Francine on her appearance, who did, indeed, look beautiful. Red-blond curls framed her freckled face, which held a smile as large as all outdoors. Her green silk gown matched her eyes, and it swept the floor in the back when she walked. *So grown-up,* Emma thought. Inclining her head toward her sister, she gave a short little laugh and said conspiratorially, "You're going to set those Bond Street bucks' hearts to racing."

"I hope so," Francine said unashamedly.

Emma smiled, then looked at the clock standing in the corner chiming out the appointed time for the little gathering. The big double doors were open, showing the night, and beyond the sloping gardens, the sea. On the road that curved so as to approach Craigmont by the Sea head-on, a row of elegant carriages, their lanterns burning, rushed to make the deadline.

Consuelo's highly liveried butler stood stiff and formal by the door to announce the guests in, and outside, liveried grooms waited to take the horses' reins.

The greathall was soon full of elegantly dressed, bejeweled women, and elegantly dressed men. Consuelo introduced Emma and Francine as her dear, dear cousin's daughters.

Mrs. Fitzherbert came with Princess Charlotte and Lady de Clifford, the lady in waiting to the Princess. A footman was sent to fetch Prudence and her governess, and while waiting, Emma assessed the Princess: Her pale blue eyes showed sadness, and she had very white skin. She was tall and gangly and poorly dressed. Emma had heard that the Prince of Wales had to be begged for money to clothe his daughter. Pity tugged at Emma's heart. She questioned why she felt pity for a child who was heir to England's throne. Prudence came, and Emma watched her give the precise courtly curtsy Consuelo had taught her. Childish laughter came from the Princess. There was something magical about their meeting. Souls in common, Emma thought, and she wondered if it could be because both of their mothers were thought to be a little insane.

When it was whispered about that the Princess was present, the crowd stilled, and then came a great sweep of curtsies from the women, and the men bowed. A clear voice announced, "Please do not stop your joyous partying because of me."

Then, as if she had not been curtsied and bowed to, and as if she were any other little girl in England, Princess Charlotte took Prudence's hand. "Crowds bore me. I'd much rather be with just you."

With Lady de Clifford and Prudence's governess trailing close behind, they moved from Emma's hearing. She turned to speak with Mrs. Fitzherbert, thinking the woman could be the Prince of Wales's mother instead of his illegal wife. She was pleasantly plump, with a big bosom, but she had redeeming qualities, Emma quickly noted. Tenderness laced her soft, cultured voice, and her smile was friendly. Deep, compassionate eyes looked back at Emma, eyes that spoke of having lived life to its fullest, and of having suffered to the fullest when things turned around.

As they often did in her relationship with the Prince, Emma mused. On-dits of his conduct toward Mrs. Fitzherbert were so outrageous they had many times reached Fernwood.

After no more guests seemingly were to arrive, Emma drifted away and mingled with the crowd. Sir Arthur Stewart was conspicuously absent, and n where was His Grace to be seen. Emma could not stop the tiny stab of disappointment squeezing her heart. She moved on, chatting about nonsensical things with the Brightonites, those people who thought Consuelo deFleury gave the most delightful little gatherings. Which looked anything but little to Emma, and she was pleased when the music started, drowning out the din. Turning, she was face to face with Consuelo, who had a semi-handsome man in tow, and Emma knew immediately that it must needs be Sir Arthur Stewart. He was smiling, his face was smooth, almost too much so.

Consuelo gave her elaborate introduction, and Stewart, giving a fancy leg, exclaimed, "Lady Winslow."

Feeling her face turn scarlet, Emma mumbled an acknowledgment.

"May I stand for this dance?" he asked, still offering a charming smile.

It was then that His Grace, as if he had dropped from the tall ceiling, stood there, saying emphatically, "Long ago Fate decreed that Lady Winslow would dance this dance with me."

While Consuelo and Sir Arthur sputtered, the Duke held Emma's small hand in his overpoweringly large hand and moved out onto the dance floor. He looked back once, to give Consuelo a wry grin and a wicked wink, and to savor the astonished look on Sir Arthur Stewart's pretty face.

"Why did you do that?" Emma asked. "You ruined my chance of making a good first impression on the gentleman Consuelo has chosen for me. I'm wondering if I shall ever have a choice."

"That pretty face! Why, Lady Winslow, you can do better than that." His Grace laughed joyously. He held her hand high, moved back from her, then moved forward to meet her,

171

his feet and her feet keeping perfect time to the music. Emma was enjoying herself immensely. Dancing was heavenly, and His Grace was so handsome in his velvet evening coat and fawn breeches, his pristine whites cravat lying in elegant folds. This night he dressed like a Duke, she thought. His blond pomaded hair glistened in the candlelight, and his hazel eyes were brilliant with laughter.

Emma's dancing was short-lived. His Grace guided her to an open doorway, danced them through to the outside, then quickly started running, practically dragging Emma behind him.

"Wh . . . where are we going?" she wanted to know.

No answer came, and when Emma rebelled and dug her heels into the ground, he picked her up, threw her over his shoulder—like a sack of feed—and headed for the stables. There, they were joined by the Duke's trusty valet Dodge, and hitched to a one-seated conveyance without a top was the Duke's great black horse. His Grace thrust Emma onto the seat and then sprang up to sit beside her. The portly valet mounted the horse to ride as a postilion.

"I demand to know where you are taking me," Emma said, growing angry. "I was having a perfectly good time at Consuelo's little gathering, and I demand to be returned."

"You demand too much, m'lady. I cannot forebear cheeseparer Stewart fawning over you."

"Are you afraid he will win my favor?"

His Grace laughed. "Pray, Lady Winslow is much too bright to let that happen."

"Then it is a fight between you and Consuelo?"

"I could not let her win." He looked at Emma, tenderness brimming his eyes. "Mostly, I wanted to be with you, my love."

They had entered the woods.

Emma shuddered from fright; the darkness seemed to swallow her up. "I don't like the darkness of the woods," she

172

said. She remembered too vividly the dream, the whispering trees. . . .

His Grace reached for her hand and held it firmly. "Don't be frightened. I would not for the world let harm come to you."

For some reason, which Emma could not understand, she believed him and they jostled along in silence. Long before it was in view, she heard the roar of the sea and smelled the fresh salt air, a relief from the musk of the dense woods.

Almost instantly then, there it was, miles and miles of dark-blue water, and a little way off shore, a ship, not the one she had seen anchored the day she was lost, but a much larger ship, rocked in the moonlight.

On the beach, a small skiff was tied to a stake driven into the sand. Emma's heart gave a little jump. "Are you kidnapping me?"

"Only until Consuelo's little gathering is over. We shall return to Craigmont when those sapsculls have departed."

"Most especially Sir Arthur Stewart."

His Grace gave a wry grin. "You are not only beautiful but smart as well. If only you were not so demme stubborn."

"*I* am stubborn! You are the one who refuses to be outdone by Consuelo."

The valet pulled the black horse to an abrupt stop, and His Grace hopped out, offering Emma his assistance, lifting her onto the sand. And in so doing, her bosom brushed his heaving chest. Emma was sure that had His Grace's valet not been present she would have been thoroughly kissed.

In the skiff, His Grace sat facing Emma, their knees touching. "So I can see you every moment," he said.

On a third seat the valet, his back to His Grace and Emma, handled the paddles. Fortunately, Emma thought, the water was not rough. In a teasing mood, she smiled at His Grace, and said, "Did you command the sea to be still?"

His Grace laughed. "No, but I do thank the Lord for the calm waters."

After that, Emma silently savored the beauty of the sea, feeling the wind in her face, and finding herself quite happy. This was much better, she thought, than being under Consuelo's critical eye. She thought about Francine. *Is she having a good time? Has she met the rich husband?*

"What are you thinking about?" His Grace queried. "Not about Stewart, I hope."

"No, not about Stewart," she answered truthfully, then said teasingly, "However, I did so much want to be fawned by him."

His Grace's countenance changed instantly from happy to blustery. Frowning ferociously, he asked, "Why?"

A tiny laugh spilled from Emma's throat. "I did not mean it, Your Grace. I was only seeking levity."

That seemed, she thought later, to set the mood for the evening. His Grace held her hand, squeezing it affectionately, and kissing it with lips that burned her flesh like fire.

A delicious chill passed over Emma, and she felt a tidal wave of warmth flow over her. She quickly cautioned herself to be careful that she not let the moonlight and the romantic "kidnapping," affect her overly much. When they neared the anchored ship, she peered closely. LADY EMMA, in bold shiny letters, was printed on its side. She shifted her gaze to His Grace, who was smiling proudly.

"When did you change the name of the ship?" she asked.

"Months ago, when I first fell in love with you, I had commissioned the ship built. She was only recently finished." He leaned forward. "Her name has always been LADY EMMA. For you."

"Months ago? You've only known me a few weeks."

"I fell in love with you when I heard your brother speak so fondly of you." His eyes never left her face. He wanted so much to tell her that she must needs know the truth; he wanted to see forgiveness. He saw instead that obdurate set return to her countenance, and he knew that underneath the surface anger simmered and hissed like hell's own fire.

It was still too soon to speak the truth to her about her brother. He would bide his time, he planned, then turned his thoughts away, seeking to bring the earlier levity to the wonderful night. "While Consuelo was planning her little gathering, I was planning one of my own. Not wanting to start gossip about you, my dearest love, my former governess Dowager Countess Maria Lankford is aboard. She is highly respected among the Ton, and her presence will quell any on-dits about this night that might spread through the upper orders. I've also asked that she take charge of you and Francine when you are in London and see that you are properly presented.

" 'Tis a shame," His Grace added, "that Consuelo refuses to go into London; she has enjoyed preparing the wardrobes so much."

He laughed then. "I've never seen her take to anyone the way she has taken to little Prudence."

Emma could not tell him that she often felt pangs of jealousy over that. In truth, she was quite ashamed of her feelings. "Thank you for being so considerate of my reputation," she said to His Grace. "I'm sure Countess Lankford will prove a real asset when we are in London."

"We will stay in my townhouse in Grosvenor Square. I will be close by to see that your needs are taken care of, and keep away fortune hunters."

"Fortune hunters! Do you really think some young buck, or even some old jackanapes, would come after my hundred pounds?"

"And don't forget your fowls and animals," His Grace said, laughing. And then he became somber. "Not after your hundred pounds, but after you. With your beauty, Emma, pounds are not necessary." And His Grace really meant it.

Never had he seen her more beautiful; moonlight danced on her face, and the stars danced in her black hair. He swallowed past the lump in his throat and reached to rake a finger down her petal-soft cheek.

"Stuff," Emma said. "I've never thought myself a beauty."

"But you are."

Thinking about the euphoria she'd felt when dancing, Emma said, "I would love to have danced more."

"You will," His Grace promised.

Upon boarding the ship, Emma heard the soft notes of a flute. "Where is the music coming from?"

"From a flutist, for dancing. But first we must needs meet Countess Lankford."

Emma curtsied. She immediately liked the Countess, who was pleasantly plump, had gray mixed with brown hair, and walked with a cane. Emma would guess she was younger than Consuelo, but looked older. From a ribbon attached to the shoulder of her plain but pretty gown hung a lorgnette which she lifted immediately, looking at Emma and dropping it after only a moment.

"I've known Ashton since he was a pup," the Countess said, laughing lightheartedly. Her voice resonated through the ship's large, well-appointed cabin, almost as elaborate as a room at Craigmont.

"When I locked Lankford out of my room, she took herself off to London and married a rakehell by the name of Lord Spencer Lankford," His Grace said. "He was the sixth Earl of Worthington."

"He *was* a rakehell, a loveable rakehell," the Countess said, laughing some more. "And then our kind maker took him."

"Do you have children?" Emma asked.

"No." There was sadness in her voice. "Only this one." She placed her hand on the Duke's arm. "Ashton, I promised to come aboard to quell gossip, not to chaperon. You are on

176

your honor this night. I will repair to my own elaborate bedchamber and get some sleep." And then she asked, "The Lady Emma will return to London this night?"

"As soon as the lights go out in Craigmont, announcing that Consuelo's little gathering has ended, I shall return Emma to her rooms. I shall remain at Craigmont to protect Emma from Consuelo's wrath."

Boisterous laughter ensued. Countess Lankford looked at Emma. "Those two have been outwitting each other for thirty years, from the time this one was in swaddling clothes. But I'm just happy to at last see him smitten, and I wholeheartedly approve his choice."

This embarrassed Emma. She thanked the Countess, who added, "He could not have done better had he let me pick his soul mate."

"But I'm not —" Emma's words were stopped by a frown from His Grace, and the Countess took her leave. Emma was alone with His Grace, the ruthless Duke who swore they were betrothed when they were not. She looked around and saw that at the end of the cabin, fine crystal, and delicate china graced a table draped with a white cloth. An epergne of fresh flowers and tall candles completed the picture, and a silver pail held a bottle of champagne. Emma smiled. She'd never thought the studious Duke a romantic. The smell of food cooking caught Emma's attention, and the Duke's as well. "I would not want you to go hungry," he said. He pulled Emma into the circle of his arms.

"The chef will serve us later. Now, I wish to finish our dance." There was barely room to dance, but His Grace waltzed elegantly with her, grinning wickedly. The satin gown moved sensually against her skin. She let herself go, let her heart skip and sing, feeling tears sting her eyes, and when the waltz was over she did not want to stop dancing. His Grace took her hand and they walked together up onto the deck.

The wind chilled Emma but she shuddered in silence. His Grace, sensing her discomfort, removed his coat and wrapped it around her, and his arms held her close to him, as he shared his body warmth, which was tremendous. They began dancing again, keeping time to the music that wafted ever so softly from below. And this time, when they danced there was no separateness, as there had been below deck; their feet, their bodies, and their hearts moved together. Emma turned her back on the thick woods and their darkness, and she forgot momentarily the aching darkness in the core of her being.

She forgot because for this night alone she wanted so much to forget. She felt as though she were in a vortex, being whirled about in some sort of fantasy world. Tilting her head back, she looked at the blue, blue sky, from which a million stars winked their blessings, and the man and his dog in the round silver moon tipped their cups in a magical salute.

The ship sat on a blanket of black undulating velvet.

Their eyes met and held. "You look no more than seven and ten years, m'lady," he said, and Emma answered quickly, "And you look no more than one and twenty."

"Then let's turn back the clock. You've had seventeen summers, and I've twenty and one," His Grace said.

Emma remembered when she had been seventeen, how she had wanted a London Season, a husband, then children. That seemed years ago, and for this night she would forget *that* time when she was seventeen. This night, she would go to Almack's, or to some fancy drawing room in Mayfair to sip tea and listen to delicious on-dits. And she would dance with lots of young bloods who sought her hand in marriage.

*In the end, I will choose the Duke.*

A second chance, that was what this night would be, a second chance to be seven and ten. Happiness flooded her face; she felt it burning. Laughing, she said, "We can be young and gay and sing and dance all night. We can pretend that yesterday never happened, that you never gambled with my brother, and that Charles is not dead."

"I wish you could forget, Emma. If not forget, forgive—"

"Shhh," she said. "This night, yesterday never happened."

The ship rocked. His Grace, accustomed to sailing the seas, planted his dancing feet securely to the deck and held Emma even more tightly. She felt his hot breath on her cheek, and she heard a tiny groan escape his lips as they sought hers, and she kissed him with abandonment.

His Grace looked down at her for a long moment, his heart in his throat. After tonight, his future wife would no longer want to come-out into society, where bucks and bloods would fawn over her. He could visualize Sir Arthur Stewart sitting at her feet, looking at her adoringly, with calf eyes. Yes, tomorrow his Emma would laugh and say she had never wanted a come-out, that only to please Consuelo had she agreed to one in the first place. That settled, they would set the date for their wedding. . . .

## Chapter Fourteen

"Of course I will have my come-out, pea-goose," Emma said to His Grace the next morning at Breakfast. They were alone, sitting across the breakfast table from each other. The others were sleeping late or having breakfast in their rooms, Emma reasoned.

"But last night, Emma, you seemed so happy, so much in love," the Duke said.

"Stuff. A romantic interlude. What gel would not be romantic on a ship named for her, the man handsome beyond bearing, the stars and the moon glaring down on her."

Emma gave her silver laugh, and His Grace, anger sparking his hazel eyes, asked, "Was that what happened, a romantic interlude? I could have sworn you returned my love. Do you deny that you kissed me?"

Remembering the last time she had denied kissing His Grace, Emma said with alacrity, "No, I do not deny it, nor do I deny enjoying it. What gel would not—"

His Grace raised silencing hands and said sarcastically, "I know! I know! What gel would not enjoy being on a ship with a handsome man . . . handsome beyond bearing. What gel would not enjoy kissing that man? Mayhaps had it been Sir Arthur Stewart you would have kissed him in the *same* manner."

Emma smoothed the teasing grin from her face. "I regret infinitely that last night I could not have been in two places at once."

"What do you mean by that?"

"This day when Van Winters was helping me dress she said Consuelo's little gathering was a huge success, that Sir Arthur Stewart stood for dances with every gel there, even dancing with some of them twice."

"I don't give a demme about the *little* gathering. You are evading my question, Lady Winslow. Would you or would you not have kissed Stewart in the same manner you kissed me, your future husband?"

Emma pretended to think on the matter. She was enjoying the bantering. His Grace glared at her. "You are testing my patience, Lady Winslow."

"I'm still thinking," Emma replied. And she was. His Grace's voice was not at all seductive, as it had been last night. But that had been a flight into a fantasy world, and she would always treasure it, but this day she must needs face reality.

*And still ahead is a set-down from Consuelo.*

Emma was sure of it, and beneath the levity, which she was enjoying immensely, dread rested heavy inside her breast.

While His Grace pecked the table with the ends of his fingers, Emma teased him further, "I really am trying to give it due consideration, Your Grace. What do you suppose would happen if I *should* kiss Sir Arthur Stewart—"

"You would be taken against your will . . . and soiled beyond redemption." He recalled how last night he had fought with his desire, how the ache had been so painful that once he had had to excuse himself and go above stairs and walk on the deck in the cooling wind. Mayhaps he should not have been so honorable.

He watched as Emma took a bite of her eggs, chewed and swallowed, and then she said, "I must needs be careful. When Sir Arthur Stewart kisses me, I will kiss him back only a small bit."

"Good day, Lady Winslow," His Grace said, flinging his serviette onto the table.

He rose from his chair, and his long strides took him quickly through a doorway that led outside. After he was gone, Emma sat deep in thought. He was so devilishly handsome in his exquisitely tailored riding clothes, and the undulating muscles under his skin-tight breeches would send any gel's heart to throbbing, she secretly admitted, a tiny bit ashamed. She remembered last night's kisses, recalling them too vividly. Now, her face flushed hot. It seemed His Grace had awakened a sleeping giant inside her that was raging to break loose.

Being three and twenty, Emma knew the giant was unadulterated passion, that special emotion that was not spoken of among the upper orders. Not spoken of, but felt, she mused.

*I must needs quell the feeling, I must needs not have such needs, I must needs forget it happened. . . .*

But trying with all her might did not help; the thoughts came, like the tidal waves of a mighty sea. She and His Grace had hardly touched the wonderful supper the chef prepared for them, capons stuffed with apples, and other delectable fare.

They had drunk champagne and danced, laughing, and near the end of the magical night, they kissed deeply and held each other.

*So against propriety.* Once His Grace left her and went abovestairs, giving no reason. It had been as if he feared to speak, afraid he would break the spell.

But the spell was now inevitably broken, Emma told herself. She could no longer pretend to be seven and ten, and His Grace *was* the ruthless Duke who tricked her brother into adding the silly codicil to his will. As if she were property, not a person.

Emma felt empty, and this brought a terrible homesickness for Fernwood, where life had been simple, and happy, without His Grace's kisses, and most especially without Consuelo deFleury.

And Emma did not forget the troubling, recurring dreams

for which she could not find a meaning. Quick little foot-steps pulled Emma from her reverie. Looking up, she saw Prudence descending the stairs. This day she wore a blue dress with black bows; lace-trimmed pantalettes hugged her ankles. "Good morning, Auntie Em," she said, giving Emma a big hug before filling her plate from the sideboard and coming to sit beside her.

"I'm happy to see you," Emma said. "I was getting lonely sitting here all by myself."

"I've been visiting with Miss deFleury."

Emma raised a quizzical brow. "Oh! And what did you and Miss deFleury visit about?"

It was amazing to Emma that at times she still got lost in the maze of one hundred or more rooms, yet, Prudence rambled all over the manor and seemingly never lost.

"About Princess Charlotte," Prudence said. "Miss de-Fleury said that Charlotte is a very lonely little girl, but I already knew that. The Princess told me about her Mama, who lives at Blackheath. Some people think she is crazy, when she is not, according to Charlotte. When she asks to see her Mama, they — and I don't know who they are — claim she is indisposed. But Charlotte knows better. She said if it were not for her grandpa, King George, she would never get to see her mama. The King's a little daft, and says eh what after everything, but, according to Charlotte, he is sweet and kind."

"My, she did impart a lot of information. I'm happy you had a nice visit with the Princess."

"Oh, the best. We are soul mates. If it were left up to the Princess she would probably give the throne to the poor people of England. She is often scolded by her lady in waiting, Lady de Clifford, for talking with the common folk when they are out riding."

Between taking bites of food into her mouth, chewing, and swallowing, Prudence went on to tell Emma that the Prince, Princess Charlotte's Papa, had had a tunnel built from the

Pavilion and Mrs. Fitzherbert's house, so they could be discreet about the Prince's visits." Prudence paused, then went on, "Auntie Em, Charlotte stutters when she gets excited. Did you know that?"

"Prue," Emma said worriedly. "One does not discuss family matters with outsiders."

"Oh, but I'm not an outsider. Charlotte said so. She has no one her age to talk with, so she says I can be part of the royal family. And she wants to be part of my family here at Craigmont. She thinks it is wonderful that I am allowed to eat with grown-ups." She took more eggs, then a sip of tea.

Emma was visited with the feeling that mayhaps Princess Charlotte was far too sophisticated for eight-year-old Prudence. But as she had admitted to herself before, what she knew about children one could put in a thimble. "What did Consuelo have to say about your being a part of the royal family?"

"That it was a capital idea. Then she laughed and hugged me and told me she wanted me to be happy at Craigmont. I told her I was like Princess Charlotte, that I wanted to see my mama."

"And?"

"She's going to take me to that special hospital where His Grace had my mama moved to. She said it was a wonderful place and that Mama was getting the best of care."

"And when is Consuelo going to take you to see her?" Emma asked.

"When we all go to London for yours and Francine's presentations at Court, and your come-out into society."

A family conference later in the belowstairs drawing room that day confirmed what Prudence had said. Consuelo deFleury *was* going to London. Emma's heart sank to her toes; she had hoped to get away from Consuelo's disapproving looks, and her veiled criticisms.

Across the room His Grace was thinking that Consuelo was going to London to push for an engagement between Emma and Pretty Face Stewart. Would the woman not give up? He hated to think that he must needs spend the next eight weeks or so outwitting her. And why in the devil did she not mention last night? Stretching his long legs out in front of him, he listened intently.

"I shall remove to London with my girls," Consuelo said. "I must needs be close at hand to see that your wardrobes are as they should be, and supervise little Prudence's activities. I've promised to go with her to see her dear mama, and that will be the extent of my movement about Town."

His Grace spoke quickly. "I don't take your meaning, Consuelo. Surely you don't plan to stay in the background . . . like a servant."

"I do, indeed. Countess Lankford will perform the duties of chaperon. She has a wonderful reputation with the Ton."

Pity welled up inside His Grace. He could not help it; it was so unfair. "There's nothing wrong with *your* reputation."

"Oh, that doesn't matter; they cut me—"

"That was thirty or so years ago," he said, adamantly. "Fustian, Consuelo, they won't even remember. They treat me with the greatest respect, and I'll wager they won't even remember what happened that long ago."

"They treat you with respect because the Ton mamas want a rich son-in-law. Well, maybe while the Countess Lankford and I are perusing the bloods for husbands for Emma and Francine, you can find a wife for yourself."

His Grace jumped to his feet and glared unblinking at Consuelo. "Lady Emma Winslow is my betrothed, and I have no desire to search further."

"Please," Emma said. "Do not talk about me as if I were some inanimate object sitting here in this chair." She looked at Francine, who was grinning broadly.

As if neither His Grace nor Emma had spoken, Consuelo continued, "The womenfolk, including Lankford, shall live

185

in your palatial home, Your Grace, but you will live elsewhere."

Still on his feet, His Grace sputtered, "I am being ousted from my own home?"

"You can't stay there. *They* will think Emma is one of your conquests, and that would ruin her chances of finding a fine husband. The claim that she is betrothed to you won't carry any weight."

His Grace started to say that he would be her husband, but, knowing the futility of words, he refrained from doing so.

Tuning out the chatter about which gown would be worn to which ball, he sat back down and became very, very silent, letting a plan materialize in his keen mind.

The plan formulated, a slow smile found its way onto his worried face, and, at the moment deferring to Consuelo, the Duke excused himself and hurried to his bookroom, where he searched the To Let section of the *Times*. Finally his gaze fell on an ad which appealed to him. It read: "Suitable for a gentleman or Member of Parliament. Servants quarters."

The address was Upper Brook Street, fashionable enough to suit His Grace's taste. He called his valet and handed him the paper. "Dodge, go right away and engage the flat. If the furnishings are not suitable, then arrange with the owner that I use my own. The place must needs be tastefully done."

"Your Grace," the valet said. "It is so unlike you to be finicky about such things. Only your bookroom—"

"A pox on the bookroom. I shall not be needing books."

The valet stared at him, unsmiling, and worriedly.

" 'Tis simple. I've learned there is something more important than books. I want the flat to be seductively done up."

"Seductively?"

"Go, Dodge, go, this minute. Return tomorrow with a grand tale of success."

The valet shook his head and prepared to take his leave, and after he was gone, His Grace paced the bookroom floor, swearing ferociously. The thought of Pretty Boy Stewart laying a hand on his beautiful Emma could bring his anger past the boiling point in no time at all.

"Desperate men take desperate measures," His Grace said aloud, pacing some more.

# Chapter Fifteen

Consuelo deFleury ordered the carriage brought around, and word passed from one servant to the other as rapidly as if the house were on fire, and some of the more privileged, like Van Winters, knew that this day Consuelo would call on Mrs. Fitzherbert in Brighton, and that Lady Prudence Winslow would accompany her. She had sent for the child.

"She never stays in Brighton over long," Consuelo said to Prudence in her receiving room. "If we delay going she might be gone. And, too, we leave for London two days hence. So time is of the essence."

Prudence hurriedly asked, "When will we visit dear Mama?"

Tears glistened on her long lashes, and creepy chill bumps formed on Consuelo's arms. "We will see the Countess but not right away when we arrive in Town."

"Why not?" asked Prudence.

Consuelo smiled and hugged Prudence, and Prudence thought she was so very fortunate to have grownups to whom she could turn when things turned black. But no one took Mama's place, not even Auntie Em. She returned Consuelo's hug affectionately. "When *can* we go, Miss deFleury. Mama will be so happy to see me, and I to see her."

"We will go as soon as we get settled in His Grace's townhouse," Consuelo said. "But now, we must needs leave for our morning call."

"I must needs tell Auntie Em," Prudence said, and left before Consuelo could tell her that she would send a servant to tell Emma.

Upon hearing about the morning call, Emma frowned. How strange, she thought, first Consuelo had announced she would be going to London and now she was making a morning call. On-dits simply could not be relied on, she decided. She mentioned this to Prudence, and said, "I wonder what brought the change."

"I'll ask her if you want. I asked her one day why she wanted to be a recluse."

Emma laughed. "You didn't! No, Prue, please don't tell her that I want to know why she has suddenly begun leaving Craigmont."

"I would imagine she just grew tired of staying in this beautiful old house by herself . . . with just the servants."

"Have a good time with the Princess," Emma said, giving Prudence a playful swat on her behind. The dress Prudence wore could have been made in Paris, Emma thought. Layers of thin white gauze touched her ankles, and the gauze was gathered below her chest with a sash made of black ribbon and tied into a big bow in the back.

Prudence ran down the stairs and out the front door, then climbed up into the carriage without help from the footman who was waiting to give the driver office to go. She felt very proud to be riding in the grand carriage. They traveled through the sloping gardens toward the sea. The sun was blindingly bright until they swung to the left and entered the woods.

"Do the woods scare you?" Prudence asked Consuelo.

"No, child, they comfort me. When I first came to Craigmont to live I so often walked in the woods, sat under a tree, on the wonderful soft, cool moss that grew from the darkness."

"Do you do that now?"

"Not overmuch. I've learned to accept my life. One must do that, accept what one cannot change."

Consuelo wanted to tell Prudence that she must needs accept that her mama would never be well, that one seldom recovered from insanity. She did not do that, for her heart was too tender. But she felt strongly that it was not right to let the child keep on hoping. Consuelo changed the subject. "Tell me about your lessons, Prue. Do you like your tutor?"

"I love my lessons, and I like my tutor."

"And your music? Do you enjoy studying the pianoforte?"

Prudence quickly replied, "I'm not overly fond of my music lessons, but I will keep taking them. Mama wanted me to have them, and I can tell her when I see her."

Consuelo could not reply, the lump in her throat was choking her. She looked into the darkness in the woods lest the little girl see her tears.

"Miss deFleury, how can Princess Charlotte have two mamas?" Prudence asked. "She said that she did, that the Prince married Mrs. Fitzherbert, then married her mama. Charlotte claims she loves them both, but her real mama the most."

Consuelo heaved a deep sigh and plunged in. "Caroline of Brunswick is Charlotte's true mama. Mrs. Fitzherbert is the Prince's true friend. Years back they did go through a marriage ceremony, but the King refused to recognize it as a marriage. Maria believes they are married, else she would not accept the Prince into her home. They are like a family. In a way, Charlotte is a very lucky little girl, to have two mamas."

"Then you and Auntie Em can be mamas to me, and Francie, too. Then I will have four mamas, but just one main mama."

*Sometimes she speaks like a child.* thought Consuelo.

Recognizing the rivalry developing between the two girls on the numbers of mamas each had, she smiled to herself. If the Princess had two mamas, then Prudence must needs have four.

"I think that's a capital idea," Consuelo said, then laughingly added, "Just don't decide that because Charlotte is heir to the throne that you must needs have a throne to inherit."

"Oh, I don't give a fig about that."

Silence came then inside the carriage, and the eerie darkness settled on the woman and child, happy and content not to talk but to feel the warmth one gave to the other. This strong, innocent little girl, old before her time, had certainly struck a chord in her heart, Consuelo thought. Prudence leaned against her, and Consuelo held her close as they traveled through the dark woods, finally coming out into the light.

Soon the coachman pulled the high-stepping horses to an abrupt stop in front of a beautiful old house with lots of windows. Consuelo thought that Fitzherbert's house looked like the owner, friendly and mellow with age. A groom took the reins, and a footman let down the step. A fancy-dressed butler announced them in.

Consuelo had been here before on two different occasions, but she was amazed no less this time than she had been when first she viewed the room. It was as if each small, infinitesimal thing *should* go where it had been placed, with loving consideration, and blue ruched silk covered the walls, the lovely gilded furniture, sofas, settees, and deep, comfortable chairs, all of which sat in the places they seemingly had been made to sit. Wonderful, expensive paintings hung on the walls.

Moving regally, like a queen, Maria Fitzherbert came toward them with an outstretched hand, taking Consuelo's and holding it.

"I'm always so happy to see you, Consuelo, and today you have your little charge, and a pretty little gel she is."

Prudence gave a half-hearted curtsy and looked about.

"She's in with Lady de Clifford," Mrs. Fitzherbert said. "The Prince of Wales is expected momentarily and Lady de Clifford is working on Charlotte's appearance." A frown marred her pretty face. "He expects so much from the child."

"Then we must needs leave," Consuelo said quickly.

"There's no need for that. You have met the Prince before."

"Yes, but—"

"There's nothing to it. I wish you to stay." Maria stopped for a moment, her eyes somber and cast down. "I sent a missive asking that he come."

They went to sit by large, open windows that overlooked a small garden. The room was dappled with summer sunlight. *"He* will not stay long, and then a repast will be served."

"Maria," Consuelo said, "I feel strongly that we should leave. This obviously is a very private matter."

"I will not hear of it. I will, however, consent that you remove to the next room with the Princess, after he has paid his respects to her. It's imperative that he give more consideration to the Princess, more of his time. I plan to speak with him on the subject, also on the delicate matter of her clothes. The poor little thing dresses like an urchin. I hope he will take notice of Prudence's fine frock."

There was nothing for it but to stay, Consuelo decided, seeing that Maria wanted the Prince to witness what a child Princess Charlotte's age should wear. Consuelo could not help but feel pleased. It had been she who had coaxed Prudence out of those awful black mourning clothes. A pox on propriety. A child should not be burdened with such tomfoolery.

The Prince came, exuding charm, commanding with his very presence. Consuelo gave a perfunctory curtsy. She thought him handsome, and she sensed immediately his fastidiousness. He dressed with flair. His tight buckskin breeches were smooth and his legs in their fine stockings were enormous. He had masses of curling hair from which an exquisite perfume gave a faint odor, and diamonds glittered on his white hands, she noticed when he lifted her up from her curtsy.

He then went to Maria and looked lovingly into her eyes, while asking, "How is my love today?"

"She is most definitely fine, but your daughter needs your attention." Her soft voice was authoritative in a subtle way. "She will be in directly, and pray, treat her with kindness. She has become quite unruly, as she does when she does not receive attention from you." After a slight hesitation, "Or from her mother."

A scowl appeared on the Prince's pink, verging on red, face. "That woman . . ." And then he stopped and mumbled something Consuelo could not exactly understand but which sounded much like the gel reminded him of her mother. Consuelo had read about his hatred for Charlotte's mother.

Maria asked that they sit, and they did. After the Prince had lowered his hefty frame into an oversized chair, which, Consuelo was sure, was reserved just for him, the conversation was strained, and Maria's eyes darted often and furtively toward the door. The Prince directed his attention to Prudence. "Do you like your studies?" he asked, and when Prudence answered in the affirmative, he probed further about her riding.

She answered in a precise, grown-up way, adding, "My Papa, the seventh Earl of Wickersham, died recently in an accident."

"I share your sadness," the Prince said, and Consuelo was happy that he did not mention *how* the late Earl had died.

Prudence did not mention her mother.

Finally the door opened and Princess Charlotte entered, followed by her lady in waiting. Consuelo noticed that this day the little girl leaned slightly to one side.

The Princess gave a strained, self-conscious curtsy. "Go . . . good morning, Papa."

He did not tell her that she need not stand on ceremony with him, nor did he take her hand and lift her up. When she was straight, her adoring gaze focused on him completely, as if not another person in the room existed. The Prince looked at her only fleetingly, visibly recoiling and giving a forced smile. "How are you, Charlotte?" he asked.

"I'm fine, Papa, now that I am with you."

Grudgingly he took her on his knees, and the happiness on her face was so blatant that it would make anyone cry, thought Consuelo, who wanted to smack the Prince.

He discussed with the Princess the same topics he'd discussed with Prudence, her studies, her riding lessons. When answering, Charlotte's voice was a little loud, but it was not until she said, "Please, Papa, when can I see Mama?" that the Prince drew back, as though he had been touched by something unthinkably dirty.

He dismissed the Princess imperiously by lowering his knees, making it impossible for her to remain on his lap. "I did not mean to offend you, Papa."

"You did not offend me, my dear," he said, but his words had the ring of a lie.

Consuelo could see that the damage had been done; it had only taken one mention of Charlotte's mother, the woman whom the Prince had been forced to wed. Consuelo looked at Maria Fitzherbert whose face had gone deathly pale. Lady de Clifford stepped forward, reached for Princess Charlotte's hand, and said, "Come, you must needs not tire the Prince."

Charlotte jerked away from de Clifford. "I am not tiring him. Five minutes of my time in one whole month would not tire anyone. He does not like me because I'm my mother's child. It's that he does not want to discuss my mother." Her voice rose, then broke. She looked at the Prince pleadingly, tears streaming from her eyes. "Why are you keeping me from Mama? Why can I not see her. She loves me . . ." Loud, hysterical sobs drowned the Princess's words as she ran and pressed herself against Mrs. Fitzherbert and hid her face.

Maria laid a shaking hand on Charlotte's head, and when the Princess demanded to know *why* the Prince did not like her, his own daughter, Maria did not deny it, and Consuelo saw the pain on her beautiful, softly maternal face.

Prudence went to Charlotte and said consolingly, "You will soon see your mother. You must needs appeal to His Majesty King George. I hear he is a kind man . . ."

From under long dark lashes Prudence gave the Prince a scolding look, and then she and Charlotte quit the room, the Princess's sobs growing fainter.

Consuelo shook her head. Only children dared express their true feelings with the aristocracy. She rose, curtsied to the Prince, then went to join Prudence and Charlotte. She prayed that Maria Fitzherbert would give the Prince the royal set-down he deserved.

"Why could you have not been kind to her?" Maria asked.

Tears streamed from the Prince's eyes. "I cannot help myself; please, my love, do not punish me further with a scold. It's *that* woman I can't stand, and Charlotte is so much like her."

Maria cradled his head on her bosom. "She favors you in appearance, and everyone speaks of what a handsome man you are."

This only brought on another onslaught of tears.

"Don't cry, my love." Maria said. "Mayhaps if Charlotte wore better clothes, perhaps a gown like the late Lord Winslow's daughter is wearing, she would not remind you so much of *that* woman. Then you would enjoy time spent with her. I know you love children. And what is wrong with her visiting her mother? Who made that decision?"

"The Queen. She has no mercy, and she lives in deadly fear that Charlotte's mother will be a bad influence on her. She says that Charlotte must needs be made to act like royalty, that she will be queen some day . . . since there will be no more children sired by me."

"Mayhaps you could visit the Princess of Wales just once to beget a son—"

"No! I could not bear it. It was only after I had drunk myself into a stupor that I could consummate the marriage. I tried to have a male heir, and I got a hoyden. No, no, a thousand times no. Never again will I touch crazy Caroline."

Maria felt sorry for the Prince. What he had said was true. She could not, however, bear that Charlotte was being made to pay for the hatred between her parents. "Mayhaps if you should leave a few pounds when you leave, I will speak with the modiste who sews for Consuelo deFleury."

"You know I do not carry money, but I shall have a small amount, which is all I can spare at the moment, delivered to you."

That was the best she could do, a new frock, maybe two, for the Princess, Maria told herself. She could not force the old Begum to let Princess Charlotte visit her crazy mother.

After the Prince left, Consuelo deFleury and Maria Fitzherbert enjoyed a comfortable coze, and a very elaborate repast was served on a huge silver tray by a maid who scurried from the room in a rush of black bombazine.

Laughing and chattering could be heard from the other room where the Princess and Prudence were enjoying their own flat cakes and tea, plus many other delicacies.

Consuelo spoke softly so they could not hear her, and she was careful that a servant was not about. "Tell me, if you may, did you persuade the Prince to do better by the Princess?"

Maria shook her head. "I fear not. I've never witnessed such hatred, such revulsion as he has for the Princess of Wales. Unfortunately, Charlotte is so much like her. He is even speaking of petitioning Parliament for a divorce."

Consuelo clucked, and changed the subject. "Is he searching greener pastures?"

"Not at the moment," Maria said. Happiness showed in her deep-set eyes.

"I only hope he continues to be faithful to you. Mayhaps he learned his lesson with that terrible Lady Jersey."

Many times, when the Prince had turned from Maria to someone younger, Maria had traveled to Craigmont to pour out her pain to Consuelo. So she felt comfortable in her inquiry, and the conversation went on about the Prince, and about what was happening in Brighton. London did not interest them, for Brighton was ripe with on-dits.

The normal thirty minutes for a call had long passsed, and Consuelo rose to go, calling to Prudence to prepare to leave.

"Oh, must you?" the Princess asked, bounding into the room. She was followed by Prudence, who did not bound but walked in a very ladylike manner.

"I'm afraid we must," Consuelo said.

When it seemed that the Princess would again become extremely unhappy about their leaving, Prudence placated her with, "Don't fret, Charlotte. When we are in London, we will go together to visit your Mama. I shall ask His Grace Ashton deFleury to speak with your grandpa. They are very good friends."

They said goodbye, and when they were in the carriage on their way back to Craigmont, Consuelo cautioned Prudence, "One does not interfere with the affairs of royalty."

To which Prudence answered, "The Princess is the same as any other little gel who wants very much to see her mama. I'm sure the Duke will be happy to help."

# Chapter Sixteen

Emma awoke to sunshine streaming through the window, a soft breeze brushing her face. The dream had come again, the whispering trees, the men on the cross, and the child with blond curls praying over a lighted candle. This night, the incessant whispering had grown louder and louder, until, in an attempt to escape, she had run into the dark woods, and had become lost.

Now she was fully awake, and the words, "Father, forgive them, for they know not . . ." pounded against her brain. What did the dream mean to her? Why did it keep recurring? Why could it not leave her alone?

"Why . . . why . . . why?" she sobbed, and the sound echoed in the silent room. Rolling over onto her stomach, she buried her face in a silk-covered pillow and swore angrily. She wanted so much to return to Fernwood where she was loved by the servants, by Francine, and even little Prudence. She recalled the night the terribly neglected child had arrived at Fernwood. She had asked to sleep with Emma, and she had let her, holding her tightly, and Prudence had cried until she slept.

Now, Emma wanted to be comforted. She wanted someone to tell her the meaning of her dreams. She heard a scratch on the door, it seemed far away. This day, everything, everybody was out of reach, and she had never felt so alone in her life.

The scratch turned to a loud knock and Emma jerked herself up and called, "Come in." It was Hannah, she knew. No one at Craigmont scratched for admittance.

When the door opened slowly and Emma saw the loyal maid standing there holding her breakfast tray, just like at Fernwood, Emma came perilously close to bursting into tears.

"Oh, don't cry, m'lady. Just because I brought yer breakfast." Hannah placed the tray on a table by a window then went to assist Emma out of bed.

"I don't need help," Emma said, pushing the maid away.

"Then, what is it, m'lady? Are you ailing?"

"No, Hannah, I'm not ailing. It's just that I had a bad dream and I'm very homesick for Fernwood."

"And right yer are, to want to be back at Fernwood. Thet's the reason I brought yer breakfast, fer a chance to talk with yer, and to make sure yer not poisoned."

Emma raised a questioning brow. "Talk to me about what? Have I done something to be poisoned for?"

"It's just that Miss deFleury wanted so much for you to make a good impression on Sir Arthur Stewart, but yer weren't here to do it. Gossip has it thet she's terribly angry with yer. Why did yer leave the wonderful party?"

*Hannah wants to know where I went, so she can tell the other servants and win their favor.*

Why not? Emma thought. She leaned toward Hannah and whispered, "His Grace took me to see his wonderful new boat and we danced until the wee hours of the morning."

Hannah's eyes widened. "He didn't! Yer didn't! But what about propriety, and Sir Arthur Stewart?"

"There will be time in London to impress him, if I should want to."

"I'm fer the Duke," Hannah said, pressing her lips together and shaking her head.

Emma went to sit by the window, and to eat the breakfast Hannah had brought. She looked at the loaded tray and thought that mayhaps she had meant to take the tray to His Grace. From the huge fare of eggs, ham, stewed kidneys, and scones, she picked a scone and slathered it with butter and jelly, then poured coffee into a cup. Pulling in a deep breath, she smelled the delicious aroma, while gazing at the sea. Unaware that Hannah had left, Emma called to her, then laughed. Hannah could not wait to tell where *her* Emma had gone the night of Consuelo's gathering, and Emma hoped that someone would tell Consuelo deFleury.

The hours after finishing her breakfast passed unbelievably fast for Emma. She wrote in her diary, visited with Francine, as she did daily, and went to check on Prudence. Francine passed on on-dits about the London Season, and from Prudence, Emma heard about her visit to Mrs. Fitzherbert's, where she had even met the Prince.

"Charlotte does not believe the Prince is overly fond of her," Prudence said, her gray-green eyes filled with sadness.

"I hope she is imagining that her Papa doesn't like her," Emma said. (She had heard that he truly did not like his own child.)

"I pray so, too," Prudence said.

Emma changed the subject and they talked about the upcoming trip to London, where Prudence would see her dear Mama.

"I count the days on my fingers," Prudence said, and just speaking of it seemed to lighten her mood.

Emma told her goodbye and went to the stables to check on her animals and to gather the eggs, bringing them to the chef, who promised to bake her a cake.

Not once had she found seven eggs in the corner nest as she had dreamed, and then later found.

Lost in the labyrinth of her own unquiet thoughts, Emma, for the lack of anywhere else to go, returned to her room, where she found that her new wardrobe had been delivered. Absolutely gorgeous gowns were spread everywhere, on the bed, on the sofas and chairs in the sitting room. Hartshorn

Van Winters stood with her hands on her hips. "See what Madame has done for you," she said, as if daring Emma to be ungrateful.

"I do appreciate her generosity," Emma said, and she did. Overwhelmed, she went from one group to another and fingered the exquisite fabrics. She had stood for fittings, but had not seen the finished garments. There were carriage dresses, dinner dresses, evening dresses, garden and morning dresses. In another group, Emma found opera dresses, riding dresses, and walking dresses. Pelisses of varying colors, mantles of different fabrics, and elegant spencers were there for Emma to examine. She picked up a Kashmir shawl and buried her face in it. It was so beautiful. "Where would I wear this?" she asked.

"To the evening affairs, when it is cool," Van Winters answered, then added, "Now, we must needs get on with your instructions."

Emma was sick to death hearing about *how* to go on in society. She decided to pry, and she went to stand before Van Winters, looked her straight in the face, and said, "I don't take the meaning. All I've heard since first learning my dead mother had a distant cousin with whom my sister and I were to live has been that Consuelo deFleury was practically a recluse, never going into London, and seldom venturing into Brighton. Now, word has it that she's going to London."

Van Winters pursed her lips. "That is true enough."

Emma could see that it was not going to be easy. "Then why is she going to London? Dowager Countess Lankford has agreed to chaperon Francine and me. Miss deFleury will not be needed —"

"She will see that the Countess does the right thing by you, and she will pass on your husbands."

Emma turned away and walked across the room. She started to say she did not want a husband, but she had said that before, to no avail. And the thought came to her that mayhaps she could enjoy a come-out if Consuelo were not there breathing her dislike onto her like a coiled snake about to strike.

Emma thought about Francine, whose wardrobe was equally as grand as hers, she was sure, and if they stayed at Craigmont little Prudence would have advantages she, Emma, could not have given her at Fernwood. Even His Grace had seemingly fallen in love with the little girl. On his ship, he had confided in Emma that Countess Margaret Winslow had been removed from Bedlam to a private hospital, and that an excellent French doctor had been engaged to treat her nervous condition.

All these things Emma could not dismiss, and the fact that she intended to deceive His Grace did not bother her a whit. He had tricked her brother. *Why do I have to keep reminding myself of that trickery?*

Emma turned back to Van Winters, who had started packing garments into huge trunks, and said worriedly, "Miss Van Winters, do you think that mayhaps I should say in London that I am under twenty? The Ladies Winslows are practically unknown in society. No one would know."

"Whatever for?" Van Winters asked.

"I feel so ancient. The other gels, they will be nearer Francine's age."

"I'm here to tell you that you will outshine all of them . . . that is if you can get your manners down pat, as I'm trying to teach you."

This elicited a smile from Emma. The strange lady's maid was quite kind at times. "I do appreciate your help, Mrs. Van Winters. I will not disappoint you."

"Or Miss deFleury. Remember, she will be there to observe."

Taking a deep breath, Emma said, *sotto voce:* "Pray do not remind me, and please, Lord, let Francine find a rich husband tomorrow."

Departure day arrived. On the circle driveway stood a fourgon loaded with a mountain of trunks, Consuelo's own chef, several housemaids, and lesser servants.

Another carriage held Hannah, Van Winters, two other lady's maids — one for her and one for Francine — Prudence's governess, and her tutor.

Hannah, who had simply refused to stay behind, was perched on the box with the driver. Word had come down from Consuelo that carriage dresses and appropriate bonnets were to be worn, and that she, Francine, Prudence, and Emma would ride in the Duke's crested carriage, and would lead the procession.

Consuelo arrived, and Emma stood with her, waiting. She had chosen a printed mulberry muslin, with a matching bonnet that framed her face in what she thought a pleasing way. The color was flattering to her fair skin, and to her delight, she had found among her new things a parasol of the same fabric.

"Ashton's carriage will come any minute," Consuelo said, and then she added almost under her breath, but loudly enough for Emma to hear. "I haven't seen the scoundrel in two days."

Emma knew she was fuming about His Grace outwitting her the night of her "little gathering."

A handsome carriage did at last come, but there was no crest on the panels. A liveried footman jumped from the back and let down the step. He offered a hand to help the ladies in.

Consuelo stood her ground. "I ordered His Grace's carriage. We must needs enter London in style . . ."

Just then Emma heard the crack of a whip, and the sound of horses' hooves hitting the white gravel on the driveway. She turned, but not before seeing Consuelo's mouth fall open. Riding in the crested carriage was His Grace, grinning his wry grin.

He tipped his hat to Consuelo, and the driver deftly jockeyed the four sleek black horses, groomed to glossy perfection and dressed in elaborate harness, to the head of the procession.

The Duke bounded out of the carriage and came to stand before Emma. Giving a fancy leg, he said in pretended seriousness, "My love, your carriage awaits."

Before Consuelo could object, if, indeed, she intended to do so, His Grace picked Emma up and placed her in the crested carriage. Without the assistance of a footman, he agilely sprang himself aboard, gave the driver office to be off, and sank into the plush red velvet squabs beside Emma, taking her small hand and kissing it with great ardor.

"Did you stay awake all night planning to outwit her?" Emma asked.

"No, I stayed awake all night thinking of a way I could have you to myself, and to prevent your riding five hours in her company. I could not bear it should she hurt your feelings."

Emma pulled her hand from his grasp. "You know this is against propriety. We are not chaperoned. If we ride into London thus, it will ruin my chances of . . . it will ruin Francine's chances of finding a suitable husband. It's very important that I do nothing beyond the pale."

Raising himself up, His Grace stretched his neck and looked back over his shoulder. "I believe that three chaperons follow us, not to mention Hannah and the driver of the carriage."

He was enjoying himself immensely. He took her hand again, holding it this time in a firm grasp, leaving no chance of it again being jerked from him. He kissed her fingertips and deliberately sat so close that his thigh rubbed her thigh, and he let his gaze blatantly linger on the top of her lovely white bosom. "You are so lovely," he said.

Emma felt her face turn scarlet; the by now familiar warmth returned to the pit of her stomach and moved over her body in waves. Looking away, she said pertly, "I'll thank you not to stare."

His Grace did stop staring, because his desire suddenly became torture. And his thoughts did not help. Jealousy rode him like a tidal wave. Consuelo audaciously planning for *his* Emma to marry Pretty Face Stewart was beyond bearing, and he was sickened to his stomach by the thought of it. Turning to look at Emma, he saw that her eyes were closed and her head was nodding. He scooted to the far end of the banquette and gently placed her head in his lap, and they rode thus for a long time. Brazenly, he caressed her breast, while her bosom rose and fell with her breathing. *Demme honor,* he thought. He was weary of being honorable.

But when Emma stirred and awakened, he jerked his hand away, as if he had committed an unforgivable, despicable sin. Which indeed he had, he told himself. He heaved a deep sigh. He must needs marry her soon.

The news of their arrival preceded them. The *Times* and the *Gazette* had reported two days before that His Grace, the Duke of Attlebery, was shortly expected in London, along with his mother, Consuelo deFleury, who had deserted London some thirty years ago, and with Ladies Emma and Francine Winslow, who would be formally presented to society at a ball at His Grace's mansion in Grosvenor Square. No mention was made of Lady Prudence Winslow. Consuelo was furious that her presence was noted and went to find Countess Lankford. "I did not want my coming noticed," she said.

Countess Lankford replied with alacrity, "I tried to keep it from the papers, but you know the Ton mamas. Anything pertaining to His Grace is news that cannot be squelched. And, too, I was obliged to send out announcements of their coming-out ball. There was no way *that* could have been kept secret."

"I only wanted my coming to go unnoticed," Consuelo said.

Emma had little interest in who knew they were coming to

Town and wandered away to inspect this beautiful dwelling which was beyond anything she had ever read about. She was sure that nothing in Paris could compare. Four stories of understated elegance was how she perceived it. Thinking she was alone, she rubbed three fingers along the rich rosewood balustrade that framed the curving stairway. She then examined her fingers to see if the servants had done their job. Laughter floated over her shoulder. Turning, she saw His Grace watching her. "Did they do their job well? If not, tell me and I shall dispense with them on the spot. Mayhaps have them shot."

Embarrassed, Emma spoke quickly. "I would not want to cause anyone to be shot, or to lose his job. A position in your household, I am sure, is an enviable one."

"I have a very efficient man who calls himself "the butler," really his name is Gorgnow, Gork for short, who is in charge of all four floors. I do not have time to run a household. I sleep, eat, and read here. My time from that is spent at work. I'm sure you have heard that I am a working Duke."

Indeed, she had. She remembered Ian bringing that on-dit to Fernwood. "I've heard that about you."

"It is only of late that I have put a man in charge of my shipping affairs. And that is only until I help you find a husband for Francine." He grinned. "After that, I will take time to make you my wife, and I shall take you on a very lovely honeymoon. A tour of the Continent, mayhaps." He raised a questioning brow.

Which Emma chose to ignore. "You don't have parties?"

She looked at the spacious foyer, large enough she was sure, for two hundred people.

"Never," His Grace said. "Why should I entertain people I hardly know, or care to know." He became very serious, and pain showed in his eyes. "Frankly, Emma, I do not care for the Ton. Their so called morning calls are gossipy broths, and gossip is seldom truth. I hope they are kind to you."

Emma knew he was thinking of Consuelo and how she had

over thirty years ago been cut by the Ton. She let the subject drop and followed him as he showed her around his home. Only his book room seemed appropriate for him.

"This is where I am most comfortable," he said. "So far the house is a place where I stay. It is not a home, but someday, with a wife and children, I hope that will change. I built it with that hope in mind. Just as I built my luxury ship."

Emma caught the loneliness in his voice and was seized by a bit of conscience. Should she tell him the truth of her intentions? She decided not. But she would, she promised herself, as soon as Francine found a husband.

# Chapter Seventeen

Ashton deFleury was not prepared for the stir Lady Emma Winslows' arrival in Town caused. It was as if the whole of the Ton was holding its breath for her arrival. On-dits had it that the Duke of Attlebery's promised wife was now residing at Number Ten Park Place in Grosvenor Square, that she was strikingly beautiful, that His Grace, at one and thirty, was so smitten with his first love he was acting like a schoolboy.

That alone made the Winslow's arrival a hot topic. Every blood of the Ton wanted to best her.

Even the color of Emma's hair, and her eyes, was being bandied about; long black tresses that shone in the dark, eyes the color of violets, and a waist that a man could span with one hand. "And she's smart, too," they said.

This had been passed about by Lord Maxmillion, who had caught a glimpse of Lady Emma Winslow at Consuelo's "little gathering" at Craigmont, and he also passed word that none other than Sir Arthur Stewart was a contender for Lady Emma Winslow's hand. Bets were made at White's on who would win.

And there were those betting that His Grace Ashton de-Fleury would cry off before time for him to become leg-shackled, for never before had he been inclined to become leg-shackled to any chit.

"I'm betting he won't cry off," Lord Peter Wiltshire said. "He likes 'em pretty, if we can judge by his mistresses."

"Ain't never seen him with one that wasn't pretty," said Lord Wilson. "But I'm betting he'll cry off."

"He can't cry off, if he's really spoken for her, and she has accepted. It would ruin his reputation," said another young blood, obviously not aware of Ashton deFleury's reputation of not giving a demme about what the Ton thought.

Loud laughter ensued, and Lord Wilson said, "When has His Grace Ashton deFleury cared about what any of us thought? I'm still betting he don't let black hair and blue eyes sway him. I hear she ain't dowered, and His Grace loves that folding stuff called blunt."

And so the betting went.

His Grace learned about it when one day he strolled into White's for the sole purpose of learning what was being said about the newly arrived Ladies Emma and Francine Winslow. He was slapped on the back, scolded for not coming to the club more often, congratulated on his choice of his affianced, and then told that he might not win her after all. "Gentlemen are standing in line at Number Ten for a glimpse of her," Lord Wilson said, and he added knowingly, "Sir Arthur is there now. And I think Maxmillion."

Lord Peter Wiltshire spoke up. "Mayhaps there will be contenders other than Sir Arthur Stewart. I might take a go at her. I could edge out any mentioned."

Feeling the hair rise on the back of his neck, His Grace glared at them. "She's spoken for," he said, but the conversation did nothing to allay his jealous fears that he might lose Emma. If only he could have kept her at Craigmont. He left the Gentlemen's club immediately to rush back to Number Ten to protect what was rightfully his. He would call Stewart out and shoot him if need be.

In front of his own palatial home, where he was not allowed to stay for propriety's sake, His Grace found Stewart's equipage at the curb, and through the window of the first-floor receiving room he saw Stewart and Lord Maxmillion. And Emma. He raised his quizzing glass for a closer look.

Emma sat on a small settee, Maxmillion beside her, and Stewart was sprawled on the floor at her feet, staring adoringly up at her. *Like a dying calf,* His Grace thought. He went inside and handed his hat to the butler who had swung wide the huge double doors, as if, His Grace thought, he had been waiting for His Grace to come save the damsel in distress.

She looked like anything but a damsel in distress to His Grace. A silvery laugh floated out to ring in his ears.

"Thank you, Gork," His Grace said.

"I'm glad you're here, Your Grace," the butler responded giddily and bowing. Then, raising a brow, he nodded toward the receiving room.

"I know. I've already seen," His Grace said, and his long strides moved him quickly to stand before Emma and her admirers. Maxmillion even had the audacity to be fingering the end of her long black hair.

His Grace greeted them graciously, if not enthusiastically, and bowed to Emma.

She jumped to her feet, stepped around Stewart, and bobbed a quick curtsy. "Your Grace," she said demurely.

He took her hand and, without fanfare, started walking toward the door, practically dragging Emma. "Did you forget that we were to ride in the park, love? We must needs hurry. It is my wish to show my promised bride to the upper orders."

He looked back and nodded to the two gentlemen with startled looks on their faces, who were both now standing, their hands on their hips.

"I am not your promised bride," Emma said from between clenched teeth. In a low conspiratorial voice, she continued, "I believe the agreement was that after a husband for Francine had been found, *my brother's* contract would be renegotiated."

"I've changed my mind," the Duke said, taking his hat

from the butler and scampering out the door, still holding Emma's hand and walking two steps ahead of her.

His smart black tilbury, hitched to a smart black horse, awaited at the curb. He lifted Emma into it, measuring for himself whether a man could span her waist with one hand.

"You dragged me from my guests," Emma scolded, not minding nearly as much as she made her voice indicate. His Grace was splendidly appealing when he was angry, she thought, looking at him from the corner of her eye. A thrill washed over her, and she scolded herself for being so school-girlish. She laid that to lack of experience, and, although she tried not to, she thought of her brother who had kept her at Fernwood until she was practically an ape-leader. Little wonder she felt thrilled when the Duke of Attlebery touched her. She wondered if she would feel the same should *another* man kiss her. But she would never know, she told herself, for it was obvious Ashton deFleury would scare off any such suitor.

Feeling gay and happy, she listened to the horse's hooves hitting the cobbled street, and she laughed when the tilbury took a corner on one wheel.

And His Grace laughed with her. This was a new experience for him as well. Never before had he ridden in the fashionable five-o'clock squeeze in Hyde Park.

"I've heard that one cannot tell a Cyprian from a lady of quality during the squeeze," he said.

"I've heard they are painted dolls," Emma replied.

They joined the procession of grand carriages carrying grandly dressed women and their abigails, and/or their companions. Grandly dressed gentlemen rode fine horses, some even rented from Tattersall's if the gentleman happened to be short of blunt at the moment. So Emma had read.

Emma saw an especially beautiful woman eying the Duke—she had noticed that *every* woman, beautiful, ugly, young, or old, eyed His Grace Ashton deFleury, even practically hanging out of the carriage to do so. She asked, "Is she your mistress?"

211

"Who?"

"That gel staring at you."

His Grace looked around. "Good God, no. She belongs to the Duke of Melborne. I suspect she is looking at you."

"If you will look at her, I am sure she will wave."

"I don't want her to wave."

"Do you have a mistress?"

He smiled and said teasingly, "You should not speak of such things. But the truth is I gave up my mistress when I fell in love with you."

Emma frowned. "I wish you would stop speaking of loving me. You have not known me long enough to be in love with me, not real love." She added for her own benefit, "Being thrilled is not the same as being in love."

He gave her a tender look. "I've known you much longer than it takes a man to fall in love. I think I told you that I fell in love with you when your brother spoke so lovingly about you, even before I first saw you that Easter morn. Lord Winslow—"

The anger stirred inside Emma, and she said crisply, "Don't speak to me about Charles. Please . . ."

Her voice broke, and the Duke reached to squeeze her hand, saying no more, and wondering if ever he would tell her about Charles. He could not force it, he told himself, for nothing was worth making her angry with him.

For a short while they rode in silence, each taking notice and commenting about the carriages, the beautiful gowns the women wore, knowing none of them. His Grace was satisfied just letting them stare at Emma, with him at her side. And then he had an idea that made him smile. Guiding his horse from the procession, he circled the tilbury and headed for his rented apartment on Upper Brook Street. There, he penned an intelligence to Consuelo, telling her that Emma was with him and would be home sometime before the cocks crowed at daylight.

Pulling the bellrope, he summoned his valet and gave the

missive to him. "Deliver this immediately to Number Ten Park Place to Consuelo deFleury, and wait for a reply."

"Yes, Your Grace," the valet said. Grinning broadly, he left immediately.

Emma was aghast. "You're a scoundrel—"

"I know," he said, laughing, and he took her in his arms and kissed her, deeply, pouring all the love there was inside of him into her, and he prayed that she would be stirred as she had been on *Lady Emma*. There was no question about how his body would react, and he wished that he were more in control. But he could not touch her without being ravaged with desire, and already delicious, traitorous heat churned in his loins. He swore under his breath and kissed her again, and when she kissed him back with great feeling, he began to tremble. Against her warm, soft lips he whispered, his voice gravelly with emotion, "Don't worry, love. I've taken precaution. I asked that Countess Lankford return with Dodge to chaperon us."

Emma was disappointed but did not say so. *I'm acting like a shameless harlot.* His Grace released her, and bent to stoke the fire, for the evening had become quite cool. He sat on the floor and pulled Emma down to sit facing him, and they sat in the shimmer and leap of the firelight, chatting amicably until Dodge returned, Countess Lankford in tow.

"You scoundrel," she said, laughing. Approval was in her eyes for Emma to see.

"You came just in time," His Grace said teasingly, and the Countess handed him Consuelo's reply, which he quickly opened and read aloud: "Ashton deFleury, return Lady Emma to Number Ten at once. Your conduct is deplorable, and should you continue conducting yourself in this manner, not a gentlemen in Town will want to husband her."

His Grace laughed uproarishly and asked his valet to see that supper was prepared. The table was to be set with the finest china and crystal, and candles were to be lit. He finished with, "And bring lots of champagne."

* * *

The day following, Emma and Francine were in Emma's sitting room having a coze. It seemed to Emma that Francine was interested in anything and everything other than finding a husband. "London thrills me," the redhead said, reminding Emma of a child of twelve instead of a young adult of seven and ten years.

This day, Francine was brimming with gossip. Emma stood by a window, listening, and Francine sat on the floor painting her toenails with gilt polish. She stopped for breath occasionally, then started again, "Sister, did you know that the Duchess of York keeps *one hundred* dogs, and when the Duke brings guests home the dogs get the best place by the fire. They live in the country, in Surrey, and the Countess takes *one hundred* dogs on midnight strolls. Don't you know the smell in the house must be offensive?"

When Emma did not answer, Francine scolded, "Emma, are you listening to me?"

"I'm sorry, Francine, I was thinking, but do go on. I promise to be more attentive."

And Francine did go on, but it was not until she spoke of His Grace Ashton deFleury that she got Emma's full attention.

"They call him the Randy Duke."

"What did you say? And where are you getting all this gossip? I am sure that gossip is all it is."

"I said that once a year the Cyprians have an elaborate ball, and only the gentlemen of the Ton can attend. They say that the Randy Duke always attends with his mistress, a certain beauty by the name of Mavarene Hall."

She tilted her head, looked at her toenails, and mused aloud, "Mavarene, isn't that a pretty name?"

Emma whipped around. "I don't believe a word of it. He would not blatantly flaunt a woman of that inclination."

"Oh, all the Ton bloods do. They say the ball is a gentleman's delight. Of course ladies of quality can't attend. I've been thinking that this year I will go in disguise."

"You will not! I forbid it! And I will have no more gossip about His Grace. He has been quite generous toward us, especially toward you and little Prudence. You must needs show your appreciation. He's offered to dower you, which will make it much easier to find a suitable husband."

As if Emma had not spoken, Francine asked, "Have you heard that His Grace is the illegitimate son of our King? And that is why he made Ashton a Duke. All kings do that, make their by blows Dukes."

Emma's mouth fell open. "Who told you that? And it is not so. He told me—"

Francine laughed mischievously. "My lady's maid loves to pass on on-dits. What did His Grace tell you, Sister, and was it last night? You know Consuelo was furious that His Grace took you away from Sir Arthur Stewart, and then of all things, took you to his private residence. You're acting rather disgraceful, you know."

With that, Francine left. And later that day Van Winters passed to Emma the same information. "Madame was furious with you," she said, scolding in a backhanded way with a disapproving look.

Emma shrugged her shoulders. She had had about all she could take of Consuelo's criticism. After all, at Craigmont it was His Grace who had kidnapped her and taken her aboard his ship, and then yesterday he had practically dragged her from her guests. Of course, she conceded, she did not have to spend the whole of the evening at his residence. He had not held her prisoner. And they had been chaperoned, if one could call Countess Lankford a chaperon. Last night she had removed to a small sitting room to read a book, and to eat supper alone.

Emma dismissed Van Winters. Something else had popped into her mind, which bothered her tremendously, and she had no one with whom to talk. Francine was entirely too giddy and frivolous to understand, and would most likely think it wonderful and too exciting to bear. So she must needs keep her own counsel, she told herself, and she admitted that His Grace's kisses were far too disturbing for her liking, and she liked them too much to ask him to stop. Making promises to herself that she could only pray that she could keep, such as forbidding His Grace to kiss her in that delicious way, Emma sat for a long while. She remembered too clearly that it was *after*, not during, His Grace's kiss that she thought of her anger toward him, and toward her brother. She simply would not be alone with His Grace, and the next time he tried to kidnap her, or drag her from her guests, she would resolutely dig her heels in and refuse to go. After all, she was twenty and three, not exactly a child.

In another part of the Number Ten, Consuelo was not overly concerned with her son's antics. She had long ago given up trying to outwit him. She had promised Prudence to take her to see her mother. She dreaded going; she feared Countess Winslow would not recognize the child. Yesterday she had sent a missive saying they, Miss Consuelo deFleury and Lady Prudence Winslow, wished to visit with Countess Margaret Winslow on the morrow. Word had come back that they would be welcome.

So this day she sent word to Prudence that they would leave as soon as the child could prepare herself, and only moments passed before she heard a light knock on her door and, looking up, saw Prudence standing there, a big, broad smile on her sweet face. Over her pantalettes she wore a blue dress with black bows and black slippers. A black bow was buried in her blond curls, and clasped in her little hands were red and white roses, still wet from the morning dew.

"I shall tell Mama the black bows are for mourning. She was very adamant about my mourning Papa." The smile faded for an instant. "I hope she knows me. At the last she didn't. That's why they took her away and sent me to Fernwood to be with Auntie Em and Francie."

Consuelo tried to prepare her, saying gently, "Darling child, your mother is getting the best of care. Keep that in mind, and if she can be helped, she will be, in the place where she is staying."

After Countess Winslow had been moved from Bedlam, Consuelo had made enquiries concerning her new residence and had learned that its reputation was of the best. And Dr. Reneau had been brought from France to treat the Countess. Consuelo admired her son for his thoroughness. He never left a task half done.

Happiness returned to Prudence's face. "His Grace told me the name of Mama's new place is *New Hope.* Isn't that a wonderful name? And I *know* Mama will know me. I've petitioned the Lord—"

"Prue, honey, *you* cannot dictate to the Lord."

Prudence sighed. "I've never seen so many doubting Thomases. Even Auntie Em. When she comes to be with me when I pray she tries in a veiled manner to prepare me for failure. Well, I believe, and I guess that is good enough."

Consuelo envied Prudence's childlike, unshakable faith, and she said no more to her about her mother not getting well. Mayhaps it was better for one to anticipate and be happy while doing so, than to doubt that anything good could happen. She herself was having a difficult time venturing out into London. His Grace had left his crested carriage for her use, and for Emma's and Francine's as well. In Town he used his tilbury.

But the crest would only draw attention, Consuelo decided. The sumptuous carriage that brought her into London would fare well enough. She would sink low in the squabs and mayhaps no one would see her. She scolded herself. After thirty years, no one of consequence would know her.

New Hope was located on the outer circle of Regent's

Park, near Hanover Terrace. Consuelo had read of Nash's wonderful transformation of the area from St. James's Park to, and including, Regent's Park, and she found herself leaning forward to view those changes. It was only when she realized she was totally visible that she sank into the squabs and wished she were back at Craigmont. Prudence was oblivious of anything except getting there as fast as the four horses could take them, and when they came in sight of the two-story building, which was once a palatial home with a wrap-around porch, she squealed with joy.

A simple sign on the manicured lawn stated simply, NEW HOPE.

The coachman pulled the horses to a stop, and a footman hopped down from the back and let the step down.

When they were on the ground, Consuelo, tears begging for release and a lump forming in her throat, hugged Prudence and suggested that they enter silently and not awaken those who were asleep.

"Mama won't be asleep," Prudence said, squirming to free herself of Consuelo's embrace.

Unable to trust the child not to storm the place, Consuelo reached for Prudence's hand and held it tightly as they walked toward the inviting porch. At the door they sounded the brass knocker, and a pleasant-faced young gel smiled at them from the inside. "Come in," she said, and they entered.

Prudence, now steely calm and silent, clung to Consuelo's hand, as if now that she was here she was afraid.

"We are here to see Countess Margaret Winslow," Consuelo said.

"I know," the gel responded, "I am her private nurse." Then, looking at Prudence, added, "I would know this little blonde anywhere. The Countess talks of her precious daughter all the time."

Prudence's sad face suddenly came to life in the most fantastic way. She laughed, and the laughter spread to her big gray eyes. "I knew it! I knew it! Mama has not forgotten me."

"May we see the Countess now?" Consuelo asked.

The nurse took Prudence's hand. "Yes. But mayhaps you should not come, Miss deFleury. If you are needed, I will come for you."

They went into the next room, into which Consuelo could see from where she sat in the small reception room. The Countess stood in the middle of the room, w 'nging her hands. Consuelo lifted her lorgnette and stared. The woman was frail, and anxious, but her beauty was startling, even though she was dressed in white from head to toe and her blond hair was brushed straight back from her face. When she saw Prudence, she dropped to her knees and reached out her arms. Her pale face suddenly became radiant.

"Mama, Mama," Prudence said, flying into her arms.

Consuelo looked away. It was their own private world. The nurse came out and said that the visit would help the Countess, who had been making wonderful progress under the expert care of Dr. Reneau.

Later, Prudence and her mother went out onto the grounds and walked, hand in hand, and when the allotted time was up, Prudence brought the Countess and presented her to Consuelo. "I've told Mama how wonderfully well you and Auntie Em and Francine treat me."

The Countess smiled but did not speak. Her eyes moved furtively, as if she were afraid of something.

Later, the nurse told Consuelo that it was normal, that often they were afraid when meeting strangers. "Her confidence will return," the nurse said. "Right now, the only thing she is sure of is her daughter's love. I hope you will bring her again."

A thought came to Consuelo, but it was just a thought, and it would take planning. Prudence went into the adjoining room, and Consuelo saw her shower kisses on her mama's cheeks, telling her goodbye. In the carriage, Prudence said, "I hope Princess Charlotte gets to visit her mother; it is so wonderful. It makes one feel whole."

Consuelo knew that her next act of mercy would be to take the Princess to Blackheath to see her mother, Princess Caroline, and of course little Prue would want to come along.

Somehow it made Consuelo feel wonderful.

## Chapter Eighteen

The day Ladies Emma and Francine Winslow were to be presented at Court came almost before they were ready. It was such a monumental step, and the dress so outlandish that Emma dreaded the ordeal more than she looked forward to it. Francine thought it divinely wonderful and came rushing to Emma's room to ask how in the world they could ride in a carriage wearing those hoops. "I'm glad His Majesty will be in London. I think it would be quite a long walk to Windsor."

"What do you mean, walk?" Emma asked. It was true the King's madness came upon him more often now, keeping him at Windsor Palace—some said locked in a padded room—but she had no intention of walking anywhere.

Francine gave Emma a look that plainly accused her of not thinking. "Have you seen those hoops? When we sit down they will show our underclothes, not to say hike up and blind us. They fit close on the side and loop out in the front and back."

"Then we won't wear the hoops in the carriage. We shall take them and unobtrusively put them on before going before the King."

"In front of everyone? Sister—"

Emma laughed. "Why do I get the feeling that you are pulling my leg? Of course we won't put them on in front of everyone. His Grace will arrange for a dressing room. Being a close friend of the King's, he will only have to send a missive. I'm sure Consuelo has already thought of it."

"Are you sure His Grace is not the old mad eh what King's by-blow?"

"Out, out," Emma said. "Enough of your tomfoolery. Have a maid dress you, your *lady's maid,* for only she will know which layer comes next."

On Emma's bed the different layers reached halfway up the tall headboard. She rang for Van Winters and asked that she have water for a bath brought, and after her bath she would begin dressing, with Van Winters' help, of course.

"At this hour?" Van Winters exclaimed.

"Yes, at this hour. I do not like to be rushed, and I fear it will take hours to dress my hair and place the ostrich plumes."

Emma looked at the huge colorful feathers and wagered silently that her head could not possibly hold that many feathers, that if it did she could not possibly hold her head erect. Seven were mandatory for court presentation, but more could be worn if desired. It had been Consuelo's decision that "her girls" would wear more. "Some wear four and twenty," she had said, and Emma understood. Consuelo thought two dozen plumes bad taste, but twenty would only push the boundary.

"Won't you go, Consuelo?" Emma had asked and was immediately sorry. Consuelo turned pale, and her eyes watered. "No," she answered, simply and matter-of-factly. "Countess Lankford will be your sponsor."

Now, her body bathed and powdered, the outlandish court dress on, with the exception of the hooped underskirt, Emma sat before the looking glass and watched Van Winters dress her hair. First, she clasped the long black hair behind Emma's ears, letting it fall to her shoulders. A garland of white roses was then twisted upon a ringlet of pearls and placed like a crown on her head. A diamond comb, diamond buckles, and white silk tassels were added.

Emma thought that mayhaps someone had stolen the crown jewels, but it did not matter to her if they had. She was entirely too old for this. She had heard that no one over seven and ten was being presented, except herself. If she did not have to consider Francine's future . . .

Then came the long colorful feathers, reaching up to hide most of Van Winters's face. "It takes a well-trained lady's maid to do this," she said proudly.

"How many have you done?" Emma asked, hiding her smile.

Van Winters sniffed. "This is my first, but Miss deFleury sent me and your sister's maid to the stylish plumier, Carberry, and we learned. And he also gave us the longest and fullest feathers."

Pursing her lips, Van Winters worked meticulously, and when the feathers were placed to her satisfaction, she stepped back to admire her work.

Emma giggled, and when Francine burst through the door, looking, with the exception of the red-blond curls and freckles, like her twin, they fell on each other and laughed hysterically.

Van Winters mumbled something, which sounded much to Emma like, "Country gels."

Instead of staring at her own reflection in the looking glass, Emma stared at Francine. Emma had seen the court dress in its making, but she had not seen the finished product, and she thought it quite fetching.

The shortest and top skirt was made of silver-spangled tulle decorated with a garland of flowers. It was turned up and tucked so the garland draped crosswise all around the skirt. The tuck openings had a flower bouquet set in silver lace. Bracelets adorned Francine's arms, and jeweled brooches, too, found a home on the high-waisted bodice that showed a goodly amount of bosom.

It only took Van Winters moments to add those same touches to Emma's arms and bodice, and then she declared that Emma looked absolutely marvelous.

Little Prudence and Hannah were sent for. "Oh, Auntie Em, you look beautiful," Prudence said. "And Aunt Francie, too."

Hannah ah'd until Emma was sure her throat would be sore.

And then Consuelo came. Tears of approval glittered in her eyes. "My gels will be the most beautiful there," she said, but when asked again to accompany them, she refused.

The procession of grand carriages traveled down Piccadilly to St. James's. In His Grace's crested carriage, the two sisters sat on one banquette, and loveable, pleasant Countess Lankford sat across from them. "You look lovely," Emma said to her, and the Countess smiled and thanked her. She, too, was dressed to the nines in a becoming gown of deep red satin. Her gray-streaked brown hair framed her very pretty face.

From the onset, Francine hung her head out the window and stared, and reported.

"Sister, every carriage has three footmen, dressed in the grandest livery. I can't believe it. They have ridiculously huge bouquets in their lapels. And you should see the carriages! They are positively elegant, and pulled by high-stepping horses wearing their Easter parade harness."

Emma pulled Francine upright. "Francie, you don't have to let *everyone* know that we are from the country."

Countess Lankford spoke. " 'Tis honorable to be from the country. Most of these gels are. Some professional has trained them not to act like it. So let Francie look and enjoy. Mayhaps she will never be so thrilled again."

"Only when I get married," Francine said, and the words brought comfort to Emma. Francine *was* thinking of a husband.

Silence ensued inside the carriage. For a short while.

Ahead, Emma saw splendid scarlet-clad cavalry parading atop jet-black horses. Guns were fired and trumpets sounded. Goose bumps formed on her arms. The Countess was right, she thought, nothing could ever be more thrilling. She listened to the clopping of the horses on the cobbled street, enjoying the sound.

And then Francine offered another on-dit, this time about the old King. "I was told," she said, "that when Lady Sarah Lennox's name was sent in as a candidate to be privately presented at King George's Court that the eh what King asked if she had another name that might be used. It seemed that he had once had a fancy for a Lady Sarah Lennox and he feared it might have an exciting effect upon him. And when —"

"I fear you are about to say something derogatory about His Majesty, and I think it poor taste," Emma said.

"No, it's not derogatory at all; it just shows the old King is human. But only *he* would ask for such a favor."

Countess Lankford was smiling.

"I'll wager you know the story," Francine said, looking at the Countess. "You tell my proper sister."

" 'Tis not a story; 'tis true. The King's first love was Lady Sarah Lennox, a great aunt to the Lady Sarah Lennox who was to be presented. The old King asked if his love's niece was pretty, and when he was told that she definitely was pretty, and that she resembled her great aunt, he asked if there was a second name that could be used, for he thought the excitement of seeing someone who reminded him of the first Lady Sarah Lennox might be too much for him. But there was no second name for her ladyship and she was presented as Lady Sarah Lennox."

Grinning broadly, Francine said, "There's more. Don't tease."

So the Countess continued the true story: "When Lady Sarah was taken up to the King, he begged her to allow a blind old man the privilege of passing his hand over her features."

225

"She didn't," exclaimed Emma.

"Yes, she did, and later she remarked that she could not refuse, knowing the reason for his request."

"I would have, too," Francine said, and laughed when Emma gave her a stern look.

They were soon to St. James's and their hoops were quickly added to their attire, and inside the huge room where they waited to be presented, Emma's eyes could not drink in the sight; it was beyond bearing. Gloriously attired young gels, each sporting a plume, afforded a fantastic sight. She felt like a spectator, not one of them. As she watched, the whole room became a vast field of undulating feathers, in all the colors of the rainbow — blue, green, red, yellow, violet, even pure white. Sunlight through the windows glittered on the diamonds the gels wore, and also on their mamas' diamonds.

So great was the excitement that one gel fainted, and her well-attired mother hovered over her, fanning her with a delicate fan. Other mothers, or sponsors, raised lorgnettes to examine the plumes of *other* gels to be presented.

"You're prettier than anyone here," Francine whispered to Emma, and Emma responded, "I'm older than anyone here, except the mothers and sponsors."

"Don't think about that, for you certainly don't look older."

"Thanks, little sister."

Emma laughed tentatively and felt better by knowing Francine was concerned enough to try to encourage her. She thought Francine positively beautiful and knew that finding a husband for her would be no effort at all, especially with the dowry His Grace had offered. *That* was uppermost in Emma's mind.

Finally, it was Emma's time to be taken to the King, and to the old Begum sitting beside him. Emma steeled herself, smiled, and gave a courtly curtsy as she had been taught, and for a moment she chatted with the King, finding him lucid but with a faraway, almost mad look in his eyes. He mentioned that she was Ashton deFleury's special friend, and Emma found herself blushing. She wondered if Ashton had told His Majesty, or if gossip had reached the old man's ears.

"He didn't feel me up," Francine said when she returned from her presentation, and Countess Lankford laughed and hugged both the girls. A sumptuous tea was served, and at last the wonderful, glorious event was over, and Emma thought that she would not have missed it for the world. It was only fair, she told herself, to thank Consuelo deFleury, and His Grace, of course, for making their appearance at Court possible. She made a mental note to do so.

# Chapter Nineteen

Emma was not surprised when two days later the London morning papers reported that His Majesty had been returned to Windsor due to another spell of his "sickness." She genuinely felt sorry for the old King. Rumors were flying that he would be declared incompetent to rule, and that the Prince of Wales would become Prince Regent. She knew this would not set well with His Grace, who had more than once expressed dislike for the Prince because of his spendthrift ways and his lack of morals.

"The man has the morals of a bitch dog in heat," His Grace had said, and not apologizing for his crude comparison. And on the subject of the Prince keeping Princess Charlotte from her mother, Princess Caroline, His Grace could become quite livid.

How fortunate that the Court presentation had taken place when it did, Emma thought. As far as she was concerned it had been a huge success. Francine's eyes shone when she talked about it. This pleased Emma very much. She started thinking about the come-out ball, which would be that night. At Number Ten Park Place, the elegantly engraved invitations had read.

When she looked at the invitation she had been given to keep as a memento she could not believe it was actually speaking of her, or, for that matter, of Francine. Never could she have done so well by her sister.

Keeping her mind focused on Francine's chance of a good marriage, Emma looked at the calendar of events which Countess Lankford had arranged. After the come-out ball, invitations would be forthcoming, the Countess had said. She was well-known among the quality, and Consuelo had been wise, Emma thought, to turn the planning over to her. Vouchers to Almack's had even been obtained, and the patronesses had given permission for Emma and Francine to dance the waltz. She was sure this was the Duke's doing.

Even though Consuelo deFleury had made it known she did not like Emma, Emma was saddened that she would not be attending the come-out ball. She had furnished the wardrobes, and, from behind the scene, had worked diligently for the party to be a success. No doubt the flowers for the ball had cost a fortune. The last time Emma had peeked, already there were mountains of white roses in epergnes placed strategically around the great foyer and the adjoining ballroom.

That Consuelo had turned the planning over to someone else, did not mean that she did not care about the parties "her gels" would be attending, Emma mused. Yesterday, when they had returned from Court, Consuelo and Prudence, along with Hannah and Van Winters, were waiting wide-eyed to hear all about the King and the old Begum, and Francine had delighted in relating every fanciful detail.

Of course the Duke had been waiting, too, standing on the sidelines, grinning, his thumbs in his waistcoat pockets. And he had seemed particularly interested when the discussion had turned to the Princess Charlotte not being allowed to see her mother.

"I hear the old Begum is the one who objects most strenuously to Princess Charlotte seeing her mother," Francine said. "She says the environment of the Princess of Wales's home is not conducive to the training of a future sovereign."

"It doesn't matter about that," Prudence said, her little face solemn. "Charlotte should be allowed to see her mother."

Emma had looked at the Duke and saw his smile fade, while a concerned frown appeared on his brow.

But now it was time to think of the ball, Emma decided. Her gown was stretched across the bed, and her long black hair was twisted and tied around white rags. "So there will be just a tiny bit of curl," Van Winters had said. Every time Emma caught a glimpse of herself in the looking glass, she laughed.

Having nothing to do but wait, for she had been shooed out of the kitchen, the ballroom, and the dining room, she went to her writing desk and penned a message to Samuel, the groom who was in charge of her chickens and animals, promising him a nice gift if he would see that they had excellent care. "I pray that someone at the stables can read," she said aloud as she put the missive in a silver salver for a maid to post. Then, seating herself by a window, she stared out at the mews where the horses and carriages were kept, and at the minuscule garden below.

Flowers bloomed profusely, and she could almost hear the tiny patches of grass popping and cracking as the green blades grew taller and taller, so the gardener would soon have to crawl on his knees and trim them to the exact, proper level. She longed for Fernwood and its open spaces, the hillocks covered with trees, the moors, the servants. In short, she longed for the simple life, her life, when she was in control.

A knock on the door drew Emma's attention, and when she bade the knocker to enter, a footman did so and handed Emma a sealed missive. "From His Grace," he said, bowing then leaving quickly.

Emma stared at the missive. Why would His Grace be writing to her? Why did he not just come and say what he had to say?

"Open it, pea-goose," she said, and quickly did her own bidding, reading aloud: "My Love: Tonight, when gentlemen pay undue attention to you, will you please tell them that the come-out is for your sister Francine, and that you have already been spoken for? This will save you embarrassment, as well as myself."

At the bottom of the page, as if it were an afterthought, he had added, "My heart aches for the time when your sister is safely married. Then I will take you to wife, to hold and love forever."

He had signed it simply Ashton deFleury.

For a long moment, Emma just stood there, thinking. His Grace was a smart, intelligent man, too smart to think he could *plan* her life without consulting her. He had taken advantage of her brother. She was sure His Grace knew that Charles could not gamble himself out of a henhouse.

Hearing a knock on the door, Emma looked up and saw Hartshorn Van Winters with her etiquette book under her arm.

"Put the book away," Emma said. "If I don't know how to act by now, after all your gruelling sessions, I will never know."

"Are you saying you refuse to go over these instructions —"

"Not one more time. I don't care a fig about the Ton does this, and the Ton does that. I am concerned about Francine. Has someone taught her to dance?"

"Yes, indeed," Van Winters said. "The gel is a natural. They say her feet know just what to do. Too bad she has those freckles and red hair. They just ain't the thing with the Ton."

Emma felt like a mother hen whose chick had been attacked, and she expressed herself accordingly. "Don't you dare say *that* to Francine. Consuelo has convinced her that her freckles and red hair are an asset. Besides, she only has a smattering of freckles across her nose."

Looking totally contrite, Van Winters promised, "I will speak to the other servants and see that they don't say anything about Francine's freckles and red hair, especially not when she's about."

"Francine's smile, and her personality, is far more important than her freckles, or the color of her hair," Emma said.

" 'Tis true, I am sure." Van Winters lifted a brow. "What about what they are saying about you?"

"What are *they* saying about me?"

"That you are a bluestocking, much too smart for your own good. Gentlemen don't like that, and it will keep you from getting a husband."

"Where did you hear that?"

"It seems Miss deFleury voiced that opinion to someone and an upstairs maid heard—"

"That's enough," Emma said. "Servants' gossip does not interest me." A long pause, and then, "Why would Consuelo deFleury call me a bluestocking?"

"Because you are always reading, and because you do not have an interest in the Ton. It's even being bandied about that you think society foolish, that you are of the opinion that time could better be spent promoting causes, such as schools for climbing boys, or food for hungry children. I did not believe it until you refused to let me drill you on the proper way to go on in society. Now, I have no choice but to believe that you are . . . well, different."

Emma laughed. "Think what you will, but I make my point when I remind you that Beau Brummell is supposedly in charge of *who* makes it in London's society. How ridiculous! Does that speak well of society?"

" 'Tis the way of the Ton."

"By-the-by, when will the eccentric dandy have a chance to pass on my possibilities of being accepted by the quality? Will there be an audience set, when I will go and bow at his feet?"

"I suppose tonight. He will be at the ball, I am sure. It will be good if you are exceptionally nice to him."

In her mind's eye Emma could see His Grace's anger exploding when she was "exceptionally" nice to the dandy. "Useless," the Duke raged when the Beau was mentioned in his presence. "Never worked a day in the whole of his life. His pretty hands show it."

Emma recalled that the other person with the capability of making His Grace Ashton deFleury explode in rage was Sir Arthur Stewart, reportedly a contender for her hand, and Consuelo's choice for a husband for her. "Cheeseparer, Pretty Face Stewart," the Duke called him.

A smile found its way onto Emma's face. Mayhaps the come-out ball would not be completely boring.

Van Winters stood with her hands on her hips, shaking her head in obvious despair. Finally, as if she could read Emma's mind, she blurted out, "Now, m'lady, don't do anything foolish . . ."


That night, at the head of the curving stairway, Emma held His Grace Ashton deFleury, the Duke of Attlebery's right arm, Francine his left. "Ladies and Gentlemen," the staid, highly liveried butler called out over the din, "Lady Emma Winslow, and Lady Francine Winslow."

Emma felt her knees shaking. As a sea of faces turned to stare, a lightning bolt of anticipation seemed to sweep through the crowd, followed by a great deep silence and an occasional gasp.

"Slowly," His Grace said as they started downward.

The sisters wore identical gowns, except for the color.

Emma's was a deep purple, and Francine's a deep green, the colors chosen to complement the color of their eyes.

The elegantly simple, low-cut gowns cupped their bosoms, fell softly and seductively over suggested curves, then trailed behind them when they walked. The sleeves were short and puffed, and showed youthful shoulders. Francine's riotous red-blond curls were just that, riotous.

Emma's glossy black hair was caught at the crown in a mass of curls entwined in pearls and diamonds.

Her eyes perused the crowd.

She knew people only by pictures she had seen of them; Beau Brummell was there, and the Prince, both standing not far from the bottom step. The Beau's loud whisper floated up to assault Emma's ears. "Beauties, ain't they?"

"Where has His Grace been hiding them?" the Prince asked, inching closer to the stairway, as if he meant to stand in Emma's path to the dance floor.

"In the country," said the Beau.

"Which one's his?"

"The black-haired beauty. Look at those eyes," Beau Brummell said, his voice now loud enough for all to hear.

Emma felt her face flush hot with embarrassment, and when she heard Francine giggle she suddenly wanted to strangle her.

"Don't let the fools fluster you," His Grace said, almost under his breath, and down they went, gracefully, haughty, exuding confidence Emma did not feel. She saw a handsome young blood staring at Francine, smiling, and then he started walking toward her, parting the crowd as he did so.

His Grace bent his head to Emma. "Lord Melvin Harthgrow, from an excellent family. His eyes are on your sister."

"I didn't think they were on me," Emma retorted for His Grace's ears only.

Francine's foot had barely touched the last stair step when Lord Harthgrow stepped up, gave a fancy leg, and practically asked the Duke to introduce them. And then he asked to stand for the first dance. His intentions were blatant, and Emma saw it. Her heart sang with happiness. She wanted so much for Francine to have a wonderful time at *her* come-out ball, and she wanted Francine to find a rich husband.

As Lord Harthgrow led Francine toward the dance floor, Sir Arthur Stewart stepped up, gave his own fancy leg, and asked Emma if he could stand for the first dance.

Turning, she smiled demurely up at His Grace. "I beg to excuse myself." She felt his fingers bite into her arm. She no longer held his arm; he held hers in a viselike grip.

"This dance is spoken for," His Grace said, and he swept Emma into his arms and danced his way to the dance floor, parting the guests who dared stand in his way.

For some explicable reason, Emma, at that moment, looked up at the stair landing. Consuelo was peering down on them, holding her lorgnette to her eyes and smiling, as if everything was going according to her plan.

"You are very rude," Emma told His Grace, and he laughed and replied with aplomb, "I've never claimed to be nice."

The Duke pulled her closer to him and looked into her violet blue eyes. "You are ravishing tonight," he said, and instantly felt himself losing control. "Dear God," he prayed, and then swore under his breath. It happened every time he was in proximity with her. Ravaging, unbidden desire surged through his body, causing him to miss a step. He quickly apologized, silently swore again, while frowning at her.

"Why are you frowning?" she asked.

"I'm frowning because there are so many people around. I prefer having you to myself."

"If we were alone, you would be kissing me . . . shamelessly."

*And making love to you,* thought His Grace. Aloud, he said, "And you would be kissing me back."

"You take unfair advantage."

His Grace gave his wry grin. "How can you accuse me—"

"Always, when you kiss me it is in some romantic spot, aboard a ship, for instance, with abundant moonlight and whispering breezes."

"How about in the stable yard? You can't claim *that* as a romantic spot. No, my love, you kiss me because you want to kiss me, not because I've taken unfair advantage as to the place in which we happen to be. How about now? Shall I kiss you here with all the Ton to see?"

Emma's steps moved in perfect unison with His Grace's steps. "You wouldn't dare."

But Emma knew he would dare. He did not care a fig what the Ton thought, and obviously he was anxious to put his seal of ownership on her. Ownership was the key word. Searching the crowd, she sought out Sir Arthur Stewart's eyes, and smiled at him.

"You dance and flirt very well," His Grace said. "Where did you learn—"

"In the country. When I was three and ten."

Just then he danced her by an exit door, and the next thing Emma knew she was in the small garden directly below her bedchamber window, being thoroughly kissed. "Did you learn to kiss like that when you were three and ten?" His Grace asked.

Without giving Emma a chance to reply, he claimed her lips again, and when he was through, he told her with no hesitation, "You, my love, have never been kissed like that."

Emma could only smile, for her head was swimming, and her heart was beating so fast she could not speak. His Grace did take unfair advantage, she thought, and, even though her body was aflame, she lifted her face again for

236

another delicious kiss, saying against his lips, "We must needs return . . . before we are missed."

His Grace was a gentleman. After kissing her until her knees threatened to give way under her, he returned her to the dance floor and danced the next three dances with her. Once she heard from the sidelines her name mentioned, and one buck said to another, "They don't call him the ruthless Duke for nothing."

It was only when His Grace released her that Emma danced with the gentlemen who were waiting in line for their chance, Sir Arthur being the first. She caught an occasional glimpse of His Grace, dancing with the Ton daughters, and with their mamas. He looked devilishly handsome, and he often sought her out with his eyes, smiling at her, his eyes dancing along with his feet.

At last he came to claim her again, and they danced together for the rest of the evening, and when the elegant supper was served, he sat beside her for all to see.

Once Emma told him, "Stop acting like you own me."

This brought only a smile from His Grace.


The next morning, Emma learned that her behavior at the ball was beyond the pale. Leaving with His Grace did not go unnoticed. The house was singularly buzzing. She heard it first from Van Winters, before breakfast, and then from Consuelo, at breakfast. His Grace was there, too, to take his share of the blame, he said. He had invited himself to have breakfast in his own home, and was sitting across the table from Emma, a wry, Cheshire-cat smile beaming from a freshly shaven face.

Consuelo accused: "The two of you acted disgracefully, disappearing before the first dance was finished. Your Grace, I hold you responsible—"

"Why me? If Emma had not looked so fetching, and had

she not practically invited Pretty Face Stewart to dance with her, I would have never taken her into the garden to kiss her."

Emma wanted to sink through her chair. She shot him a shut-up look.

"Is that true, Emma?" Consuelo asked. "Did you openly flirt with Sir Arthur Stewart?"

"We . . . well, I suppose I did."

"Suppose! You know demme well you did," exclaimed His Grace, now laughing openly. He winked at Emma. "That, my love, will get you kissed every time."

"Your Grace," Consuelo scolded, "only a chaste kiss is allowed before marriage."

Emma heard the mirth in her voice, and she suddenly realized that the woman did not care a feather what the Ton thought about Emma's behavior. So she decided to tease along with them. "I did dance with Sir Arthur Stewart, and I found him a delightful dancer, and very witty. And also the Prince . . . and Beau Brummell. The Beau was very charming, and he said the same about me, which means, I suppose, that I am accepted by the Ton."

His Grace scowled. "As if you need his approval. My kisses did not seem to slow you down a whit. You danced with every young blood there, and they all seemed smitten," His Grace said, and then he added, "There seemed to be a hundred or more."

"That was what I intended," Consuelo said. "And from the flowers that have already arrived, and the invitations to parties and soirees, I would say that both my gels were a great hit. No doubt the Ton has not been set back on its heels in such fashion for many years."

Emma turned to her and said, "Thank you, Consuelo. It was a delightful party, a complete success. Several asked about you. Why did you not attend?"

The room became exceedingly quiet.

Embarrassed, Emma added, "I saw you watching from the landing."

Consuelo's voice was crisp. "I did not wish to attend. London holds nothing for me. I only wish to see my cousin's daughters with good husbands."

Knowing she had stepped over the line, Emma sought to make amends. She desperately wanted Consuelo to like her. Forcing a laugh, she said, "I believe Francine met her Prince Charming. He stood for dancing with her at least five times. After that, I lost count."

"More than two dances announces the gentleman's intention of paying his addresses," His Grace said. "That be the case, a half-dozen will this day be on your doorstep, my love."

"I should hope so," said Consuelo. "Emma should have a choice before settling for your pursuit."

His Grace challenged the remark. "I don't see that, Consuelo. Emma is my betrothed. When Lord Harthgrow offers for Francine, and with her dowry I think that will be soon, then Emma and I shall be wed. Being a loving sister, my love only wishes to see Francine settled before seeking happiness for herself."

But Consuelo was adamant. "I am still of the opinion that you should step aside, Ashton, and let Emma choose for herself."

Emma threw up her hands. "Would both of you stop arguing over me as if I were a haunch of beef. I am perfectly capable of making my own decision. For a long time I have thought I would never become leg-shackled, and I've many times said that I'm too set in my ways, and, at three and twenty, too old to change." She looked at His Grace. "But after Francine and Lord Harthgrow are wed, I will take your offer into consideration, Ashton. I think we spoke on this once before."

Just then Francine and Prudence entered the breakfast

room. Following close behind was Countess Lankford, who looked as if the party last night had been a little too much for her.

Consuelo immediately enquired of her health. "Tis a fact," the Countess said. "I don't feel well, and, Consuelo, I think it is fair time you think upon chaperoning the girls. Mayhaps the two of us can get them through the season."

Again the room became quiet, and Consuelo's chin formed that indomitable line. Emma watched, and wanted to go put her arms around her and tell her that she did not have to face the Ton if she did not want to. But she did not do this, for she suspected that Countess Lankford was playing a game, forcing Consuelo out of her shell, and mayhaps it was true that Consuelo had hidden at Craigmont long enough.

"I have no right to interfere," Emma said, *sotto voce*, and she turned her attention to Francine and Prudence, complimenting them both on their dresses. Francine's soft pink muslin was especially charming.

Emma asked her, "Are you expecting Lord Harthgrow to call?"

"We are going to ride in Hyde Park at five today, and tonight we will attend the Opera," Francine answered.

"I think that is wonderful, Francie. Just think, you only had to be seen to be claimed, which speaks well of your looks, and of your comportment."

Francine ladled food from the sideboard into her plate. "Stuff! I think His Lordship is desperate."

"Desperate? What do you mean?" Emma asked.

"He has already asked for my hand in marriage, and he hardly knows me. He says he will speak with you soon."

Emma could not have been more pleased. "Love at first sight. How utterly thrilling."

Obviously bored with the subject of love, Prudence

240

spoke up, looking at Consuelo, "May we this day visit Mama again?"

"It has not been a week yet, dear Prue, and the nurse taking care of your mama suggested we come only once a week."

"Then mayhaps we can call at Carlton House and take Princess Charlotte for a ride, mayhaps sneak her off to see her mama."

"Prue!" Emma exclaimed. "You won't sneak anyone off anywhere."

"I will send a missive to Lady de Clifford this day."

And it was left at that, to be settled later in the day.

His Grace rose from his chair, touched his lips with his serviette, then placed it on the table by his plate. He addressed Emma directly, "I shall make a quick call at my office, and then I shall return."

"Whatever for?" she asked.

"To protect what is rightfully mine. When Sir Arthur Stewart calls, and no doubt he will, I shall be waiting in the receiving room . . . by your side."

"Nothing is rightfully yours," Emma argued, but realizing the uselessness of words, she turned her attention to the cold food on her plate and ate silently. It was enough for her to know that Francine was on the verge of being settled for life.

## Chapter Twenty

"You were very charming last night, and very beautiful," His Grace said. True to his word, he had returned shortly to Number Ten Park Place, to sit beside Emma in the first-floor receiving room, guarding what was "rightfully his."

"More like a dog guarding a bone," Emma told him after he had stubbornly refused to relinquish his seat to any of the twelve gentlemen callers who found their way to the door, and this included Sir Arthur Stewart, who had come with two dozen red roses spilling out of his arms.

"You're a little shy of the appropriate number," His Grace told him. "Lady Emma deserves more than a mere two dozen of anything." He inclined his head toward a nearby table so covered with yellow roses that one could not see the beautiful Wedgwood vase that held them. His Grace reached and plucked a rose, then, holding his hand up, palmed it. "Your roses are of inferior quality. Just look at this yellow beauty, as large as my hand."

"Demme you," Sir Arthur said. "That was your valet following me when I went to the flower shop, and after I made my purchase he sought to best it."

With that, Sir Arthur Stewart gathered his roses into his arms and left, with His Grace's laughter sounding in his ears.

When the door slammed behind him, the butler smiled,

and Emma prayed that the floor would break open and swallow her up.

There were women callers, as well, and they left no doubt that they were there for the purpose of seeing the Duke.

"He never gives one a chance at him," one said to Emma.

And another, "His Grace has always been too busy for social calls. Until now."

Another gave a little laugh. "Lady Winslow, you must have worked magic on him."

Emma smothered a laugh. The gels' eyes were actually dilated, and their mamas' worse yet.

"Mayhaps he is just discovering how exciting morning callers can be," Emma said.

His Grace leaned back and stretched his long legs out in front of him; then, looking lovingly at Emma, said, "Actually, I'm only available for Lady Winslow. After her London Season, which every gel should have, we plan to wed—"

Emma straightened. "That is not so . . . what I mean is . . . we've only discussed the possibility."

But the damage had been done, and Emma knew it. The gels and their mamas promptly jumped up and began curtsying to the Duke and sputtering their goodbyes.

Gork, the staid butler, waiting in the foyer, opened the huge double doors, then closed them quietly behind the departing guests, a smile as big as all of London on his face.

And so went the first day after Emma's come-out ball. Francine was receiving in another room, and Emma was anxious to hear about her day, most especially about Lord Harthgrow. She asked His Grace to excuse her and went to speak with her sister, stopping at the door of the appointed room, watching unobtrusively.

Francine sat on a settee, chatting with the circle of guests, mostly gentlemen, who were drinking tea and eating scones from a huge silver tray. Flowers filled the room, and the conversation was directed at Francine. As if she had been receiving morning callers all her life, she answered with finesse the questions she wanted to answer, and dodged cleverly those she did not wish to answer. She drank her tea delicately.

Standing behind Francine was Lord Harthgrow.

As Emma watched, he smiled proudly down onto the top of Francine's red-blond head, fondly twined a finger into one of the curls, while shaking his head in agreement with whatever she was saying.

Still unnoticed, Emma turned away, and she asked herself why the Duke could not be more like Lord Harthgrow, instead of always arguing with her and kissing her. In short, acting like a rutting sheep. *Something only a country gel would recognize,* she thought. And, of course, when His Grace acted *that* way, she could not help but respond in like manner, and she should not blame herself for doing so.

His Grace had repaired to his book room and was reading one of his leather-bound books when he heard a delicate knock on his door. Looking up, he saw Consuelo standing in the doorway. He was pleased. He loved his mother dearly, as long as she did not act like a Ton mother, which he could not forebear. He smiled at her, rose to his feet, and went and took her hand, kissing it in a very gentlemanlike manner.

"Consuelo, I am pleased to see you," he said, and when she responded, calling him Ashton, he knew she was in a conciliatory mood. She was very well aware that he preferred being addressed by his given name. She only used His Grace when she was out of sorts with him.

"Ashton, I have something to discuss with you." She paused for a moment. "In truth, there are two things which need your attention."

His Grace could not imagine what she was talking about.

Surely they had laid to rest his desire to marry Lady Winslow. After inviting her to sit he returned to his chair. Consuelo sat in a matching chair, facing him.

The noonday sun streamed through a window, making shadows on the Turkey carpet, and on the rich patina of ceiling-high bookcases filled with well-read books.

"What is it?" he asked.

"First, I must tell you that Countess Lankford has taken to her bed. She does not look sick to me, so I believe she is contriving to have me accompany Emma and Francine to Almack's next Wednesday evening. I would like you to speak to her."

"And tell her she is not ill? Consuelo, I cannot do that. Besides, I think it is a capital idea that you sit in the dowager's circle at Almack's, like other sponsors, smiling proudly upon your chicks while they dance and flirt with the gentlemen of the Ton." His Grace's smile faded, and his demeanor became serious. "No harm can be done. What you feared most happened many years ago."

He remembered too well the night his father's body was found, the despair that Consuelo had suffered.

"They could dig up the past. The truth could hurt you."

"No, never. Do not let that affect your life. I'm ready for the truth to be told. I am proud of what my father did. I am only sorry it ended so tragically for you."

"Losing him was a tragedy, but I survived because I had you."

His Grace went to her again and patted her shoulder, then walked to the window and looked out. Below on prestigious Park Place, high-stepping horses, pulling crested and elegant carriages, passed on the cobbled street. The sound drifted upward, even the sound of a whip cracking over the horses's backs split the still air. He turned back into the room. "Go to Almack's. I will be there, with Emma."

245

His Grace thought of inquiring again as to why she disliked his future bride, but this was Consuelo's audience; she had come to him with two things on her mind. He would not deter her.

"I will think on going to Almack's," she said.

His Grace was pleased. "Now, for the second thing you wished to discuss with me."

" 'Tis about Prudence's mother, Countess Winslow. After taking Prudence to see her, I wrote to the wonderful doctor you brought from France, inquiring of his prognosis of the Countess. This day, I received his answer, and it is not encouraging. He doubts that the Countess will ever be able to live in the outside world again. It seems her nerves are shattered."

His Grace frowned. From what he had learned from Charles Winslow before his untimely death, His Grace had feared this to be the case. He said, "Little Prudence is advanced far beyond her years. She will accept it."

"Oh, no," Consuelo quickly said. "I approached the subject, and she was adamant. She never forgets to pray, and God *will* answer her prayers, she says. I cannot destroy the child's faith by telling her what Dr. Reneau said."

"Then let time tell her the truth. Little by little she will learn that her mother cannot be well, and gradually she will come to accept it."

A huge sigh escaped Consuelo. "That relieves me of the burden of having to tell her, I suppose. I needed reassurance from you." She rose from her chair and made her way to the door, where she turned back. "There is one other thing, Ashton. Could you speak to His Majesty about Charlotte seeing her mother? This bothers Prudence immensely."

"I had planned to go to Windsor this afternoon on another matter," His Grace said. And later, he did go, returning with bad news about the King. He had heard the rumors, but he had gone to Windsor to hear for himself, and during a long audience with Her Majesty Queen Charlotte, he had been told the awful truth, his beloved King George III was permanently mad. The Prince of Wales would rule England as Prince Regent. His Grace knew that this would expedite a great surge of spending by the Prince. Upon returning to London, he went to White's, which was his custom when he wanted reaction to an event. The Gentleman's Club was solemn, almost quiet, and not once did he hear King George III referred to as the eh what King. "He was a good King," one said in a sad voice. Another, then another echoed the same sentiment. In a way, this comforted Ashton deFleury.

His Grace then returned to Number Ten Park Place to impart the news that permission had been granted by the old Begum that Princess Charlotte could visit her mother once weekly, and that a two-hour weekly visit to her grandmother, the Duchess of Brunswick, would be allowed.

"That is wonderful news, Ashton, and you are given due credit," Consuelo said.

His Grace's reply was modestly given, "No, it was decided before I went to Windsor. It was one of the old King's last lucid requests."


A missive came the next day from Lady de Clifford, saying, although it was against her better judgment, indeed a little unhealthy, she felt, Princess Charlotte would be going to Spring Gardens to see her grandmother, and there she would also visit with her mother. Would Consuelo and Prudence please come to Carlton House and accompany them to Spring Gardens? she asked.

Prudence danced around the room and hugged Consuelo with abandonment. "I want to see my new friend again, but more important, she will see her mama," she said.

Consuelo felt buoyant. She loved seeing Prudence happy, and she thought about the transformation the child had brought into her life. She was an angel, so good and kind to everyone.

So the next day Consuelo and Prudence set out in the Duke's crested carriage for Carlton House. She had heard so much about the Prince's London home and now she would see it. She had many times seen the Prince's Pavilion in Brighton, and had thought it gaudy. In her reticule she had placed a parchment and pen so that, in private moments, she could write down what she saw, lest she forget and could not repeat it accurately. This surprised Consuelo about herself. Why would she be interested in Prinny's home, when she had visited King George and Queen Charlotte at Windsor?

"I suppose because there has been so much written about Prinny's extravagance that I am just curious," she said to herself, and when Prudence asked her what she had said, Consuelo explained her curiosity, and Prudence laughed.

"Let's go by Gunther's and get a sweet," Prudence said.

"That's a capital idea."

Consuelo, being in a high good mood, gave the direction to a footman to pass on to the coachman.

Gunther, the great confectioner, ran his business in Berkeley Square, and when the horses were pulled to a stop in front of the establishment, Consuelo thought to send a footman for their treats. But Prudence would have none of that. She hopped down onto the street and reached a hand to Consuelo. "Come on, Miss deFleury, half the fun is smelling *all* the treats. I used to come here with Mama."

It was not until they were inside Gunther's that Consuelo realized they were breaking propriety. A lady of quality does not appear in a business establishment without a lady's maid, or an abigail, the Ton strictures read. She shrugged her shoulders and laughed, for she was having more fun than she had had in a long, long time. Not one person recognized her, so she was spared embarrassing questions. In truth, she did not remember that she was supposed to be afraid until she and Prudence were back in the carriage and the horses were clopping along on the street. Prudence had begged to purchase an apricot tart for Princess Charlotte, and Consuelo had gladly paid for it.

They were soon at Carlton House and, to Consuelo's chagrin, were taken to a side entrance where doors were opened by a footman, who bowed low and with much dignity. He then took them to the Princess's apartment and announced them in.

"I wanted to see the state apartments, the fabulous dining room, and the Throne Room," Consuelo said to Lady de Clifford when they were alone.

Lady de Clifford looked taken aback, as if no one had ever before made such a request. "I will see what I can do."

Just then Charlotte came skipping out of another room and nearly collided with a table in her excitement. She still listed to one side, Consuelo noticed.

The girls fell upon each other's necks, both talking at once. Prudence gave the Princess the apricot tart and she ate it in two bites.

"Your manners are lacking," said Lady de Clifford, and Charlotte licked her fingers.

"Old Cliffy doesn't like me," Charlotte whispered to Prudence when they were alone. "She's afraid I will be like my mama. And I hope I am. Mama is wonderful. She loves me . . ."

The carriage they rode in was unmarked. " 'Tis the newspeople," Lady de Clifford explained. "Once they get wind that the Princess is to visit her mother weekly, they will publish it, and there will be no end to the people gathered around Princess Charlotte. She will be Queen someday, there not being another heir. And there never will be, not with that dreadful . . ."

She stopped, for Charlotte had turned her attention from Prudence to listen. Lady de Clifford then went on, in a different vein. "Princess Charlotte is very popular with all of England."

"Then what would be wrong with the common folk seeing their future sovereign?" Consuelo asked.

"The Prince objects."

That ended the discussion, and Consuelo did not want to pursue it further, not within hearing of Charlotte's sharp little ears. Consuelo was aware of the Prince's unpopularity with the populace, and she imagined he was jealous of his daughter's popularity. As they rode along, the Princess waved and smiled to the people on the street, and once she demanded the carriage be stopped so she could help a little boy who had fallen.

When the carriage stopped in front of a dingy old house in New Street, Consuelo was appalled. This was no residence for a Princess. Why, the Duchess of Brunswick, Charlotte's maternal grandmother, as sister to King George III had once been the Princess Royal of England.

But the Duchess made the dingy house a palace, Consuelo was soon to learn. With only two attendants, she received with dignity the homage due to her rank.

She greeted her granddaughter without a trace of affection, but that was not so with Charlotte's mother, who flew at the child, knocking her yellow straw hat from her head. "Darling daughter," she said, over and over, and the look on the little Princess's face melted Consuelo's heart.

It was plain that in her mother's arms Charlotte felt loved. It did not matter that the mother's actions were a little wild, or that her enormous black curly wig was askew, or that too much rouge painted her cheeks, or that white lead made her face look ghostly.

250

The two hours went by quickly. Consuelo, Prudence, and de Clifford, not wanting to cut in on Princess Charlotte's time with her mother and grandmother, waited in an adjoining room, but not out of sight. Seeing the interaction between mother and daughter brought a huge lump to Consuelo's throat, and tears showed on Prudence's pink cheeks.

Not so with de Clifford. She plainly resented every minute of the two hours. "I live in fear that the Princess will be like her mad mother," she said, and she stated further that it was her duty to see that Princess Charlotte was properly trained to be Queen. "Your little Prudence, Consuelo, she is a good influence on Charlotte, so proper and well mannered. It's almost as if she was sent to us."

Consuelo responded without thinking, "Prudence has such faith," and then she looked at Prudence and wondered *why* the child had come into her life when she had needed her most. And Emma and Francine, their coming had been a blessing.

*God works in mysterious ways,* she thought, and she whispered to herself, "God must have sent them."

In the same breath Consuelo scoffed at her own words and thoughts. It had been a long, long time since she had beseeched the higher power for a favor, so why would He send someone to her?

## Chapter Twenty-one

On this morning Consuelo rose early, finished her toilette quickly, then ordered her breakfast sent to her quarters. She had not slept well. She had dreamed of things best forgotten.

Something had been on her mind for several days, and she could not dismiss it. Past experience had taught her that only important things nagged her when she was asleep. Not even breakfast, her favorite meal, calmed her. Pushing the tray aside, she said to her lady's maid, "Maydean, send for a footman and have him order a carriage for me, and not one with the Duke's crest. I shall be leaving shortly." After a pause, "And I don't wish my going out alone discussed with the other servants."

Maydean pulled a pouty face. "Do you think I would tell m'lady's business?"

"Yes, I do. Now scat and do what I asked. Offer no explanation to the footman. With luck, I shall return and no one will know I've been gone."

Consuelo doubted that. She had dealt with servants too long; they thrived on gossip, at least the ones at Craigmont did, and the simple fact that she left her son's Townhouse alone, and without explaining where she was going, would be grist for their gossip mill.

The maid left, and Consuelo pulled a handsome dark blue straw hat with a high crown and wide brim down over her white hair. The hat matched her dress, which was made of dark blue lawn imprinted with tiny red roses, green stems, and leaves. Her only jewelry was a diamond-encrusted shoulder brooch from which her lorgnette hung on a ribbon. She had purposely chosen the dress, and the brooch, for simplicity. She was perplexed at her nervousness, but never before had she meddled in anyone else's life, except that of her sons when she had tried in vain to get him leg-shackled so he could produce grandchildren. Well, she had failed at that, and she prayed for better luck this time.

Consuelo had finished dressing when Maydean returned and said the carriage was waiting at a side entrance. " 'Tis proper that I accompany you, m'lady," the maid said.

"A pox on what's proper. I shall go alone, and I expect you to stay in these rooms until I return, without the company of other servants. That way, there will be no chance of gossip."

Consuelo took up her reticule, then reached for a dark-blue, painted silk fan and made her way to the carriage. She must needs have something in her hand. She scolded herself again for being apprehensive, and she thought that mayhaps it was because she was not entirely sure how Emma would feel if she, Consuelo, should succeed. But she had thought about it, had even prayed about it, and was led to believe that the path she had chosen was right.

These thoughts ran through Consuelo's mind while the carriage rolled through Regent's Park, on her way to the hospital where Prudence's mother was being kept, and when the driver pulled the horses to an abrupt stop in front of a white building with a wraparound porch, there was no more time to worry. A missive to Dr. Reneau had preceded her, and he now stood on the porch waiting for her.

He was a small man, with dark hooded eyes, and although young, his shock of black hair was already turning gray. He spoke English fluently, but with a heavy French accent.

He reached out a hand and took hers, bowing slightly. "Miss deFleury, I received your missive and am in a quandary as to what could be so urgent. Am I being dismissed for my rather pessimistic report on Countess Winslow?"

"No, of course not. I expected nothing less than the truth from you. It is another matter on which I wish your opinion."

The doctor looked puzzled. "What —"

"May we sit?"

"Of course. I beg your forgiveness." He stepped back and opened the door, and by gesticulating with his hand, invited her into the receiving room. Then he entered a room which could be nothing other than his office, Consuelo concluded, and she followed.

"The fainting bench is for Countess Winslow. She can either sit or lie, whichever she prefers," Dr. Reneau said.

After they were seated, he behind a large rosewood desk, and she in a chair facing him, he smiled and was very silent. His eyes seemed to twinkle with life.

"I've come to ask a very large favor of you. Your prognosis for the Countess is very grave. In truth, you have little hope that she will ever be entirely well."

"That is right. She has long periods of silence through which I cannot penetrate."

Consuelo took a deep breath. "Would it be possible that she be moved to Craigmont, my home near Brighton, with your coming, too, presiding there as resident physician?"

A frown knitted the doctor's brow. "That is a strange request. As you know, it would be a great responsibility financially and otherwise for you. May I ask your interest? She is not a relative?"

"In a way, yes. She was married to the son of my distant cousin, both deceased. But that is not the reason for my request. It is the Countess's daughter, Prudence. She is a bright girl, far advanced for her years, and she is happy . . . with one exception. She wants so very much to be with her mother. At Craigmont that would be possible. Not all the time, of course, if you thought it best not, but each day they could be together for short periods, to walk on the beach, or to sit in the rose garden. I cannot help but believe it would be best for the Countess, as well as for Prudence."

Reneau was quiet for a long while. Consuelo could almost hear his thoughts marching back and forth through his mind; his breath came in short spurts. Finally, leaning back in his chair, he said, "Have you thought of the expense? It would mean my giving up a lucrative practice in Paris. I agreed to come to New Hope for only a short time."

"I am aware of that, and I fear when that time is up the Countess will regress. I understand that she no longer takes to her bed for days at a time. Yes, I have thought of the expense, and I have come upon a plan I think will work. I have considerable income in my own right, and my son, His Grace Ashton deFleury, the Duke of Attlebery, owns a fleet of cargo ships. I am sure he would not bat an eye at the expense, but I prefer to do this on my own. Don't worry about your fee. When you come to Craigmont, I have something to show you, something I've been hiding for years. The treasure is yours if you will only do this thing."

The doctor's keen eyes studied Consuelo for a long silent while, and then he shook his head in the affirmative. "I, too, have great interest in this patient. I will give it a year, no more."

Consuelo, satisfied, stood and told the doctor goodbye, with the promise she would contact him again when she knew when she would return to Craigmont. In the meantime she would bring Prudence to see the Countess weekly as had been recommended.

"Please do," Dr. Reneau said. "Countess Winslow showed encouraging improvement after her daughter's first visit."

This lifted Consuelo's spirits considerably. Her trip to New Hope had been a success. Now she would tell Emma, and after that, impart the good news to Prudence. Consuelo found herself smiling when she anticipated seeing the look of joy on the child's face when she learned about the new arrangements.

Now, another problem faced Consuelo, that of chaperoning Emma and Francine to Almack's Assembly on Wednesday evening, two days hence. Countess Lankford was still moping, saying she did not feel well and insisting that Consuelo go in her stead. And His Grace had said he thought she should go. *Mayhaps he is right. Like the hidden treasure, I've been in hiding long enough.*

London did not appeal to Consuelo, and she craved to return to Craigmont. But since she had come, she mused, she should do her part to launch Ladies Francine and Emma Winslow into society. She wondered why years ago it had hurt so much when the Ton had cut her. Now, if only Francine's future could be settled. And Emma's. *Ashton will not let Emma be courted by anyone besides himself,* she thought, smiling behind her fan. She was cognizant that several suitors had called and had been run off by His Grace.

In front of Number Ten Park Place, Consuelo saw four carriages at the curb, as had been the usual since the come-out ball. She did not see Ashton's tilbury and was glad. She wanted to speak to Emma alone, if she were not engaged with foolish morning callers.

A footman helped her alight from the carriage, and inside the house she observed Francine in the receiving room, with a circle of callers sipping tea and eating scones. Lord Harthgrow was at his usual place, standing behind Francine and fingering her hair.

Consuelo asked the butler, "Gork, is Lady Emma receiving?"

"No, Madame, I believe she returned to her rooms after a late breakfast."

Consuelo went directly to the second floor, knocked on Emma's door, then entered in response to Emma's invitation. She had in mind dismissing Van Winters if she were there.

Emma was alone, sitting by the window, embroidering. Consuelo laughed. "What are you doing?"

Emma threw the small piece of cloth stretched over a silver frame down, and stood. "I'm learning to embroider."

"Whatever for? It does not fit you."

"I know. Miss Van Winters said that you thought me to be a bluestocking, and I wanted to prove I could be a Ton lady."

"But you don't want to be a Ton lady."

"I can't think of anything worse than sitting around doing fancy stitching all days and scavenging for a husband at night . . . and I must not forget, receiving inane callers when they have on-dits to pass on . . . and being preoccupied with what to wear and changing clothes two or three times a day."

Emma sat back down, and Consuelo sat in a chair near her.

"Oh, I beg your forgiveness, I should have asked you to sit," Emma said. "This day, my manners seem to have left me."

As if she had not spoken, Consuelo went on, "You much prefer reading books, or the morning papers, learning what Parliament thinks is best for the populace? Do you not?"

257

"Or driving over Fernwood's fields to see the crops growing."

"Well, dear, Fernwood is lost to you forever. You must needs accept that which you cannot change. But there is nothing wrong with being a bluestocking. There are men who prefer gels with brains."

"I don't singularly care what men prefer. It is not my wish to marry."

"But you will."

"Why do you say that? *I* have control over my life."

*Oh, but I don't,* Emma thought.

Consuelo looked straight into Emma's face. "Ashton wants to marry you, and I've never known him to fail in getting what he wants. Even though I have told him that marriage to you would be a misalliance."

Emma was suddenly defensive. "Why do you say that?"

"I have my reasons," Consuelo answered. She lifted a quizzical brow; she wanted Emma to go on and reveal her *true* feelings, but Emma was silent. So Consuelo approached the subject she had come to discuss, and she saw no reason not to state bluntly what she had done. "Lady Winslow, I have made arrangements to have Countess Margaret Winslow removed to Craigmont."

Emma leaned forward in her chair. "You have what?"

"The Countess will live at Craigmont, and Dr. Reneau, the wonderful doctor that Ashton secured from Paris, will reside there also, for a year. He has agreed."

Anger washed over Emma. Prudence was her late brother's child; *she* would decide what would be done, not Consuelo deFleury.

"I plan to keep Prudence with me—"

Consuelo did not let her finish. "At Craigmont, the precious child can see her dear mama every day. You know, as I do, that her little heart pines for this. And I cannot help but believe it will be the best thing for the Countess, and

Prudence will have as nearly as possible a normal existence. She will, of course, continue her studies with her tutor."

*But why do I feel that my life has been snatched away from me, that someone else is in charge?* Emma thought. She had no choice but to agree. She could appeal to His Grace, but he would most likely pile more guilt on her by saying that it was a capital idea, and then he would castigate himself for not suggesting it to Consuelo. Emma did not know where the blunt was coming from for this extravagant plan, and she did not care. Setting her chin in an indomitable line, she said, "I wish you luck, Consuelo. I will miss little Prue, but I cannot be selfish. I know how very much Prudence craves to be with her mother, and she is fortunate to have you make these wonderful arrangements."

"Thank you, Emma," Consuelo said.

Looking closely, Emma saw something she had never seen before, the look of satisfaction of someone who had done something wonderful. Not only was the sadness gone from Consuelo's large hazel eyes, they were positively glowing. This made Emma feel good.

Consuelo rose to go. At the door she turned back and said, "Countess Lankford claims she is too ill to attend the Assembly Ball at Almack's this Wednesday evening with you and Francine. I will go in her stead."

Emma stared unbelieving at her, then lied through her teeth, "I am happy for that," and when the door had closed, she drew in a deep breath, picked up the embroidery hoop, and slung it across the room. And then she did not deny her tears. Another evening ruined by Consuelo raining her dislike on her.

Meanwhile, Consuelo continued down the hall, then climbed the stairs to the next floor and went to Prudence's room, where she found her and her tutor, their heads bent over a book.

Prudence jumped up exuberantly and ran to her. The tutor looked disgruntled by the interruption but left when Consuelo asked to have a private moment with Prudence.

"What is it, Miss deFleury?" Prudence asked. "Do you have word about mama? May we go today to see her?"

"Yes, I do have word about your Mama," Consuelo said. She sat down and took Prudence onto her lap. It seemed strange. So many years had passed since she had held a child close. Taking a deep breath, she began, and when she was through, Prudence's little arms were locked around her neck and her wet cheek was pressed against hers.

"Oh, Miss deFleury you are the most wonderful woman in the world . . . besides Mama, and Auntie Em . . . and maybe Francie."

Although a lump the size of an egg had formed in Consuelo's throat, she managed a laugh. Her heart felt as if it would at any moment burst inside her. She hugged Prudence fiercely and released a torrent of tears, until they dripped from her cheeks, and Prudence wiped them away with the palms of her little hands.

Finally, Consuelo said, "I'm in very good company when you compare me with your dear mama, and your aunts."

"I knew God would answer my prayers, I just knew it," Prudence said. "Before Mama got so sick, she taught me to pray in Jesus's name, and she read from the Bible that if we have the faith the size of mustard seed, our prayers will be answered. My faith is as big as a mountain. God will make Mama well by next Easter."

A shiver passed over Consuelo. She recalled vividly Dr. Reneau's discouraging prognosis. She did not know how to explain to an eight-year-old that moving the Countess to Craigmont did not mean the Countess would be well before next Easter, maybe never; it just meant that mother and daughter would see each other more often, and that the

Countess would continue to get expert care from Dr. Reneau.

*I can't promise more than that.*

"Prue," Consuelo said, then stopped for a long moment to measure her words. They had to be just right. "To have your Mama close, and to be with her a part of each day, will be a miracle. Maybe that is the most God can give you."

Prudence shook her head in exasperation. "God does not do *anything* halfway. Miss deFleury, you are just like Auntie Em, you don't have enough faith."


On Wednesday when they were going to Almack's assembly rooms, Emma listened to Francine's chatter about the wonderful "London Season," and to Prudence's happy talk about the wonderful news about her mama moving to Craigmont.

Prudence had visited Countess Winslow at New Hope a second time, and had been allowed to tell the Countess the good news. Now, Prudence could not stop talking about it. And there was something else she was excited about. She and Consuelo had gone for another visit with Countess Charlotte at Carlton House, and this time they had been shown the state apartments, and the throne room, and the elaborate chandeliers.

"They were so beautiful, and the Princess is the most sympathetic and generous person," Prudence said. " 'Tis little wonder the people love her." Emma hugged Prudence and told her she was happy that her life had taken a turn for the better. And she meant it, for the image of the lost little girl coming to Fernwood with her small satchel was ever in Emma's vision.

That same day, she listened to Hannah read, the result of Prudence's teaching. "I never dreamed I could learn to read, and she won't allow me to say yer for you. So if I forget, will you help me, m'lady, and remind me that I am to speak correctly?"

Emma said she would and had laughed with the loyal little maid who had stopped tasting her food to see if it was poisoned.

Now, it was time to dress for the Assembly Ball. Curiosity was the bigger part of Emma's anticipation. Her gown, as all of her wardrobe had been, was singularly spectacular. Without ringing for Van Winters she slipped it over her head, looked into the looking glass, and gasped. It was made of very soft rose silk, and rosebuds of the same color rimmed the low decollette. Tiny puffed sleeves barely covered her shoulders.

Satin ribbons made tiny bows under the high waist and fell to the gown's hem. Matching slippers, with satin rosebuds, graced her slender feet.

An ivory stick, encrusted with jewels, held the rose silk fan she would carry, on loan from Consuelo.

She then rang for Van Winters to dress her hair and was quite adamant about how she wanted it to look. There would be a mass of curls atop her head, and corkscrew ringlets would frame her face. The gel staring at His Grace the day they had ridden in Hyde Park had the same look, matter not that His Grace had said she was a courtesan.

The frown on Van Winters's face told Emma that she did not approve, that it was too daring, and the frown grew more fierce when Emma told her she wanted to blacken her brows.

"What in the world for? Your brows and lashes are as black as His Grace's black horses's tail."

Emma ignored Van Winters's protest, and suddenly had a notion to shock the maid even more. "And I think I would like more rouge."

An exasperated sigh was the maid's answer. She pursed

her lips and set to work. When she was through, Emma giggled and felt quite sophisticated.

"I hope His Grace approves," Van Winters said, shaking her head doubtfully.

"And Consuelo? Do you think she will approve?" Emma asked, and the maid answered resignedly, "Only time will tell."

Emma dismissed Van Winters and sat down to wait to be summoned to come belowstairs.

But instead of waiting for her belowstairs, as was usual, His Grace this night came to her rooms and knocked lightly on the door. Emma bade the knocker come in and was surprised to see His Grace standing there. She anxiously searched his face for a reaction but could not discern if the look was of approval, or if he was in total shock. He took her hand and kissed it, and for a moment she thought he would kiss her. But he stepped back and let his gaze move up and down over her body. She heard him catch his breath.

"Your gown is lovely," he said, rather wistfully, without his wry, charming smile.

She was pleased with the way he looked, so handsome in his evening attire, so debonair. But too demme sure of himself, she mused. Gallantly, he offered her his arm, and she hooked her arm through it and they walked together down the curving stairs and across the foyer to the big double doors, held open by the butler. Gork then bowed and handed His Grace his *chapeau bras,* which he folded and placed under his free arm, thanking the butler.

In the crested carriage His Grace sat on the banquette beside Emma, with Consuelo and Francine sitting across from them. The lanterns were burning, showing luxurious royal blue velvet squabs. And the clothes they were wearing took Emma's breath away. It was all too much for her.

Consuelo was dressed to the first stare, in a bloodred

263

gown shot with platinum. The straight skirt was pulled to a bustle in the back. The red gown contrasted sharply with Consuelo's white hair. Very becoming, Emma thought, and the nervousness Consuelo had exuded earlier had seemingly disappeared. Her conversation was lively. The new gas lights that lined the street were absolutely amazing to her. "What a change since last I was here," she said.

She then changed the subject entirely, "I will never wear one of those horrid turbans the dowagers wear while sitting around in a circle watching their charges dance. How singularly silly."

"I hope you will allow me to stand for a dance with you," His Grace said.

Consuelo laughed. "I predict that you will spend the evening fighting the young bloods off Lady Emma. Your future bride is extremely lovely this night. After this, all of London will be on her doorstep. You will most likely have to call half of them out to stop their suit."

That was the first reference Consuelo had made to Emma as His Grace's "future bride," and Emma wondered about the change. It could not be that Consuelo deFleury had suddenly thought her acceptable for her *only* son.

"Please," Emma said, "let me fight off my suitors. I've never been allowed the privilege."

Emma was referring to her late brother's refusal to allow gentlemen to pay their addresses to her when she was the desirable age to wed, and she was certain that by the intonation of her voice His Grace took her meaning.

His Grace frowned, but did not respond, and Emma turned her thoughts to Francine, who looked lovely in a gown of yellow satin. It seemed that Francine was a little subdued, or that her thoughts were elsewhere. Quite a departure from her earlier gay moods when she was dressed to the nines and going out. Emma wondered why Lord

Harthgrow had not offered for Francine, so strong was his suit.

In front of the assembly rooms in King Street, off St. James's, the driver jockeyed four handsome bays for position. Upon seeing the panels emboldened with the Duke's crest, other carriages moved, and the two footmen riding the back jumped quickly down and helped the passengers to alight. They were thanked properly by His Grace, and another highly liveried servant parted the crowd so that they might enter the rooms with the honor due a Duke. Inside, they were met by a very fashionably dressed woman.

"That is Lady Jersey," His Grace said, and he took the slender hand she held out to him. Even so, she managed to curtsy to him without dipping, all the time smiling right up into his face. Emma observed this with derision.

"Your Grace," Lady Jersey said, " 'tis such an honor to have you come to Almack's."

Emma wanted to spit.

Then His Grace made the introductions all round, with great aplomb, calling Emma his affianced. But before he could step forward and claim Emma, Sir Arthur Stewart stood before her asking permission to stand for the dance. Not waiting for an answer, he hurriedly swept her away from the Duke and out onto the dance floor. Stealing a backward glance, Emma saw the terrible glower on His Grace's face and laughed. Because of his past actions, she expected him to come raging out onto the floor and claim her, but he didn't. It was not until she had danced five dances with different gentlemen that he finally, and very politely, asked to stand for a dance.

It was a waltz, and he could dance it beautifully, Emma learned, as she followed his lead. Unlike the night on his ship, there was room for him to move, which he did gracefully, taking Emma with him. When they were halfway through the dance, she realized that other dancers had stopped dancing and were watching. Emma felt her face burn. Once she almost missed a step.

"Show them what a determined, stubborn, unforgiving country miss can do," His Grace whispered, and she did, for she forgot her feet and pondered on His Grace's remark. What a strange mood he was in. When the dance was over, he thanked her, then went to dance with Francine, who did not seem to be lacking for partners.

When he left Francine, he stood before Consuelo, who had been sitting in the dowagers' circle, watching through her lorgnette. Pride showed on her face, and she smiled up at Ashton when he asked her to dance, then followed him to the floor. After the Duke's obvious dismissal of Emma, bloods of the Ton, young and old, lined up to dance with her. She was danced with gracefully, stumbled over, told that she was beautiful, and fawned upon. So this is what His Grace had been protecting her from, she thought. But she found the attention exhilarating and let it show in her smile, and in her eyes. She even found that flirting came naturally, and several times she used her fan to advantage, as she had seen other gels do.

Time passed speedily by. As on the wings of a bird in flight, Emma thought, when at midnight, Consuelo and Francine came and said it was time to go. "Where is Ashton?" she asked. "I've not seem him for quite some time."

"He left over an hour ago," Consuelo said worriedly. "He asked Sir Arthur Stewart to escort us home."

Emma was shocked beyond bearing.


"Enough is enough," His Grace said as he whirled his brandy round in his glass. This was his third long drink since leaving Almack's assembly rooms and coming to his rented flat. Dodge, his valet, sat crunched sleepily in a chair, a blue robe wrapped around his portly figure. He had been jarred out of bed by His Grace's booming voice demanding he come talk with him.

"Enough is enough of what, Sir?" Dodge asked.

"I've had singularly enough of her flirting, batting those long eyelashes at men, like a frog in a hailstorm." He got up from his chair and started pacing. "You should have seen her, Dodge, and you should have seen the men lined up to dance with her—"

"You should have jerked her off the dance floor."

His Grace stopped in the middle of the room and glared at Dodge. "And taken her outside and kissed her until her knees were weak. I've tried that. I thought she cared a little. Her kisses seemed to say she did, but I was wrong. The kissing just awakened that certain something at the core of every woman . . . which they all deny, even to themselves."

"Well, now that 'tis awakened, it seems to me that all you have to do is feed it with more kisses."

His Grace went back to his chair, poured himself another brandy, and took a big gulp. Inside his breast, his heart was breaking. He did not like to give up, for defeat did not come easily to him . . . but tonight . . . tonight was beyond bearing. It had started when he went to her rooms to fetch her. Never had she looked so radiant, so alive, so determined. And then in the carriage when she said that she had never been given the chance to choose with whom she would dance, he had known that he had been wrong. She was not rightfully his. She never had been, but he had been too hardheaded, too . . . too obstinate, to listen.

"I'm letting her go," he said, as much to himself as to his valet. He wanted to hear the words, then mayhaps the pain would go away.

"You are not giving up! My advice to you—"

His Grace raised a hand. "Pray, spare me more advice. What you've given me heretofore has failed. But I was wrong from the start. I was wrong when I enticed her brother to the gaming tables. I knew he could not gamble. And I was equally wrong when I insisted that he promise me his sister's hand in marriage. But at the time, I did not see another way. I'd begged for an introduction."

"Mayhaps he tricked you into falling in love with her by extolling her virtues. Mayhaps that was his wish."

"Lord Charles was too naive to trick anyone. He sincerely believed that Emma was too stubborn to wed any man. A brother could love her, but not a husband, to whom she must needs be submissive." His Grace went on reliving the past. The walls had heard it before, and he did not care how many times Dodge had heard it. He would say it again.

"I've never wanted a submissive wife. I would be bored out of my skull. Emma is a bluestocking, erudite, independent to a fault, not enamored with society."

And then he added, almost wistfully, "Exactly what I wanted for a wife."

Dodge looked at him pityingly.

His Grace took another gulp of brandy, and the valet cautioned, "Sir, you are going to be as drunk as a wheelbarrow if you don't stop that swigging. May I suggest that tomorrow you call on the lady in question—"

"Never. She made it plain tonight that she never intended to marry me. I've never in the whole of my life been so humiliated," he raved, and he wasn't through. Jumping to his feet, he strode across the room, then back again, stopping only to blurt out more condemnation on his love.

"No one can claim that I cried off. She did it herself, for all to see. So I gave her to Lord Arthur Stewart. Let's see how he handles her stubbornness . . . and her unforgiving heart. I fear not so well. She is so angry with her brother there is no room in her heart for love."

"And you? What do you plan to do with all this love that has crippled you? Spit it out?"

"I'm going on the Grand Tour, and you are going with me. We'll take the *Lady Emma,* visiting ports of call. Until now, I've forgone all the pleasures other gentlemen have enjoyed. Mayhaps my time has come. I refuse to stay here and have my nose rubbed with Lady Winslow's flirtations."

"Mayhaps you can return in time to attend the Cyprians' Ball and choose another paramour," the valet said hopefully.

"I don't want another paramour. Not after loving Emma. She will always be my Easter Lady, for it was on that very special morning that I first saw her. Until then she had been only something I longed for, a hope, a dream."

And then His Grace added, "Demme that dream."

# Chapter Twenty-two

At Number Ten Park Place, in an upstairs salon, Consuelo deFleury and Countess Lankford were having a coze over steaming cups of tea. The Countess's health had improved drastically after the ball at Almack's, and Consuelo scolded her, "You were never poorly. Your aim was to get me to go to Almack's. Now admit it. You certainly use that cane to advantage, leaning on it when there's no need."

The Countess gave a hearty laugh. " 'Tis true. You have kept yourself hidden long enough, Consuelo. It's time you put your past behind you, and I am not speaking only of your shunning London."

"The past is never left behind," Consuelo quickly said. "It is with one always. But I agree that it is time that I no longer let it rule me. Ashton said as much." She stopped for a moment, then went on, "I've certainly learned that society is an empty shell. Years ago, I thought it so important."

"You didn't enjoy yourself at Almack's then?"

"Oh, my yes. And I was treated with great warmth from Lady Jersey. Of course that was because of Ashton having been made a Duke. Nobility is everything. They don't even seem to mind that he made his blunt from the trades."

For a long moment the Countess was silent, her brow

wrinkled as if in deep thought. Consuelo waited. She had known the Countess since before Ashton was born; they had gone together to Craigmont, and she could almost read her thoughts. She said to her, "You shouldn't be afraid to ask me anything. I won't think you are intruding."

"I want to word it carefully," answered the Countess. "I feel that I am treading on sacred ground, but are you still afraid?"

"No. As Ashton said, the worst that could happen has happened, and he no longer thinks that the truth could harm him." She gave a little laugh. "In truth, he was never afraid. But I feared for him."

"How you've kept the secret all these years, with only old King George knowing, is beyond me."

"And you knew. You were there when I needed someone with whom I could talk, someone I could trust. You are family, especially to Ashton."

"I guarded your secret with my life. There were times, after I moved into Town, when I wanted to blurt out that Ashton was *not* the King's by-blow, but I realized it was best the gossipers think so."

The conversation ended there, for a knock on the door and a servant entering with a missive brought the pleasant coze to an end. "The post just came, madame," the servant said.

The missive was from Dr. Reneau, and Consuelo opened it quickly. She read silently. When she was through, she looked at Countess Lankford. "I'm glad your health is much improved. I have to remove to Craigmont straight away. You must needs chaperone the gels."

"Why? What on earth has happened?"

"Dr. Reneau says that Prudence's mother has become agitated at the delay of leaving New Hope. This happened, it seems, after she was told that she and Prudence would be living at Craigmont. She has no reasoning, and her only

271

thought is to be with her precious daughter, wherever that might be. I think we should depart for Craigmont. To bring her here would be a mistake."

"I agree with you. It would not do for her to regress, and that could happen."

"We'll leave today. As soon as I can gather Prudence and the servants. Hannah will stay with Emma, I am sure. I will pen a missive to Dr. Reneau, telling him that he may follow with his patient two days hence. That will give us time to prepare Craigmont for their coming."

Consuelo quit the room immediately, and soon thereafter the household was in sixes and sevens. Every servant was drawn into packing and loading carriages. Emma did her part by helping Prudence prepare to leave. "Don't worry, Auntie Em," Prudence said as she ran about gathering her things, "Mama will hear my prayers."

And then Prudence penned a missive to her new friend, Princess Charlotte, and told her she hoped she could visit with her when the Princess again came to Brighton.

Emma would miss her niece terribly, she knew, and had Consuelo asked her to return to Craigmont with them, she would have done so without hesitation, leaving Francine to finish the Season. Or to do that which was inevitable— marry the nice Lord Harthgrow. Of course she, Emma, would return for the wedding.

These thoughts went through Emma's mind, but they did not materialize, for Consuelo did not ask her to return to Craigmont. Upon parting, she said to Emma, "Ashton is probably too busy for social activities at the moment. Mayhaps some big crisis with one of his ships. But I wager he will be on your doorstep, or rather on *his* doorstep, before another sunset."

Emma managed a smile, waving as the carriage pulled away from His Grace's townhouse. Another carriage, loaded with servants and baggage, followed close behind.

272

Emma was glad that Van Winters had chosen to return to Craigmont. She could do quite well with Hannah.

Emma felt lost when the carriage was out of sight, and the next week passed slowly. And still no Ashton. Sir Arthur Stewart was around more than Emma wanted, and she finally told him that his suit was hopeless. Other Ton gentlemen were turned away as well. She wanted so much to tell His Grace how terribly sorry she was for her behavior at Almack's. Her head had been turned, she would tell him, by so much attention, which was a new experience for her. Surely he would understand, she mused more than once, her feeling of remorse growing.

But she did not feel badly enough about her comportment to accept his *demand* that they marry as soon as Francine found a husband.

"If only he had not been so adamant about *his* wishes. If only he had realized that my brother had no right to barter my life away," she said to Countess Lankford, and then she told what had happened at Almack's, and how sorry she was for her flirting.

The retort was plainly spoken, "Gel, you never miss the water 'til the well goes dry. You should not have flirted with other blades right under his nose. Now, you most likely will pay the price. Ashton can be very stubborn when he gets his hackles up."

"I know very little about men," Emma said, and then she asked, "Will you go with me?"

"Go with you where, child?"

"To Upper Brook Street, his rented flat. I could write, but I'd much rather be looking him in the face when I apologize. I would go alone, but that would not be proper."

The Countess laughed, but underneath she felt sad, for, as she looked at Lady Winslow, she saw beneath her sophistication a kind heart that had been seared by life. When she had first seen His Grace's intended, that night on his luxury ship, she had thought her a proud, spirited beauty, but since coming to London, she had blossomed into a full-fledged beauty.

Little wonder the Duke was so terribly smitten, Countess Lankford thought. To Emma, she said, "What you are saying is that I may go along to make things proper, but that you would appreciate my finding a book to read in some obscure corner while you and Ashton talk."

Emma joined in her laughter. "Something like that. You are so wise."

"It comes with experience, Emma. I was married to a rakehell, but before he died I learned to wrap him around my finger. You must needs study the male animal if you wish to succeed."

Emma had heard about the Countess's turbulent marriage. "Do you miss him?" she asked.

"Of course I miss him. One misses a cold if it hangs on for years."

They laughed together and decided that if Ashton de-Fleury had not made an appearance by nightfall they would call on him.

"If we go during the day," the Countess said, "he will be at his office or at the docks where always one or more of his ships is being loaded. I don't think it a capital idea to go there."

"If he isn't home, we shall wait for him," Emma said determinedly, and the Countess smiled at her and shook her head.

"I believe I am looking at a gel in love."

"I am not in love," Emma said vehemently, adding, "I was wrong, and 'tis my wish to admit it."

They parted and Emma went to her rooms. She wanted to talk with Francine and sent Hannah to fetch her, but the maid returned and reported that Francine had gone out. So Emma took up her embroidery again, and again she became disgusted and threw it aside. Her thoughts went back to her brother, and like a coiled snake, simmering anger raised its head, even though Charles was dead. *Were it not for him, I would be at Fernwood.*

Emma admitted to missing the Duke. She no longer thought of him as ruthless; she had witnessed the good he had done, especially for little Prudence, and he had volunteered to dower Francine. Still, she wished her heart was lying dormant, as it had all those years at Fernwood.

Emma had a dreadful thought that His Grace might have left on one of his ships, going to India. She prayed that that would not be so, and she watched the clock for the time she would dress to go to him. There was time for tea and sandwiches, which she had a servant bring to her room. She sent for Francine the second time.

"Lady Francine is not in her rooms," Hannah said when she returned. "And her lady's maid is not about. I hear she has a thing for one of the grooms. She's probably at the stables."

"So be it," Emma told Hannah. "I'm going out. Will you please watch for Francine's return and tell her that I wish to visit with her this night before retiring. Most likely she is with Lord Harthgrow."

"I'll wait in her rooms, that way I won't miss her," Hannah said, leaving immediately.

There was nothing for it then but for Emma to get dressed, and long before it was time to meet the Countess belowstairs she stood before the looking glass admiring another new dress from her wardrobe, a deep blue sarcenet with tiny flowers embroidered on the sleeves and around the hem. Shamelessly she looked at her bosom pushed above the neckline and wondered what it would feel like to have His Grace press his hot lips against the white quivering flesh. With rocking clarity, she recalled his kisses and wanted so much for him to be there to kiss her again, and again, with that deep torturous feeling, nurturing that part of her body he had awakened. Tears blinded her, and she wiped them away with a delicate handkerchief with lace trim.

The need that His Grace had stirred inside her moved slowly over her body. Her flesh simmered, and hot blood suffused her face, and the rest of her body. An ache began in her thighs, pulling at the core of her.

Emma quickly quit the room and went belowstairs and sent a footman to tell the Countess she waited there. She did not like this; she did not like it at all. She must needs be at all times in control of her body, her mind, her needs. Most definitely she was not, she told herself, and fought to gain that which she had lost. Mayhaps after she had spoken to His Grace this terrible feeling of contriteness would leave her; mayhaps that terrible need to have him kiss her and hold her in his long strong arms would go away also.

Countess Lankford came soon, and they set off for His Grace's rented residence. A liveried coachman sat on the box, a footman rode the back. Emma and the Countess sank back into the velvet squabs, and neither spoke as London passed them in the twilight. Emma was glad for the silence. She barely noticed the houses they passed, the candles being lighted to push away the dark, or how they sparked the windows. Unlike His Grace's fabulous townhouse, the houses, for the most part, were plain, very ordinary.

The coachman pulled the horses to a stop in front of one such ordinary house, and Emma leaned forward to stare. Even in the growing darkness, she could see the sign on the door: "Fine apartment to let."

This could not be the place, she thought. But it was, she soon learned.

"Wait here," the Countess said when the footman let

down the step, and she went straight away and banged on the door with the knocker.

An upstairs window opened and a man in a nightshirt stuck his head out. "Air yer lookin' for a place to let?"

"No," the Countess answered. "We are in need of speaking with His Grace Ashton deFleury, the Duke of Attlebery."

"He ain't here. Left a week back."

"Where—"

"How am I to know? He didn't say." The window slammed shut on his words.

"Well, that's that," Countess Lankford said as she regained the carriage. "He's not here, and there's no sense in waiting."

"Where do you suppose he's gone?" Emma asked.

"Mayhaps to India. He's done it before, and sometimes six months would pass before anyone would know for sure. Consuelo grew used to his independence. Always though, the post would bring a missive . . . when His Grace took time to write. You will be hearing from him."

"What would happen if Consuelo needed him?" Emma asked.

"She could go to the business. Ashton's man there would know."

"Then, mayhaps we can go—"

The Countess reached to give Emma a pitying pat. "We cannot do that. He would not tell unless it was an emergency, and, Emma dear, an apology is not an emergency."

"I have no one to blame but myself," Emma said. Her thoughts were different. *How dare His Grace do this?* Her anger grew, and she told herself that tomorrow it would not be so important that she apologize. He most certainly did not deserve to know how she felt. Thus, with this resolve, she returned to Number Ten Park Place.

"I will put him out of my mind," she told the Countess.

"Tomorrow my need to say I'm sorry will not seem so important."

The Countess gave a doubtful smile.

Emma went on: "I must needs concentrate on Francine. I have been neglectful of her the past week. I've not even noticed who called, or with whom she left the house."

They parted, saying they would see each other at breakfast the next morning, and as Emma walked to her rooms, she pensively recalled that Francine had not sought her out to talk each day, as she had done in the past. Emma knew intuitively that something had gone terribly wrong. And she had been too busy with her own feelings to notice.

"Hannah," she said as she opened the door.

"Yes, m'lady."

The voice had a far-away dead sound, and Emma stepped quickly inside the room.

"What is it, Hannah? What's wrong?"

Hannah handed her a sealed envelope. "She's run away to Gretna Green."

Emma ripped at the envelope. "Run away? How do you know? The missive is sealed."

"Her lady's maid told me. Said she left by first light."

"Why did she not tell me, the maid, I mean?"

"As I said, she's gone on the groom, and she has windmills in her head."

Emma was not listening. She stared at the paper she held in her hand, feeling the blood drain from her face as she read aloud:

Dearest Sister: I've loved the Tonnish time in London, but I was never really a part of it. I'm glad that we came. I would not want to wonder the rest of my life what it was like to be on the marriage mart. Except I was never on the marriage mart. Before we left Fernwood, Gregory and I had an understanding that

I would send for him when I was ready to marry. And then when I sent for him and he came, he said that he had waited long enough. So, this day, we are running away to Gretna Green. I'm so excited, dear Emma. Please wish me luck.

She had added a postscript.

Lord Harthgrow only wanted the dowry His Grace so generously offered. It seems that the Harthgrow family is in bad straits. And there was something else — he had no notion of giving up his mistress. He made that singularly plain. Not that I ever for one moment considered marrying him. I told him that I did not care how many mistresses he kept.

Emma found a place to sit. Staring dry-eyed at the floor, she murmured, "Gregory . . . Gregory Banks."

Lady Emma Winslow had never felt so alone in her life.

# Chapter Twenty-three

Emma stopped thinking of her anger toward her brother; it was a constant, insidious thing, and it needed no kindling. She had lost Prudence and Francine; it was Charles's fault. She was not at her beloved Fernwood; it was his fault. The unrelenting anger so smoldered beneath the surface that she did not know how to go on with her life. Everything she had planned so meticulously had gone awry.

No word had come from Ashton. Prudence had written from Craigmont, saying that she had received a missive and that he was on the Grand Tour, on his ship *Lady Emma*.

"It seems," Prudence had said, "that Mama is much improved, and my studies are going well." She had closed by asking Emma to return to Craigmont, saying she loved her very much.

A missive had come from Francine, and her happiness literally jumped off the pages, Emma thought. She could not be sorry that her plan for Francine had not worked, and she wrote back, saying as much.

Now, she must needs find employment, Emma one morning decided. She hated to admit that she had been reluctant to leave Number Ten Park Place for fear a missive would come from His Grace. She scolded herself for even thinking he would write. Of course he had not cared for her as he had claimed, else he would not have left her to be gone such a long time. She ached for him; she needed his strength, his smile, and admitted after much soul-searching that she loved the ruthless Duke dearly.

Emma wanted very much to return to Craigmont, but she knew she could not again face Consuelo's rejection. The post had brought Countess Lankford word from Consuelo. The Countess, however, had not imparted the news to her, and Emma determined not to pry. She had a vague, inexplicable feeling that a conspiracy existed between Countess Lankford and Consuelo. They had been bosom bows for over thirty years.

Emma felt alone . . . alone . . . alone. For companionship she wrote in her diary. Every day.

Even the strange dreams had stopped. It was as if everything and everybody had given up on her.

Well, she had not given up on herself, she mused this particular morning. She dressed demurely, pulled her hair back from her face, donned her most handsome hat, an unadorned, high-crowned straw with a wide brim, and went to visit with Countess Lankford, who, Emma had learned, had permanent rooms in His Grace's palatial townhouse. In answer to her soft knock, Emma was told to enter.

"I must needs find employment," she told the Countess immediately, her gaze moving furtively over the room.

Countess Lankford wore a long morning coat of dusty rose silk. She sat in a large, comfortable chair, her cane nearby.

Looking at Emma as if she had windmills in her head, the Countess asked, "Doing what?"

Emma was taken aback. She knew her skills were inadequate, but she was willing to learn. "I aim to apply to Madame Franchot to work as an apprentice. I understand that she is the foremost modiste in London. Since I am not living at Craigmont, as my dead brother decreed, I cannot depend on the stipend he designated for me. I only have one hundred pounds, and that will not last long once I get a place of my own."

"A place of your own? Why—?"

Emma was quick with her answer. "I cannot go on living in His Grace's house."

"I don't know why not. He's not here to stop you."

" 'Tis a matter of principle. I am not a beggar."

Countess Lankford went to Emma and embraced her. "Darling child, you are of the nobility, and entirely too pretty to be hired as a modiste. Any woman in her right mind would recognize the danger of your being snatched away by some eligible gentleman and carried off to the altar."

Tears came then, tears Emma had been holding back for a long time. So often she had had to swallow in order to breathe. She wanted only one man, His Grace. How foolish she had been not to have recognized that she loved him when he was pursuing her so diligently. How foolish she had been to flirt with Sir Arthur Stewart and the other bloods of the Ton. But she had not been cognizant of male vanity, that it was unforgivable to throw something precious like love back into a gentleman's face. For all to see.

There, on the Countess's soft bosom, Emma sobbed her heart out, and drew comfort from the hand that compassionately patted her back. "I'm glad that I have you, Countess Lankford. I appreciate—"

"Shhh," the Countess said. "Everyone needs someone who understands. If you wish to make a try at becoming a modiste, I will not discourage you. As I said, you are of the nobility. And it would not be fair to Madame Franchot to mislead her. What if Ashton should return and claim you? I wager you would not be so stubborn . . ."

"Please don't remind me," Emma said.

They went to sit by the window. Countess Lankford pulled the bellrope, and when a servant came she ordered tea and scones. "Any day you will receive a contrite missive," she told Emma.

"I believe not," Emma said. "He has written to Prudence, but not to me. He has his hackles up, and that is that. And there is no way I can write to him . . . should I want to."

The tea and scones came, and they sat for a long time, while Emma talked. She told her about the wardrobe she had made for her and Francine, how she had sold her mother's precious things for one hundred pounds, and lastly she told her of how her brother had failed to produce an heir, forcing her to relinquish Fernwood, her precious home, to a distant cousin.

"It seems you have been like the dog chasing its tail," the Countess said.

"I don't take your meaning," Emma responded.

"The dog knows what it wants, his tail, and he goes around in a circle, but never quite achieves his goal."

Emma gave a small, empty laugh. "It seems that way. But I had nothing to do with my brother promising me in marriage to the Duke, to pay a gambling debt. I felt sure His Grace had tricked him—"

"And you were so angry about leaving Fernwood that no one would tell you what to do."

"How do you know?"

"Because I am a woman, and because I know human nature."

"I will never forgive Charles," Emma said.

"That is a mistake," the Countess answered, then quickly went on. "One must needs forgive. Always. I know. Once I let anger drive me, using it as a shield against pain. And I was like you, determined to be independent."

Emma for the first time saw the pain behind Countess

283

Lankford's kind eyes, her understanding smile, pain softened by time. "What happened?" Emma asked.

"When things were at their worst, I met Consuelo and she hired me for her unborn child's governess." She paused and took a deep breath. "I might as well tell you the whole of it. I was engaged to be married and he cried off."

Emma sat forward in her chair. "Why?"

"His family. They were on bad times, and they insisted that he make a marriage of convenience."

"How dreadful," Emma exclaimed.

"Lady Winslow, things happen and one must make the most of it. I worked for Consuelo until Ashton decided he did not need a governess, then I returned to London and married. I had saved, but it was Consuelo's generosity that afforded me entrance back into society, making it possible that I marry well. She furnished a handsome dowry."

"Your anger—"

"It, and the pain, went away in time. So you must needs give yourself time, gel. Do not opine over much."

"In the meantime live in Ashton's home, like a poor relation, with no means of support. I want my own place."

It was like reliving her own past for the Countess, and she understood perfectly how Emma felt. "Then go to Madame Franchot. Mayhaps she can give you work that can be done secretly, thus not jeopardizing your future. However, His Grace would not object to marrying a modiste. In his words, he doesn't give a demme what the Ton thinks."

"You are so sure I will marry the Duke."

"I know Ashton," the Countess said, smiling.

Emma rose to go.

"Should I go with you to see Madame Franchot?" Countess Lankford asked.

"No," Emma said. "I will take Hannah."

Then, realizing that she might have hurt Countess Lankford's feelings, Emma said, "It's just that I want to do this on my own. Madame Franchot might favor me because of you."


A week later, at Craigmont, Consuelo deFleury held a missive from Countess Lankford and fumed. Her son had done exactly the opposite of what she had expected. Imagine poor Emma sewing in the dark of the night for a modiste, while His Grace Ashton deFleury flitted over Europe with his valet. It was fortunate for the jackanapes that he was so far away, else she would be tried for murder.

"Have a carriage brought around," she told Maydean, her lady's maid, who left immediately to tell a footman.

Consuelo dressed hurriedly. It was a six-hour journey into London, and it would be pushing the horses to make it before dark, with two changes.

But make it they did. At twilight she was pounding on the huge double doors of Number Ten Park Place with the brass knocker, and when the doors did not instantly open, she gave it more resounding whacks.

"Madame," Gork said, extreme surprise showing on his face. "May I help you?"

"You can. Please tell Lady Emma Winslow that Consuelo deFleury is here to see her. I shall wait in the receiving room."

The butler cocked a quizzical brow, bowed, then left.

In less time than it took Consuelo to situate herself comfortably in one of the many chairs, Emma stood before her, the look of wonderment on her face even more pronounced than on the butler's.

"I've come to set things straight," Consuelo said. "I've been entirely wrong."

"I don't take your meaning," Emma said.

"Well, sit and I shall tell you the whole of it, and I shall start by telling you that I have never been more angry with Ashton deFleury than I am at this moment. He has no right to be flitting all over Europe, leaving you alone. Sit down, gel."

Bemused, Emma sat. In defense of His Grace, she said, "I humiliated him at Almack's. I went to Upper Brook Street to apologize and he was gone."

"That's Ashton for you. But he should have stayed put and thought things through. 'Tis so unlike him to do something like this."

"I think he knew I planned to trick him," Emma said. "I was so angry that I took great pleasure in *pretending* I was interested in marrying him. In truth, I had no such plan. I wanted him to furnish a dowry for Francine so she could make a good marriage."

The confession made Emma feel good. In retrospect, she was at a loss on how she could have acted so deceitfully.

Consuelo studied her appraisingly for a few minutes, then said, "Don't try to take the blame. Ashton is thirty and one; he should recognize a gel in love."

Emma started to deny it, but knew it was of no use. Consuelo was too wise for that. So she was silent, waiting for her next order. That did not mean she would do it, she thought, but she wanted Consuelo to play her hand.

"Have Hannah pack your things. We are returning to Craigmont. And return that sewing to Madame Franchot."

"I will not," Emma said, her anger flaring. "I hired out to do a job, and I intend to keep my word."

"Then take it with you. When it is finished, it will be sent back to the modiste."

Emma set her chin in a stubborn line, stared straight into Consuelo's eyes, and asked, "Why do you want me to return to Craigmont? I was there, and you made it plain that you did not like me. You told Ashton that marriage to me would be a misalliance. Now you order me to come home with you. I don't take your meaning."

"You will, for I intend to explain on our journey back to Craigmont. And I will tell you other things as well, things very few people know. The time is right that I share my secrets."

# Chapter Twenty-four

"Are you sure it is not your wish to go with us?" Consuelo asked Countess Lankford.

"No, I shall return to my country home. It's boring and peaceful," answered the Countess, laughing.

"Then promise to come for Christmas."

"I promise. By then, Ashton will have returned."

"I certainly pray so," said Consuelo. "Else I shall send the Bow Runners after him."

Emma went to the Countess and hugged her. "Thanks, Countess, for your kindness."

The Countess gave her a hefty hug in turn, saying, "Take care, Lady Winslow, and remember our little talks. Experience taught me a lot. Anger does not render good. It may have cost you Ashton."

Emma felt herself pale, but she could not release her anger, forget what her brother had done. It was impossible. "Please come for Christmas," she said, and then she climbed, with the help of a footman, up into the carriage to sit opposite Consuelo.

Hannah was perched on the box, and had been for the past half hour, as if she feared she would be left.

As soon as the horses pulled away from Number Ten

Park Place, Emma expected from Consuelo the explanation she had promised, but this was not to be, for Consuelo seemed determined to talk of other things. "Little Prudence is doing marvelously well," she said.

"About her mother, how—"

"She sees only the doctor and Prudence. She does, however, walk in the gardens and on the beach with them. From what Dr. Reneau has learned, then imparted to me when I pried, Countess Winslow became deeply melancholic soon after Prudence was born. He's had other patients that this has happened to, but none have remained out of touch for so long. And some patients turn against their child, but this Countess Winslow did not do. She turned on her husband instead. The kind doctor believes she has passed the point of no return."

"Does Prudence still talk of an Easter miracle?" asked Emma, deeply concerned.

"Yes, at times, but it seems that her faith never wavers. It makes me dread for Easter to come."

"I want so much for Prudence to have a normal life, to be a little girl, not an adult as she has been forced to be."

"Things are better on that score. Since returning to Craigmont, she rides every day." Consuelo laughed. "And she feeds your animals, which, I regret to say, are multiplying by leaps and bounds. The geese returned with a gaggle of goslings, and the pigs are no longer pigs. They are now huge hogs, and they have four piglets. If it were not for Prue's objection, we would eat them."

"At least one thing turned out as I planned," Emma said.

"What do you mean by that?"

"I had planned to let them multiply and then sell them. That was part of my plan to becoming independent."

Consuelo gave a questioning look. "And what was the other part? The part that didn't work."

"To find a rich husband for Francine, and then I would become a modiste and take care of little Prudence."

Consuelo clucked and shook her head. "Sometimes I think God has a plan for our lives."

Emma remembered the painting of her that His Grace had done, the wind blowing uncontrollably against her and his saying that fate was stronger than she. "Ashton called it Fate."

"What is Fate except God's plan?"

Emma could not answer that. It had been so long since she had prayed, since she had thought about what she believed.

Consuelo went on, "Prudence went seabathing in Brighton, with Princess Charlotte. They spent one whole day at the beach."

"At last she is having children fun. Sometimes she is so grownup it scares me. The dipping must have been fun to hold her and the Princess's attention for one whole day."

"Prudence talked of little else for days."

Emma had heard that, for a price, anyone who desired sea immersion could enter a bathing machine, which was a wooden box on wheels pulled by a horse. In the box, safely hidden from prying eyes, one made ready to bathe. Ladies donned caps and long-sleeved shifts. She was not sure what gentlemen wore.

The bathing machine would then be backed from the beach into the ocean. Dippers, always a woman for a gel, waited halfway up the steps to assist. After the dip, the bather would again enter the box and change clothes as the box was being drawn back onto the beach by a reliable man carefully guiding the horse.

It sounded like fun to Emma. She smiled and thought that mayhaps she would be "dipped" someday. With His Grace guiding the horse, of course. She was almost certain he would not be reliable when it came to peeking. She could envision his wry grin when he was discovered cheating.

After that, a long silence ensued. The countryside passed in a blur for Emma. The crested coach was passed by hired equipage, all taking note of the Duke's standard emblazoned on the panels and tipping their hats. It was a pleasant day, and the bright autumn sun kept Emma warm. She listened to the country sounds, so familiar to her ears, and waited for Consuelo to tell her why she disliked her so much.

Finally, when the silence became suffocatingly unpleasant, Emma looked her straight in the eye and asked, "What did I ever do to you?"

Surprisingly, tears brimmed Consuelo's large hazel eyes and spilled down onto her cheeks, her chin slightly quivering. It took her a moment to answer, and then, "Nothing. And I am so ashamed."

Taken aback, Emma waited.

"You know, I am sure, about Ashton's reputation. He would not forebear a smothering mother." A light laugh escaped her throat, and her eyes shone through tears. "That's what he called me when he was in leading strings, then, when he was older and learned about the Ton, he refused to let me be a Ton mother when I became too bossy. He said more than once that he would let me know when he was ready to become leg-shackled. Well, I was not satisfied with the time he was taking. I wanted grandchildren in the worst way. So cleverly, at least I thought it was clever, I arranged for him to meet eligible gels. Having been apprised by gossipers of how beautiful his mistress of the moment was, the gels I picked were gorgeous creatures. Unfortunately, they were empty-headed.

"The result was that Ashton castigated me ferociously

and told me that he would never wed a gel I chose for him. I believed then that I must needs pretend to dislike any gel he chose for his wife, should he *ever* do that.

"I was about to give up when he came to me and told me that he planned to marry you. Immediately I had you investigated and was most impressed with what I learned. Erudite, capable, and determined, my investigator said. And beautiful beyond measure.

"So I unwisely treated you badly, dear Emma, in hopes that Ashton would indeed marry you. I never wanted you to marry Sir Arthur Stewart. I only wanted to make Ashton jealous. He has such a keen mind that I had to pour it on thick. Should I have shown my true feelings, he might have thought that I had arranged the whole affair. It was stupid of me . . . will you forgive me?"

Emma was so relieved that she could not stop her eyes from clouding with tears. She reached for Consuelo's hand, clasping it with great feeling. "I forgive you, but I was terribly hurt."

"That proves you are sensitive."

"In some areas. In others I am very hard."

Emma was thinking of the lingering, smoldering anger she held dearly to her heart against her brother. But she did not want to discuss those feelings with Consuelo, so she said sincerely, laughing a little and heaving a deep sigh, "What a relief to know that I am not totally objectionable."

"You're not, my dear, and I am in a deep pucker about Ashton's behavior. Just wait until I get my hands on him."

The two women then rode in pleasant silence, only occasionally saying something of little consequence to each other. At a posting inn, the road-weary horses were exchanged for fresh ones, and a repast enjoyed. A great burden had been lifted from Emma's heart, and she saw no reason to further rehash what had happened. They spoke briefly about the Season, and Emma thanked Consuelo again for her great generosity, and she laughingly said, "I must have been fighting Fate when I wanted Francine to find a rich husband. Seemingly, she is extremely happy with Gregory."

It was not until they were nearing the end of the journey, as they entered the woods, that Consuelo leaned forward and said conspiratorially, "Lady Winslow, I want to tell you something."

The look on Consuelo's face brought Emma up. "I'm almost afraid to ask what, but I promise to listen."

"It's about Ashton's lineage."

For some inexplicable reason Emma did not want to know about His Grace's lineage. With them estranged, she thought it none of her business. "Mayhaps Ashton feels that his lineage is not my affair."

As if she had not spoken, Consuelo continued, "As the mother of my grandchildren, you have a right to know about Ashton's father, Luis Maurier."

Emma's mouth fell open. "Not the famous French artist?"

"Yes, and he was something else, a spy for England, as was my father, Avery deFleury."

Emma again objected, "Why are you telling me this?"

"You will marry Ashton, Emma, when his temper has had sufficient time to cool, and I want you to know so that, if I am not here, you can tell my grandchildren."

"Do you not think Ashton would tell—"

"No. It is too hurtful for him to talk about. Besides, it is my story. I want to tell it."

Then, as if she had slipped back in time, Consuelo deFleury settled back against the luxurious squab of her son's crested carriage and began:

"My father was French, my mother English. Even

293

though my father loved his country, he hated Napoleon, but I was seven and ten years before I knew how much he hated the little Emperor. This night I learned he was a spy. He brought Luis home with him and they sat up all night talking. Luis was twenty years my senior, but I fell hopelessly in love with him. I did not know that he also was working for England. King George III was his close friend, I later learned, and they conspired. It would not have mattered had I known. I loved him and that was that. War between France and England was inevitable, and due to the danger involved, Luis and I were secretly married by a priest who was engaged in the same underground work. There was no official license, or record of our marriage. For security reasons, I kept my maiden name. I didn't care about that either; we were married in the sight of God, if not the state. Then began the happiest time of my life. But it was all too short. One month later I was pregnant with Ashton."

Consuelo stopped then, as if to savor that moment in time when her world was right. Emma watched the enraptured look on her face, the tiny happy smile, and waited until again words would come.

"My father insisted that I leave France," Consuelo said. "Through my deceased mother he owned Craigmont, but for appearance sake, and this I will never understand, he wanted me to live in London for a short while. I was skinny as a rail, and my condition did not show."

She looked at Emma. "You know the story there. Word somehow leaked out that I was unmarried and enceinte. The Ton is very unforgiving. At less than eighteen summers, I did not bear pain well, so I hired Countess Lankford and we repaired to Craigmont, where Ashton was born."

"Did you not ever see his father again?"

"Oh, yes, nothing could keep us apart. He risked his life to anchor his ship off the Sussex Coast and make his way to the cabin I had built for him in the woods. We had many happy hours there. He continued his painting, and when Ashton was old enough, he was a wonderful teacher for his son. Ashton inherited his talent."

Emma asked, "Is he . . . where is—"

"Dead. But they did not get him, as they did my father, but the wind did. When Ashton had had eight years, Luis was anchored several miles off the Sussex Coast when a storm blew up and sank his ship. My husband drowned, as did his captain, the only other man aboard. I was expecting him, and was apprehensively watching because of the storm. Days later I found his body, and that of his captain washed ashore."

"How dreadful for you," Emma said, at a loss for adequate words.

"My heart broke, but I did what I had to do. I went for Lankford and Ashton, and we buried them in the woods, and spread leaves over the fresh dirt, leaving the graves unmarked."

"Why Ashton? He was so young. Why did you want him to witness such sorrow?"

"I wanted him to accept that his father was dead so that he would not sit on the big rocks and watch for his ship."

"And did he?" Emma asked.

"Yes. But he never went back to the cabin to paint. He set aside one of his rooms and painted there."

"And you never told anyone you were married."

"Ashton and Lankford knew, but no one else. I feared that retribution would be taken on Ashton. As years passed, I saw no need to tell. I had grown used to the seclusion of Craigmont. Then, because of the contribution his father made to England's cause, His Majesty King George made Ashton a duke, an honor he did not wish to accept, exclaiming vehemently that he had done nothing to deserve a dukedom. I was adamant, however, and he acquiesced."

A smile flashed when she said, "It is the only argument I ever won with my son."

*Chapter Twenty-five*

Emma was happy to return to Craigmont. It was strange, she thought, how it felt like coming home. And she had only been there a short while before going to London. She told herself that mayhaps it was because Prudence was there, and the child made her feel loved. Every day they visited the farm animals together, fed them, counted them, and laughed. The tiny goslings grew into tiny geese for Prudence to feed, and to occasionally hold, becoming so attached to her that they returned nightly to the stables.

Emma continued her sewing, despite Consuelo's protests. She could not be idle, she told Consuelo. They went to the theater in Brighton, and Emma often walked on the beach. But never near the cabin. She felt that that was Consuelo's own sacred ground.

The invaluable Maurier paintings that the cabin for years had held were donated to a Paris Medical Institute of Dr. Reneau's choosing, in payment for his care of Prudence's mother.

Newspapers carried the story, but no mention was made of where the paintings had been all these years, or of the artist's life. This was a relief to Consuelo, who exclaimed that she felt so good about the paintings going to a worthy cause that she now planned to approach Ashton about doing something similar with his own paintings. It would be perfectly all right for the populace to know he was an artist, and that he was the legitimate son of Luis Maurier.

Autumn quietly slid into winter, and still Emma had not heard from Ashton. A missive from him to Consuelo said that he had left the Tour and had gone to India, where there was trouble with his business, and that he would return early spring.

Emma started counting the days, but with each day, hope died a little more, painfully. The days were interminably long. Her need to apologize for her actions at Almack's became unimportant, simply because she was sure His Grace no longer cared. If he cared, he would write to her, she reasoned, sobbing into her pillow.

Then, Christmas came with great celebration. The young Princess and Mrs. Fitzherbert made a courtesy call, and Countess Lankford came as she had promised, then stayed over. Emma was glad; she felt more comfortable sharing confidences with the Countess than with Consuelo. After all, Consuelo was Ashton's mother. Sure that the Countess Lankford would not tell, Emma told her most intimate desires to her.

"I must needs leave," Countess Lankford said one day. "I shall repair to His Grace's place in Town. Winter is on the verge of becoming severe, and the townhouse is warmer and more comfortable than my house in the country. Won't you go with me, Emma?" she asked.

"No," Emma said without hesitation. "I explained why last fall when I was there. I will not be his charity case. He has been away so long that now he must needs come to me . . . if he still wishes to do so."

Countess Lankford shook her head but did not offer a lecture, for which Emma was grateful. She sent with her several bodices on which she had sewn pearls, ribbons, and other ornaments, to be delivered to Madame Franchot.

Upon parting, Countess Lankford tried again, in a subtle

way, to entice Emma to come to Town with her. "His Grace is supporting a school of learning for lads whose families are so poor that the boys have to work to buy food. Ashton gives them their weekly wage for going to school. I plan to work there when the weather is fair. You could help, Emma." She smiled. "And we could make morning calls. I hear gossip is rife about His Grace crying off when he was supposed to wed a pretty gel from the country."

"I am sure I would not enjoy that. For he did not cry off. It was I who spoiled everything. Now, I can't understand why he is staying away so long." Emma's voice broke, and she got a consoling pat from Countess Lankford.

Climbing up into her carriage, the Countess gave the driver office to be off. Emma watched until they made the sweep and turned into the woods, then, turning, she went back into the house, which reeked of loneliness, and of idleness.

Restless, Emma could not help but long for Fernwood, where she was busy every hour of the day. This once again brought to fore the simmering anger she had for the past months clung to so passionately. Had Charles had an heir she would not be at Craigmont praying for the return of a man who had *thought* he wanted her, and then had found out he was mistaken. That he had taken his mistress with him when he left London haunted Emma immensely, and as time went on, she believed more and more that this was so. A country gel knew about those things. As lusty as His Grace appeared to be, he would not be without a companion this long. The thought became so painful that she thought of little else, except Fernwood, where her heart had lain dormant inside her chest. The need to return there increased monumentally.

One such spell of homesickness lasted several days, and Emma finally made plans to visit Fernwood. She had promised the servants she would return, and she so wanted to see Francine. Their correspondence had been sporadic because Francine was so busy being a happy wife. Emma wondered if Francine still painted her toenails with gilt lacquer and thought that no doubt she did. The thought brought a smile, and she felt that she would burst if she did not see her sister.

The longing grew until at last Emma went to Consuelo and asked to borrow traveling equipage. She would drive, and Hannah would go with her.

"Of course you may have a carriage *and* a driver," Consuelo said. "But let's not speak of borrowing. What is here is yours to use anytime you wish."

Emma was again struck with Consuelo's generosity, and she seemed so happy these days. Bringing out into the open about her years-ago secret marriage, and the giving of the Mauier paintings to a worthy cause had seemingly lifted a great burden from her. Now, Consuelo deFleury's only complaint was about her stubborn son. Whom she would strangle when she saw him, if ever that should be, she more than once avowed to Emma.

Emma knew better. Consuelo deFleury adored His Grace Ashton deFleury.

The journey to Fernwood did not materialize. The night before Emma was to leave a late winter storm struck with vengeance. And that same night, the dream came again; the crosses, the whispering trees, the child praying over a candle.

Emma awoke burdened with the desire to know why the dream kept coming to her. It was as if a dark curtain had, for no reason that she could discern, fallen before her eyes, obliterating the light. She went to get her diary to see how long it had been since she'd had the dream, finding it several months. This was the only recurring dream; the others, the one about the seven eggs in the nest, and it had come true, and the one about her brother and His Grace having

300

orns and her wearing an armor, she had only dreamed once. Emma shuddered and suddenly she was visited with he overwhelming desire to go to the woods and look for he answer in ruins of the Abbey. As if some mystical force were drawing her there. But she couldn't go, she told herself, for this day she was going to see Francine. Her trunk was packed.

She went to the window and opened the curtain, and it was then that she learned of the storm. The world looked as if a brush had painted it white. Tree limbs, laden with snow, swung low to the ground, also blanketed with snow. A pale gray steam rose up from the sea. She noticed that the room had become cold, even with coals simmering in the grate.

After washing and dressing as quickly as possible, she went belowstairs to breakfast. Mayhaps if she discussed the dream with Consuelo, she could interpret it for her. But Consuelo was having breakfast in her room, a footman said as he handed Emma a missive. "It came last evening, m'lady," he said sheepishly, "His Grace's solicitor, a Mr. Prescott, brought it."

Emma stared at it for a long moment. There was no return address, but she recognized His Grace's sweeping script. Her heart lurched then slammed against her ribcage. "Then why was it not delivered to me last evening?"

"You had repaired to bed, so Van Winters said," the footman replied, leaving quickly.

Her hands shaking, Emma ripped the envelope open and began to read, saying the words under her breath.

My dear Emma:

I spent more time on the *Lady Emma* thinking than I did doing the Grand Tour, and I know now how foolish I was to expect to manipulate you into marriage. You told me you did not wish to marry me, and I should have believed you. Your late brother had

301

told me enough that I should have known you would dig in your heels when someone began to dictate terms to you. I am sorry for this crass treatment.

Also, I feel I would be remiss if I did not tell you the whole of it about your brother. I tried several times to speak to you of him, but was immediately bluffed out by your anger. You vow to never forgive him for not producing a male heir to inherit Fernwood. It was not his fault, Emma, for after Prudence was born, his lordship was locked from his wife's bedchamber. Her madness had come on her, and she wanted no one around her except the baby to whom she had given life. Lord Winslow loved his wife with every fiber of his being, and it was over her that he fought the untimely duel, not about some lightskirt as the gossipers would have it. A practically unknown blood made a disparaging remark about Margaret's illness, and your brother called him out.

Lord Winslow wanted an heir to Fernwood as much as you did, Emma. His life was hell. I know. I was his friend and confidante. With respect due you, Emma, I can only say that you are wrong to be so angry. As you know, madness unfortunately carries a stigma which most families cannot accept. They keep loved ones locked away for years, secretly. Lord Winslow did not do that, even though he was ashamed.

And that shame kept him from inviting you and Francine to his home in London, and from allowing you a London Season.

Please, Emma, try to understand and pray find it in your heart to forgive. Charles's heart broke long before yours did. If you believe this, then mayhaps yours will mend, and there will be room for love.

Emma stared at the sheet of parchment, longing to read

love words, finding nothing except that he had misjudged her. She wanted to read about his longing to see her, his dreams of holding her, passionate words whispered against her lips.

At the bottom was simply, "Ashton deFleury."

Emma sat for a long while, the missive crumpled in her hands. She no longer wanted to talk with Consuelo, and she no longer felt the need to go to the abbey ruins, for the black curtain no longer veiled her eyes. The answers were there for her to grasp; God, through a dream, had told her to forgive for she knew not the truth. Shame for her past weak faith washed over her as she rose from her chair and went immediately to thank little Prudence, that angel of mercy, for her prayers. Once Prudence had said, "Auntie Em, His Grace asked that I pray for an Easter Miracle for him, and I said that I would. He seemed so terribly lonely. Like me."

Emma was sure the child had prayed for her as well, and as she climbed the stairs, then walked the long halls, she pondered on why it had practically taken a whack on the head by an axe handle for her to realize that an unforgiving heart was a closed heart. She had shut out His Grace's generous love.

# Chapter Twenty-six

"I've kept it as a shrine long enough, I shall have it demolished," Consuelo said.

They, she and Emma, were walking along the sea, returning from the cottage where the paintings had been kept, and where she had years ago met secretly her secret husband.

"The memories are still poignant, and they always will be, but one can't live in the past," she added.

"Thank you for taking me there," Emma said, and then she asked, "The man I saw on the ship the day I was lost, do you think he was looking for Luis Maurier? Mayhaps since his death was not reported, the French government is still looking for him."

"I suspect it was a lecherous old seadog ogling a pretty woman through his spyglasses. It was so long ago that the spying and all that work happened. Most likely the files have been closed. I pray so."

Emma's thoughts went to the day Ashton had found her on the beach, the day she had been lost in the woods. His kisses still burned like fire on her lips. Since the one intelligence, there had not been a word from him, and the modicum of hope that she had held inside her heart that he would return to her had painfully died. She had been waiting for the weather to clear so that she could go to Francine. This day, for the first time in three weeks, the sun was shining and the wind off the sea was warm.

"Your husband's grave," Emma said. "You say it's unmarked. Do you still know where it is?"

"Oh, yes. It's under a special tree, marked in a way that only Ashton and I would know, and Countess Lankford. I still go there, sometimes at night, taking a rose. He always brought a single rose when he could manage to come."

Emma had several times from Prudence's room seen Consuelo picking a rose and disappearing into the woods. And she had wondered where she was going.

"Why at night? Aren't you frightened in the woods at night? Even in the daytime, they are so dark."

"Darkness can't harm you, Emma; unless there's darkness inside your heart. It shuts out the world, and I am alone with my love."

They walked along, basking in the sunshine, talking little but communicating, Emma thought, in that way women seemed to do. With the mention of the darkness in the woods, Emma could not help but remember how frightened she had been of the smothering darkness, and she wondered if possibly it had been the darkness inside her heart where anger for her brother lingered, fermenting, blinding her to the goodness of life.

And the life he had planned for her and Francine had been good since leaving Fernwood, she belatedly realized. She thought about what *could* have happened had not Consuelo taken them in. London could have been cruel beyond bearing. Even little Prudence's coming, thought to be such a disaster at first, had proved to be a blessing, opening Consuelo to herself and her self-centered life.

At last, Consuelo said, "Ashton has returned to London. I received a missive from Countess Lankford."

Emma felt her heart jump to her throat. She waited for Consuelo to say he would soon be coming to Craigmont, but she did not. Emma asked, "Ho . . . how is he?"

305

"According to the Countess, he is doing splendidly well, works all day, coming in late at night."

Emma felt a small, hot lick of jealousy, but knew she had no right. She had turned His Grace away. Nonetheless, she was jealous, and she was angry. Why could he not come to Craigmont so she could tell him that she was sorry for her flirting, for her coldness, and for her terrible, terrible anger against her brother. She had learned her lesson, she would tell him. And never again would she listen to gossip. She had been so sure that Lord Winslow had simply been too wild in his ways to produce an heir, and she had been so wrong.

"Should I go to Town and speak with Ashton? Tell him I'm sorry for humiliating him in front of the Ton," she asked Consuelo.

The answer was a quick, "No. Let him come to you if he wishes to see you. Then you can tell him. Men like to be the aggressor." Consuelo stopped for a moment, then went on. "Ashton must needs share his part of the blame. He is so stubborn, and in the affairs of the heart, this does not always work."

Then a pause. "And he should have courted you, won you on his own, not flapped that demme codicil of your brother's will in your face."

"That did make me terribly angry," Emma admitted.

But she did not want to discuss it further, for there was nothing to gain, she told herself. What had happened had happened. She doubted very much that if she went to His Grace and got down on her knees, which she was not about to do, that he would believe she really regretted what she had done. She remembered the painting he had done of her, her fighting the wind, and his saying that Fate had decreed they be together, and for her to fight it would be like fighting the wind.

*Now it is His Grace who is defying the wind.*

So there was nothing to it but to try again to make plans for her future, Emma mused. She could not remain idle, and the distance from Craigmont to London was too great for her to keep sewing for Madame Franchot. Should she go to London, she would lose her stipend from her brother's estate, and there would not be enough money from sewing to live. She would be forced to live in some mean place in a dangerous part of Town.

The thought came to her that she was well-read and may-haps, like Countess Lankford, she would become a governess.

When they reached the house, she hugged Consuelo, and said, "The weather has warmed. Tomorrow, I shall go to Fernwood, and then to see Francine. I want so much to see her, and another Easter is upon us. I will stay over for the holiday."

That night, Emma packed carefully, at the last adding a gown she had not worn. It was made of *Jonquille,* a new fashionable yellow, and she had a silk hat and parasol to match the dress. Remembering that last Easter Francine had said that if she did not wear a new gown that a crow would befoul her old one, Emma smiled, and she wondered if this year Gregory would lift Francine in a chair on Easter Monday.

So much had happened since then, Emma thought, and she wanted very much this moment to be in the carriage, on her way back *home.* Still, when she at last went to bed, she had to force herself to think of Francine, instead of Ashton. His Grace's wry grin and his beautiful hazel eyes lingered at the boundary of her thoughts, and in the night she awakened several times to ponder, and to check the time. One such awakening was caused by a vivid dream. It was her wedding night, and His Grace was holding her. She was naked, and it was naked flesh against naked flesh, desire matching desire. Moonlight invaded the room, and the darkness, while His Grace made unrestrained passionate love to her.

"I will teach you about love, dear Emma," he said, and she had let herself go, becoming his willing pupil. Even now, fully awake, her breasts ached for his touch, and her distended nipples pushed against her thin gown.

As with all dreams, Emma thought, this one ended, and she was alone. By sheer willpower, she drifted into a fitful sleep, her face burning, her body aching for her dream man, her precious Ashton.

Morning came at last, with brilliant yellow sunlight dancing across her bed. Sitting up, she looked beyond the window and saw the blue-black sea roiling leisurely, breaking against the shore with rhythmic booms.

Van Winters came to help her dress, And to pry, Emma was sure. Upon returning to Craigmont, Hannah had again taken up her job in the kitchen, not to keep her lady from being poisoned, she confessed to Emma, but to be near Oliver, a footman to whom she had taken a fancy.

"Why are you in such a hurry?" Van Winters said as Emma pulled a red velvet traveling dress over her head.

"I'm anxious to see Francine is all," Emma answered.

Van Winters took her shoulders and pushed her into a chair in front of floor-to-ceiling looking glass. "No need to be in such a hurry. Breakfast won't be for another half-hour."

The brushing began, and then the twisting.

Emma sat, stoically silent. She did not care what her hair looked like, nor did she want to argue with the maid.

"Will you be seeing His Grace?" Van Winters asked, nonchalantly, as if it were of little consequence whether or not Emma answered.

"Fishing for something to feed the gossip mill?" Emma asked, raising a dark brow.

"I would never gossip about m'lady. But I just thought—"

"It doesn't matter. I will tell you that I will not be seeing His Grace Ashton deFleury. So you can pass the word along to the others. Since coming to Craigmont I've become quite used to abovestairs and belowstairs gossip."

Emma rose and gave the maid a hug. "I will miss you Van Winters. You've proved to be much more efficient than I expected. Take care of yourself."

"But, m'lady. You'll be coming back," Van Winters said, looking fondly at Emma.

It was the first time that Emma had faced up to the plan that had formulated in her mind. She would not be coming back to Craigmont to live. It was imperative that she find employment.

"Mayhaps," Emma said, and then she asked Van Winters to have a footman load her trunk onto the carriage.

Belowstairs, Emma looked at the lovely breakfast dining room, then out at the sea. The sloping gardens were beginning to show signs of life, and buds on the trees were near bursting into bloom. Almost a year had passed since she had come to Craigmont, she thought, and in that short span of time she had learned to love a truly great man, and also a truly great woman. She said to Consuelo, "I will miss you."

"Your home is here, Emma. Don't ever forget that. I expect you to return."

Just then Prudence's joyful chatter could be heard, and she bounced into the room. A mote of light in a shaft of sun, Emma thought.

"Auntie Em," she said, running to hug Emma. "Mama is so much better. I told that she would be well by Easter."

Emma could not stop the tears that brimmed her eyes. "Dear Prue, Easter is only three weeks away."

"Don't doubt, Auntie Em. God can work swiftly. Don't you remember He moved a mountain, and He fed the multitude with only a few fish."

Once Prudence had told Emma that her Mama, before she became terribly sick, had read the Good Book to her every day. And then, after Prudence learned to read, she had read to Countess Winslow.

*Her faith is carrying her through this terrible ordeal,* Emma thought, and, as before, she listened, not willing to tell the child her petition to a higher power might not be answered.

Consuelo had been exceptionally quiet during the exchange, Emma noticed, but when Emma rose from the table, bent and kissed Prudence on the cheek, telling her goodbye, then went to the waiting carriage, Consuelo followed her out onto the veranda.

In a kind, quavering voice, she said, "I wanted so much for you to be the mother of my grandchildren. I would go and personally strangle Ashton for his stubbornness, but it would do no good. He doesn't take advice from his mother."

Giving Consuelo a quick peck on the cheek, Emma felt the choking sensation return to her throat, and she forced a little laugh. "His Grace is no more stubborn than I, Consuelo. Thank you for your kindness."

And then, with a footman's help, she climbed into the carriage. Hannah was on the box beside the driver.

In Number Ten Park Place, London, His Grace paced the floor of his magnificent book room and stormed at Countess Lankford, "Will you please stop telling me what I should do. When I left London, after that dreadful night at

310

Almack's, I vowed I would never again court Lady Winslow. I made a sapscull of myself over a pretty skirt, but no more. In truth, I'm thinking of reestablishing myself with my former paramour."

"Your Grace, that will be over my dead body," the Countess said brazenly, and calmly. "When you were eight, you locked me *out* of your room; now I will lock you *in* your room until you come to your senses."

# Chapter Twenty-seven

Emma was going home.

The carriage moved through the dense woods, and in the cold, clean darkness, there was the sharp smell of spring. Overhead, tree limbs leaned to each other, touching, making an arch over the road. Emma drew in a deep breath and, looking out, saw beauty she had not recognized as beauty upon her arrival at Craigmont, and she no longer felt threatened by the darkness. She knew that the deep, dark woods had for many years stood guard over Consuelo deFleury's secret.

The road twisted and turned, until ahead of them there was a thinning of the blackness and the faintest glimmer of white light. The gatekeeper opened the great iron gates, letting the carriage roll through, and as iron clanged against iron behind them Emma felt an overwhelming sense of timelessness. It seemed that she had been gone from Fernwood forever; yet, it had been less than a year. And in that short span of time, Craigmont had reached out with loving tentacles to clasp her to its protective bosom, as it had Francine, and little Prudence and her dear Mama, Countess Margaret Winslow. She tried not to think of Ashton, but found it impossible to push his handsome face from her mind. She breathed around the pain in her heart. To keep from becoming sentimentally morbid, she mentally called him a jacka-napes, a rakehill, even a scoundrel.

His Grace was none of these, she knew, but it helped to conjure up unkind images of the man who had stolen her heart and then left to tour the Continent before she was ready to admit he had stolen it. When they came to the road that veered to the right, and would have taken them to London, she was tempted to give the driver office to drive to Number Ten Park Place in Grosvenor Square. She would go to Ashton and call him all those names.

When she tried to imagine what he would do, she smiled, knowing he most likely would still her rapier tongue with a kiss, until she kissed him back and her knees went all weak, and then he would tell her not to ever deny she had kissed him, thoroughly and completely.

Emma did not go, of course, but she spent the rest of the journey thinking about the kiss she would receive should she do such a foolish thing. Only once or twice did she remind herself that she was twenty and three — twenty and four now, for she'd had a birthday — and much too old to act in such a schoolgirlish fashion. Her thoughts made for a pleasant journey.

The sun was sinking in the West when they reached the village of West Wycombe in the South Chilterns, and twilight hovered over the valley that held Fernwood Manor. Emma's heart welled full when she looked at the beautiful old house, its many windows framing flickering candles. She listened to the gathering night sounds, frogs croaking in the nearby pond. It was the same; yet, it was different. It was not her home.

She had come to keep a promise to the servants, and this she did quickly. They clamored around her, all talking at once. Her family, but not her family. They worked for some-one else now.

"I'm happy to see all of you," she told them.

"We miss yer," Ian, the coachman, said, "but the new lady

313

is nice as ken be. Too bad they're not home to greet yer."

When there was no one listening, he whispered to Emma conspiratorially, "They didn't put yer in a dungeon, did they?"

Laughing, Emma assured him that she had not been in a dungeon, and after only a short time, in which she told the servants she was happy in her new life and was glad they were being treated kindly by the new owner of Fernwood, she asked her driver to take her to the Banks's home. She had written ahead that she was coming, but did not give the date.

"Their land runs with Fernwood, to the South," she told her driver, and he turned the horses in that direction, and soon a sprawling old house loomed up out of the darkness, homey, welcoming, with a gray slate roof. Until this moment, when she was really here, Emma had not fully known how much she had missed Francine, and she thought her heart would burst with anticipation. Here was the child she had raised, now a married woman.

Emma did not have to wait long. The driver pulled the handsome horses to a jolting stop in front of the house, and instantly, as if she had been watching, Francine burst out the door, running to the carriage, her red-blond hair flying behind her. "Sister, I knew you would come for Easter," she squealed as she reached for Emma and hugged her fiercely.

In the days that followed, Emma found Francine extremely happy but unchanged. Gregory had a gaggle of brothers and sisters whom she mothered, and as Easter approached she painted eggs for the workers' children. On Easter eve she ordered the servants to clean the house in preparation for the Lord's coming, just as she had done at Fernwood. A bloodred goose egg lay by Emma's plate on Easter morning.

"The red represents the Lord's blood that he shed on Good Friday," Francine said.

"Thank you," Emma said, touched.

Francine and Gregory had their own apartment in the big house, and this suited Francine just fine, she said. Gregory was away, she further explained, and would be gone for Easter Sunday, but he had promised to return on Easter Monday to lift her in a chair, for which he would receive a real kiss, not a peck on the cheek as he had last Easter Monday. "He's such a wonderful husband," Francine opined, making Emma smile.

Emma had written to Countess Lankford, telling her she would be staying with Francine until after Easter. She had hoped that the Countess would tell Ashton, that he would come to the Banks' place to see her. It seemed to her that after all these months the last small hope would have died, but her thoughts kept coming back to him.

His Grace had not come, and she had not heard from him, nor had she heard from the Countess, making Emma think that mayhaps she had returned to her country home in Oxfordshire.

On Easter morning, wearing a new frock of printed lawn, Francine said, "I certainly hope you have a new gown this year. Else a crow will befoul your old dress and people will hold their noses and turn away from you."

Emma laughed. "You are making that part up, Francie."

" 'Tis logical. Who would want to smell—"

"Hush! I do have a new gown, a pretty yellow one."

When Emma was dressed in the yellow dress and had donned her new yellow hat, Francine ah'd until Emma thought surely her throat would be sore.

"If only the stubborn Duke of Attlebery could see you, Sister. You are beyond the tenth stare," Francine assured Emma.

"Let's don't speak of the ruthless Duke on this beautiful Easter morning. I wish to enjoy myself," Emma retorted.

As they went to the waiting coach, Emma stopped in the garden and picked a fistful of Easter Lilies. "For Brother's

315

grave," she said, feeling happy that this year she did not carry the burden of anger inside her. "One should always seek out the truth," she told Francine, "not listen to gossipers."

"I'm so thankful you learned the whole of it."

"I would not have, had it not been for Ashton."

"You should love him for that, if for nothing else."

"Oh, there are other reasons, but that does not mean I can't be angry with him for staying away so long, and for not writing."

"Are you sure that he will someday come back to you?" Francine asked.

"No, but I keep pretending, so my heart will stop breaking," Emma said.

In front of the Church of St. Lawrence, a young lad greeted them with, "The Lord has risen." In unison, Emma and Francine answered, "The Lord has risen."

The lad took the horses' reins and guided the carriage away, while Emma and Francine went to Lord Winslow's grave and placed the flowers at the base of the tombstone. For a moment, Emma knelt and asked God to forgive her sin of judging another human being. Then they went inside the church, where they sat in the family pew.

This day the church was exceptionally quiet, Emma noticed. People went to the altar and knelt, leaving a white lily, until they were strewn everywhere. She looked at the familiar font, around which twined a serpent, the symbol of evil. At the top was a silver-gilt bowl, with four doves perched around its rim, drinking the waters of life. Emma felt at peace as her gaze was drawn to her brother's grave. Instantly, she sat forward on the pew to stare. Standing beside the grave were little Prudence and her mother, Countess Winslow, who was wearing a dark blue dress with white flowers. Prudence's white dotted dress stopped just above her ankles, showing lace-trimmed pantalettes; a matching bonnet framed her pretty little face. The black mourning bows were missing. As Emma watched, they knelt, the Countess on her knees, Prudence in her familiar crouch, leaning back on her heels. A small distance away, Consuelo stood with her hands crossed in front of her, her head bowed.

Extreme joy swept over Emma, so much so that she could hardly contain herself. Unashamedly, tears rolled from her eyes when she blurted out, "Fran . . . Francie, look . . . look out at Brother's grave."

Francine grabbed her hand and squeezed it so hard Emma felt nails digging into her flesh. "Oh, Sister," Francine said, "the Lord did give little Prue her Easter miracle. I can't believe that Margaret has ventured out."

"Or Consuelo," Emma said.

In a little while they left the grave and came to sit in the family pew, Prudence beside Emma, but still holding her mother's hand.

In the back of the church, His Grace Ashton deFleury glared at the back of Emma's head, willing her to turn and look at him. The music started, and voices rose in celebration of Easter, and still, he stared. Beside him sat Countess Lankford, saying crossly, "Why did you not go and sit beside her?"

"And have her ask me to leave in front of all these people? I don't take humiliation well."

"Pea-goose, she would not ask you to leave. She loves you. She wants to tell you she is sorry for flirting with Sir Arthur Stewart at Almack's."

"Strange that you would say that she loves me. Her nostrils flared when she denied it to me. I was just so besotted that I would not believe her."

"She's besotted with you, too," whispered Countess Lankford.

To which His Grace declared, not too quietly, "If you are wrong, Countess, you will be banished to a prison ship for the rest of your life."

"On what charges?"

The Duke grinned. "I'll think of something."

Giving up on Emma turning to look at him, His Grace decided to listen to the vicar, and found himself engrossed in the Easter message, and when the service ended, he felt a sense of well being. He made a mental promise to himself that he would attend church more often. Of course he would, he told himself, when the children were old enough he and Emma would take them to church, and afterwards on a picnic. . . . In his pocket was a special license for him to wed Lady Emma Winslow . . . if she did not turn him down.

Solemnity was in order as the crowd filed out past His Grace and Countess Lankford. They sat at the very end of the pew, near the middle aisle, waiting. Finally, Emma rose, and the others rose with her. His Grace's heart stilled, for it appeared that Emma would turn and lead them through an exit where they would not pass by where he and Countess Lankford were sitting. He hated the thought of getting up and chasing after her. But he would, he decided.

Then, Emma turned and started down the middle aisle, and His Grace heaved a deep sigh of relief, and when she was even with him, he reached behind a rather portly woman and took Emma's arm.

She jerked, but he held on tightly, pulling her toward him.

"You jackanapes," she said, hiding her joy. "What are you doing here?"

"I know a certain vicar who is terribly hungry. He wishes to get this ceremony over with."

"What ceremony?"

The Duke stood, his big frame towering over Emma. He could not smile, so serious was he. He was very much aware that Countess Lankford, Francine, Prudence, Countess Winslow, and Consuelo were gathered round, all grinning and acting as if they were about to shout. Even the vicar, peering over the heads of the others, was smiling.

*This would be easier if we were alone,* His Grace thought,

but he plunged right in. Taking Emma's hands, he held them to his lips for a long, lingering moment, while looking down into her big blue eyes.

*Demme, I'd like to kiss her.*

In a choked voice he brazenly asked, "Will you marry me, Lady Winslow?"

"Is it a love match?" she asked.

"Demmet, I love you very much."

Emma, smiling, returned his gaze, batted her long, black eyelashes at him, and said, "Then, I will marry you, Your Grace."

Then and there, the Duke kissed his Easter Lady, and she kissed him back, after which all concerned marched toward the altar.